THE COMING THING

a novel by
Anne Billson

By the same author:

Novels
Dream Demon (a novelisation)
Suckers
Stiff Lips
The Ex

Non-Fiction
Screen Lovers
My Name is Michael Caine
The Thing (BFI Modern Classics)
Buffy the Vampire Slayer (BFI TV Classics)
Let The Right One In (Devil's Advocates)

e-books
Billson Film Database
Breast Man: A Conversation with Russ Meyer

Copyright © 2017 Anne Billson

ISBN-10: 1544247818
ISBN-13: 978-1544247816

THE COMING THING

'Mr Bond, they have a saying in Chicago: "Once is happenstance.
Twice is coincidence. The third time it's enemy action."'
(Ian Fleming, *Goldfinger*)

'For three films, anyone who even considers inconveniencing
Damien is put in the position of a Tex Avery cartoon character
whose path has been crossed by a black cat and is thus doomed to
be pulped by a falling battleship.'
(Kim Newman, *Nightmare Movies*)

'The best lack all conviction, while the worst
Are full of passionate intensity.'
(W.B. Yeats, *The Second Coming*)

Prologue
The Hospital

There's a blob of greyish stuff on my shoulder. I make a move to wipe it off, then realise to my disgust it's a small piece of someone's brain, at which point the wiping turns into a convulsive scrubbing action and I think I'm going to be sick.

Where am I? Oh yes, in front of the big window on the landing, next to the lifts. The glass is reinforced with wire mesh, to make it more difficult for desperate patients to defenestrate themselves. Even so, there's a crack across one corner, as though someone tried, and failed, to do just that.

I can see the Skoda, still parked in the courtyard below. Last time I saw Les Six, he was no longer in any state to drive. Perhaps he took a bus home. Perhaps he managed to flag down a cab. Or perhaps he just crawled into an empty room and bled to death. I examine my own feelings about this, and decide that not only do I not care, I don't care about not caring. I wonder if it's possible that I don't even care about not caring about not caring, but decide things have gone far enough.

I've been telling myself to ignore the reflection in the window, but my eyes are too tired to listen to instructions from my brain and come to rest on it anyway. I could be a misshapen lurching creature from a monster movie, something cobbled together by a mad scientist with a whimsical sense of humour. The left side of my head is held together by a patchwork of soggy sticking plasters, and not just any old sticking plasters, but sticking plasters covered with green and purple dinosaurs.

Maybe I should get out of here while I still have the use of my legs. That would be the smart thing to do. But Nancy is my friend, and what are friends for if not to hold your hand while you're in labour? All I have to do is hang on, and try not to bleed to death.

She's going to die. I think we both know that. What's coming out of her is too big, too powerful, and it's going to tear her apart. I just hope it doesn't tear me apart as well.

*****

I break the news that I couldn't find any proper drugs, and offer Nancy one of my Extra-Strength Dolibans instead, but she ignores me, and it's true it wouldn't make much difference anyway; she needs something stronger. She isn't paying much attention to anything except what's happening inside her. Her face is all shiny, and she's muttering to herself again.

'Not my fault,' she says. 'He took me by surprise.'

I feel the familiar shooting pain in my sinuses, and chip in quickly. 'It was no-one's fault except Delgado's. He knew what he was getting into.'

She tries to haul herself into a sitting position. I should probably help, but I don't want to touch her. Once again I'm feeling pressure mounting in my head, like water building up in a blocked hosepipe. Oh please God, not another gusher. I'm not sure how much more blood I can spare.

'What about your exercises?' I say. The breathing exercises I once sneered at for being hippy mumbo-jumbo? Well, I'm ready to give them my blessing now. Her eyes focus on something I can't see, and she starts chanting under her breath. Probably some of that New Age witchery they drummed into her at Wormwood. But miracle of miracles, it seems to do the trick. The pressure recedes, and moments later she's propped up against a pile of blankets and looking quite chipper, under the circumstances. Like a hotel guest expecting breakfast in bed. Crisis averted. For now.

'Bloody hell, Belinda. How long does this go on for?'

'Not much longer,' I say, trying not to think of Les Six's last words. *Could be days.*

'It would help if... I don't know, if you could take my mind off it. Tell me a story.'

'What kind of story?'

'I don't know. You're the writer, Belinda. But you never let me see anything thing you've written.'

'You never asked.'

'That notebook you're always scribbling in?'

'It's at home.'

The almost imperceptible narrowing of Nancy's eyes is accompanied by a twinge behind my left temple, as though an acupuncturist has inserted the tip of a needle into my brain and is preparing to slide the rest of it in.

'No, it's not. You'd never leave that behind. I looked for it once, when you were out. But you'd taken it with you. You always take it with you.'

So she did go through my stuff! I knew it!

'It's not finished,' I say.

'I'll be dead by the time you finish it,' she says. I can't tell if this is a figure of speech, or if she means it literally.

'Some of it's about you.'

She rolls her eyes. 'Of course it's about me! Because let's face it...' She lets the sentence hang, and I can feel my face turning pink..

I finish the sentence for her. 'My life isn't as interesting as yours?'

'I'm probably not going to make it anyway,' she says. 'What have you got to lose?'

Only blood, I think. *Lots of blood.*

'OK, but there are gaps, so you may have to chip in,' I say as I reach into my bag. There's a faint click as I press RECORD on the brushed chrome Miniguchi microcassette recorder.

'Well?' says Nancy.

So I draw out my leather-bound journal, in which all but the last few pages are filled with my impeccable script. Enough inconsistency to make it legible, just enough sweep in the ascenders and descenders to make it easy on the eye. Nancy's view is upside-down, but it doesn't stop her from letting slip an envious little sigh as she says, for what must be the hundredth time, 'You have such lovely handwriting, Belinda.'

'Don't say I didn't warn you.'

She chuckles, and I shudder, because what with the shiny face and stringy hair plastered against her scalp, she reminds me of a Death's Head. 'You think I don't know what you did, Belinda?'

And my blood freezes in my veins, which I guess is one way of stopping the haemorrhage.

—

PART ONE
BABYLON

Chapter 1
The Soho Slasher

Nancy didn't find about her pregnancy the normal way.

There were signs, though she recognised them only in retrospect. For example, there was that time she felt sick in the middle of telling the tour group from Illinois what the Soho Slasher had done with the severed head of his third victim.

Maybe I shouldn't be going into such horrible detail, she thought, leaning against the Temple of Ishtar for support. She heard one of the women asking, 'Is she OK?' but it was as though the voice were muffled by a heavy blanket. She wondered if she were going to throw up. *Oh please. Not here. Not in the museum. Not in front of everyone.*

'Should we call an attendant?' asked Mr. Entwhistle.

'Smithsonian's better,' said Mr. Kreuger. 'They've got moon rock and the Spirit of St Louis.'

'She's very pale,' said Mrs.Plotnik, whose own skin was a dark bronze, the texture of leather.

The nausea didn't last long. Nancy raised her head and saw the group gazing at her in collective concern. She felt a fleeting wave of affection for all of them, even Mr. Kreuger and Mrs. Plotnik.

'She looks better now,' said Mrs. Lurie. 'Doesn't she look better?'

Nancy straightened up, as though nothing had

happened, and life went on as normal. She had things to do, people to meet, auditions to attend, red carpets to walk. But the red carpets were in the future. First, she had to convince the tour group that the British Museum was the most thrilling place they'd ever visited. Even more thrilling than the Smithsonian.

She took up where she'd left off. 'That statue over there, the one holding the fly-whisk? You'll notice the head is missing.' She lowered her voice until it came out dark, thrilling and a little bit fruity, just the way the American tourists liked it. 'Well, it was that very statue that inspired the Slasher's next atrocity. So if you'd follow me, please.'

As she was turning to lead them on to the next attraction, someone grabbed her by the wrist. It was Mrs. Plotnik. She was looking at Nancy with the strangest expression, as though the harmless old lady had been occupied by something quite unsettling which was peering out at her through pale and filmy eyes. Nancy hoped the old biddy wasn't having a stroke.

'*I know.*'

'Know what?'

Mrs. Plotnik gave her one last beetle-browed look, then something seemed to pass out of her and she became docile again and pottered off, leaving Nancy rubbing her wrist. The old lady's grip had been like iron. Later, she wondered if Mrs. Plotnik had already sensed that, deep within the darkest and most secret recesses of her innermost being, something was stirring. And we're not talking about the sandwich she'd had for lunch.

There were approximately one month, three weeks and twenty-two hours of normal life left to her.

*****

It wasn't a bad part-time job. Better than waiting tables.
To begin with, she took them around to the usual
attractions: St. Paul's, the Tower, Buckingham Palace
and so forth. The reaction was always the same: initial
excitement over the age of the buildings, swiftly
followed by disillusionment and a certain amount of
tetchiness as repetition set in. Nancy took it personally.
It wasn't just her city they were judging, it was her
presentation of it, her performance. She looked on it as a
challenge. She would hold their attention if it killed her.

One day, in an effort to maintain interest levels,
she went a little over the top in her descriptions of how
the Bloody Tower had earned its name. A Mr. Van Fleet
was sufficiently impressed to chip in with, 'How about
Jack the Ripper?'

Nancy turned towards him with a warm smile.
'How about him?'

'Didn't he operate round here?' *Operate* was
perhaps not the most fortuitous choice of word. But at
the mention of Jack the Ripper, there was a rustle of
excitement.

'Not around the Tower of London, no.' Nancy felt
the beginnings of a frown impinging on her smile. But it
wasn't enough to put off Mr. Van Fleet, who had single-
handedly built his own recycling plant out of a couple of
used car batteries and a broken vending machine.

'Where, then?'

They were all looking at her expectantly, so she
told them. *Whitechapel.* There was a pause while this sank
in. They'd never heard of Whitechapel. They stood
poised like a pack of lost retrievers, ears pricked and

noses pointing in all directions, trying to work out where it might be.

'I guess we could go there,' said Nancy. Her words were greeted by a murmur of approval, but her heart sank; she knew in advance how it would turn out. Sure enough, collective enthusiasm ebbed as the minibus crawled through traffic-clogged streets to Spitalfields. They huddled in a shop doorway, trying to avoid the drizzle, while Nancy told them what she could remember about Jack the Ripper and his exploits. The tour group was unimpressed.

'Isn't there a museum?' asked Mrs. Stivers, a sweet-faced old lady with a purple-rinsed perm. 'Don't you have a Ripper Experience, something like that?'

'You want to experience having your entrails ripped out?' Nancy said, and immediately regretted it. She wondered whether to propose a tour of the London Dungeon, but it was nearing lunchtime and Mrs. Stivers, who didn't seem at all offended at Nancy's outburst, had already redirected her energies into explaining to Mrs. Riffenbecker that what she wanted was a plain white bagel with lo-fat cream cheese and oak-smoked salmon and absolutely no poppy seeds.

'There's a Jack the Ripper pub in New York City,' said Mr. Van Fleet.

'Glad to hear it,' said Nancy, who blamed him for the whole fiasco, 'but I'm sure you'll understand why we can't go there right this minute. Anyway, as I was saying, apart from the five official victims, there were also a couple of other murders which the police...'

'Only five?' Mr. Vasquez said. 'Our own Ted Bundy bagged three times as many.'

It was at this point that Nancy decided it might be

easier to make things up. The advantages were many. The stamping grounds of her imaginary serial killers would all be in the vicinity of the hotels, so they wouldn't spend so much time sitting around in traffic jams. And she could easily rustle up tales of bloodshed that would make Bundy sound like a rank amateur. Plus it would keep her on her toes, impro-wise.

Regaling tour groups with tall tales about fictional mass murderers wasn't the kind of performance she'd had in mind when she'd decided to make a career out of it. But then neither had she ever imagined she would end up playing a water-lily, a low-ranking nun or Scarlatti's second wife. Time was running out. If she didn't catch that big break soon, she would be too old. But she never gave up. Nancy's optimism never failed to amaze me. Even before all this happened, she was always convinced she was going to be big. Though I don't suppose she meant big like this.

Chapter 2
The Kitchen Devil

Nancy's flat was on the fifth floor of a block which squatted like a raw stump at the corner of Natal Place, as though the adjoining buildings had been hacked away with a machete. The tenants were a combustible mix of old-timers who had been there since the Jazz Age, when the place was built, and young trendies requiring a nest within flopping distance of their central London nightlife. Nancy's uneasy relationship with her downstairs neighbour, Mrs. Feaver, was typical; all over the block, young and old were locked in petty feuds about loud music, or leaving the front door on the latch, or putting out rubbish bags on the wrong day.

On the morning of the day when everything changed, she woke with a mouth so parched her tongue kept sticking to the roof of her palate. She was used to hangovers, but this was a doozy. Which was strange, because she hadn't drunk that much, plus she'd remembered to eat. Perhaps that shrimp curry had been off. Her stomach was roiling with hunger, but anything she swallowed came straight back up again. The sounds of regurgitation were amplified by the acoustics of the lavatory bowl. She wondered if Mrs. Feaver could hear; if so, she was probably already reaching for her broom to bang on the ceiling.

Nancy perched on the edge of the bed, resisting the temptation to climb back in. She was supposed to be meeting a tour group at the Durward at nine, and she couldn't very well do that with her head between her knees. So she pulled on the clothes she'd left on the floor the night before and, feeling as though her head had been pumped full of Crazy Foam, groped her way out of the flat. It was a question of willpower. She could make it, just so long as she concentrated on small goals, such as placing one foot after another. One foot, then the other. That was it. She was walking.

She set off towards the Durward. It was 08h52.

There were approximately six minutes of normal life left to her.

*****

The one-foot-after-the-other tactic seemed to be working. She managed to cross the road without being knocked down by a bus. The Durward was only minutes away when she spotted the poster on a bus stop and immediately, instinctively, knew what would make her feel better.

LAYERS OF DEEP DARK CHOCOLATE WRAPPED AROUND A MOLTEN CORE OF FUDGE.

There was a newsagents a few yards away. Despite the poster outside his shop, the man behind the counter had never heard of Fudge Tub, so Nancy had to settle for a strawberry-flavoured Frooty Pop instead. As soon as she was outside she pulled off the wrapper, but after only a couple of licks her gut heaved ominously and she knew it wasn't going to work. It was Fudge Tub or nothing. She lobbed the unfinished Frooty Pop at a rubbish bin and moved on, checking her watch. There was no time to embark on a confectionery hunt. She would just have to hold out till lunch and hope her group didn't make too many elaborate demands in the meantime.

One minute to nine. If she didn't look sharp she was going to be late. She stepped up her pace, still taking it one step at a time, but faster now. It seemed to be working, but she was concentrating so hard it took longer than it might otherwise have done to notice other pedestrians were getting out of her way. As it was, the first thing she noticed were their feet - breaking step, swerving, changing course.

She raised her head and saw a businessman staring at her. No, staring at something *behind* her. A woman in a blue woolly jacket met her gaze and opened her mouth to say something, then changed her mind and hurried on. Nancy wondered if she'd gone out with a stream of toilet paper stuck to her shoe. Or maybe she'd got her skirt tucked into her knickers. It was possible; she'd been too busy trying not to throw up to pay much attention to grooming.

And then she glanced over her shoulder and saw what everyone else had been looking at.

Ordinarily the man behind her wouldn't have attracted much attention, though his unexceptional grey suit did seem exceptionally crumpled, as though he'd slept in it. But right now it was hard to ignore him, because he was clutching a knife. It looked like a Kitchen Devil.

Wow, thought Nancy. No wonder people were getting out of the way; there was probably some innocent explanation for the knife, but in the circumstances it seemed sensible to follow their example, so she wheeled round in a wide semi-circle and started walking in the opposite direction. Now she was walking *away* from the Durward. This was going to make her late, dammit!

As she reached the shop where she'd bought the Frooty-Pop, she decided she'd gone far enough, and turned... The man with the knife had changed direction too. He had followed her back up the street, so now they were facing each other, and he was coming closer.

Nancy felt strangely serene, still cushioned by her hangover. There was no indication the stranger's change of direction had been anything other than coincidence. If someone wanted to attack you with a Kitchen Devil, they weren't going to do it in broad daylight, not with a blade the size of *Africa*. Not on a busy street in the rush hour. Things like that just didn't happen. Not to her.

And yet there he was.

Nancy wondered what to do. Stay where she was? Run? Too embarrassing, especially if she'd misread the situation. Go back into the newsagent's and wait until he had passed? This struck her as the most rational option. But then, as the man in the grey suit drew nearer, she saw his eyes were fixed on her, and there was saliva gleaming on his chin, and her morning lurched into uncharted territory. None of this was happening. None of it was real.

The man in grey stopped about eight feet away from her. For an endless suspended moment, they stood and stared at each other. Passers-by slowed to watch, as though this were some sort of street theatre unfolding before them. Then the man mumbled something. Out of force of habit, Nancy looked at her watch and told him the time, which reminded her all over again that she was running late.

I'm not even supposed to be here.

The man looked wildly around, as though expecting support, and when it wasn't forthcoming he gathered up his wits, like odd pieces of pastry, and pressed them into some sort of shape. And then he opened his mouth and began to babble, and this time Nancy could hear what he said quite clearly. But even then, it didn't make sense.

'Whore of Babylon!'

Nancy said, 'I think you must be mistaking me for someone else.'

She spotted a thin line of blood trickling from one of his nostrils, and, all of a sudden, being sick in public no longer seemed like the worst thing that could happen. She never found out if he knew his nose was bleeding, because in the next instant he shook his head like a wet sheepdog, so violently the air was filled with droplets of blood and saliva, and she was vaguely aware of people shrinking back, out of range of this insanitary drizzle, and then she stopped seeing anything except the man in front of her as he shifted his weight from one foot to the other and adjusted his grip on the knife and charged at her, like a bull.

She felt a pang of regret so acute that, for a split-second, it was as though the knife had already found its mark. She wasn't even famous enough for an obituary; she'd be lucky to end up with a couple of inches at the bottom of the home news. She could see it now in her head: MAN GOES BERSERK ON LONDON STREET, STABS WOULD-BE ACTRESS TO DEATH.

Then time stood still, and it was just her, and she

realised it was true what they said about your past flashing in front of your eyes. Scenes from Nancy's life zipped past like pictures in a flip book: twirling around in a sugar-pink tutu to the applause of family and friends, costumed as an elf in Santa's Grotto, her mother hurling an empty bottle at her father's head and missing, first kiss, forgetting her lines in that school production of *The Crucible*, boyfriends, married men, auditions, dressed as a hooker and saying 'Oi mister, fancy a shag?' on that TV cop show. Faster and faster, till the past finally caught up with her: last night's shrimp curry, throwing up in the bathroom, Southampton Row, the Fudge Tub poster, the strawberry-flavoured Frooty-Pop...

An invisible finger slowed the carousel and touched a series of interlinked images. The Frooty-Pop. Licking it. Throwing the lolly at the bin, but she was distracted, and so her aim was off...

She was jerked back into the present. The man in grey was still charging towards her, but now she felt calm and in control, and an odd phrase popped into her head. *As it is written, so shall it be done.* Light glanced off the blade. It looked sharp as a laser, and it was coming closer. No longer six feet away. Now five feet. Now four...

The man tried to close the gap between them in one last mighty, tendon-stretching lunge. The effort was evidently too much for the blood vessels in his nose, which stopped trickling and started to gush. As his looming image blotted out everything else, Nancy found herself focusing on small but sharp details, such as the grimy tear-tracks on his cheeks, the small tuft of tissue stuck to the side of his jaw where he had nicked himself shaving, the whites of his eyes tinted pink like Tequila Sunrise.

Quietly, she registered her own eerie calm in the face of impending oblivion and felt proud of the way she was keeping her head in a crisis. It was just a shame this would be the last crisis she would ever have to face. Because there was no way he could miss. *Ah well*, she thought.

And then his heel came down heavily in a gleaming puddle of pink. It was as though he'd stepped on a discarded roller-skate. His left leg shot out at an unexpected angle. He flung his arms out, letting go of the knife, and flapped around like a flightless bird, slithering around on one foot, a comical look of surprise on his face as he struggled to regain his balance. But the foot slid out from under him, and he crashed backwards on to the pavement and lay there, mouth silently opening and closing.

It might have ended there, had it not been for the knife. According to the laws of physics, it should have clattered to the ground as soon as he'd loosened his grip, but he must have inadvertently given it a last minute googly-like twist because it arced into the air instead, rotating lazily on its axis like a caveman's bone. When it could go no higher, it did one last lazy flip before starting to tumble back to earth. It tumbled straight towards the man on the pavement. His eyes opened wide as he tied to focus on the object falling towards him.

There was a dull ping as the steel struck the pavement and the knife skittered away before coming to rest at the feet of a woman in Birkenstocks. The man in grey didn't make a sound. He kept staring into the air, as though wondering where his weapon had gone. It was some moments before the cut in his neck peeled slowly open, like a freshly sliced pomegranate exposing its fleshy pink insides.

There was a shocked hush. Then it was as though someone had opened a valve. The water fanned out like fine spray from a garden sprinkler, except it was red. All the onlookers stepped back, almost as one, and everyone said *oooh*, as though they were watching a firework display.

At the same time, the screaming began.

This was no time to get hysterical, thought Nancy. Someone needed to slap that woman, make her stop.

Only when the man's body had stopped twitching did she realise the screaming was coming from her.

Chapter 3
The Shrimp

She was hungry and nauseous and still hungover. The smell of antiseptic was overpowering. She was lying on a narrow bed, wearing nothing but a paper gown which rustled when she moved. She tried to sit up, but her head began to swim.

'Wouldn't get up if I were you.'

She turned her head and saw a middle-aged man in an unbuttoned white coat. He was holding a clipboard.

'You had a shock, but you're safe now. Nothing to worry about.'

'What happened?'

'We gave you a sedative,' said the man in the white coat, and added, 'A perfectly safe one. No need to worry.'

Why did he keep saying there was nothing worry about? Why couldn't she remember anything? And where was she?

He seemed to read her mind. 'You're in St. Cuthbert's. I'm Dr. Webster. Chief obstetrician.'

Obstetrician. She knew that word. But before she had time to think about it, a montage of impressions zipped through her head. Grimy tear-tracks, a small tuft of paper tissue, Tequila Sunrise, blood fanning out like the fine spray from a garden sprinkler...

'Oh dear,' she said. 'Is he dead?'

Dr. Webster shook his head. 'The two of you are

fine.'

Nancy found this hard to believe. The last she'd seen of the man in grey, he'd been painting the town red with his carotid artery. 'But he lost so much blood.'

Agitation played across Dr. Webster's features. 'The fellow who attacked you? I'm afraid there was nothing we could do for him.'

Nancy was confused.

'Not a friend of yours, I hope.'

'Christ, no.' She shivered at the memory of those red-tinged eyes with their fanatical gleam. 'Who was he? Why was he...?'

But the doctor was already moving towards the door. 'You need to rest, you've had a shock, but there's no reason you can't go home. One of the nurses will take you to a phone so you can call your husband.'

'I'm not married,' said Nancy.

'Partner, then.'

'I don't have one of those either,' said Nancy, noticing the clock on the wall. It was the first time she'd been able to focus on it properly; the small hand was pointing to the right. She'd lost an entire morning. She had a poignant vision of elderly American tourists still waiting anxiously in the lobby of the Durward.

'I have to go,' she said. This time she made it as far as a sitting position before the room began to ripple, like the prelude to a movie flashback.

Dr. Webster's hand was already on the doorknob. He turned back with a sigh. 'Father, whatever.'

'My father's dead.'

Dr. Webster reluctantly let go of the doorknob and arranged his face into a suitably solemn expression. 'My condolences, Miss... It is Miss, isn't it? Miss, er...'

'Seven years ago. I'm just about over it. But you said I can go home?'

'We just thought you might want to let the father know,' said Dr. Webster. 'Your baby is fine.'

Nancy found herself staring at a poster pinned to the wall beyond the doctor's shoulder. SMOKING STUNTS YOUR BABY'S GROWTH.

'Excuse me?'

With infinite patience, as though issuing directions to a foreign tourist with only a shaky grasp of English, Dr. Webster repeated, 'Your baby is fine.'

*****

They had to give her another sedative. By the time she woke up again, Dr. Webster had been replaced by a younger, more callous-looking colleague, whose lip curled each time Nancy protested that she couldn't possibly be pregnant because it had been one year, four months and twenty-six days since she'd last been in direct contact with a man's reproductive organs. She could tell by the way the doctor raised one eyebrow that he thought she was in stupid-girl denial. It was a relief when he left.

The rest of the afternoon might have been happening to someone else. She couldn't get a signal on her phone. A nurse came in and made her drink a lot of water and then took her into another room, where she slapped a dollop of green gel on to Nancy's stomach and started spreading it around with a small squeegee.

'Now... look.' The monitor displayed a swirling green constellation sprinkled with planets, meteors and a couple of starships. '*Look!* the nurse said again, her face lit by an evangelical glow. She pointed to a tiny crescent in the heart of the galaxy. 'That's your baby!'

Nancy gripped the edges of the couch and said, 'No.'

The nurse's face took on a green tinge as she leant closer to the screen. 'You never noticed your periods had stopped?'

'It's one of the shrimps from last night's curry,' said Nancy, staring at the tiny crescent until her eyes felt ready to pop.

The nurse chuckled and patted her on the head.

*****

Later, when Nancy had emptied her bladder and been led back to the room where she'd woken up, she found a print-out of the scan lying on the bed. She sat there for what seemed like a very long time, staring at the picture the way one stared at photographs of motorway pile-ups, trying to work out which twisted scrap of metal belonged to which vehicle, until the nurse came back into the room. 'Not dressed yet?'

When Nancy said she wasn't feeling well, the nurse's manner turned brisk. 'Chop chop, we need the room.'

Nancy began to pull her clothes back on, trying not to look too closely at the rust-coloured stipple on the pastel pink top. She wanted to burn these garments and plunge into a hot bath and scrub every inch of her body clean.

A woman with frizzy orange hair like Ronald McDonald poked her head around the door and said, 'Verity Wilson to see you.'

The first nurse looked up from a jug she was rinsing. 'Friend or family?'

'Reporter,' said Ronald.

Nancy's ears pricked up. 'What do they want?'

'What do reporters usually want? To screw you over, I expect!' The nurse laughed, but Nancy felt a flush of optimism. Perhaps she could salvage something from this wreck of a day. Perhaps she would end up in the news after all, not as a victim but as a heroine. BRAVE ACTRESS SURVIVES KNIFE ATTACK.

'You don't have to see anyone,' said the nurse.

' I should go home and change,' said Nancy, looking down at her clothes. 'I'm covered in...'

'Send her packing,' said the nurse. 'Nancy doesn't feel like talking.'

'No, wait,' said Nancy, but Ronald had already disappeared.

'Tabloid scum,' said the nurse. 'You don't want anything to do with them.'

Nancy's eyes filled with tears again. Was that it, then? Her last chance to be famous, and she'd flunked it by worrying about her appearance. She began to weep. The nurse gave her a starchy hug.

'There, there,' she said. 'We'll keep the jackals away.'

This only made Nancy sob more, but her tears dried up when Ronald poked her head around the door again and said, 'Another visitor, my darling. And no getting out of this one.'

'No problem,' said Nancy, blowing her nose. It was going to be OK after all. She would play the heroine, the plucky survivor, the One Who Got Away. She peered into the mirror over the washbasin, splashed water on her face and tried to smooth down her hair. She'd looked worse. She took a deep breath and turned towards the door, where a large, red-faced man in an ill-fitting suit was leaning against the jamb, panting. His tie was covered in mallards.

As if in response to a silent signal, the nurse slipped past him, out of the room. Nancy put on her best smile.

'Won't take long,' gasped the red-faced man, collapsing into a chair. He took out a handkerchief and started dabbing his forehead. 'Lift full of walking wounded so took the stairs. Time I lost some weight.'

'I need to lose a few pounds myself,' said Nancy. It was true her clothes had been feeling a bit tighter than normal, but that was because she'd been eating too much, not because she was pregnant.

The red-faced man looked at her sharply, as though she'd insulted him. 'If this isn't a good moment we can put it off till later.'

'This is fine,' she said. 'What about photos?'

He continued to stare, without blinking, and so fixedly that she started to wonder if there were something wrong with his eyesight. At last he said, 'No CCTV. Swiss tourist with a camcorder, not best quality. Pity there were no Japanese, they always have cameras. Some blurry footage of the aftermath, nothing of the incident itself.'

'Which paper did you say you worked for?'

The red-faced man looked at her oddly. 'I'm sorry. Let me introduce myself. Detective Inspector Church.'

Nancy felt her face turn as red as his.

'You OK?' he asked.

She nodded. *How could I have been so stupid?*

'We've already spoken to a number of witnesses,' said Church.

'There were loads of them. No-one lifted a finger.'

Church shook his head sadly. 'That's how it is these days. People think it's a domestic and don't want to get involved. Sorry to bother you like this, but there are a few things I need to ask while your memory's still fresh. Did you recognise the man who attacked you?'

'No.'

'You didn't see or talk to him before today? Never spotted him hanging around outside your house or in the street?'

'You think he was a stalker?' asked Nancy.

Church's jowls wobbled as he shook his head. 'Today was the first time you met him?'

'I wouldn't call it *met*, exactly,' said Nancy. But I've never seen him before, no.'

Church was scribbling into a notepad. 'So the first time you saw this individual was when he attacked you? Did you say anything that might have set him off?'

'*What?*'

'Sorry, phrased that badly. Not suggesting you were to blame. But did you exchange words?'

Nancy thought back. *Had* she said anything? 'I told him what time it was.'

Church nodded as though she'd just confirmed what he already knew.

She bit her lip. 'And he called me a whore.'

The detective's eyes narrowed. Up until that point, he'd looked like the sort of uncle who would dress up as Santa Claus and hand out gifts to underprivileged children. Now he just looked mean. 'Any idea why?'

Nancy became flustered. 'Some men think all

women are prostitutes.'

Church's gaze had strayed down to her strappy pink Suzy Hendricks with kitten heels, and now he was eyeing them judgementally, as though they were cheap hooker footwear.

'I can't wear flats,' she said. 'My tendons have shrunk.'

He was scribbling in his notebook again. She sensed disapproval coming off him in waves. So what if he didn't like her shoes? How would he like it if she were to sneer at his mallards?

'OK, you noticed this chap following you. Then what?'

'He had a knife.' She found herself short of breath. 'And then?'

It took several false starts before she could actually get the words out. 'Then... I don't know... He... *ran* at me.'

'We know he ran at you,' said Church. 'What we'd like to establish is why he never reached you.'

Reluctantly, she tried to play it back through her head, the way everything had flashed through her head during the attack. But now the memory was spotty and incomplete, as though someone had already got to the video and cut out most of the connecting footage. She vaguely recalled her attacker skidding on something, and wondered whether to mention the strawberry-flavoured Frooty-Pop she thought she'd thrown away. Had she missed the bin? What if he'd slipped on that? She suddenly felt guilty, even though she was the innocent victim here. Maybe it was better not to mention it.

'I don't know,' she said. 'He tripped? I don't remember.'

Church nodded as though that was exactly what he'd been expecting her to say. 'Was there anything to suggest he was in pain?'

She went back into her head and saw the moist face, with its pink-tinged eyes. And blood trickling, no, *gushing* from his nostrils. That was one vision that hadn't been deleted. She already had a feeling she would be seeing it again, in her nightmares.

'His nose was bleeding.'

'Yes.' Church tapped his pen against the edge of his notebook. 'Everyone remembers the nosebleed.'

'Then why are you asking?' said Nancy.

'Just a formality. But beyond that, no two witnesses agree. One said the perpetrator stabbed himself. Another that he tripped and fell on the knife. Another...' He looked Nancy in the eye. 'Someone insists you seized the knife and slit his throat with it.'

Nancy breathed in sharply. 'That's ridiculous.'

'We know that, Miss, er, Loughlin. Evidently the would-be perpetrator met with some sort of freak accident before he could touch you. The autopsy may tell us more. But it seems you were lucky.'

Nancy didn't feel lucky. Lucky people didn't get attacked by knife-wielding maniacs in the street.

Church flipped over some pages, and she finally caught a glimpse of what he'd been scribbling - no words at all, just an impenetrable thicket of crosshatching. He tapped his Biro against his front teeth. 'One more thing. I'd appreciate your telling me if this name rings any bells. Karl Petersen. That's Karl with a K, Petersen with three Es.'

Karl Petersen. Nancy repeated the name to herself several times, unsure of how she was supposed to react.

Church was waiting for her to say something, so she asked if the name was German.

'American. Have you spent time recently in the United States?'

'New York, last Christmas.'

'Not since then?'

Nancy shook her head.

'Ever been to Pittsburgh?'

'What?'

'It's where Karl Petersen got his driver's licence.'

This struck her as the most peculiar detail yet. 'Why would he fly all the way to London, just to attack a complete stranger?'

Church nodded to himself. 'That's what we're trying to find out. Seems you were just in the wrong place at the wrong time. Would you like to talk to a Victim Support Group?' He jotted something on a page of his notebook, ripped it out and pressed it into her hand before hauling himself to his feet.

'Wait,' said Nancy. 'What's going on?'

He paused in the doorway as though something had only just occurred to him. 'No plans to leave the country? No further trips to New York?'

She shook her head. 'Why?'

'Just a formality,' Church said again. 'Have a good day, Miss Loughlin. We'll be in touch.'

*****

Have a good day. He'd been kidding, of course. Nancy couldn't see how her day could be any worse. While she was waiting for the lift, she checked her mobile; still no signal. Maurice would be hopping mad about the tour group; she needed to explain what had happened. Maybe once she'd got over the shock, it would make an entertaining anecdote. *You know, that time I was attacked by the crazy American guy with the knife...*

Seven floors down, as the lift doors opened on to the reception area, she forgot all about her phone. Right in front of her, sandwiched between an accessories franchise and a hamburger outlet, was a tuckshop window displaying a stack of Fudge Tubs. She was *so hungry*. She bought one and started digging in even before she was out of the shop. As the small plastic spoon delivered its payload, her mouth was filled with a sunburst of soft ambrosia which dissolved on her tongue and slithered down her throat, leaving a trail of sweetness in its wake. Instantly, she felt suffused with a burst of energy. It was a sugar rush and she knew it wouldn't last, but it felt like a miracle all the same. The nausea had gone, the headache too.

As she stepped out of the shop, the second spoonful had an even more dramatic effect. The day blew up in her face, leaving her temporarily blinded. As the darkness began to disperse she saw she had company. Standing in front of her was a scrawny blonde in a tight black leather skirt and stilettoes so high they cast Nancy's kitten-heels into shadow. The blonde reeked of Miss Dior, and something else, something less pleasant. Next to her was a baby-faced man who looked barely old enough to have started shaving - until you noticed the creases around his eyes. He was clutching a bulky camera; it was the flash on that which had blinded her. They were both staring at Nancy with unconcealed interest, but it wasn't until she started to move, and they moved right along with her, that she realised they were operating as a team.

'How you?' asked the blonde, as though life were too short to waste on verbs.

'Ever seen the guy before?' asked the man.

Nancy spotted a microcassette recorder nestling like a silver kidney in the blonde's palm. She took another step. There was something wrong with this woman. She sensed a deep, dark cave where hundreds, no, thousands of minuscule creatures were swarming like centipedes. Or bats, because they were clinging to the ceiling. The image was so alarming that she stopped, frowning, and the couple, who'd kept on walking, had time to backtrack.

'Oops!' chuckled the blonde, 'Nearly lost you there!'

Nancy studied her face, trying to discern further traces of the decay inside her, but the impression had gone.

'Nearly gave us the slip,' said the photographer, raising the camera again.

Nancy raised an arm to cover her face. 'I'd like a minute to do my make-up.'

The blonde thrust the silver kidney under her nose, as though it were something she might want to smell. 'Any idea why he attacked you?'

Nancy pushed the recorder away, but the photographer was pressing in again, camera at the ready. 'What did Church say?'

Nancy caught a whiff of alcohol on his breath. To her surprise, she found herself breaking it down into separate components: four or five pints of Black Monk, a couple of neat MacLugloch and at least two glasses of Sherpa's Pride. She stared at him in astonishment and said, 'You shouldn't mix your drinks like that.'

'What?' He lowered the camera.

'Just give me a minute,' said Nancy, trying to throw them off balance with an unexpected zigzag movement.

'We're on your side, love,' said the blonde.

What was happening? Her sense of smell had gone into overdrive. Overwhelmed, Nancy started walking back towards the lifts. No, wrong way. She wheeled round in an unnecessarily large circle, dimly aware the three of them had started to attract attention. A man with a bushy beard had stopped to watch, and a small Chinese woman in a trim navy trouser suit stood on tiptoe and clapped her hands.

Once again, the blonde wasn't wasting words. 'Better off with us. Bastards from the Mucker won't be so honourable.'

'Where did you learn karate?' asked the photographer.

Karate? *OK*, thought Nancy. *Let's do this.* She took a deep breath and turned to face them and gave them a short, dramatic account of the knife attack, allowing tears to well up in her eyes, letting her voice catch in her throat now and again, for dramatic effect.

'And how you feeling now?' asked the blonde, still proffering her silver kidney.

'A bit shaky,' said Nancy. 'That guy obviously needed help.' She gave them her age, told them she'd studied at the Shuna North Academy for the Performing Arts, and turned her head slightly, to give the photographer her best angle. He fired off a flurry of shots. The blonde pressed a namecard into Nancy's hand and leant closer.

'Verity Wilson' she said in a stage whisper. 'This Clive Mengers.'

One again Nancy sensed something lurking beneath the Miss Dior. She began to feel nauseous again. She needed another Fudge Tub, and fast. But first she wanted to go home, and change.

'Call me,' said Wilson.

Nancy stepped into the revolving doors. Wilson and Mengers lost valuable seconds trying to jam into the compartment behind her. There was a taxi waiting at the kerb. Nancy got in and slammed the door.

'Let's go,' Nancy said to the driver, who was looking at her doubtfully.

'How about a lift?' yelled Wilson, face pressed against the window.

Nancy said, 'You should tell your doctor. If they catch it in time you'll be fine.'

Wilson reeled back as though she'd been slapped, and the cab moved off.

'Who was that?' asked the driver, changing into third gear.

'Reporter,' said Nancy, feeling quite pleased with the way things had gone, but wishing she'd bought more than one Fudge Tub.

'You a celebrity?' asked the cabbie, eyeing her in the rearview mirror.

'Not yet,' said Nancy, and even as she said it, an internal voice whispered: *famous last words.*

Chapter 4
The Pink Dot

She didn't make the front page. Just a couple of paragraphs under a tiny picture. The caption read, 'No loss of appetite!' The picture of her shovelling Fudge Tub into her mouth was so unflattering she was thankful they hadn't printed her name.

Of course Maurice forgave her for not turning up at the Durward. 'Please don't tell the Americans you were attacked,' he said when she called round at the office. 'They're already antsy enough about the IRA and football hooligans. Are you sure you don't want some time off?'

'I'll be fine,' she said. 'I mean, how many times can you get attacked by knife-wielding maniacs in one lifetime? I think that's my quota filled.' So she went straight back to shepherding tour groups, as though the man in the grey suit had never bled to death on the pavement in front of her.

And if her waistband was getting uncomfortably tight, and the only foodstuff she could keep down was Fudge Tub, she didn't let it worry her; in fact, with all those extra calories it was hardly surprising she was putting on weight. Detective Inspector Church called her the next day, and again a few days later to verify a few minor details, but the entire incident felt increasingly like something that had happened to someone else. Later, she would reflect that that was about the size of it;

she *had* been someone else back then. Without being aware of it, she had already left her old life behind.

The following week, she got a call from Anthony, her agent. He'd fixed her up with an audition, the first in months. 'You're perfect for it, sweetie,' he said. 'Les Six is hot right now.'

The name sounded familiar, but she couldn't place it.

'Made a splash in Edinburgh a few years ago,' said Anthony. 'Politically correct to the point where it wasn't politically correct any more. But Rudy says he's mellowed since then. Gone more mainstream.'

'Thank God for that,' said Nancy.

She hung up with mixed feelings. Auditions were brutal at the best of times, but now her self-esteem was especially low. She had eight days to lose weight and rebuild morale. But every attempt to replace the Fudge Tubs with fruit or vegetables or protein ended with her throwing up. Surely she couldn't survive on Fudge Tub alone? She checked the list of ingredients on the side of the carton - apart from powdered cream they were mostly e-numbers, plus some foreign-looking symbols that reminded her of hieroglyphics she'd seen in the museum.

Finally, after a dreadful weekend in which her every attempt to eat sensibly was immediately followed by painful retching, she forced herself to think back to what they'd said at the hospital, to the words she had been studiously ignoring for nearly a week. *Your baby's fine.* Maybe there *was* something to worry about.

She stood sideways in front of the mirror and tried to study her reflection objectively. Her stomach did look a bit more prominent than usual, though if she stood up straight and put her shoulders back it was as flat as ever. It was all a matter of posture. She couldn't be pregnant. It just wasn't possible. To get pregnant, you first had to have sex.

So why did she keep throwing up? Gas? Stress? An ulcer? *Worse?*

Her stomach was gurgling like a faulty cistern. She was so hungry she couldn't think. She went around the corner to the newsagent's for Fudge Tubs and a paper, then popped into the chemist's for something to combat the nausea. On her way to the counter, she passed a shelf displaying packets marked Gravitask, Euclava, Anamene. All she needed was confirmation that Dr. Webster and the nurse and the ultrasound machine at the hospital had been wrong. She bought one of the kits and took it home and peed on the white plastic wand, as instructed. Two pink dots would mean she was pregnant, but she was confident they would never appear.

She'd barely sat back down again before both miniature portholes on the wand were already pink. Her heart stopped, but only for a second. The leaflet said four minutes. There was still time for the colours to change. And as the seconds ticked by, she saw they were indeed changing. Gradually the pink deepened, like the underside of clouds around a sunset, until both dots were glowing dark red, the colour of dried blood. One of the dots stayed red. The other turned sepia.

Nancy kicked the table-leg in annoyance. What the hell kind of stupid test was this anyway? She read the instructions again. There was no mention of any colour other than pink. She looked back at the sepia dot. The colour was still changing. The sepia darkened. She peered more closely, and saw it was no longer a dot; now it was a tiny, intricate picture of a curious creature with feelers and six legs, but unlike any insect she'd ever seen. She didn't get the opportunity to examine it further, because there was a dull pop, like a champagne bottle being uncorked. She felt a sudden blast of heat and jerked backwards as the room filled with the stench of singed hair and melted plastic.

On the table, what was left of the wand was sizzling like oil on a griddle, emitting evil-smelling fumes. The smoke alarm in the hallway began to shriek. Nancy emptied a bottle of water over the table and dragged a chair into the hallway to fan the alarm with a newspaper.

Later, after she'd opened all the windows and the smoke had disappeared, she sat and gazed in glum fascination at what was left of the pregnancy-testing kit, which was now oozing all over the table like avant-garde artwork. She had to scrape it off with a knife.

*****

She went to see her doctor that afternoon. She provided him with a urine sample, but he didn't need to wait for the results to inform her that she didn't have gas, or an ulcer, or cancer. She was definitely pregnant.

Chapter 5
The Apocalypse Kit

This story is as much about me as it is about Nancy. It might not seem like it right now, but trust me, I'm just as important as she is.

Like Nancy, I was starting to worry about life passing me by. But at least she still had a few windows of opportunity, whereas all mine - thanks to the time I'd spent in Croydon and my failed marriage and more false starts on the career front than I cared to remember - had been boarded up and nailed shut, one by one, like coffin lids. Sometimes I thought my friendship with Nancy was the only thing standing between me and the void. I teetered on the edge of nothingness, just *this much* away from vanishing completely.

People hardly ever noticed me. In the bookshop, customers would wander around, searching desperately for assistance, and I could be jumping up and down in front of them, waving my arms and yelling, *'Hello there! Can I help you!'* and still they would stare right through me. I was the Invisible Woman. The Ghost at the Banquet, except I wasn't dead. If I'd been a character in a fairytale, I'd be the fairy they forgot to invite to the christening, the one who would turn up at the last minute and inflict some sort of hideous curse on the baby. Except I would never have done that, and even if I had I don't suppose anyone would have noticed.

But the way people looked right through me made

me think I'd missed my calling in life. I should have been a spy. Or a private detective. Or a journalist. Something where being able to blend into the wallpaper might have been an advantage. As it was, people had trouble remembering my name. Maurice, for example, was always getting it wrong.

Let me tell you about Maurice and Phoebe. After me, they were probably Nancy's closest friends. They represented everything I despised, though I almost certainly spent more time thinking about them than they did about me. To them, I represented... nothing. Nancy's loser friend.

Maurice was almost as rich and famous as his father, though all he'd done was to be born into the right family, one where celebrated writers or film-makers would always be popping round for tea and patting little Maurice on the head and chuckling at his childish aperçus, in the process bestowing on him the sort of social savoir faire than can't be bought or learned. It was the sort of upbringing that automatically placed him on another, more exotic planet, one for which Phoebe had been granted a resident's permit by marriage. I could only gaze at it from afar, dreaming of distant kingdoms peopled by fabulous beings whose names were familiar only from the newspaper articles and gossip columns I perused with gritted teeth. Nancy shuttled back and forth between the worlds, forging connections, winning people over with her easy-going charm, and sometimes I managed to hitch a ride alongside her, but I couldn't survive there on my own for long. The atmosphere was too rare.

It wasn't fair. What did these people have that I didn't? Apart from good looks, money, fame and glamour? Apart from famous parents? Apart from gold jewellery and garish designer togs and handbags trailing fringes and small furry knick-knacks and tiny padlocks? They didn't have good taste, that was for sure. Taste was the one area where I ruled. It wasn't everyone who could distinguish a genuine T. Vernon Isopod from the common horde of cheap Taiwanese imitations, or who could zero in on the Spud Williams candelabra nestling amongst the rusted bric-a-brac on a flea-market stall. I loved that candelabra, but it would have taken up half my living-room. So I cleaned it up and gave it to Maurice and Phoebe, whose loft was vast enough to accommodate a fleet of Chinooks. The next time I tagged along there with Nancy I was pleased to see it taking pride of place on their dining table.

I didn't go round there a *lot*. I couldn't call Maurice and Phoebe friends, not exactly, because the only thing we had in common was Nancy. They were always perfectly nice to me, but I'd lost count of the times I'd had to reintroduce myself to Maurice, even after I'd given them the candelabra. I felt awkward in their company, like a gatecrasher, unless I could somehow steer the conversation round to trends in decoration - the use of sawdust as floor covering in fashionable bars, or the sudden unexpected popularity of handwoven Tunisian towels - in which case they would hang on my every word, eyes open wide, mouths agape.

Phoebe was my sworn rival, though I don't think she was aware of it. She had what I wanted - a glittering career, which she'd managed to forge out of a low-ranking university degree and barefaced ambition, and a handsome, well-connected husband. She wrote a weekly column for a national newspaper, where she would describe the minutiae of her existence in mind-numbing detail - her social round, beauty regime, nanny problems, parking tickets. She popped up regularly on TV arts programmes, regurgitating other people's opinions as though they were her own. Once I heard my own views on fitted carpets emerging, as if by magic, from her glossy lipsticked mouth. It made me want to put my foot through the TV screen.

But Phoebe's career gave me hope. She didn't possess any particular talent; she wasn't outstandingly beautiful, and she didn't write especially well. She had parlayed a career out of nothing. And I could do that! Because I didn't have any particular talent either.

What's your talent? Nancy and I had once had a teacher called Mrs. Andrews who had asked this question incessantly. *What's your talent?* It was her catchphrase. We all called her Mrs. 'What's Your Talent' Andrews. Or at least I did. Everybody, Mrs. Andrews claimed, had a special gift. In some cases, it was academic brilliance; in others it was social, or artistic, or athletic. Or it could entail being good at things like housework or (and this made the class snigger) knowing how to please your husband.

Mrs. Andrews's question gave me sleepless nights. I would lie awake and worry about it. What *was* my talent? What *was* it? It seemed to me I'd never been terribly good at anything. I hadn't been terribly bad at anything either, so I couldn't even claim distinction there. I approached Mrs. Andrews with my problem. What did *she* think was my talent?

'Don't worry, Brenda,' she said. 'One day you'll find out what it is. You'll see.'

Finally, out of desperation, I decided I wasn't bad

at writing. Over the years, I'd worked hard at polishing my literary skills, though they hadn't got me very far. I'd written criticisms of contemporary design, and humorous vignettes about life as a cult survivor or a bookshop assistant. I sent some of these pieces off to magazines and newspapers, but had yet to receive a reply, even though they were better written than Phoebe's columns. My pen name was 'Gabrielle de Rospin', a near-anagram of Belinda Rose Pringle. While messing about with the Scrabble tiles, I also came up with the phrase, 'Lo, pale rider begins' which seemed appropriately apocalyptic, what with the end of the century looming and Alain going on about the computer bug he was convinced would kick in at midnight on December the thirty-first and make planes fall out of the sky.

'It'll be the end of civilisation as we know it,' he said as we unpacked a boxful of *Millennium Panic*, an opportunistic paperback with collapsing skyscrapers on the cover.

'Don't be daft,' I said.

'I thought you'd be more worried, being so religious and all.'

'I am *not* religious.'

'But Croydon...'

'Alain,' I said in a warning tone, 'You *promised* never to mention Croydon.'

It was my own fault. This was what happened when you had too many glasses of wine in the pub after work and spilled your dirty little secrets to your co-workers.

'What was it Wonderboy told you about signs?'

It was just as well there weren't many customers,

because I started yelling. 'You want signs, Alain? I'll give you signs! Bad rulers, civil discord, war, drought, famine, plague, comets, sudden deaths of prominent persons and an all-round increase in general sinfulness! Not to mention stupidity!'

Alain took a step back, as though he thought I was going to hit him, and for a second I wondered if he were going to burst into tears. But after a tense moment, he clapped his hands together and began to chuckle, a little too cheerfully. 'That's it, then. The end of the world is definitely nigh. You know what, Belinda? You really are a piece of work. Remind me never to get on your wrong side.'

I thought my wrong side was exactly where he'd just been, but the outburst had drained me, so I slunk off to sulk in the Cookery section.

*****

It was true no-one knew what was going to happen after the Millennium. Doom-mongers warned of rioting in the streets, and crazy new death cults, and incurable viruses. The Just Published shelf was crammed with novels set in post-apocalyptic landscapes strewn with rubble and corpses. The Amazon jungle was being hacked down and the ice-caps were melting. London seemed safer than most places, but I didn't trust the Thames Barrier. Flooding on a Biblical scale was always on the cards.

So to be on the safe side, I put together an Apocalypse Kit. I didn't tell anyone about this because I knew it would make me seem paranoid. But you couldn't be too careful. The contents:

1) One Space Blanket in superfine gold foil.

'Windproof. Chillproof. Waterproof. Also reflects radar.'

2) One packet of sticking-plasters. The chemist was out of beige that day, so - on a whim that would later cruelly rebound on me - I plumped for children's plasters decorated with green and purple dinosaurs. I always intended to replace them, but somehow it slipped my mind.

3) One matchbook bearing the Bar-F logo (a modern design classic).

4) One packet of Extra-Strength Doliban.

5) One horn-handled Étripouille folding knife with stainless steel blade, of the sort traditionally used by French peasants to slice off boars' testicles.

6) An Edison Samurai, with spare ink cartridges.

7) Two small tins of tuna.

8) A cereal bar which I later ate and forgot to replace.

Unlike Nancy, I was adept at spotting signs. For example, I had a premonition that something big was about to happen to her, that maybe something big was *already* happening, and that if I didn't watch out, it would happen without me. In September she fell off the grid, all my messages went unanswered and I assumed she'd gone off on holiday. But finally, on the tenth of October, she answered her phone.

I sensed immediately that something was wrong. She didn't sound herself. Yes, she was fine. No, she hadn't landed a starring role... Not yet, anyway; there was an audition coming up. Then her voice wobbled, and I knew it wasn't just pre-audition nerves.

'These last few weeks...' She trailed off into an uneasy silence, then sighed and said, 'There was this guy... The police, Belinda... He had a knife... It was...' She began to cry into the phone.

'I'll be right over,' I said.

*****

As soon as she opened the door I knew it was serious. The flat stank. Her hair lacked bounce. There were mauve circles around her eyes. She was wearing a sweatshirt and tracksuit bottoms, the sort of outfit one might expect to see on Mr. and Mrs. Slob, but not on Nancy Loughlin. It's true she'd never shown much enthusiasm whenever I'd tried to interest her in some of the more rigorous Belgian or Japanese designers, but she usually managed to assemble her flighty boho-chic look with a modicum of flair. Strangest of all, she'd put on weight. Nancy was a human twiglet. Now, though, she was looking... OK, still skinnier than a normal person like me, but unusually lumpy for someone whose default setting was stick-insect.

Knowing how often she forgot to eat and unwilling to forgo my own supper, I'd done some shopping on the way there. We exchanged chaste kisses and I took my bag into the kitchen. As usual, her fridge contained little of merit: the usual cheap Chardonnay, a greenish-grey lump that might once have been cheese, six lip pencils and about a dozen Fudge Tubs.

I stared at the Fudge Tubs, perplexed. I'd seen a poster featuring a busty supermodel laughing maniacally as she raised a spoonful to her lips. I'd even sampled one, for research purposes, but it had been too sweet and artificial-tasting, even for me. Later, I would wonder if the range hadn't been placed on the market just for Nancy. She was the only person I ever saw eating them.

And eat them she did, all the time. She was a Fudge Tub junkie.

I shut the fridge door with a shudder. 'Just as well I brought supplies.'

'I'm not hungry,' said Nancy.

'I am, though. You don't mind if I eat something?'

'Be my guest.'

I opened the Beaujolais I'd brought with me and we took our glasses back into the living-room, which is where I discovered the source of the bad smell. The melamine surface of the table was disfigured by a scorch mark as big as a pudding-plate. The thought of such vandalism so casually inflicted on any piece of furniture, even one as mass-produced as that, made my buttocks clench involuntarily. 'Have you taken up drugs again?'

Nancy perked up. 'You have drugs?'

'When do I ever have drugs?' I prodded the scorch mark. To my horror, the fingertip came away coated in black sludge. I tried to wipe it clean with a tissue, then had to wash my hands thoroughly, with lots of soap, to get rid of the lingering odour.

I'd been thinking our conversation would simply pick up where we'd left off on the phone, but she seemed reluctant to open up, so I prepared tagliatelle for the both of us. After I'd cleaned my plate, Nancy was still pushing her food around, trying to make it look as though she'd eaten some. Finally she gave up the pretence, and sat back and lit a cigarette.

'I thought you'd given up,' I said.

'I started again.'

'Try the salad.'

'I've had enough.'

'Maybe just a mouthful?'

'I'll throw up.'

'Remind me to go to a little more trouble next time.' I started clearing plates away to hide my annoyance.

Nancy sighed and blew out smoke. 'Sorry, Belinda. It's just this last week has been an absolute nightmare.'

This was my cue to be a good listener. I dumped the plates in the sink and grabbed the bottle of Beaujolais. Observing that although she was off her food, she was having no such problem with alcohol, I poured us both another glass.

'So what's up?' I said, sitting down again.

She lit another cigarette and started talking. Once she'd started, she didn't stop until she'd told me everything.

*****

I gazed at her in wonder, feeling slightly intoxicated, though not from the alcohol. The knife attack was extraordinary enough, but my friend being pregnant had knocked me for six. I wasn't yet sure if it was good news or bad, but I wanted to know more about the pregnancy test.

'What kind of insect?'

'Feelers and lots of legs. Like a beetle.'

'Pregnancy tests don't do that.'

'This one did.'

'Why didn't you call me?'

She shrugged. 'I didn't feel like calling anyone.'

'You called Maurice.'

'That was work.'

'And this maniac just attacked you out of the blue,

for no reason? I didn't see anything in the papers.'

Nancy pulled a tabloid from one of the stacks she kept lying around. She'd always been a bit of a hoarder.

'Well no,' I said. 'You know I don't read *that* one.'

She found the page and passed it over.

WEST END KNIFE ATTACK. From our reporter, Verity Wilson. A crazed immigrant attacked an unemployed blonde glamour model with a knife on a West End street yesterday before accidentally stabbing himself and bleeding to death. Police are looking into the incident, which they described as a domestic squabble.

'I'm shocked,' said the victim, who was shaken but unharmed. But it certainly didn't appear to have affected her appetite for sweets!

Then there were some quotes from a police spokesman about knife violence and what steps were being taken to combat it.

'He was an immigrant?'

Nancy shrugged. 'Do I look blonde to you? American, apparently. On a tourist visa though.'

I relaxed. Nancy would surely think twice about sharing any more information with this Verity Wilson person. Even I could have done a better job than that. *My* headlines would have been much more sensational. PREGNANT ACTRESS ESCAPES DEATH BY INCHES! CRAZED ATTACKER DIES IN FREAK ACCIDENT! STREETS OF LONDON DRENCHED IN BLOOD! PREGNANCY TEST EXPLODES!

'You didn't tell this reporter about, you know, being pregnant?'

'I haven't told anyone except you,' she said.

I looked at her sceptically. 'And you never noticed your periods had stopped?'

'We're not all as organised as you, Belinda.' She said this as though it were an insult. It was true I could predict the onset of my period almost to the day, but Nancy's always took her by surprise, as though each one were a never-to-be-repeated aberration. Her girlfriends would invariably end up rummaging around in their bags for spare sanitary products to give her. I'd lost count of the tampons I'd donated over the years.

'I've got better things to do than mark my diary in red ink,' she said. I glanced down at my bag, where the corner of my journal was peeking out from the folds of an olive-green pashmina. She didn't know I kept a journal. *Or did she?* It wasn't the red ink I was worried about. It was the other stuff, about her. Some of it was less than complimentary.

Nancy leaned back and lit yet another cigarette.

'You shouldn't be smoking,' I said. This was ironic, *I'd* always been the maternal one. Nancy had never wanted children. Now my motherly instincts kicked in and I leant over to snatch the packet of cigarettes away. She tried to grab it back. We tussled for a while. She won, but I was pleased to see the packet was squished out of shape.

'You'll stunt its growth,' I said.

'Christ, Belinda, I'm not going to *keep* it.'

'Who was it? Maurice?'

Nancy insisted she and Maurice were ancient history, but that didn't stop them canoodling in public. Their continuing intimacy had always struck me as abnormal. Most couples who split up turned into deadly enemies, like me and Roger, whom I never tired of slagging off to anyone within earshot. But Nancy and Maurice were still so chummy I sometimes felt like a gooseberry in their presence. They even snogged in front of Phoebe, who always pretended not to mind.

'It wasn't anyone,' Nancy said in a voice so tiny I had to strain to hear it. 'I haven't had sex for over a year.'

I tried to wrap my head around this, and failed. I couldn't imagine Nancy not having sex. 'What about that sculptor? The one who looks like a tree?'

'Ugh, no.'

'That nice black dancer?'

'Winston? Gay. Fact he never goes anywhere without his boyfriend is a bit of a giveaway, I'd have thought.'

I circled back to Maurice. Of course it *had* to be Maurice. Who else could it have been?

'Does Phoebe know?' I was already imagining what effect the collapse of Phoebe's marriage would have on her column. Her readers would go wild for it. There was no way I would be able to compete. It was years since the collapse of my own marriage, and now my feelings about it were sealed away, tragically unexploited, in an airtight vault to which I no longer had access.

'It wasn't Maurice,' said Nancy. She looked so pathetic, sitting there with her lifeless hair and puffy eyes that I went over to give her a hug, taking care to avoid the drooping cigarette jutting from her fist.

'It's OK,' I said. 'We've all had one-night stands. We've all got caught up in the heat of the moment, and forgotten to take precautions.' In fact I hadn't forgotten, not ever, but I also sensed that now wasn't the time to tell her off for being flaky.

I felt her stiffen in my arms. '*It wasn't a one-night stand!*' She was trying to shout, but her voice was muffled by my jumper. *'It wasn't anything!'*

'Sure.' I withdrew my embrace and sat down again. 'So I guess it's some sort of immaculate conception. Except you're not exactly immaculate, are you.' She gave me a look I pretended not to notice.

I tried again. 'How many weeks?'

'Eighteen? No, nineteen.'

I felt my jaw plummet. '*Nineteen!* How could you possibly *not* notice you missed *four periods?'*

'First month doesn't count, apparently. Anyway, I miss them all the time. Stress.'

Or anorexia, I thought uncharitably. 'No blackouts? Date rape drugs? Lost weekends?'

'Nope,' she said.

'But let's say Maurice is the leading contender.'

Nancy sighed. 'Let's not.'

'Who else could it be?' I insisted. 'Think!'

I'd pushed her too far. 'I've been doing nothing *but* think for the past week! For Christ's sake, do you think I don't know a shag when I've had one?'

Normally I would have shouted straight back, but I could feel one of my migraines coming on and had to go into the kitchen for a glass of water to wash down one of the Dolibans from my emergency kit, making a mental note to replace them in the morning.

In the months to come I would have to replace them again, many times.

*****

For the next hour, we went round in circles, covering

the same ground over and over again, like steeplechase runners getting wearier with each lap. She insisted the pregnancy had just 'happened', while I kept repeating that pregnancies didn't 'just happen' and that, sooner or later, she would have to face up to it. It was getting late. Since it didn't look as though Nancy would be finishing the tagliatelle any day soon, I spooned what was left into an airtight container and stowed it in my bag. As we polished off the Beaujolais, I asked what she was going to do. She told me she'd made an appointment at a clinic just off Harley Street. She turned her best pleading face towards me. 'I might have to borrow.'

'What about the N.H.S.?'

'Too slow.'

'Yeah, I guess you have left it a bit late. Does Maurice know?'

'He thinks I'm ill.' She laughed. 'I threw up in the National Gallery yesterday, right in front of your dragon painting.'

I burst out laughing too. Cornelius van Haarlem's *Two Followers of Cadmus Devoured by a Dragon* showed a dragon chewing a naked man's face off and sinking its claws into what was left of his companion, whose already severed head lay trailing fibrous tissue in the foreground. It was the sort of gruesome image I'd thought would send appreciative shivers of horror down the spines of Nancy's tour groups, which was why I'd told her about it.

I took advantage of her positive mood swing to say, 'Why not keep it?'

She stopped laughing. There was a weighty pause, and then finally she said, 'You're kidding.'

'I could babysit,' I said.

'Jesus, Belinda.'

The words slipped out. 'I could adopt it.'

Nancy stared at me, aghast. 'You think I'd go through all the *pain*, of having a baby and then just... *give it away?* To *you?*'

'Better than getting rid of it. Like a disposable bunch of cells.'

'Oh shut up.'

'Adoption would be the ideal solution,' I said.

She snarled, 'If you want to adopt, there's nothing stopping you. Plenty of unwanted children out there.'

'But not *this* one,' I said, warming to my theme. '*This* one is different. Can't you feel it?'

'I'm feeling it all the fucking time,' she said. 'Forget it, Belinda. I'm not having a baby just because *you're* feeling broody.'

'It's not as though you've got a career to harm,' I pointed out with unnecessary cruelty.

She winced. 'That's not entirely true.' She lit yet another cigarette, and told me about the audition.

'Congratulations,' I said. 'I see you've got your priorities straight.'

She ignored my sarcasm. 'I just wish I didn't look like shit.'

'You'll be fine,' I said. 'What's the play?'

All she knew was that it was a musical.

'You can sing?'

'I can do whatever is necessary.'

Chapter 6
The City of Dreadful Night

The audition was at Carlo's Place, a cavernous backroom behind a fashionable pub along the road from Maurice and Phoebe's loft. Nancy recognised some of the actors who were lounging about smoking and looking so relaxed she deduced they must have already auditioned. She nodded to them and started smoking too. After twenty minutes, a needlessly harassed young woman with a clipboard called her name and ushered her through a set of swing-doors towards the stage area, where the darkness was pierced by a single spotlight.

Nancy positioned herself in the patch of light and squinted towards where she imagined Les Six would be, but the light was shining directly into her eyes. She heard coughing and shuffling, but no-one spoke up. This was typical; no-one ever told you what they wanted, and she knew it didn't make the slightest difference anyway, because they'd already decided the instant you'd walked on stage whether or not you they wanted you..

Unless this time they were looking for someone with initiative, someone with the ability to improvise. Nancy planted her feet firmly on the ground, took a deep breath and said, 'WHAT WOULD YOU LIKE ME TO DO?'

Either her sense of hearing had been heightened by the tension or it was a trick of the acoustics, because now she could make out voices. Three of them, all men.

They were discussing her merits and demerits, as though she were livestock at an agricultural show.

'Marion said this one was a looker. Jaz?'

Jasper Andrews, thought Nancy. Had to be. She felt a small shiver of excitement.

'She *is* supposed to be lowlife.'

'Not *that* low.'

'Hair would be nice if she styled it properly.'

The truth washed over Nancy with depressing inevitability. It wasn't an actress they were looking for. It was a sex kitten. The disappointment felt bitter on her tongue. Only a few weeks earlier, glamour-puss had been her middle name. Only a few weeks earlier, and she would have walked it. *This is only temporary*, she wanted to tell them. *I'll be back to normal next week*. She shielded her eyes and tried to peer beyond the front seats. Maybe it was time to seize the day.

She took a deep breath and let it out slowly, pushing the air up from her diaphragm. One two three four. And expelled, with the air, all her doubts and fears. Five six seven eight. She was an empty vessel, waiting to be filled. She was clever. She was a fifteenth century noblewoman disguised as a man.

'The quality of mercy is not strain'd it droppeth as the gentle rain from heaven upon the place beneath it is twice blest it blesseth him that gives and him that takes...'

'Hello?' said one of the voices.

'Tis mightiest in the mightiest it becomes the throned monarch better than his crown his sceptre shows...'

'What are you *doing?*'

She stopped and squinted again.

'Portia's speech from *The Merchant of Venice*.'

She heard an exaggerated sigh. 'Yes, we can hear that. But *why?*'

Another outbreak of muttering, though this time she couldn't make out more than an odd word here and there.

'...pants...'

'...too fat...'

'...nice tits...'

The tits remark gave her hope. She wasn't proud. Whatever it took. She thrust her breasts out as far as possible (was it her imagination or were they bigger than usual?) and stood there like a drab bird trying to attract a more colourful mate.

A figure materialised in front of her, backlit so brightly it might have been an alien. 'Page forty-four,' it said, holding out a sheaf of paper.

She heard someone else say, quite clearly, 'Waste of time.'

No it's not, thought Nancy. She grabbed the manuscript and immediately started to read.

'Saw her last night, I did. Wearing a pretty new bonnet and tipsy with it, all lit up and laughing, like the gal was in love. Laughing she was, and saying, see what a jolly bonnet I've got. And look at the poor bitch now.' Nancy pretended to look down at something laid out in front of her. 'Just look at poor Polly lying shrunken and white on the slab, grinning with her extra mouth, throat slashed from ear to ear...'

She hesitated, suddenly convinced there was a fourth pair of eyes watching her from the void. Someone coughed. She squinted in the direction of the noise, but thanks to the dazzling light the only thing she could see were dancing clusters of red and green pinpricks.

'Thank you, Miss, er, Loughlin.'

No. They weren't going to get rid of her that easily. She riffled through the pages until she spotted some lyrics. She set them to the first showtune that popped into her head, which happened to be *I'd Do Anything* from *Oliver!* The words didn't fit, but she wasn't going to let a thing like that put her off.

> *Some say we're way below*
> *The very lowest of the low*
> *That the East End is the kind of place*
> *Where the gentlefolk don't go*
>
> *It's the pits, it's shit, it's underlit*
> *Your throat's at risk of being slit*
> *In the city of dreadful night*

All of a sudden she knew what the musical was about. *The Soho Slasher!* But how would Les Six know about that? She'd made him up... It was hot beneath the lights, but her brow felt chilly. She stared in horror at the corpse of the man in grey, his throat yawning open like a sliced pomegranate. Suddenly her ears were filled with the roaring of a crowd, as though the home team had just landed one in the back of the net..

*****

She was flat on her back, and there was a bald gremlin crouching over her. But this time, she was ready for him. She brought her knee sharply up into his groin. The man said 'Oof!' and keeled over, applying both hands to his testicles, his face the colour of chicory.

There was laughter from the void, and clapping.

The bald man curled into a foetal position. Nancy sat up and said, 'I'm sorry, I thought you were attacking me.' She scrambled to her feet, trying to smooth down the back of her skirt.

'All right there, Les my boy?' said the voice she thought was probably that of Jasper Andrews. 'Still capable of fathering children?'

Her heart sank. She'd just kneed the playwright in the nuts.

Another voice shouted in an American accent, 'Man, you were pussywhipped.'

Les Six grunted in pain. Nancy was furious with herself. Now she would never get the part, not even if she were the last actress on earth. Six manoeuvred himself into a kneeling position and gasped, 'Thank you for reading.'

More laughter and applause.

'Would you like me to read some more?' asked Nancy, holding out a hand to help him struggle to his feet.

'Christ, no.'

She took this as a signal the audition was over, and probably her acting career as well.

'We'll be in touch, darling,' the invisible American said with all the sincerity of a hardened roué after a one-night stand. He lowered his voice, but she could hear him saying, 'Who's next? Has the luscious Carlotta dragged herself out of bed yet?' As Nancy retreated backstage, she passed a dark-eyed brunette who'd been waiting in front of the swing doors. The luscious Carlotta flashed the cruel, confident smile of someone who knew her chances had only been enhanced by the debacle she'd just witnessed.

'You were fabulous,' she said as Nancy passed. Nancy felt a rush of irritation mixed with envy - *she's going to get it* - and at the same time felt a familiar wave of nausea rising from the pit of her stomach. *Oh God*, she thought. *Here we go again.*

'Sorry,' she said, charging through the doors. Behind her, she heard a startled yelp as they swung back and slapped Carlotta on the bottom, propelling her pell-mell on to the stage.

Nancy felt a thin ripple of satisfaction. *Was that an accident, or something I did?*

Either way, it was the best thing that had happened all day.

*****

I commiserated with her later in the Bar Gee.

'There'll be other auditions,' I said.

'That was my first in *months*,' she said. 'And once it gets out that I kneed the playwright in the testicles they're not exactly going to be lining up with offers.'

I watched curiously as she got down to the serious business of mainlining Marlboro and glugging Chardonnay. Occasionally, I took a sip of my Pinot Noir.

'You *sure* you're not going to keep it? Because I don't think you should be smoking and drinking like this.'

'I'm seeing a doctor tomorrow afternoon.'

'I bet he tells you to stop smoking.'

'An abortion doctor,' she said.

'Damn.' The last tiny droplets of hope trickled out of me. I'd been hoping she might change her mind after all.

'Don't start up again.'

I made an effort to be positive. After all, it was Nancy's choice, not mine. 'Do you want me to pick you up afterwards?'

'No, tomorrow's just a preliminary. It's Monday I need someone to take me home.'

I couldn't help myself. 'Are you sure it's what you want?'

'We already talked about this.'

'I'm paying for it.'

This was a low blow. Nancy stubbed out her cigarette and immediately lit another. 'For heaven's sake, Belinda. If I'd known you were going to be such a pain, I would never have told you. I'm sorry, truly sorry you can't have babies, but you can't expect me to provide you with one.'

I bit my lip and backed down. 'I'm sorry, OK? Of course it's your decision. I just don't want you to do something you'll regret for the rest of your life.'

She guffawed. 'No regrets, I promise you. But if you find it distasteful, I could always borrow the money from Maurice and Phoebe.'

'No, of course I'll help out,' I said quickly, not wanting my rival involved. 'Forget what I said about adoption. It was... sort of a reverie. Forgive me.'

Nancy smiled sadly. 'You would have been a wonderful mother. You could still adopt, you know.'

I blinked back tears and tried to smile back at her. 'It wouldn't be the same.'

Nancy squeezed my hand, and I was touched to

see that she too had tears in her eyes.

I permitted myself to wallow for a while, drank more Pinot Noir than was wise, and started talking about things I shouldn't have done, like Croydon, and my ex, and the disastrous miscarriage that had put paid to my ever having children of my own. Nancy ended up feeling so sorry for me she offered to make us Dry Martinis the next evening. And because I thought it might provide me with one last chance to change her mind, I accepted eagerly. She even lent me her spare keys, in case she was late getting back from her appointment at the clinic.

Which is how I met the man who would later cut off one of my ears.

Chapter 7
Enemy Action

Nancy's day started badly and got steadily worse. By the time she left for her appointment, the wind couldn't seem to make up its mind which direction it was coming from, and kept blowing cold drizzle into her face. There were no taxis to be seen, but the very thought of being trapped between malodorous bodies on the underground made her feel queasy again. She bought a magazine and a newspaper from the stall outside the station. The headlines were grim. NHS CRISIS: SHOCK HOSPITAL CLOSURES! SNAKE ALERT IN REGENT'S PARK! JELLYFISH PLAGUE HITS SOUTHEAST!

She gave this last item the once over; the water supply in parts of Essex and Kent had been contaminated by tiny transparent jellyfish, almost invisible to the naked eye. The already overstretched emergency wards were being swamped by people who'd sustained multiple stings on their hands and faces and in their gullets. Those in affected areas were being advised not to drink or wash in water that hadn't been strained.

Nancy's low mood got even lower. Buying the newspaper had been a mistake. She dropped it into the nearest rubbish bin, ignoring the beseeching gaze of an old man trying to sell her a heart-shaped silver balloon from a bunch the wind kept threatening to snatch out of his grip. While she was there, she stripped the shrink-wrap from the magazine and dumped it into the bin as well, along with a small rainforest's worth of free catalogues and flyers. Just as she was turning away, she saw a man in a pinstripe suit reaching into the bin for her discarded paper, and felt unreasonably aggrieved, as though he'd been lurking on purpose, ready to freeload.

Her skirt snagged on something. She looked down and saw a small, grubby child tugging at it, egged on by a woman in a headscarf standing a few feet away. Nancy wrenched herself free and hurried into the station, dogged by a sense that things were falling apart. The feeling persisted all the way down the escalators.

The platform was already dangerously crowded, but it wasn't long before she heard a low rumble and felt the displacement of air that heralded an approaching train. Aware that if she wasn't quick off the mark there might not be room for her in the carriage, she worked her way towards the outer edge of the platform, past an old man who hadn't dry-cleaned his clothes for several months, a fat lady who smelled of marmalade, a cluster of loud youths with backpacks, and a gaggle of adolescents who ought surely to have been at school.

Someone bumped her from behind. *Stupid backpacker*, she thought. She'd barely regained her balance when she felt herself bumped again. Once, twice, thrice. She realised with mounting incredulity it was deliberate. She was being prodded forward by someone in the crowd. Slowly but surely, they were jostling her towards the edge of the platform.

Just as the nose of the train burst out of the tunnel, she felt another push. She planted her feet firmly, determined to resist, and caught a glimpse of something shiny floating past: a silver balloon, borne aloft on the warm air current.

And once again she found herself looking at the slide-show of her life and times. This time the early memories zipped past so quickly they were subliminal, but now they'd been updated: blood spraying out of Karl Petersen's neck, the hospital, the exploding pregnancy kit, the audition, the man in the pinstriped suit fishing her discarded newspaper out of the bin, the grubby child, the escalator...

She felt herself snatched back into the here and now, and the voice in her head was saying, *As it is written, so shall it be done.* One moment she was pitching forward, and the headlines flashed through her head like a montage from an old black and white film. ASPIRING ACTRESS SURVIVES KNIFE ATTACK ONLY TO PERISH TRAGICALLY IN FREAK UNDERGROUND ACCIDENT! The next, she was no longer toppling but sashaying to one side in a snake-hipped manoeuvre that wouldn't have looked out of place on *Come Dancing.* But there was no time to feel smug, because she had to swivel yet again to avoid the grubby child pushing past in pursuit of the balloon.

The tall man behind her had no such luck. The child became entangled in his legs. The tall man twisted round, trying to break free, windmilled his arms, sailed backwards off the platform and landed flat on his back across the rails. The impact made blood squirt out of his nose like ketchup from a plastic tomato. Nancy just had time to note that he was wearing a grey suit, and had a fleeting impression of him struggling to sit up, shiny white face staring up, mouth starting to move, but she didn't get time to work out what he was trying to say, because the train was suddenly *there*, and thundering so loudly that she must have imagined the *squelch* as it mashed into him.

The train stopped and the doors slid open, but now her dancing skills had deserted her. Her legs refused to move out of the way as she was buffeted by disembarking passengers. She saw the child reunited with its balloon, and the mother thrusting her hand out towards oblivious passers-by. No-one was behaving as though anything were amiss. She wondered whether to scream, just to mark the fact that something had happened, but her instinct told her it was better not to draw attention to herself. Her presence at one violent death had been bad luck; witnessing a second might seem to some people like carelessness.

There was an inaudible announcement over the speaker system. People were looking around, bewildered, suspecting a problem but unable to see what it was. Nancy knew she had to get away before police arrived. She finally forced her feet to move and joined the swell of passengers shuffling towards the exit. There was shouting from further down the train; she glanced back just in time to see the driver lean out of his cab and vomit over the platform.

Well at least it's not me *throwing up this time*

The escalator was out of order, so she joined the long column of travellers toiling up the steps towards the daylight, at one point pressing back to allow a stream of uniformed staff pass on their hurried way down to the platform. She made it outside just as a member of the transport police was sealing off the entrance with yellow tape. The drizzle felt cool on her face. She moved away from the gathering crush, leant against the wall, closed her eyes and breathed deeply.

One two three four. That was better. She sensed someone in front of her and opened her eyes.

'Are you all right? Do you need to sit down?'

The concerned citizen who was peering at her looked vaguely familiar. He was shielding his head with a newspaper.

'That's my paper,' she said, surprised.

'What?'

'I saw you take it out of the bin.'

She wasn't accusing him, just stating a fact, but he was angry and embarrassed. 'Lady, you threw it away.'

She wanted to tell him he could keep it, but he stalked off before she could summon the words. The exchange left her unsettled, so she bought a Fudge Tub from the station kiosk. Before she had time to open it, a cab drew up and three men climbed out. She barged in front of a young Japanese couple standing patiently at the kerb, and climbed in.

'I'm pregnant!' she yelled back at their bemused faces.

'Congratulations!' the driver said as he pulled away. 'When's it due?'

'Never!' she shouted, feeling dangerously light-headed.

He breathed in and said, 'Blimey, sure you've got enough perfume on?' Before she could reply, the driver's phone rang and he immediately started bickering about something that had happened to someone's wife the previous evening at the Pig and Whistle.

As the cab inched down High Holborn, she swallowed a spoonful of Fudge Tub and felt the familiar sugar rush flowing through her system. It was so addictive it *had* to be illegal. But it delivered the much-needed boost. Mad knifemen? Homicidal tube-travellers? Screw them. She was ready for anything fate could throw at her.

Fate took aim.

The next incident took place as they were approaching Oxford Circus. She heard a screech of tyres and looked up to see a Ford Fiesta barrelling out of a side street. The cabbie swore and swerved, sending her careening against the window, but the slide show started up in her head again, and she knew it didn't make any difference what anyone did now. *As it is written, so shall it be done.* Her instinct told her she was safe and the Fiesta driver was doomed.

Her instinct was right. One moment they were on a collision course, the Fiesta looming close enough for her to make out the bloodshot whites of the driver's eyes. The next, he was wrestling with a plastic bag that had blown through his open window and wrapped itself around his head. He took his hands off the steering-wheel to claw at his face, stamping on the brakes, but his feet must have connected with the accelerator by mistake because the Fiesta shot across the junction, sending out a shower of sparks as it scraped a metal barrier, and scattered a crowd of pedestrians before embedding itself, with a lazy shower of glass, in a shop window display. The impact wasn't loud; it was like a foot stamping on an empty cardboard box.

'Bloody tourists,' said the cabbie.

Nancy twisted in her seat to get another look, just in time to see the last moments of a haunting tableau vivant: the driver caught in mid-struggle, trying to extricate himself from the clinging embrace of a display mannequin which had pinned him to his seat like an over-possessive mistress. Then the crushed engine ignited with a mighty whoosh and the car and its contents were lost to view behind a curtain of boiling steam.

She turned back to her Fudge Tub. This time, she felt detached, more of an observer than a participant, the solid walls of the cab sealing her off from outside events.

The rest of the journey passed without further drama. She felt unnaturally calm as she ran through a series of unlikely scenarios in her head. Perhaps she'd inherited a fortune without knowing it, and now rival legatees were trying to bump her off. Perhaps she had unwittingly offended a member of a powerful crime syndicate. Perhaps it was jellyfish in the water supply.

But there had three attempts on her life now, because she had no doubt the Fiesta driver had been aiming at *her*. Ascribing it to coincidence was stretching the bounds of probability. This was personal. What was so special about her? Yes, she was pregnant. But so were hundreds, no thousands, no *millions* of other women around the world. What made her so different?

There was only one thing she could think of. All those other women had had sex.

And everyone who had tried to kill her had died.

She wondered if the two things were connected.

*****

After the examination, Nancy sat facing Dr. Madison in his office as he consulted his notes. He was frowning.

'Ah yes, it's clear that allowing this pregnancy to come to term would pose a grave risk to your health.'

Tell me about it. Nancy thought of the Fiesta driver,

then realised what was required of her and nodded.

'Definitely.'

Dr Madison looked up sharply. 'I'm not kidding. The foetus really is showing signs of irregular development in several significant respects. I can't be more specific without further tests, but...'

'I just want it to be over.'

Now it was Dr Madison's turn to nod. 'Then I don't see a problem.' He turned his blue-eyed gaze on her. 'Would you like to see a counsellor?'

She shook her head. She didn't need counselling. She just needed her body back, and as soon as possible. She filled out her cheque and made a note of Monday's appointment in her diary. 'You can't make it any earlier?'

'Afraid not. You're not our only patient.'

'Of course not,' said Nancy, wishing she hadn't sounded so eager.

'By the way,' he said as he held the door open for her to leave. 'Love that perfume. Anarchie?'

'That's right,' said Nancy. She'd been especially generous with the spritzing that morning in an attempt to counter the everyday odours pressing in on her. 'Too much?'

'Not for me, I love it. But best leave it off next Monday. You don't want our anaesthetist sneezing when he's trying to stick needles into you.'

He saw her face and said, 'Oh, don't look like that. I was *joking*.'

*****

The drizzle had stopped, leaving the air smelling of damp grass. Now the day was all brightness and birdsong and sunlight glancing off random windows. There was a skip in Nancy's step as well. She smiled at passers by and paused to pet a small dog that had been tied to some railings. The end of the ordeal was in sight. Life would soon be back to normal, and she would be free to face the future and drink deeply of whatever life had to offer. She wouldn't waste a minute of it. This pain-in-the-arse pregnancy was at least teaching her to count her blessings.

There were vacant cabs aplenty now, but she decided to walk. She lit a cigarette and inhaled deeply. As soon as the abortion was over she would quit smoking again, but in the meantime - why not?

But things weren't back to normal, not yet. If the car crash at Oxford Circus had reminded her of a low budget action movie, the rest of the afternoon turned into a Roadrunner cartoon. She was Roadrunner. The men in grey were Wile E. Coyote.

The first one made his just as she was passing beneath some scaffolding. He was fifty yards away, bounding towards her, drawing what looked like a syringe from his inside pocket. Her immediate instinct was to scoot for cover, but instead she forced herself to slow down and see what would happen, and she saw the images in her head, and the voice inside her said, *As it is written, so shall it be done.*

There was a series of small convulsive reports from somewhere overhead, but Nancy's eyes were fixed on the man in grey, so she had an unobstructed view when a large cube of white marble plummeted to the ground like a meteor, taking half his head with it. Only when other passers-by stopped to stare in shock at the pink stuff oozing out of his splintered skull did she see the cube was an ornamental clock trailing uneven lengths of rope. She tilted her head and saw two ashen-faced builders peering down from the scaffolding, one of them sneezing uncontrollably. His colleague gave him a look that said, *Now you've done it.* A small crowd was gathering: a couple of businessman, a man in a High Visibility jacket, and a fat woman in a floral-print dress pressed forward to get a better look. A man in shirt sleeves leant out of a nearby window to tell everyone he had rung for an ambulance. But there was nothing to be done. The fellow on the ground was beyond help, so Nancy walked away. None of this was really happening. It wasn't real life, it had to be a movie.

She'd barely had time to recover when the next man in grey appeared. There was a knife in his hand, not a Kitchen Devil this time, but before Nancy could identify the brand he'd already lost his footing and fallen sideways into the path of an oncoming number 73 bus. Who would have thought that such a solid-seeming object as a man's head could end up wrapped like a pancake around one of those front wheels? But there was no time for this vision to sink in, because now a lanky man in spectacles was striding purposefully towards her, and she'd only just had time to register the glint of sunlight reflecting off whatever he was pulling out of his inside pocket when there was a frenzied barking and a brace of Rottweilers appeared out of nowhere and launched themselves at his throat. She hurried on and didn't look round, not even when the screaming began. *As it is written, so shall it be done.*

She was trembling. Her nerves were shot. She needed a stiff drink. Or several. So she adjusted her route home and stopped off at the Bar Zoom.

Chapter 8
Jules Delgado

At first I thought Nancy had forgotten to lock her front door again. She was always leaving doors unlocked, or losing keys, or leaving windows open so the rain came in and soaked whatever was inside, which on one occasion was a book on Surrealism I'd lent her. By the time I got it back it was as warped as one of Salvador Dali's watches.

So when her door swung open before I'd even had a chance to turn the key, I tutted and compensated for her earlier oversight by double-locking it from the inside. Which was poor judgement on my part, because there was already someone in the flat, and it wasn't Nancy. I walked straight past the blue nylon rucksack leaning against the wall, and straight into the living-room.

The first thing I noticed about him was his hair, which was long and black and gleaming. He'd made himself at home. Judging by the pile of discarded magazines and half-finished bottle of Chardonnay, he'd been waiting for some time. He was installed in Nancy's favourite armchair, feet up on the coffee table, ankles neatly crossed and toes elongated by winklepickers, the like of which I had not seen since my ex had briefly played bass in a beatnik revival band. He was wearing a white shirt buttoned to the neck, without a tie, and his suit was charcoal-coloured, and so well cut it made my eyes water. His were hidden behind sunglasses. Maybe he thought they made him look glamorous. I wasn't about to argue; he was easily the most glamorous person I'd ever set eyes on. And ridiculously handsome, like a rock star. Clearly he was one of Nancy's actor friends; I couldn't think of any non-showbiz milieu that would have tolerated looks like those.

He wasn't the first of Nancy's friends I'd ever fancied, but this was different, I could feel it. More than fancied, in fact; I decided almost instantly that I was in love. But it was a love fated to be unrequited, of this I was already certain. He was so far out of my league it made me dizzy and I had to prop myself up against the sitting-room doorframe.

'Hello,' I said.

I could have sworn he'd noticed me long before I opened my mouth, but he gave an exaggerated start, as though it had been the greeting that had alerted him to my presence. He set the bottle down and got to his feet and covered the space between us in two bounds, almost - but not quite - leaving me no time to notice he wasn't as tall as he'd appeared while sitting down with his legs stretched out. He was actually quite short. But a couple of inches taller than me, which is what counted. Or it might have done, had I been in his league. It wasn't as though I fancied my chances, but I couldn't help imagining what it might be like to wake up with a face like that on the pillow beside me.

The finishing touch - he whipped off his shades as he came, folding them up and slipping them into his breast pocket in a movement so streamlined it was as though he rehearsed it in front of mirrors.

'How *are* you?' he asked, as though we were old friends.

'I'm fine,' I said. 'How are you?' I stuck out my hand, but instead of just shaking it, he grasped it warmly in both of his and gazed directly into my eyes, as though realising that I was, in fact, the most fascinating person in the world.

Yep, that'll do it, every time.

His eyes were brown, but surprisingly pale, with an orange nebula exploding outward from the black hole of the pupil. I found it difficult to tear my gaze away. There were whole galaxies in there, and I yearned to explore them.

'Busy,' he said. 'So many projects we have to finish before the Millennium.'

He spoke with a fake-sounding accent. Posh American, if there were such a thing. I wondered if he were practising for a role; if so, he would need a dialect coach.

'I know what you mean,' I said, thinking about my ever-present Apocalypse Kit, yet sensing that whipping it out to show him might be a little premature at such an early stage in our relationship.

He finally relinquished his warm grip on my hand. 'Jules Delgado,' he said. 'My pleasure.' And he flashed a smile that turned my knees to jelly, despite giving me a flash of gold fillings that made me think of Mexican drug barons. Not that I'd ever met any.

I couldn't remember Nancy ever mentioning a Jules, but her friends were legion; the ones I'd actually met were only the tip of a very large social iceberg. I wondered how many others she'd doled out keys to. Flustered by his awesomeness, I parked my bag and, trying to buy time, announced I was going to make myself a cup of tea, and did he want some. He trotted after me into the kitchen, which was so tiny we were smooshed up against each other as I went through the ritual of selecting the least chipped mug in Nancy's cupboard. I can't say I was displeased by his proximity, though in that small space it became apparent he was fond of garlic.

He said, 'I don't drink tea.'

I said, 'I don't drink... *tea*,' in an approximation of a Hungarian accent.

He chuckled. 'You English are adorable.'

'What part of *America* are you from, Jules?'

'Here and there. I've been all over, one time or another. But originally Pasadena.'

'That's nice,' I said, intent on my tea-making.

'I'd like to tell you something about myself,' he said. 'I owe you that much.'

I didn't think he owed me anything, but said, 'Be my guest.' He stuck to my heels like a shadow as I trotted back into the living-room with my tea. I perched on the sofa, but Delgado, instead of reclaiming the armchair, hovered by the doorway, as though preparing to make a dramatic entrance. Even though he was already in the room.

'My mother was a Hollywood movie star,' he began, and immediately responded to my unspoken question. 'I don't suppose you would have heard of her. Her career never really took off. She made a couple of movies in the sixties, forgettable pieces of fluff no-one bothered to see and everyone quickly forgot about. But the industry was already changing, and her looks were too old-school for the seventies brats. Which didn't stop her partying with some of them. I think it was at that time she developed her taste for rough sex and drugs, and as a consequence fell in with some pretty unsavoury characters. Anyhow, she ended up marrying the most powerful lawyer in town, partly I suspect to fund her habits, also I suspect as a smokescreen, but you know what? Darren Lipsky wasn't my father. I doubt he and my mother ever had sex. His predilections were more... recherché. He wasn't interested in other adults...'

I nodded knowingly, to show how worldly I was. 'Don't tell me. He liked little girls. Or little boys.'

Delgado gave me a pitying look. 'No. What he *liked* was Pyrenean Mountain Dogs. Newfoundlands. Irish Wolfhounds...'

'A big dog lover,' I said, trying to sound blasé. 'I expect he liked Great Danes too.'

'Not Great Danes. They had to be not just big, but shaggy. He liked having something to grip.'

'I see,' I said. This was all very exotic, and scarcely credible. I wondered if it were a dramatic monologue he was preparing, but couldn't remember any big dogs in Arthur Miller or Tennessee Williams.

'Anyhow, my poor mother had to get her kicks somewhere. My father - my *real* father - was the gardener.' He shuddered visibly, and for a split-second his face looked almost ugly. 'It was a decadent household. The gardener, the fancy Italianate villa, the dogs...'

'Poor dogs,' I said, thinking this monologue needed work.

'I don't suppose it did them lasting damage. Lipsky wasn't... a *large* man, if you get my meaning. And he liked them big, the bigger the better. It was probably why my mom preferred Chihuahuas - she knew they would be safe from her husband's predations. She used to shield their eyes, but she never thought to shield mine; I once came across him sodomising a St. Bernard in the utility room.'

'So... all these sexy dogs were running all over the house?' I asked, trying and failing to picture it.

He gave a little sigh, as though my imagination had fallen short. 'Of course not. He picked them up off the street. And then afterwards, once he'd had his way with them, he took them back to where he'd found them. I daresay their owners, if they *had* owners, never even noticed their absence.'

I wondered if he were using some fashionable new street-argot. Perhaps, in certain circles, *dog* was a euphemism for prostitute; maybe the various breeds were code words for age, race or proportions. I just kept nodding, trying to make it look as though I knew what he was talking about.

'He never closed doors; I think he wanted to be seen. And of course it warped my young and impressionable mind. You know what my first sexual experience was?'

'I can't imagine.'

'My best friend's Cocker Spaniel! It was Lipsky's fault. He encouraged me in ways you can't possibly imagine. Before my voice had even broken, I'd had carnal relations with dogs, most of my toys, items of furniture. And plants, lots of plants.' He shook his head, as if to say yes, I know this needs more work. As if to say, if even *I* can't believe what I'm saying, how can I expect an audience to suspend its disbelief?

'Have you ever fucked a cactus?' he said, baring his teeth.

'Not lately,' I said, trying to sound jaded. I couldn't

tell if he were shaking his head or nodding it. Some of Nancy's actor friends were a little strange, but Delgado was the strangest yet. I just hoped she hadn't slept with him. If Nancy had slept with him, I wouldn't be in with a chance. Not that I stood much of a chance anyway. But it was fun to dream. And hadn't he said he thought English people were adorable? Well, I was as English as they came, apart from a Scottish grandparent on my mother's side. I began to fantasise a relationship between the two of us, one in which I would be able to show him off to Maurice and Phoebe and their high-flying friends, to prove I knew glamorous people too. Just so long as he didn't blow it by launching into one of his monologues. Like the one he was spouting now.

Something he said yanked me out of my daydream.

'...looks as though he was wearing a flamboyant floral headdress, a large, ungainly thing a small child might have fashioned out of red and pink crepe paper in a misguided attempt to emulate Carmen Miranda's headgear. But it isn't *on* his head, it *is* his head, or at least *what is left of his head*...'

I breathed in sharply, making a noise like 'Whaaaa?' and wondered how long I'd been dreaming about us being a couple. Long enough to miss the point where Jules' speech had taken this unexpected diversion into Grand Guignol. He appeared to be experiencing a traumatic flashback, but was unable to tear himself away and return to the safety of the here and now. As far as acting went, it wasn't bad; it was just the dialogue that needed more work.

'...then I see what I've skidded on isn't one of my mother's sapphire earrings tangled in a chain of fine white gold, but one of her beautiful blue eyes, trailing stringy gristle...'

'Oh my God,' I said.

'Are you OK? Your face is yellow.'

'I'm fine,' I said, taking a sip from my mug to steady my nerves. The tea was cold.

'You need to hear this story,' he said. 'Because it's important for you to know where I'm coming from. My mother's Chihuahuas have been decapitated, and their severed heads placed in her empty eye sockets.'

I tried to imagined how that might have worked, and failed. The head of a dog, even one as small as a Chihuahua, would surely be much too big to fit into an eye socket. This entire yarn was becoming more untethered by the second.

As if he'd once again read my thoughts, Delgado said, 'The heads have been *hammered* into the sockets. But that is nothing compared to what my father has suffered. My *real* father, that is, the gardener. His head left on a gatepost, and as for the rest of him... The things you can do with cheesewire. The things you can slice down the middle.'

'Oh my God,' I said again, not sure how to react. He surely must have been aware how unhinged this sounded, even as a drama class exercise. 'You poor thing,' I said, trying to steer our conversation back to normality. 'How old did you say you were?'

'Fourteen. And you know what? I saw it in a dream.'

'I'm not surprised. Hammered Chihuahua heads would give anyone nightmares.'

'I mean I dreamt about it *before* it happened.'

'OK,' I said, now starting to wonder if Jules

Delgado was perfect boyfriend material after all.

But then he shook his head in a roundabout movement, as though to shrug off a dark hood, and smiled at me. Back to his old charming self. 'But enough about me,' he said. 'Let's talk about *you*. You're prettier than I expected.'

This wasn't a line I'd heard often. In fact, I'm not sure anyone had ever said anything like that to me before. I decided it might be worth overlooking the weirdness. 'I am?'

His smile morphed into a wry look. 'Though, if you don't mind me saying so, that outfit doesn't do you any favours.'

I flinched. He'd been doing so well, but this was like a slap in the face. The quality of his suit had suckered me into thinking he had good taste. 'It's a Vandersmissen,' I said. 'From Antwerp.' But to judge by the lack of reaction, I might as well have been speaking in tongues. 'You really *are* American, aren't you,' I said, the truth dawning at last. Much too late.

'How far gone are you?' he asked. 'Three months? Four?'

This took a while to sink in, then finally, belatedly, the penny dropped into the echo chamber of my empty head and rolled around there noisily. He thought I was pregnant. Ah yes. Of course.

He thought I was Nancy.

I sipped my cold tea for a while, playing for time while my thoughts raced in circles like tiny Ben-Hur chariots. Up till now I hadn't been taking Nancy's story about being attacked as seriously as I should have done. At last I wrangled the tiny mental chariots into a tidy line. I looked at him carefully, but he didn't appear to be armed.

I said, 'That bloke with the knife, I forget his name. Friend of yours?'

Delgado slipped his hand into his inside pocket and I tensed. But he wasn't drawing out a weapon - just a long, thin cigar. He peeled off the cellophane, foraged in his inside pocket again, and this time extracted a cigarette lighter with a Union Jack on it.

'Erm, I'm not sure you should do that,' I said.

'Do what?'

You shouldn't smoke a cigar, because Nancy will smell it when she gets back. But obviously I couldn't say this. And so what if Nancy smelt it anyway?

'He works for me,' said Delgado. '*Worked*, I should say. Poor Karl. I told him not to do what he did, but there was no reasoning with him.' He blew out a small cloud of blue smoke. 'I must apologise. I realise you can't help being pregnant with the Antichrist any more than a leopard can change its spots. But you have to understand that we can't allow this *thing* to come to pass.'

I stared at him, vaguely aware my mouth had dropped open but unwilling to waste precious willpower on closing it.

'You must understand that if men like Karl can't kill what's inside you, you must do it yourself.' He smiled again, as though he'd just suggested I dye my hair. 'For the future of mankind. I'm sorry, but that's the way it is.'

My jaw dropped even further. 'Erm,' I said, not knowing where to start.

Delgado balanced his cigar on the edge of the table, and pulled a small black notebook out of his pocket. He flipped off the elastic and flicked through the pages till he found the one he was looking for, flattened it out and read out loud:

'Bad rulers, civil discord, war, drought, famine, plague, comets, false prophets, sudden deaths of prominent persons and an increase in general sinfulness.'

It all sounded so familiar.

He looked up, as if expecting applause. 'But if you prefer all this in a more reader-friendly format, I put it in my last graphic novel, *The Anti-Antichrist*. I'll have my people mail you a copy.'

'What?'

He chuckled. '*Comic book*, if you like. I'm no snob. But it's the best way of disseminating a message to the widest possible readership. Not everyone has time to read books these days.'

I'd wandered into a Looking-Glass World where the normal rules no longer applied, where Nancy's actor friend was... But I had to remind myself he *wasn't* one of Nancy's actor friends. In fact, they'd never met. As far as he was concerned, *I* was Nancy. 'How did you know about... the pregnancy?' I asked.

'I dreamt about it,' he said.

'Like the Chihuahua dream?'

'I often dream about the future. It's my blessing, and my curse. I dream of eternal suffering in the netherworld. A man wrapped around a giant wheel. Another with an arrow in his eye. A woman's head separated from her body and put on display in a palace of ice. A man in a gold robe, with his head on fire, flesh melting from the skull. Horrible visions. X-rated visions.'

Later I would wonder if Delgado really did have the gift of prophecy. But that was after these things had happened, more or less. In most cases less, since his descriptions were so vague. It could have been coincidence.

'And you I saw enthroned in The House of Ishtar, thronged by worshippers.'

This was obviously a fabrication. If he really had dreamt about Nancy, he would have known I looked nothing like her. Then again, thinking it over, it was conceivable he *did* dream about me. Because, as I said, this story is as much about me as it is about Nancy.

'The house of Ishtar. Goddess of Fertility, Queen of Heaven...'

I remembered something Nancy had told me about her morning sickness. 'The Temple of Ishtar!' I said. 'The Museum!'

'Your followers were old and wizened, their necks and fingers adorned by gold and precious jewels.'

'Rich American tourists with Rolexes!'

He looked irritated. 'I am telling you what I saw.'

'So you... let me get this straight... You described this dream to your friend, and it made him want to kill, er, me?'

'We were trying to come up with a civilised solution, but Petersen was headstrong. They all are. Sometimes it's a pain, being surrounded by people like those guys. Easy to sway, but once they've got an idea in their head there's no stopping them.'

I was beginning to think I knew where Jules Delgado was coming from - and I don't mean Pasadena. Because I had met someone like him before, someone who'd also had the golden gift of persuasion. None of us had ever questioned his edicts, no matter how crazy they'd been; we'd just fallen over themselves trying to win his approval.

'How many of you are there?'

'Four shy, after today's bloodbath.'

I felt my eyebrows shoot up, so high they threatened to quit my forehead altogether and take off into space. '*Today's bloodbath?*'

'Oh yes, I've already heard what happened today. People around you keep dying, Nancy. Don't tell me you haven't noticed.'

I started feeling afraid again, but whether for me or for my friend, I couldn't tell. She could be back at any second, and I had to get rid of this nutjob before she came home and he realised I wasn't who he thought I was. I hadn't impersonated her on purpose, but now I wasn't sure how to explain the situation to either of them. I kept thinking of hammered Chihuahua heads.

'I'm sorry people got hurt,' I said. 'And I really think you should leave now.'

'*Hurt?*' His amicable mask slipped, just a little bit. 'Bidlack's head was mashed like a tick's, according to Arbogast. And Koslo... He swore blind he knew how to operate a stick shift.'

I began to feel dizzy again. 'But if they were trying to kill me...'

'Not you, Nancy, *it*.'

Delgado's eyes fell to my stomach. He was once again trying to make out the shape of my pregnancy. I breathed out, giving silent thanks to Vandersmissen's penchant for bunched fabric, plus the cheese sauce I'd had on my lunchtime pasta that was now making my stomach bloat. I gave thanks for these things, and for the fact that, however many months pregnant she was, Nancy was still scarcely bigger than my regular shape. I'd never been what you'd call *fat*, but then I'd never suffered from a fashionable eating order, or bothered to count calories, or gone on one of those wacky diets Nancy had been prone to, back when she'd been eating more than just Fudge Tubs. I patted my belly in what I hoped was typical mother-to-be fashion, though it was quite hard summoning maternal feelings for bunched cotton jersey.

'This child will destroy us all,' said Delgado

'Not me!' I said. 'I'm its mother.'

'All men hate their mothers! But we're not doing this out of some misguided religious fervour. We're not misogynists, Nancy! I'm pro-choice! But there *is* no choice here. If we can't destroy what's inside you, the world will end.'

Had there been a cigarette within reach just then, I would have put it in my mouth and lit up - and I don't even smoke. Pro-choice my arse. My adolescent involvement with the Croydon Sunshine Club had left me hypersensitive to any form of extremism, but now it seemed my best friend had somehow been targeted by fundamentalist lunatics. I didn't know whether to laugh or cry. Well, they had no idea who they were dealing with. Because I'd been here before, and I wasn't going to stand for it again.

Delgado was watching me earnestly. His friendly manner was more discomfiting than any outright menace.

'I know karate,' I said, just in case he was thinking of launching an attack.

'You don't need to *know* anything. *It* can defend itself. You must know that by now.'

'It's a *foetus*,' I said.

His voice sank to a whisper. 'Petersen, Bidlack,

Koslo, Roop... How do you think they died?'

'Hoist on their own petard?'

'It protects itself.'

I considered this. 'How is that possible?'

'It's the Antichrist!' said Delgado. 'Evil incarnate!'

'Sounds more like self-defence to me.'

'It won't be self-defence when it starts laying waste to humanity. You must kill it before it can take its first breath. It's the only way. Otherwise...'

'End of Days?'

He shook his head sorrowfully. 'It'll be like Hiroshima, only a thousand times worse. We can't let that happen.'

'You think it'll grow up to be President and push the nuclear button? We've got about forty or fifty years before that happens.'

He looked exasperated. 'Stop being so literal.'

'But then how will it destroy the world?'

'Earthquakes! Hurricanes! Volcanoes!'

'So Britain will be OK then, because we don't have any of those here. Well, we had a hurricane twelve years ago, but that was exceptional.'

Delgado sighed. 'A great flood, perhaps.'

I thought about the Thames Barrier and said, 'Yeah, OK.'

He wasn't expecting this. He peered at me sideways. 'OK?'

I told him I was as eager to get rid of the Antichrist as he was, probably even more so. I told him I'd already fixed a date for a termination at the Faraday Clinic. I told him that after Monday, whatever had installed itself in my womb without my permission would be history.

Delgado beamed with what looked like genuine pleasure. 'I knew you would see it our way,' he said. 'I only wish I'd come to see you earlier. We could have saved those poor misguided idiots. I tell you, once they get an idea in their heads they're uncontrollable. I warned HQ we'd have carnage on our hands, possibly an international incident.'

'Yes, I'm sorry about what, er, happened to them.'

He shook my hand warmly, once again clutching it for longer than was necessary. 'You have nothing to apologise for. You're in a difficult situation, as are we all. You do the best you can, with what you're given. And I must say, you're doing very well.'

I glowed with pleasure, forgetting once again that his compliments were aimed not at me but at someone who wasn't even in the room. I ushered him through the door and into the hallway. 'Oh, this is nothing,' I said. 'Not compared to what happened to you. And you were only fourteen...You must have been traumatised.'

If it had really happened. His story seemed too lurid to be true. And if it *had* been true, it would surely have made the international press, and I couldn't remember having read about it. I couldn't imagine the media ignoring anything as sensational as bestiality, murder and hammered Chihuahua heads.

In the hallway, he picked up the rucksack, slung it over his shoulder, and asked me which buses went to the British Museum. I told him it was about ten minutes' walk away, not worth getting a bus there, and gave him directions. He thanked me and opened the front door.

'Did they ever catch your parents' murderers?' I asked him.

Delgado turned to leave me with one last cockle-warming smile, and said, 'Oh, I'm sorry, I thought I made that clear. *I* killed them. And then I fucked the two headless Chihuahuas. In the necks, one after the other. Lipsky would have been proud.'

And he winked at me, and was gone.

Chapter 9
Antichrist

I sat there feeling numb for a while before coming to and springing into action, as though a celestial puppet-master had jerked my strings. I ran round opening all the windows, trying to get rid of the stink of Delgado's cigar. I thought I did quite a good job of fumigating, but of course the smell was the first thing Nancy noticed when she got in.

'Alain had a box of expensive cigars and gave me one,' I overexplained. 'I'd never smoked a cigar before and I was curious, but it was vile. I took a couple of puffs and had to throw it away.'

'Where is it? I'll smoke the rest.' Nancy moved towards the kitchen. I wouldn't have put it past her to start going through the rubbish, where she would no doubt find the cigar stub and wonder why I'd bothered to lie about it.

'I threw it out of the window,' I said quickly, then remembered the empty bottle. 'I drank some of your wine as well.' I was digging myself into a slithering pit of untruth. I knew even as I said it that while smoking a cigar was out of character, drinking an entire bottle of Nancy's awful Chardonnay was even more so. She gave me an odd look, as though she thought so too. Then asked if I'd been cooking with garlic. Nothing was getting past her nasal passages today, though I was surprised she could smell anything at all, what with the heavy scent she'd drenched herself in. Her taste in perfume was even worse than her taste in wine; she stank like a Wild West brothel.

'Now you mention it, that cigar did have a garlicky taste.' I can't say exactly why I'd decided not to tell her about Delgado. I just thought I ought to keep quiet about him, for now. Plus I didn't want to alarm her, and Lord knows what he'd said had been alarming, whether or not you believed it, and I still wasn't sure I did. But he had seemed sincere, which was all it needed for me to take him seriously. I knew from experience that sincere people were the most dangerous ones.

Nor did I want Nancy finding out I'd been impersonating her. She would have laughed, but I didn't want her thinking I wanted to *be* her. But mainly I didn't want to mention Delgado because he'd freaked me out. I found myself wishing I could rewind the past two hours and relive them. I wouldn't have come round to Nancy's flat, for a start.

Luckily, Nancy seemed almost as distracted as I was. I could tell she'd already been drinking. She forgot all about the promised Dry Martinis and opened another bottle of Chardonnay. As she sat back and lit a Marlboro, I noticed her hands were shaking. My hands were shaking too as I poured myself a glass. Normally I wouldn't have touched that swill with a barge-pole, but I needed to calm myself down.

'How small are Chihuahuas?' I asked in what I judged was a conversational tone.

'Pretty small. People carry them around in handbags.' Nancy drained her glass in a couple of gulps, and poured out another. 'Why? Thinking of getting a dog?'

'Go easy on the booze,' I said. 'How many have you had already?'

'Look who's talking.'

I could hardly tell her I hadn't drunk the whole bottle by myself, so there was a prickly silence, which I finally broke by saying, 'And?'

'And?'

I leaned back. 'And how was your day, Nancy? You didn't see anyone getting *mashed like a tick* or anything?'

She looked up sharply. 'What?'

'Business as usual, then? Nothing... happened?'

We played chicken. She stared at me so hard I almost backed down. But at last she looked down and said, 'How did you know?'

I shrugged wordlessly, like someone too modest to talk about their astonishing powers of precognition.

'You really want to hear this?' she asked.

'You know I do.'

'You're not going to believe it, Belinda. I mean, it's fucked up.'

And you'd never believe the conversation I just had with this freaky psycho who less than an hour ago was sitting right where you are now.

'You'd be surprised.' I tried not to flinch as she lit another cigarette. Just as well she was getting rid of the baby, otherwise the poor wee bairn would come out smoked, like ham.

'It happened again,' she said, screwing up her face as though she knew what she was about to say would tax my credulity. 'And again...' But I sat back, all ears.

*****

When Nancy had finished telling me about her afternoon, she sat back and lit another cigarette. I gazed at her in awe. My credulity had scarcely been taxed at all; I believed everything she'd told me. Her outing had made my encounter with Jules Delgado seem like a walk in the park. Maybe he really did have the gift of prediction. It *had* been a bloodbath, though he'd underestimated the body count. And of course, he'd misidentified the heroine of the story.

'They all died?'

'I didn't stick around long enough to find out, but you get hit by a tube-train, or a big lump of marble falls on your head... I don't think you'd walk away from that.'

'It was *you*,' I said.

'I never touched them!'

'You *made* those things happen.'

She glared at me. 'Accidents.'

'As Auric Goldfinger said to James Bond, *once* is an accident. Twice is coincidence. Three times is enemy action.' Half my life I'd been looking for an excuse to use that quote, though of course it was wasted on Nancy. But it was all starting to make a crazy kind of sense. 'How about if I run a few theories past you.'

Nancy flapped her hand wearily. 'Don't let me stop you.'

'OK then, listen to this. The man you said took your newspaper out of the rubbish bin? What if he'd been about to *buy* a paper?'

'I don't follow.'

'What if he had the coins all ready to buy one,' I said, warming to my theme. 'But then he got your paper for free. So what would he do with the money? Put it back in his pocket? Of course not!'

'I don't see...'

'What if he gave that money to the beggar woman?'

Nancy was looking uncomfortable. 'It's possible, but I still don't think...'

'That's what he did! And what if *she* used the money to buy a balloon for her kid? It was because of the kid going after his balloon that the killer fell in front of the train. It was the *balloon* that saved you!'

Nancy was shaking her head again. 'Why would a beggar waste money on a balloon?'

'Oh, who knows? Maybe she'd already made enough for the day, and decided the kid deserved a treat. No, wait, there's more. The scrap of plastic that wrapped itself around the driver's face? You stripped the wrapping off your magazine, am I right? *What if it was that very same piece of plastic?'*

Nancy frowned, not keeping up. 'I threw it away.'

'But you also threw the newspaper away! The plastic could have been, oh I don't know, *clinging* to the newspaper, and then when that bloke fished it out, the plastic came out with it, and got sucked up in the taxi's slipstream until that other car came along, and then the wind caught it, and it wrapped itself around the driver's head!'

Nancy burst out laughing. 'Oh *sure*! That's *absolutely* what happened!'

'It *was* quite windy.'

'It just doesn't seem likely.'

'It's as likely as someone getting pregnant without having sex, Nancy.'

She laughed again, though this time there was a hard edge to it. 'That's unfair. All right then, what about the others? You've got it all figured out, Belinda. So explain to me how *they* died.'

We both swallowed some more of the Chardonnay, which didn't taste quite as revolting now.

'You reek, you know that?' I said at last. 'That perfume is the sort of thing a twelve-year-old would wear when she's trying to be sophisticated. And you know how certain perfumes make some people sneeze? Didn't you say the workman was sneezing? Well, what if *he* was allergic? What if he sneezed and dropped the clock?'

Nancy's eyes opened wide in astonishment. 'Oh, you mean...? No, that's impossible.'

'Wait.' I was on a roll. 'The guy who fell under the bus? What happened there? I mean, who just *falls* under a bus? '

'He slipped, I guess. The pavement was damp.'

'Maybe he slipped on something *you* dropped?'

'No, he was in front of me.'

I thumped the table in triumph. 'But you'd already been down that street earlier, in the cab, am I right? You'd already prepared the ground without being aware of it! *What happened to your empty Fudge Tub carton, Nancy? The one you were eating in the cab?*'

She stared at me, trying to work out if I were teasing, but I had never been more serious in my life.

'Even if he did slip on something,' she said at last, 'there's no way it could have been my Fudge Tub. I left the empty carton in the cab.' She sighed. 'Though it *was* banana flavour, so there is that.'

'What if the cab driver threw it away?'

'And threw it with clairvoyant precision, so it landed on the exact bit of pavement where one of my attackers would later be placing his foot. I suppose you have an explanation for the dogs too...'

She trailed off, as though she'd thought of something. 'It might have been the poodle.'

'Poodle?'

'Or Labradoodle. Tied to the railings outside a shop. Whining so pathetically I stopped to scratch its ear. When I walked on it started barking after me.'

'Poodles don't bark, they yap,' I said, thinking about Chihuahuas again, and shuddering.

'And I think the Rottweilers might have been headed in that direction to sort out the poodle, and the man in grey just got in their way.'

'The Rottweilers appeared out of nowhere?'

'There was a bald guy chasing them.'

'Like Benny Hill!'

'Not funny, Belinda. People died.'

I tried to dial down my facial expression to reflect this solemn thought. 'What's the body count now?'

She was looking distressed. 'I don't even know who they are. Why would they do this?'

'I'll tell you how many,' I said, counting them off on my fingers. 'There was the Kitchen Devil guy who made you late for work. Then today: the one who fell under the train. Then the Fiesta driver. The marble clock. The Labradoodle.'

'And the one who fell under the bus.'

What was it Delgado had said? *A man wrapped around a giant wheel?* The coincidence made my nerves tingle. If only I'd had some sort of device to record him while he'd been talking. His words were already slipping away.

'And you have no idea why this is happening?

These are momentous events, Nancy. You should be keeping a diary, for the benefit of future generations.'

'A diary!' Nancy chuckled mirthlessly. 'And what would I write in it? Gained five pounds. Sixty-one cigarettes. Alcohol units ninety-nine. Four Fudge Tubs. Three vomits. Body count five, no, six. As if people would want to read *that*.'

'It would be a bestseller!'

'Yeah, sure.'

I stared at her. 'I can't believe you're so calm. You've seen six people die right in front of you! I'd be really freaked out.'

'I didn't see all of them,' she said.

'Why are they after you? What have you done?'

'It's not that I don't *care* about people dying,' she said. 'I'm afraid that if I start caring too much, I'll start screaming again, and this time I'll never be able to stop. So I'm putting on a performance and making myself believe I'm OK. I've done a lot of fringe, Belinda. I'm used to believing in plots that make no sense.'

'What if they knew about the pregnancy?' I said. 'What if they were trying to stop your baby being born?'

'How could they know? I didn't even know it myself till *after* the first attack.'

'What if, oh I don't know, what if there were some sort of prophecy?'

'What the fuck, Belinda?'

'What if this is like *The Omen*?'

Nancy hadn't seen *The Omen*, so I described the plot, with its series of freak accidents that killed anyone who tried to harm the Antichrist. It was another of the things my ex-husband had made me watch at the stage when I'd been trying to impress him and hadn't liked to confess that I didn't like horror movies.

'That's insane,' Nancy said when I'd finished. She seemed more amused than outraged. She patted her tummy. 'You think this is the Antichrist?'

'Maybe you were drugged. Or maybe it *was* an immaculate conception.'

'All the more reason to get rid of it.'

This wasn't what I wanted to hear. 'No wait, everyone always assumes the Antichrist is a bad thing. But what if it isn't? What if he's just a product of his environment? Nurture not nature? And genes, of course. I can't answer for the father's, assuming it's not Maurice, but yours aren't so bad.'

'Thank you very much,' said Nancy.

I was warming to my theme. 'Maybe there'll be a touch of evil in there, but which of us doesn't have a mean streak?'

Nancy was looking bemused. 'You're saying this thing inside me is evil?'

I was too drunk to realise she was humouring me. And I couldn't very well tell her it was Jules Delgado who'd put the idea into my head. 'Maybe the Bible is just propaganda,' I said.

'You'd know more about that than me.'

'Why does everyone assume God is good?' I cried. 'What if He's the evil one? He does a lot of evil things. What if the reason people *think* God is good is that he always had a brilliant PR team?'

Nancy jerked back in mock-surprise. 'Fucking hell, Belinda, where is this *coming* from?' She poured me another glass of not-so-horrible Chardonnay.

'The Millennium. The jellyfish. We're living in End Times.'

'You should stop watching the news.'

'It might be for the best,' I said, examining my fingernails, which were impeccably French-manicured apart from a chip in the varnish on the index finger of my left hand. That chip annoyed me out of all proportion to its size. I was vaguely aware of Nancy leaning across the table towards me.

'Are you OK, Belinda?'

'I've had a lot to drink.'

'You're still on for next Monday?'

Monday? I blinked slowly, trying to work out what she was talking about. My head was full of Chihuahuas and cheesewire.

'If you could get there around six...'

It took me a moment to work out she was talking about me picking her up from the clinic. 'Sure, yes. I'll make sure I'm on the early shift.'

Nancy dipped into her bag and came out with a sheet of pink paper. 'You might want to jot down the address.'

'No need,' I said, looking at the paper. 'I'll remember.' And I did. I have a mind like a steel trap, even if did have a tendency to snap shut on all the wrong things. Chihuahuas, for example. And the difficulties of having carnal relations with a cactus. And, afterwards, the clinic.

Clinic.

I still can't hear that word without shuddering.

PART TWO
SCORPIONS

Chapter 1
The Unpleasantness at the Clinic

I spent the next few days looking over my shoulder, expecting to see Jules Delgado or one of his grey-suited berserkers lurking behind me, knives at the ready. In the shop, I read everything I could find about the Antichrist and End of Days, which wasn't much since our Religion section had largely been hi-jacked by New Age philosophy and books about Zen. I also checked out the entry on Chihuahuas in *The Dog Spotter's Handbook*. But none of it really helped.

Alain noticed I was twitchy and asked if I was OK. Story of my life. Alain was *always* asking if I were OK. I suppose I should have been touched.

'Of course I'm OK!' I snapped. 'Why shouldn't I be OK?'

'When I patted you on the shoulder you nearly jumped through the ceiling.'

'I thought you were someone else.'

Alain laughed. 'Who? The cops? Have you done something wicked, Belinda? You're acting like a guilty person.'

'No I'm not,' I said, a little too emphatically. I glanced sideways at Alain, who grinned back at me as though I'd given him the glad-eye. I badly needed someone to talk to; if only Alain had been a little more sensitive I might have confided in him, but the *Corpse Grinders* T-shirt was just too off-putting. I could have opened up to Nancy, but that would have meant telling her about Jules Delgado, and she already had enough to worry about. Maybe we'd be able to laugh about it afterwards, when she was back to normal.

So, in the absence of anyone to bare my soul to, I made lists, writing them out in my journal. I made a list of signs, even though I knew them off by heart: bad rulers, civil discord, war, drought, famine, plague, comets, sudden deaths of prominent persons and an all-round increase in general sinfulness. I made a list of how each of the men in grey had died, and how Nancy might have been responsible for subconsciously setting up the deaths; I had to use some poetic licence here, as I hadn't been present, and it didn't seem likely they'd *all* slipped on discarded Fudge Tub packets. I also made a list of everything I could remember about what Delgado had told me: Pasadena, Chihuahua, cheesewire, pancake, palace of ice, the dreams. The more I reread the Delgado List, the more preposterous it sounded.

And so the rest of the week slipped by, punctuated by the usual shifts in the bookshop, meeting Nancy for a drink at the Bar-F (where I made another unsuccessful attempt to persuade her to keep the baby), a botched job interview with a magazine based in Hammersmith, visiting my grandmother in the nursing home, a dispiriting reunion in Crouch End with the other Croydon survivors, who were all forging successful careers in pension planning or sales management. It was a relatively uneventful few days. Had I known it would be the last time I'd feel even remotely safe and in control of my life, I would have sought out a crash course in self-defence. Or joined a gun club and learned how to shoot.

And so Monday came around, and I clocked off early and went to pick Nancy up from the clinic, as arranged.

*****

This is what Nancy remembered afterwards: being wheeled into a room that looked more a boutique hotel suite than an operating theatre. Soft piano music tinkling out of hidden speakers. No windows, but the walls hung with soothing landscapes in pastel colours. It was almost a jolt to see white tiles and not fluffy carpet on the floor.

The anaesthetist, whose name was Arthur, asked her to count backwards from a hundred. She closed her eyes, but at ninety-three began to worry. What if they started the procedure while she was still awake? She opened her eyes to let them know she was still conscious, and saw that Arthur, Dr Madison and the nurse had all vanished. So there was no-one to stop her as she climbed off the table and padded over to the door and opened it.

The corridor was longer than she remembered. At the far end stood a large refrigerator, which was making an electronic humming sound, so loud it was almost throbbing. The humming grew louder as she padded nearer, and she began to feel an overwhelming sensation of dread. She knew there was something unpleasant inside that fridge, and she really didn't want to see it. Yet her feet kept carrying her towards it, and her arm stretched out, her fingers slid around the handle, and she pulled it and the door swung open and...

Silvery moonlight spilled out.

As it is written, so shall it be done.

'Nancy? Nancy? Nancy?'

Someone was saying her name, over and over again, the sound penetrating her brain like the buzzing of a fly that refused to be swatted away, so she opened her eyes again, and this time it wasn't a dream. She'd never moved from the operating table; she was still laid out in her loose green gown with legs apart and feet hitched up to stirrups. She had no idea how much time had passed; it might have been five minutes or five hours. But she did know that when she'd first been wheeled into the the room, the walls had been white. Now they seemed mostly to be red.

'Nancy! Wake up!'

That was me talking. Later, she told me it looked as though someone had drained all the blood out of my face and replaced it with hummus.

*****

When I pressed the bell at the front entrance, there was no answer. After what I judged to be an acceptable pause, I tried again, and, when there was still no response, jammed the heel of my hand down on all the other buttons on the panel until someone in one of the upper flats released the catch on the door without bothering to ask who I was. I could have been anybody. I could have been a pro-lifer with a nail-bomb in my handbag.

I expected the door to the Faraday Clinic to be locked as well, but it swung inwards when I pushed it. Again with the slack security. I went through into a lilac-coloured reception area. It was deserted. 'Hello?' I said, as loudly as I dared. Still no answer. I began to wonder if Nancy had got her dates mixed up.

Leading off the reception area was a dimly lit corridor, dotted with framed reproductions of Fragonard and Watteau. I walked down it, expecting to bump into someone at any second. There was a faint whiff of bleach. From up ahead came the sound of dripping water.

I poked my head around the first door and found a small office with a desk and metal filing cabinets, but still no sign of life. I knocked at the second door, not expecting an answer, so when someone said, 'Nurse?' I nearly jumped out of my skin.

Inside, propped up against pillows on the bed, a bored-looking woman was looking up from a dog-eared paperback of *Middlemarch*.

'How much longer do I have to wait?'

'I don't work here,' I said.

'Then go and find someone who does.'

'I'm not your fucking servant,' I said, backing out and slamming the door behind me. The next room had exactly the same layout as Middlemarch Woman's. No-one there, but I saw Nancy's bag on the chair and felt a flash of outrage on her behalf. Anyone could walk in off the street and help themselves to her belongings. Someone really needed to talk to these people about their security problem.

I guessed the next two doors would be locked, but tried them anyway. It was just a way to put off having to deal with the other door, the one at the end of the corridor. Brilliant white light was leaking out around the edges, as though an alien mothership had landed on the other side. My ears picked up a low electronic hum, like the faint drone of an old-fashioned fluorescent light. There was something about that doorway which made me want to turn my back on it and walk away. But I'd promised Nancy I would pick her up and take her home, and I always keep my promises. I'd seen Nancy's bag, which meant Nancy had to be somewhere around here too.

Maybe something had gone wrong. But that would have meant more activity, not this eerie lack of it. I rapped on the door, ears straining to pick up any sound beyond the ambient humming, ready to back away if I found myself barging in on some tricky medical procedure. But there was no response, so I reached out and pushed.

'Hello?' I said as the door opened inward.

Afterwards, I couldn't help wondering how things would have turned out if I hadn't opened that door. If I'd just gone home without searching any further for Nancy, and watched it on the news or read about it in the papers like everyone else, instead of seeing it with my own eyes. But opening that door was like ripping the scab off a festering wound, and a lot of ugly fluid oozed out, and no matter how much I tried to scoop it all up and push it back inside, there was too much of it, and it was too runny, and kept getting away from me.

On the other hand, they say it's not healthy to keep ugly fluid all bottled up, so maybe it was just as well I ripped that scab off. After all, it could have been worse.

I tried to imagine how much worse it *could* have been, and failed.

*****

My first impression was that some idiot had spilled a sack of offal. This would have been a stupid thing to do in any circumstances, but especially so in an operating theatre. It was only when I'd picked my way past the offal and looked back that I saw what it really was. The two different views had so little in common I could have been forgiven for not spotting it immediately. It was like one of those optical illusions in which a single image simultaneously represents two apparently incompatible subjects - a young woman and a death's head, for example, or Albert Einstein and Marilyn Monroe.

Seen from the door, it was a gleaming pile of green and purple entrails. But when I looked back, it was a man, perfectly intact, clothing unsullied, curled up on the floor as though he'd simply been overcome by fatigue and fallen asleep.

I retraced my steps and took another look from the other side, to confirm my eyes hadn't been playing tricks. My brain methodically registered the spectacle and, aware I still had tasks to perform and wouldn't be able to perform them if I were distraught, placed it on another level, out of reach. It was as much to put that vision behind me as anything more intrepid that I picked up my gaze and directed it at the rest of the room. It felt as though I stood there for hours, trying to make sense of a vast abstract expressionist installation: a touch of James Abbott McNeill Whistler, a splash of Jackson Pollock, and a few slices of Damien Hirst. Even with eyes averted, you couldn't help identifying some of the pieces.

Something at my feet caught my attention. At first sight it might have been a large earring, but when I looked properly I saw a bright blue eyeball trailing stringy white gristle. It reminded me of something, but I couldn't think what, because I knew damn well I'd never seen anything like that before. The eye looked at me, unblinking, and I stared back at it for a long time before finally tearing my gaze away.

And then it came to me. Sapphire earrings. Eyes. *Jules Delgado.* Oh Christ, I thought. He'd been here! This was all his doing. Of course it was. I had no doubt that if I were to examine the carnage more closely I'd find hammered Chihuahua heads as well.

But wait. Maybe he was still here.

Maybe he was watching me right this second.

Sensing any movement might attract unwanted attention, I tried not to turn my head as I scoured the edges of the room for crouching figures, though the lighting was so bright and its sources so numerous there clearly wasn't enough shadow to anyone to crouch in.

I was so intent on watching out for lurking killers that I didn't notice Nancy immediately. She was spread on a table in the middle of the room, like a sacrificial victim temporarily abandoned while the high priest with the knife had interrupted the ceremony to answer an urgent telephone call. She wasn't moving, but she didn't have entrails all over her, which was a good sign. My duty was clear: I had to make sure she was all right.

This, of course, meant picking my way across the floor. I felt like a pawn in some live-action anatomy-themed boardgame. Get blood on your shoes, forfeit a point. Step on a finger, miss a turn. Skid on a kidney, and it would be back to square one and lose the rest of your marbles.

At one point, as I slipped on a wet white frill and

ended up on all fours, I started giggling, and found it hard to stop. But I forced myself to focus on the assignment, which was to take Nancy home. Concentrating on that helped me get back on my feet and make it across the killing floor. That, and placing some mental distance between myself and what was all around me. And when I say 'distance' I mean a couple of thousand miles.

Even then, some nether region of my brain was prodding me, suggesting that ghastly as this was, it was also the opportunity of a lifetime, the sort of eye-witness account people would pay a lot of money to read about. All I had to do was keep a firm grip. But keeping a grip was easier said than done; more than once as I crossed that gut-strewn floor I could feel my mind straining at the leash. But just as it was on the point of slipping its collar to go galloping off into the dark, dark woods, Nancy stirred, and said something.

She was alive. *Thank God*.

'Nancy? Nancy? Nancy?'

Was she still pregnant? I looked at her stomach and it seemed flat as ever. She mumbled something and tried to turn on to her side. I unhooked her feet from the stirrups and straightened her hospital gown before retracing my steps to the reception area, where I did what any sane person would have done already, and called the emergency services.

*****

The rest was a blur. I remember leaning over Nancy and holding her hand and telling her to keep looking at me, not at the room, no, don't look at that, keep looking at *me*. Then, after several aeons, there was finally someone else there, lots of people in fact, and some of them were taking photos, lots of photos, though they didn't want me in them, which I found slightly insulting, and Nancy was being rolled on to a stretcher and wheeled away, and somebody scolded me for having tried to clean myself up with wet wipes, and someone else chided the one who'd scolded me, saying, 'Can't you see she's in shock? Can someone get over here and look after her, please?' and they'd taken my shoes away and I was being photographed at last, and wrapped in a blanket, and people kept pelting me with questions I couldn't even begin to answer.

I allowed myself to drift into a daze; it seemed easiest to leave all the decision-making to others. Then there was a brief interval of soothing blackness, then more light and a hubbub of noise. And flashing blue lights and more people, some of them in uniform. Somehow I ended up in the back of an ambulance, though I couldn't say how I'd got there. I found another packet of wet wipes and carried on trying to clean the blood off my hands. There was blood all over my knees as well.

Nancy was in the back of the ambulance with me, lying on a stretcher while a man in green overalls took her pulse. She opened her eyes and saw me and smiled.

'Hi Belinda,' she said a bit too brightly. 'How are we getting home?'

'Ambulance,' I said, though I didn't think it was taking us home, not just yet.

'I can walk,' said Nancy. 'Just give me a minute.'

'Is she still pregnant?' I whispered to Green Overalls.

'They'll give her a check-up at the hospital.'

'What's that?' asked Nancy, trying to sit up.

'Ssh,' he said, pulling the blanket up over her.

'What about me?' I asked.

'This lady here is our priority. She's had a traumatic experience.'

'But she was out of it! She didn't see what I saw!'

What I'd seen, in fact, had been one doctor, one nurse and one anaesthetist. Though by the time I'd got there it had no longer been easy to tell which was which.

*****

When we got to the hospital they plied me with cups of vile-tasting dishwater they called tea. When I finally managed to buttonhole a nurse who knew what was going on, she told me Nancy and her baby were fine. Nancy was under sedation, and was now sleeping in a comfortable bed, in a private room, with a police guard on her door. When I asked if I too could be sedated and have a police guard, the nurse laughed, though not unkindly. I was welcome to stick around, she said, but no-one offered me a bed, so I spent the night slithering around on one of the hard plastic seats in the waiting-room, keeping a wary eye on the sunken-eyed junkies and belligerent drunks, and almost going into cardiac arrest each time the doors slid open to let another one in. What if Delgado had followed us to the hospital?

Afterwards, I realised that if Delgado had wanted me dead, he would have seen to it back at the clinic when I'd been on my own. Unless he was just messing with me. Maybe this was his way of punishing me for pretending to be Nancy.

I spent the most uncomfortable night of my life in that waiting-room, waiting for the angel of death to appear and put me out of my misery. But everyone had forgotten about me, even the killers. Nancy was the star of this show, and I, as usual, was invisible. It wasn't till I was taken to the police station the following morning that a detective took the trouble to talk to me properly, which was when I learned there had been CCTV cameras trained on the building. The only people filmed going in and out had been me and Middlemarch Woman, a cleaning lady and two couples who lived in one of the flats, all of whom gave each other alibis. Which is how Middlemarch Woman and I became suspects - for all of two minutes. I was almost insulted by the speed with which they ruled us out.

During the two hours I spent with Middlemarch Woman, waiting to be interviewed, she still seemed to think I was some sort of lackey and kept asking me to fetch her coffee.

*****

The official line was that the murders were the work of anti-abortion extremists, or perhaps of the vengeful father of Nancy's unborn child, who had somehow managed to avoid the cameras.

'Have you talked to Jules Delgado?' I asked the detective, a red-faced man in a crumpled suit who doodled on a notepad when he should have been taking notes.

'Is he the father?'

'He's the killer,' I said.

The detective tapped the end of his Biro against his teeth. 'What makes you think that?'

'Because he hammered Chihuahua heads into his dead mother's eye-sockets!'

The detective tried not to look disgusted, but I saw his mouth twitch. 'Chihuahua heads? Aren't they a bit big for that?'

'I'm just telling you what he told me!'

'When?'

'When he was fourteen. Maybe it was logged as an unsolved murder, I don't know.'

'No. I meant when did he tell you this?'

I lowered my voice to a whisper. 'Last week. He told me Nancy is pregnant with the Antichrist.'

This wasn't coming out the way I'd rehearsed it. The detective was staring at me as though I were coughing up armadillos. A light-bulb went on over his head and he started flicking back through his notebook, through page after page of scrawled notes and elaborate crosshatching, until he found what he was looking for.

'Ah yes. You're *that* Belinda Pringle.' He looked at me sympathetically. 'I saw the transcripts. That must have been very... difficult, what happened to you back then. You were very young. It wasn't your fault, you know.'

'That has nothing to do with anything! That was then, and this is now. You need to talk to Delgado. Ask him where he was yesterday. I bet he doesn't have an alibi.'

'Would you like to talk to someone? I'm afraid your original case worker is no longer with us, but I can provide you with another contact number.'

I'd practically solved his investigation for him, and he wasn't listening to a word I was saying.

'Aren't you even going to take his name down?'

'Go on then,' he said. 'What was it again?'

'J-u-l-e-s D-e-l-g-a-d-o,' I spelt out. 'Check out unsolved murders in Pasadena.'

The detective jotted this down before shutting his notebook and struggling to his feet. 'We'll be in touch, Miss Pringle,' he said, opening the door for me.

Chapter 2
Lars Longa, Vita Brevis

I made my way back to the hospital and asked to see
Nancy, but they reacted as though I were trying to sneak
in and infect her a contagious disease, so I went home
and tried to take a nap, which I thought would come
easily after the night on the plastic chairs. But each time
I closed my eyes the visions were so appalling I decided
it was better to keep them open. I didn't feel up to
dealing with that right now. Maybe later... Maybe never.

I was down to work the Tuesday late shift, and it
never occurred to me to call Alain and ask for time off.
It would have been an admission of weakness. When I
left for work, I was still feeling a little peculiar.
Outwardly I was functioning normally - walking and
talking and paying my busfare as usual. More to the
point, I could see and hear other people walking and
talking and travelling on the bus, and none of them were
bleeding, and all their eyeballs and other extremities
appeared to be where they were supposed to be. So that
was reassuring.

Less reassuring was the feeling that I was being
followed; I couldn't actually *see* anyone following me, but
an unusually high number of the people I could see
appeared to be wearing wigs. As the bus went past the
Angel, my mind vaguely registered ABORTION
CLINIC MASSACRE headlines on the newsstand
outside the station, but failed to connect them with

anything I'd experienced. At work, even while I was ringing up purchases or responding to queries or looking titles up on the database, my mind kept drifting off into a no man's land of fuzzy atrocities. More than once Alain had to snap his fingers and say things like, 'Ground control to Major Belinda!'

'You look as though you've had a busy night,' he said with a leer that was as good as a wink and a nudge.

I had a pressing need to talk to someone. Anyone but Alain, who sniggered nerdily at anything connected to gynaecology. I wondered whether to call Church and ask him about those victim support groups he'd mentioned, but the dismissive way he'd treated me still rankled. As the minute hand of my watch edged ever more slowly towards closing-time and the customers began to drift away, I found myself floating, as if in a dream, towards the medical section. I started flicking through the colour plates, trying to find something that even approximated what I'd witnessed, but somehow got sidetracked by fungal infections of the big toenail. Some of the images were so unlike anything resembling regular human anatomy I began to feel even more peculiar than I'd been feeling already. I closed the book and dug my knuckles into my eyes until all I could see were black spots.

As the spots dispersed, I became aware of someone standing in front of me. An eerie calm washed over me. So this was it. I'd forgotten to keep an eye open for Delgado, and he had snuck up on me and was now going to torture me to death, right here in the bookshop. I was almost glad, because this meant it would soon be over and I could stop fretting.

But it wasn't Delgado. It was someone I'd never

seen before - not one of our regulars, but a guy in a navy blue suit who looked like a mid-level executive, not the kind of bloke you'd think would be interested in books unless they were of the *How To Grind Your Business Opponents into Dust* variety. How long had he been there, watching me dig my knuckles into my eye-sockets? I tried to focus.

'Excuse me,' he said, smiling so amiably it immediately put me on my guard. 'I'm looking for a book.' His English was impeccable, but there was a slight inflection, as though it weren't his first language. I thought he might be German.

'You're in the right place,' I said.

He wasn't daunted. '*Le Bal du Comte d'Orgel* by Raymond Radiguet, in translation of course. *Count d'Orgel's Ball*, I think it's called in English.'

This woke me up. 'You're kidding.'

The stranger looked perplexed. 'Why? You think I should try and read it in the original French? I'm not sure I'm up to that.'

I shook my head. 'I don't think it's even in print.'

His face fell. 'Lent my copy to someone who never returned it. Don't you hate it when that happens?'

I studied him more carefully. Was this guy for real? He didn't seem the bookish sort, and yet *Count d'Orgel's Ball* wasn't exactly the sort of blockbuster novel you bought at the airport to read on the beach, even in translation. As it happened, it was one of my favourite novels and I had a spare copy at home. But I wasn't about to promise that to any Tom, Dick or Harry who walked into the shop.

'He was very young when he wrote it,' I said, blinking stupidly.

'Published after he died of typhoid at the age of twenty. Jean Cocteau said he died without knowing it.'

'I love Cocteau,' I said.

The man was looking at me as though I'd just offered to have his babies, so it wasn't entirely unexpected when he asked what time I finished work.

I checked my watch. 'Twenty minutes.'

'Know somewhere we could discuss French literature over alcoholic beverages?'

'Wine bar round the corner.'

He laughed delightedly. 'Perfect. I was afraid you were going to suggest a pub.'

I warmed to him even more. I too loathed pubs. We agreed to meet in the Bar Me ten minutes after closing time. Too stunned to relish my triumph, I stared in bemusement at his departing back. He had a barely perceptible limp. I floated back to the cashdesk, where Alain was staring at me with his mouth open.

'Seven years I've worked here and I never once pulled.'

'We're only going for a drink,' I said. 'Anyway, he's not my type.'

'What *is* your type, Belinda?'

'Not suits and ties.'

'I'm still in with a chance, then.'

'Not Batman T-shirts either.'

The day that had started off badly was now ending on a high note, though there was no question of 'pulling', as Alain had put it. The stranger hadn't been bad-looking, but I hadn't been lying when I said he wasn't my type. I usually gravitated towards feckless painters and musicians, or psychopaths like Jules Delgado, and my new acquaintance looked steady and reliable, not in the least bit dashing or artistic. He looked like someone who worked in an office and talked business on the telephone. We lived in different worlds, but unlike Maurice and Phoebe's planet, it wasn't a place I longed to visit.

But he'd read *Le Bal du Comte d'Orgel*, so I couldn't help but be intrigued.

*****

His name was Lars. Not German but Norwegian, though he told me he'd never actually *lived* in Norway, just had relatives there. I told him I'd noticed the slight accent and he seemed pleased. 'I guess I must have picked that up from my parents. They came over here to get away from the Nazis.'

When I let slip, midway through our first drink, that I wasn't just a bookshop assistant but a writer, he asked if he could read something I'd written. I told him I'd think about it. When he admitted, a bit sheepishly, that *he'd* written books once upon a time, and that some of them had even been published, I must have looked sceptical, because he laughed and said, 'Not your idea of an author? Is it the suit? I didn't always look this conventional, you know. And it's true I wasn't in the Raymond Radiguet class, and I haven't written anything for many, many years. It was never a day job, just a hobby.'

'So would we have anything of yours in the shop?'

'Long out of print,' he said, 'though I daresay you might find one in second hand bookstores, if you were to look hard enough. They were published under a pseudonym, of course.'

I wondered if he were making this up, to impress me. He didn't *look* like a writer, though I wasn't sure what writers were supposed to look like since up till then I hadn't known any.

'So what was your nom de plume?'

'Mike Romeo.'

It didn't ring any bells, but it sounded like the sort of name you'd see in raised foil on chunky paperbacks on sale in railway station newsagents. Gabrielle de Rospin suddenly seemed pretentious and overelaborate. I began to wish I'd settled on something snappier, like Juliet Tango or Sierra Foxtrot.

'Sounds romantic,' I said, eaten up by envy by the fact that he'd actually written books and they'd been published.

'Not romance, I'm sorry to say. War stories. Lunkhead escapism for would-be alpha males.'

'Do you get royalties?'

'Lord no. To tell you the truth, they weren't very good. I'm sure your novels are much better.'

'I haven't had anything published yet,' I admitted.

'But you're working on it...'

'As a matter of fact I am. Not a novel, though.'

'What's it about? Or is that a secret?'

I weighed up the pros and cons. He'd said he'd given up writing, but I already had my hands full keeping Nancy's story out of the clutches of professional scribes like Verity Wilson and Phoebe Pflum. The last thing I needed was Mike Romeo muscling in on my exclusive as well.

'I don't want to talk about it,' I said, though I did, very much.

'Are you sure about that?' he asked.

Normally it would never have entered my mind to describe what I'd seen at the clinic to someone I'd known for less than an hour. Then again, there was no *normally* about any of this. I was dying to tell someone, anyone, and Lars was persuasive, and after a couple of glasses of Bordeaux, I couldn't help it, the whole thing came tumbling out.

Chapter 3
The Bunterberg Exchange

It was clear it wasn't what he'd been expecting to hear, especially from a virtual stranger. Lars was appropriately shocked and horrified. But I liked the way he put his arm around me - not making a pass but in a chivalrous gesture of comfort. He shook his head in disbelief.

'Jesus Christ, what kind of people would do something like that?'

'The insane kind,' I said. 'The kind who kill in the name of the Lord.' Because my tongue was already loosened I thought I might as well give him the lowdown on Nancy and the strange circumstances surrounding her pregnancy, then filled him in on my meeting with Jules Delgado as well, though I downplayed the Antichrist angle, remembering the look of scorn it had earned me from Church.

When I'd finished, Lars tipped his head to one side, as though to get me in focus. 'I can't believe you're so cool about all this.'

'I don't *feel* cool,' I said.

'But if you'd arrived a few minutes earlier, it could have been you, chopped to pieces on the clinic floor.'

'Quite,' I said. 'Plus Delgado thought I was Nancy, which complicates matters.'

'You look alike?'

'Not at all. She has red hair. Also her taste in clothes is rather eccentric. I told the detective about

Delgado, but he didn't seem interested.'

'If they're doing their job properly, they'll have him in their sights anyway. He was a friend of the men who died? Maybe he was out for revenge. Although...' He looked thoughtful, like someone thinking about the solution to a crossword clue. The hesitation struck me as ominous.

'What?'

'If this Delgado fellow didn't want Nancy's pregnancy to come to term, like you said, why would he kill the people who were preparing to end it?'

I hadn't thought of that. I stared into my wine and tried to make sense of it. Things seemed more nonsensical than ever, and only partly because I was drunk.

'I don't know,' I said at last. 'Maybe because they're mad? I've known some maniacs in my time, and their thought processes aren't like yours or mine.'

I was half-expecting Lars to ask me about the other maniacs I'd known, but instead he nodded sagely, and said, 'That's true. We once had a guy in the office who had a breakdown, stripped naked, and tried to stab the CEO with a stapler.'

'Everything has felt a bit strange since then,' I said. 'I think I'm probably still in shock. I'm not sure I'll ever get over it.' I was trying to sound flippant, but he was staring at me intently, as though searching for hairline cracks in my façade.

'In that case,' he said, 'I'd better see you home.'

When we got outside I asked him about his limp. 'Old war wound,' he said. 'One day I'll tell you about it. But I think you've had enough body horror for now.'

This implied he was hoping to see me again. Well,

I thought, why not? I expected him to escort me to the bus stop, but instead he hailed a cab and saw me all the way to my door, and I didn't object, because I couldn't imagine Delgado trying anything with him around. Lars looked like the sort of man who could take care of himself. And after he'd gone to all the trouble of seeing me home, it would have been churlish not to invite him in for coffee.

'Just a quickie, then,' he said, glancing at his watch. 'Mustn't miss the last train.'

I tried not to read too much into the word 'quickie'.

'After all,' he added as we stepped inside, 'It isn't every day you get to drink coffee in a Wilkie Bunterberg.'

This time I didn't even try to hide my surprise. 'How did you know it's Bunterberg?'

'My company was looking for investment opportunities, so I read up on this block when it was being built. Used to be a potato warehouse, am I right? I had no idea bookshops paid such generous wages.'

'They don't.' I told him how my grandfather had fallen out with my father and had ended up dividing his estate between me and my grandmother, whose slice was currently being sucked up in nursing home fees. 'It wasn't a massive amount, but better than a slap in the face with a wet fish.'

Lars fell about laughing, as though this were the first time he'd heard the expression.

'Though of course this is the smallest flat in the block,' I said, 'and I only get direct sunlight between the hours of seven and nine o'clock during the months of June and July.'

Lars laughed again, making me feel witty and

urbane. He impressed me again by identifying the floor lamp as Vig Munsen, and went on to enthuse about the St. Malo armchair I'd picked up for next to nothing in a Clapham junk shop, though he needed prompting to put a name to it.

'Of course!' he said, slapping his forehead. 'I *knew* there was something familiar about that curved back; I've never seen one in the flesh before. How much did you say you paid? You're kidding! My God, you did well there.'

I was so thrilled to have met someone who knew almost as much as I did about design that I handed him my spare copy of the Raymond Radiguet then and there. The gift pleased him so much he stopped checking his watch, so I opened a bottle of red and before we'd got halfway through it he started kissing me and we adjourned to the bedroom.

Underneath that suit he was a tiger in boxer shorts. And soon, not even the boxer shorts. I couldn't believe my luck. He was too good to be true. There had to be a catch. It wasn't until he'd put his clothes back on and was about to leave that I found out what it was.

Of course he was married. I should have guessed. Nobody was *that* perfect.

*****

So maybe Lars wasn't perfect, and he would never be my type, but he couldn't have come into my life at a better time. We met again after work on Thursday, and on Friday evening as well. It was just what I needed: not just a distraction, but someone I could open up to, and in more ways than one. Plus he turned out to be almost as much of a Scrabble addict as I was. We got into the habit of playing after sex; it was rare for us to actually finish a game - he had to catch his train - but it was such fun it didn't really matter.

That week I left several messages on Nancy's answering machine, but for once, I wasn't annoyed when she didn't return my calls. The prospect of seeing her again was filling me with dread. We had shared an experience of unimaginable horror, but my predominant feeling about it now was one of embarrassment. She had seen my face stripped of everything but naked quivering fear, and even though she'd been so far out of it she probably didn't remember, I felt I'd been tricked into baring my soul.

I shared these sentiments with Lars, and he seemed to understand. In fact, in his eyes, it only seemed to make me more fascinating. He couldn't believe he actually knew someone - no, that he was *actually having sex with someone* - who had been personally involved in the Abortion Clinic Massacre.

'You won't tell anyone?' I asked on our second date. 'You won't sell my story to the press?'

'Who would I tell? Eileen doesn't know about you and I intend to keep it that way. Anyway, we have plenty of money. I don't need any more.'

And so I kept banging on about the unpleasantness at the clinic, dredging up fragments and trying to piece together what had happened, and he egged me on.

'Perhaps there was another way in? A back door?'

'I don't think so.'

'And Middlemarch Woman had nothing to do with it?'

I shook my head. 'She's a snotty-nosed bitch, but I don't think so. Though of course if this were a movie, she'd turn out to be the murderer simply because she's the least likely culprit.'

'That's not true,' he said. 'If this really were that sort of preposterous thriller, the killer would turn out to be *you*.'

I laughed weakly. 'They ruled me out straightaway.'

To my surprise he seized my hand and stared into my eyes in that disarmingly candid way he had. 'Why do I get the feeling you're disappointed by that? You surely wouldn't want anyone to think you were capable of murder?'

'Of course not! It's just...' I searched for the words. 'All my life I've felt invisible. I blend into the wallpaper. I would have made a brilliant ninja assassin, because no-one ever notices I'm there.'

He chuckled. 'Then maybe it *was* you! You don't have any black holes in your memory by any chance?'

'No!' I said, laughing back at him. In fact, I did have a few holes, but I assumed it was due to my brain censoring the worst bits for the good of my mental health. I didn't share this with Lars; I'd told him more than enough about me and Nancy and Jules Delgado as it was. But the more I shared my memories of the clinic, the more I felt it slackening its grip on my psyche. It began to sound like an urban legend which had once happened to a friend of a friend. It occurred to me that talking about it was excellent therapy.

'That's right,' he said when I said this out loud. 'You didn't think I was asking you all those questions for fun, did you? I used to have a friend who served in the Falklands, and well... I won't say what happened when he tried to lead a normal life afterwards. You've been through an ordeal the average person can't even begin to comprehend.'

'Did *you* serve in the Falklands?' I asked, thinking about his limp.

'Oh no,' he said. 'My life has never been that exciting.'

I agreed with him there. Our evenings together weren't all one-way traffic. Lars told me his problems, but he was right, his life just wasn't very interesting. Eileen was a hypochondriac who drank too much, they wanted children but had never had any, and he harboured fantasies of driving across America on a motorbike, *Easy Rider*-style, though hopefully without the getting-shot-by-rednecks ending.

But I couldn't see him ever doing anything that intrepid when he was so clearly in thrall to his job, the daily commute, trivial disputes with neighbours over garden fences, occasional visits to Ikea. This is what real people did, I reminded myself. They got married, bought houses in the suburbs, took the train to work, and had dull relationship problems. I couldn't understand why anyone would want to give up writing for such a banal existence, but whenever I mentioned his books to Lars he laughed them off, and assured me it had never been a serious career, and that he didn't miss writing at all.

Besides, he said, *'You're* the writer now, Belinda.' He glanced sideways at me. 'As well as a ninja assassin.'

I breathed in sharply.

He shook his head and laughed. 'I'm *kidding*.'

Chapter 4
Desperate Living

The morning after the clinic, Nancy awoke to the feeling that she was trapped in a loop of the space-time continuum. Here she was back in the same hospital with the same people telling her she was pregnant. She had tried to put a stop to it, but it seemed there was to be no escape. She felt like throwing herself out of the window. She asked a doctor if she could set up another abortion immediately. He frowned and told her she would have to talk to the chief obstetrician. 'You're what? Twenty weeks?'

'I only found out two weeks ago, and there's something wrong with the foetus.'

'We'll do a scan this afternoon,' he said. 'Best not rush into anything. You're under enormous stress.'

'You're telling me.' said Nancy. Her memory of Monday afternoon was foggy and incomplete. She knew something had happened before the termination could take place. But what? Someone had died, and violently, that much was clear, but she didn't know how, or why, or who. Another one of the men in grey? What was *wrong* with them? They kept coming at her like lemmings.

She put her hand on her rounded stomach. 'Was it you, you little bleeder? What on earth did you do?'

Oh fuck, she thought. *Now I'm talking to it.*

*****

It wasn't just the same hospital. It was the same red-faced detective bugging her. Three people dead, he told her. All clinic personnel. *Dr. Madison*, she thought. *The nurse. Arthur the anaesthetist.* She was appalled. They hadn't been trying to hurt her; they'd been trying to help.

'Obviously, since for most of the critical period you were under anaesthetic, we don't expect you to remember much about what happened.'

'Obviously,' Nancy said through a mouthful of banana Fudge Tub.

Church looked at her evenly. 'Quite a coincidence, though. After that Karl Petersen business.'

'Tell me about it.'

'We were hoping *you* might be able to tell *us*.' He paused, as if hoping she might fill the gap with words. Nancy ignored him and carried on eating, so he asked, 'Can you think of anyone who might bear you a grudge?'

She froze, spoon halfway to her mouth. 'I was a sitting duck in there.'

Church leant forward, his blubbery features rearranging themselves into an almost hawkish expression. 'And yet you have a knack of getting off without a scratch while everyone around you is dropping like flies. Perhaps you heard about that series of freak accidents last Wednesday?'

'No,' she said.

'All Americans on tourist visas, like Petersen.' He studied the backs of his hands. 'All from Spittle Mill, North Carolina. One under a tube train. Another crushed by a bus, a third brained by a couple of idiotic builders. A fourth man was attacked by dogs; they got him to hospital but he discharged himself before we could talk to him. We managed to keep the details out of the press. Luckily they're preoccupied with jellyfish right now.' He stopped looking at his hands and stared at her so intently that she began to feel uncomfortable. 'Where were you last Wednesday, Miss Loughlin?'

'At home,' she said. 'Throwing up, I expect.'

'We already know you visited the Faraday clinic and talked to Dr. Madison.'

'Then why ask?' She felt sick. 'Shouldn't you be talking to the builders who dropped the clock? Or the dog owner?'

Church kept staring. She stared back. Why wouldn't they just leave her alone? She'd assumed things would be back to normal today, but instead they were even worse than before. Three more people dead, and her situation more hopeless than ever.

Church coughed. 'Perhaps now you'll tell us who the father is.'

She sighed. 'How should I know?'

He tried to not let the disgust show on his face, but couldn't prevent it from seeping into his voice. 'If narrowing it down to one name is too much of a challenge, maybe you could provide us with a list of possibilities.'

'I can't do that,' said Nancy.

This time, he made no attempt to hide his disdain. 'A pity you weren't this coy when you were sleeping around.'

'I didn't sleep around!' she yelled and, because she wasn't in any position to stamp her feet, flung what remained of her Fudge Tub across the room. The carton bounced off the wall, leaving a dribbling yellow stain behind it.

Church lowered his voice. 'Did someone rape you? Would you prefer to talk to a female officer?'

'I don't know.' Nancy felt tears pricking at her eyes. It wasn't fair. She hadn't asked for any of this.

'Is someone threatening you, Miss Loughlin?'

All the frustration and helplessness of the past weeks bubbled up in her.

'I DIDN'T HAVE SEX WITH ANYBODY!'

Church was overcome with exasperation. 'You'll be telling me next it was some sort of Immaculate Conception.' It was a lame attempt at sarcasm, but as he fumbled in his pocket, trying to find a handkerchief, their eyes met, just for an instant. She thought he was going to give her the handkerchief so she could dab her eyes, but instead he mopped his own face with it. There was a pause which stretched beyond awkward into embarrassing.

Maybe Belinda was right. This *was* the frigging Antichrist inside her, and it was killing off anyone who threatened it, including the three people preparing to abort it. She wondered if the cheque had already been cleared, how she would go about getting a refund, and then felt guilty thinking about money when lives had been lost. But maybe it was time to face the facts, however implausible. She was pregnant, and yet she hadn't had sex. Nor as far as she was aware had any sort of in vitro fertilisation occurred while she hadn't been looking. Might someone have slipped her a date rape drug? Had she been kidnapped and impregnated *by aliens*?

Church interrupted her thoughts in a hearty tone that sounded forced. 'But we don't believe in nonsense like that, do we? It's a myth, just like the, er... Soho

Slasher.' And he winked.

She flinched. 'I don't know what you're talking about.'

'Some foolishness the press have come up with.' This time he raised an eyebrow. 'But maybe there's more to it than they think,' he said. Before she had a chance to find out exactly what he meant, a nurse came up to tell him visiting hours were over, even for agents of the law.

Nancy was relieved to see the back of him. Her head was buzzing, and she needed time to think things over. For a moment, she had almost broken down and told Church everything, but now her instincts were kicking in and telling her to be careful. She wanted to believe he was on her side, but how could she be sure? What if the police thought it was her fault? That she was responsible for those people's deaths?

And what if she *were* responsible?

She realised she'd been absent-mindedly patting her stomach again.

'You,' she said. 'It's *your* fault, isn't it. *You've* been doing this.'

*****

The scan revealed that the foetus was only abnormal in that it seemed to be developing much faster than was usual. The obstetrician concluded Nancy had been mistaken about the date of her last period, and refused to listen when she insisted her calculations had been correct. They impressed upon her that she'd already left it late for an abortion, but allowed it could probably be arranged if her health were at stake. Drawing on the times she'd read for Ophelia and Charlotte Corday, she gave them her best impression of a woman on the edge of a nervous breakdown, one who had survived a massacre by the skin of her teeth and was hanging on to her sanity by a thread that would almost certainly snap if the pregnancy were allowed to continue. The doctor seemed more embarrassed than convinced, but booked her in for the end of the week.

Church popped back to see her, just long enough to say he was being taken off the case, which was being shifted to another department, and he doubted she would find his replacement quite so congenial. He added something she didn't catch.

'Sorry?' she asked. 'Could you repeat that?'

'You're ComSec's problem now.' He rolled the two syllables around as though they were mouthfuls of vinegar. 'Better funded than us, by all accounts. Well, good luck with *them*.' And with that, he seemed to deflate before her eyes. 'We're removing the officer outside your room; in fact, I think you're being moved into one of the public wards. But don't worry about being unprotected; I'm sure those bastards will be keeping a close eye on you.'

'Com Sec? What's that? Like telecom? Communications? Comedy?'

'They're comedians all right,' said Church. 'But not the kind you'd laugh at.'

And he smiled, a little ruefully, and was gone.

*****

On Wednesday morning, round about the time an orderly tried to change the sheets while she was still in the bed, Nancy decided she wanted to go home and got dressed. No-one paid her any heed as she signed herself out. A climbing frame had collapsed at a playground and the reception area was full of wailing infants and their neurotic parents. Nancy felt almost regretful. On Monday night she'd been the hospital's star patient; now she was just taking up space.

Outside, the rain smelled of fish and ink. Her eye was caught by the headline on the newsstand across the street. ABORTION CLINIC MASSACRE!

Time to find out what lies they're peddling about me now.

She stepped off the kerb without thinking. Three cars screeched to a halt, causing a motorbike to skid into the back of the middle vehicle. Its rider fell off and slid sideways into the path of another car, which managed to brake just in time. Nancy watched all this calmly and then, smiling to herself, sauntered across the rest of the road, taking her own sweet time, ignoring the cacophony of car horns and the fallen biker who, to judge by the way he was yelling obscenities at her, had escaped serious injury.

She scooped up a bunch of newspapers and hailed a cab. She could quite clearly smell the last three passengers. One had been suffering from acute gingivitis, another had been drinking white wine at lunch, and the third had been suffering from Type 2 diabetes. *I could launch a new career as a diagnostician,* she thought.

'Never stops, does it?' the cab driver said over his shoulder. 'Be raining jellyfish next. You heard about the jellyfish? Smuggled in by immigrants. They eat them grilled in Malaysia. Can't see them with the naked eye but heaven help you if you accidentally inhale one. Though that's what the kids are doing these days, snorting jellyfish for kicks.'

Nancy tuned him out and looked at the front pages. The story had broken too late for some of the Tuesday editions, but it was all over the Wednesdays.

THREE DEAD IN CLINIC CARNAGE!
ABORTION CLINIC MASSACRE!
DEATH COMES TO THE BABY KILLERS!

It had made every front page except *The Financial Times*, which had gone with BLACK MONDAY. Most of the papers ran editorials by writers who smugly conveyed righteous satisfaction that an abortion doctor had been horribly murdered. No-one mentioned Nancy by name, though in some reports she was a 'female patient'. Twice she was described as an 'unmarried redhead', once as a 'mystery blonde'. Elsewhere she was referred to as 'busty', a 'benefits scrounger' and a 'Saudi Arabian concubine'.

'Just goes to show this global warming theory is a load of bollocks,' the cab driver was saying. 'What the powers-that-be don't want you to know is that climate change is a recurring natural phenomenon, and that every three hundred years there's a period of extreme moisture caused by sun spots and earthquakes, and if you ask me we're in that period right now...'

Nancy felt vexed. She was glad her name hadn't been splashed all over the tabloids, but the absurd speculation and inaccuracies annoyed her. 'The Soho Slasher' was a recurring theme. She wondered if this were the official line now. Maybe the police were encouraging it. Maybe they didn't *want* the truth to come out. Whatever that the truth was.

Well, what was it? She considered the facts:

a) She was pregnant without having had sex.

b) Complete strangers had tried to kill her. Presumably because of a), since no-one had ever made an attempt on her life before, so long as you discounted that time Sally had fallen asleep at the wheel on the way back from Hastings.

c) Everyone who tried to harm her died in a freak accident.

d) Correction - everyone who tried to harm *the foetus* died. Dr Madison and his staff hadn't been trying to harm *her*.

Maybe Belinda had been on to something. This was no normal pregnancy.

'And of course,' the cab driver was saying, 'it serves those baby killers right.'

All the papers used the same quotes from the detective in charge, but Church had withheld as much information as he'd given out. There was no mention, for example, of Karl Petersen, or of any of the other American sightseers whose lives had been so abruptly curtailed. So no-one had yet joined up the dots and connected her to those incidents. But it was only a matter of time, she thought. Shuffling through the papers again, she spotted Verity Wilson's byline. How long before Wilson put two and two together and realised Nancy was the missing link between Kitchen Devil Man and the Baby Killer Bloodbath?

The road was badly surfaced, and her insides churned as the taxi lurched over a large pothole. She had to stop reading.

'Bloody council,' said the cab driver. 'Whole town is falling apart.'

The rain had stopped by the time the cab set her down. Red Lion Street had been cordoned off, so she got out on Theobald's Road. As she turned the corner into Natal Place, she saw blue light bouncing off the walls and a small crowd of people clustered around the entrance to her building. This was it, then. They were waiting for her. *Shit, how did they find out? At least give me a chance to fix my hair.*

But the crowd wasn't there for her. Something else was going on. Pushing her way towards the door, she peered through a small gap between bystanders and saw paramedics loading a stretcher into the back of an ambulance. The shape on the stretcher had been covered by a blanket, but, as she watched, an arm flopped down and swung limply for a moment. The medics quickly tucked it back out of sight and the bystanders rearranged themselves and blocked her view, but not before she'd spotted the grey sleeve.

She saw Ernie, her neighbour from the third floor, gawping along with the rest and asked him what was going on. Ernie jerked a thumb across the street, to where the coffee bar's plate-glass window was lying in fragments on the ground, roped off by a cat's cradle of yellow tape; a few remaining shards clung like stalactites to the top of the empty frame. One of the sandwich-makers, face set in a grimace, was trying to sweep the wreckage to one side. As Nancy watched, she saw a uniformed policeman bend over to pluck a pair of binoculars from the wreckage..

'Freak accident,' said Ernie.

Another one. And she hadn't even been there.

'Did you see it?' Nancy's mouth was dry. She needed a drink.

'Heard,' said Ernie. 'Like someone dropping an dinner service.'

'Who was it?'

Ernie shrugged. 'Some guy. You should have seen the blood. Christ, what a shitty thing to happen on your tea break.'

Nancy looked over at the shattered glass, some of it smeared with strawberry jam, then up towards her window at the top of the block. Had he been spying on her? Or waiting for her to come home, so he could attack her while she was fumbling for her keys? *Keys.* She rummaged in her bag, but as usual it was a black hole that swallowed objects whole. After a fruitless search, she remembered she'd lent one spare set to Belinda, and left the other for safekeeping with Ernie, who managed to peel himself away from the spectacle long enough to climb the stairs with her and fetch them.

'You all right?' he asked, dropping the keys into her outstretched hand. 'You look a little off-colour.'

'I'm fine,' said Nancy, though she was finding his Essence de Citron Vert a little overpowering.

Ernie bent over to whisper in her ear. 'Can I be godfather? I've always wanted to be a godfather.'

Nancy took a step back, surprised. Was it that obvious? 'We'll see,' she said. 'Sorry, I have to go pee.'

It had been an excuse to avoid further questioning, but as she climbed the rest of the stairs she realised her bladder really was uncomfortably full. As she reached the fourth floor there was a familiar snarling. Mrs. Feaver was waiting in her doorway, cradling her growling Jack Russell as though it were a hairy baby.

'If this keeps up I'll have to complain to the landlord,' said Mrs. Feaver.

'Nothing to do with me,' said Nancy. 'I only just got back.'

'All that clomping around, doors slamming at an hour when decent people are trying to sleep. Hoovering the floor at one in the morning! No consideration, none at all. We couldn't sleep a wink, could we Chip?'

Nancy had heard this before. She'd been accused of talking too noisily, walking too heavily, closing cupboards too briskly, playing music too loudly. But this time she had a watertight alibi.

'I wasn't even here.'

'Oh, I *know* what I heard,' said Mrs. Feaver, backing into the witchcave with her snarling familiar.

Nancy was left staring disconsolately at the closed door. Now she was being blamed for *everything*. But as she reached the fifth floor, she saw Mrs. Feaver hadn't been imagining things. The mystery of her missing keys was solved. Because there they were, hanging from the lock. And the door was wide open. She knew she could be scatty at times, but she also knew she wasn't *that* scatty.

She edged into the hallway, half-expecting to find one of the men in grey lying in wait, but the silence hung heavy and undisturbed, and her nose informed her that whoever had been there had left hours ago. She went from room to room to check, but her enhanced sense of smell was giving her all the information she needed. There had been more than one of them; one or both had slathered their hands with coal-tar soap, brushed their teeth with spearmint toothpaste, daubed armpits with roll-on deodorant, coated their lips with chapstick. And there was a whiff of cleaning products. Bleach, oven cleaner, washing-up liquid… She was so impressed by the precision of her heightened olfactory abilities that it was some moments before she noticed the state of the flat. She stared at the living-room in disbelief. Whoever it had been, they had gone to town.

The place had never been tidier. Every surface was polished and gleaming. The carpet had been so thoroughly vacuumed the colour was several shades lighter than usual. Newspapers and magazines were stacked in neat piles. In a daze, Nancy drifted through to the bedroom and found the bed made up with fresh linen. The clothes and shoes she'd left on the floor or draped over chairs had been tidied away. The bathroom and kitchen dazzled with their spotlessness. The limescale was gone, the hob scraped free of ancient grease. She went back into the living-room and sat down heavily in the armchair, which is when she spotted the last straw - three knicker-pink hyacinths poking their noses out of a pot on the window-ledge.

Nancy felt violated. Someone had broken into her flat, cleaned up, and left hyacinths.

She sat staring at the pink buds until it grew dark. And then she pulled herself together and phoned Maurice, who she knew would still be at the office, making phone calls to the West Coast. He'd been understanding about her taking so much time off work, but she'd put off telling him about the pregnancy, thinking that once the abortion was out of the way, she would be able to return to work and pretend nothing had happened. But now the termination had been rescheduled, and she wasn't even sure if she ought to go through with it. What if it ended in more carnage? Could she risk that happening?

Perhaps it was time to ask Maurice straight out if one of their drunken evenings had got out of hand. There had always been a bit of casual groping, but surely she'd remember if they'd gone further? Maurice canoodled with all his exes, but when it came down to it, she couldn't imagine him not being faithful to Phoebe, any more than she could imagine herself having intercourse with the husband of one of her best friends - least of all forgetting about it afterwards.

The thought of throwing herself on Maurice's mercy was comforting. He would know what to do. Maurice *always* knew what to do. She dialled his number and told him she'd been burgled.

'Oh my God. Hang on tight, sweetheart, I'm coming straight round.' There was a pause. 'You already called the cops, right?'

It hadn't occurred to her. He instructed her to hang up and dial 999, so she did as ordered, but the switchboard was in no hurry to connect her, and once she'd been connected and explained the nature of the emergency, the police weren't in much of a hurry to come round, so Maurice arrived before they did. Nancy let him enfold her in a bear-hug. She buried herself gratefully in his chest, breathing in the comforting blend of man-sweat and Marlboro Light, now magnified to an almost dizzying degree. In mid-hug, he said, 'At least they left you the telly.'

She looked up from the moist nest she'd made in the front of his jacket. 'So they did.'

'What did they take?' He began to stalk around her flat like an insurance investigator taking an inventory. Nancy's tears dried up as she trotted after him.

'You shouldn't have cleaned up,' he said.

'That wasn't me.'

Maurice stopped so suddenly she nearly cannoned into him. 'What?'

Tears welled up in her eyes again. '*They* did. They cleaned up my flat.'

Maurice gazed at her in wonder. 'Burglars did your housework?'

Nancy pointed to her shoes, which had been arranged in neat rows. 'They didn't take my Cherry Valances. They're worth more than anything else here.'

'How did they get in?'

'Somebody must have gone into my bag at the hospital and stolen my keys.'

He gawped at her. 'Hang on. You've been back to hospital?'

She took a deep breath. 'You know the Abortion Clinic Massacre?'

In an incongruously camp gesture, he raised both hands to his face and gasped, '*That was never you*! Nance! What's going on?'

'I wish I knew,' she said. She told him about the pregnancy. After a while, he stopped trying to interrupt.

'No, we did *not* have sex,' he said when she'd finished. His mouth was set in a grim line. 'You think I would take advantage of you like that? You think I would take advantage of *anyone* who was so drunk they couldn't remember it? I can't believe you'd think I could do that. Don't you know me at all?'

He was upset. Nancy tried to explain, but before she had time to apologise, there was heavy knocking at the door. She opened it. There were two of them. Plain-clothes detectives - both small, blond and very imperfectly formed, like fumbled clones of Alan Ladd and Veronica Lake. Nancy stared at them in shock - not because of how they looked, but because of how they smelled. It was them! *They* were the burglars! And now they had the nerve to saunter into her flat, peering around politely as though they'd never been there before.

'Nothing's been touched?' said Veronica, stifling a yawn.

'*Everything* has been touched,' said Nancy.

'How did they get in?' asked Alan.

You know perfectly well how you got in.

Nancy said, 'Well, I'm on the fifth floor, so not likely to be through the window.'

Maurice scowled at her, but Alan gave no sign of having noticed the sarcasm, and continued to stroll around the living-room as though he were at a plainclothes cocktail party. His eye fell on the stash of newspapers. He picked up the top one: BLOODBATH AT BABY-KILLING CLINIC!

'We don't have time for that,' said Veronica. She tried to snatch the paper away. There was a sound of rending newsprint as the front page ripped down the middle. 'Sorry about that,' she said to Nancy.

'It was you, wasn't it,' said Nancy.

'Yes, I'm sorry about tearing your newspaper,' said Alan.

'You stole my keys.'

'Nancy...' said Maurice.

Nancy went into her chilliest leading-female-role-in-the-Scottish-play manner. 'I'm sorry this has been such a waste of time for you. Though I'm not sure why you bothered to turn up in the first place. You already knew what you were going to find, because *you were here last night*.'

Veronica adjusted the angle of her head in a manner that was almost menacing. 'What are you suggesting?'

Maurice gave Nancy a despairing look and took the detectives to one side. The three of them bent their heads in a huddle. Even with her enhanced hearing, Nancy couldn't make out what they were saying, but they kept glancing in her direction. Probably deciding which asylum to have her committed to.

'Let's go,' said Veronica, straightening up. 'Would you like us to send someone round to advise you on security?'

'Bit late now,' said Nancy.

'Up to you,' Veronica said with a shrug.

Maurice escorted them to the door and there was another round of huddled muttering before they left. He closed the door and turned back to Nancy. 'What's got into you? It never pays to be cheeky to the filth. You never know when they'll get it into their heads to plant something.'

'Of course!' said Nancy. '*That's* why they were here!' She ran into the bedroom and began to rummage through her clothes, reducing the neatly folded garments to their habitual jumbled heaps.

'Come and sit down,' said Maurice, watching her from the doorway.

'It was the police,' she said, pulling a half-eaten packet of gum out of one of her coat pockets.

Maurice took the gum and popped a piece into his mouth. 'Sure it was. The badges were a dead giveaway.'

'It was the police *who broke in*.'

Maurice shuffled in embarrassment. 'Why would they do that?'

She rounded on him. 'You want me to tell you what you had for lunch? A Four Seasons pizza. And a doughnut.'

Maurice chewed thoughtfully. 'The doughnut was mid-morning.'

'A doughnut covered with *chocolate icing*.'

'Nancy, this is getting out of hand. I never said anything before, because the clients seem to enjoy it, but all that stuff about the Bloomsbury Bodysnatcher...'

'The Soho Slasher,' said Nancy. 'The police think the clinic massacre was the work of The Soho Slasher. But I made that up, you know I did.'

'Slasher, Ripper...' said Maurice. 'Of course some hack is going to slap one of those labels on the killer. Standard alliteration. The Fitzrovia Flayer. The Holborn Hacker. The Clerkenwell Cutthroat...'

'This is real, Maurice.' Somehow, the conversation had got away from her. In desperation, she grabbed his hand and laid it on her stomach. 'Feel this.'

He kept the hand there for no more than a split-second before snatching it back, as though his fingers had been burnt.

'I can't get rid of it,' she said.

'Aw hell,' said Maurice, continuing to chew, but lighting a cigarette as well. His mouth seemed to want to work overtime.

'And I'm going to have to go through with it. I have no choice.'

'There's always a choice, Nancy.'

She snatched the cigarette from his mouth and took a long, deep drag on it. He watched disapprovingly.

'Look, if you really are pregnant...'

She fell to her knees and started rummaging through the newspapers, cigarette dangling from her lips, shedding ash.

'If I'm pregnant? *If?*'

Her rummaging grew frantic, until finally she sat back on her heels and wailed, 'They stole my picture. *That's* what they were here for!'

Maurice lit a second cigarette to replace the one she'd taken. 'We'll get you another picture,' he said, sounding as though he wished he were somewhere else. Anywhere else.

'The ultrasound picture. This is not a normal foetus, Maurice...'

'Oh Nancy. Just because the abortion didn't work out...'

She stood up to face him in a fury. 'It didn't just not work out,' she shouted, stamping on the floor. 'It left *three people dead!*'

The ground beneath their feet shuddered to the rhythm of Mrs Feaver thumping on her ceiling, probably with the end of her witch's broom. Maurice grew distracted. He fluttered his elegant fingers, checked his expensive watch, made a lame excuse about having to meet Phoebe in the Bar Raccuda, and left in such a rush he forgot to take his cigarettes with him. Nancy drop-kicked the packet across the floor before retrieving it. She slumped into a chair and lit another Marlboro, trying to fend off tears of frustration.

When she'd smoked the cigarette down to the filter, she went into the kitchen, found a half-full bottle of sherry the burglars had restored to visibility, switched on the television and sat on the floor in front of it, staring at a late-night arts programme but lacking the will to turn up the volume so she could hear what the smug talking heads were saying. When the sherry was gone, she went back to the kitchen cupboard, found a tin of ready-mixed gin and tonic, and started on that. She would end up permanently pickled, like her mother, and then Maurice would be sorry. They're all be sorry. She would show them. But show them how?

She would live dangerously.

She thought about it. Through some inexplicable quirk of fate, she seemed to be invulnerable. So where was her sense of adventure? *Now* was the time to go scuba-diving. Hang-gliding. Mountain-climbing. What could go wrong? The foetus wouldn't let her fall. Or maybe she could go for a midnight stroll around one of London's parks. Potential muggers and rapists would fall victim to freak accidents, and serve them right. She could turn vigilante. Clean up the city, fight crime. Maybe she should start thinking about a superheroine costume... The idea made her giggle. A pregnant superheroine! Had there ever been one of those before?

But in her heart, she knew she would end up doing none of these things. Scuba-diving? Hell, all she felt capable of right now was sitting in front of the TV, drinking gin. She sighed and lit another of Maurice's cigarettes.

Smoking, now. That was a dangerous sport. The foetus didn't seem to mind that, or it would already have made her stop. And smoking had the added advantage of taking the edge of her supersensitive sense of smell. Being able to smell everything was more of a curse than a blessing. Christ almighty, people stank.

*****

Her last memory of that evening was a disquieting one.
From the living-room window, she'd always been able to
peer into the flats over the sandwich bar - in particular a
room on the fourth floor that was usually occupied by
hippy foreigners who could never be bothered to install
curtains. Not that there was much to look at, apart from
paunchy ponytailed guys smoking joints, or laughing
girls who shrieked to each other in Spanish and dropped
keys to visitors in the street below. None of them ever
thought to tilt their heads so they could look up at
Nancy.

That night, though, it was different. As she turned
off the lights, getting ready for bed, she noticed
someone in the room across the street. It was dark in
there as well, but Nancy could just about make out the
form of a large woman in a floral-print frock, sitting on a
straight-backed chair that barely seemed wide enough to
support her bulk. She was facing the window, looking
out into the night. That was all she was doing - sitting
and staring.

She didn't appear to be looking up at Nancy's flat,
but Nancy tugged the curtains over her own window,
just in case.

But even with the curtains drawn, she could sense
the fat woman sitting in the room across the street,
staring out of her window. Sitting and staring.

Chapter 5
The Bar Chester Chronicles

Before the end of the week, the Clinic Bloodbath story had already gone off the boil. With no new developments, it dwindled to a few paragraphs on the inside pages: mouthy columnists sharing their thoughts on abortion, speculation as to where the Soho Slasher would strike next, and some musing as to whether his name should be changed to the Marylebone Mangler since the Faraday Clinic was technically north of Oxford Street.

Detective Church called, but was clearly not interested in pursuing the Jules Delgado angle and instead asked questions pertaining to my precise movements before and after my arrival at the clinic. I wondered if I were a suspect after all, and, remembering Lars's observation, decided this wasn't altogether displeasing. When I asked Church if I were being watched he denied it, but in such a way that convinced me he was lying. I didn't mind. So long as I was under police surveillance, Delgado wouldn't be able to get to me.

But I knew I had to face Nancy before it got to the point where I would never be able to look her in the eye again, which would make it difficult if I was to be her official biographer. I kept putting off phoning her, but in the event it was she who called me, to invite me over on Sunday. I felt a flash of elation when I heard her on the other end of the line, swiftly followed by a resurgence of the awkwardness I'd been feeling all week. What exactly *was* the accepted etiquette for conversing with someone you'd last seen semi-naked in a room full of dead people?

'Maurice thinks I'm taking the piss,' she said.

This was music to my ears. The longer Maurice, and by extension his wife, my rival, could be kept on the sidelines, the better for me. This was *my* story.

*****

It was only three in the afternoon, but Nancy was already sipping from a tumbler of whisky when I arrived. I poured myself a small measure and went back with her into the bedroom, where she was sifting through a heap of clothes, shaking her head sorrowfully as she held up a stretchy gold tube I assumed was a stocking before realising with a shiver of distaste it was supposed to be a dress. 'Nothing fits any more.'

'Don't you have anything a bit baggier?'

She shot me one of her looks. 'Oh yeah, I may have some monk's robes here somewhere.'

I sat back on the bed with my ankles crossed and said, 'So how are you doing?'

She plucked sadly at a sliver of a T-shirt. 'I fixed up another appointment. For an abortion.'

'Oh no,' I said.

'Then cancelled it.'

I restricted myself to saying, 'Ah,' but felt like bursting into applause. She had finally seen the light!

'Looks like I have to keep the wretched thing.' She sounded like someone announcing a funeral.

'You've made the right choice,' I said, trying to cheer her up.

'I never *had* a choice. I just don't want anyone else to die.'

'You think the men in grey will leave you alone now?'

She sighed. 'I have no idea. But that's beyond my control. Actually, all of this is beyond my control. It's like I'm on a runaway horse. All I can do is cling on, and pray.'

'Praying might be a good idea,' I said.

'I don't mean *literally*.'

'Was it the men in grey who killed those people at the clinic?' I asked, thinking of Delgado. He was their leader, wasn't he?

'I don't think so.'

'Then who?'

A wave of acute distress passed over her face. 'I'd rather not talk about it.'

'You think *you* did it? Something you set up without being aware of it, like the others?'

'How? I didn't leave empty Fudge Tub cartons strewn all over the clinic for them to slip on and accidentally impale themselves on scalpels, if that's what you mean.'

'Actually, it was more disembowelling than impaling.'

'Let's not talk about it,' she said again.

I felt slightly hurt by her refusal to hear the details of my ordeal, which as Lars had pointed out had been much more horrible than hers, but she'd already changed the subject and was telling me about her keys being stolen. When she told me they'd been stolen by the police, who had used them to get into her flat and clean up, I was sceptical. 'Why would they do that?'

'They were looking for my scan. They wanted proof.'

'You sure they were cops? You said Church had been taken off your case.'

Nancy shrugged. 'I don't know. Maybe they were from... I don't know. Those other people. ComSec.'

'Maybe they're a cleaning company.'

'You wouldn't be so flippant if someone broke into your place,' said Nancy.

I told her she was being paranoid. But she had every right to be paranoid, I added, because someone really was out to get her.

'That makes me feel *so much better*,' she said.

In any case, if a cleaning company really had tidied up Nancy's flat, there was no longer any sign of it. The place had reverted to its usual state of disarray. I went round emptying overflowing ashtrays into a rubbish bag and watched in discomfort as Nancy continued to chain-smoke, letting the ash on her cigarettes build up into friable grey tubes which broke off and fell to the floor.

'I thought you didn't like strong smells. How can you bear this fug?'

'You don't understand,' she said, prodding the air with her cigarette. 'Smoking is the only thing standing between me and olfactory overload.'

'It's bad for baby,' I said.

'Not for *this* baby. I think *this* baby likes it.'

'That's what all the pregnant smokers say.'

She patted her nicely rounded stomach. 'I can tell by the way it kicks.'

'It's moving?'

'Well, no-one has managed to kill it yet, so yeah. It's getting bigger, I can feel it. It's starting to shift around.'

The way she'd patted her tummy had been almost affectionate. I realised I was staring, and wrested my attention away. There was a stack of newspapers nearby. I started leafing through the pages of the top one. 'They still don't know you're the mystery redhead. Or *mystery blonde*, as they call you here.'

'Why should they?' said Nancy. 'Anyway, I'm yesterday's news. They've moved on. The latest jellyfish infestation. The hostage crisis in Aberystwyth. Is Lala Messidor going out with Reuben D. Pimp?'

I tutted. 'Anyone would think you didn't *want* to be famous.'

'When I'm famous, Belinda, it'll be on *my* terms. For something I've done, not for something that has been done to me.'

'The publicity would boost your career! People would pay to see you.'

She sighed. 'How many roles for pregnant actresses can you think of?'

She was looking so downcast that I suddenly twigged what had happened. 'You didn't get that part.'

She made a face. 'They went with Carlotta Reese. I think they'd already decided before I even did the audition. I think she's sleeping with Les Six.'

'That's a shame,' I said. 'Maybe if your name had been in the papers they would have picked you instead.'

As I looked through the newspapers, there was one byline in particular that kept leaping out at me. It seemed more strident, more persistent than the others.

'Story by Verity Wilson,' I read. 'Pictures Clive

Mengers. Those jokers you met at the hospital, right? Do *they* know you're the mystery blonde?'

'No,' said Nancy. 'And they're not going to find out.'

I peered more closely at a picture of that looked as though it had been lifted from CCTV footage. The details were blurry, but the location looked familiar: police cars and an ambulance outside the Faraday.

'Hey, that's me! Coming out of the clinic.'

Nancy glanced over my shoulder. 'Could be anyone.'

'But it's me! I know it!'

I'd never had my picture in the paper before. There had been lots of press about Croydon, of course, but they'd managed to keep me and most of the other girls out of it. Seeing myself in print now was intoxicating, even if I did look all fuzzy; I couldn't understand why Nancy was so determined to keep a low profile.

I asked her if I could keep the page. She nodded her assent, a little bemused, and I carefully tore it out.

'Do you think I should phone the paper and tell them that's me?'

'Absolutely not,' said Nancy. 'If you talked to the press I'd kill you.'

She laughed as she said it, but I didn't much care for the turn this conversation was taking and changed the subject. I'd been itching to tell her about my new boyfriend anyway.

'Hey, guess what,' I said. 'I met someone.'

'That's great,' said Nancy. 'About time you moved on from whatsisname. Ronnie? Robbie, was it?'

'Roger.'

'Good for you,' she said. 'Is he nice? What's his name?'

'Lars. His parents are Norwegian.'

'I knew a Lars once. Or was it Sven?'

'He's nice,' I said. 'But he's married.'

'Aren't they all,' said Nancy.

She was smoothing out a sliver of semi-transparent fabric I saw to my horror wasn't a silk scarf but another dress. 'So pretty,' she whispered to the fabric. 'Now I'll never be able to wear you again.'

*****

I had to go home and do some paperwork before I got too ratfaced on Nancy's whisky, but we agreed to meet up the following evening at the Bar Chester, a favourite hangout of minor celebrities I'd been dying to check out. I would never have dared go there on my own, but Nancy was my golden ticket; she knew the head barman. Of course, I was almost a celebrity myself now, in a way, even if no-one would ever recognise me from the CCTV image.

'Will Maurice and Phoebe be there?'

I decided to ask Lars if he wanted to join us. Despite his boring lifestyle, he was good company, and I thought it might be fun to show him off in public. Maybe he would get mistaken for a suit-wearing hipster.

'Could be,' Nancy said, not seeming to care one way or another. 'I know Phoebe likes their Monkey Glands.'

'I'll bet she does,' I said.

That night I left a message on Lars' answering service, suggesting he join us, but when he called back in the morning it was to say he had to go straight home that night. Eileen was cooking; they were expecting people for dinner.

'Neighbours, and deadly dull,' he groaned. 'I would much rather be spending the evening with you. I miss you, Lindy.'

Lindy. He was the only person I allowed to call me that. Alain had tried it once, and I'd threatened him with a pair of scissors until he'd sworn never to do it again.

*****

So it was that, on Monday after work, I found myself perched on one of the Bar Chester's wrought iron stools, which had seemingly been designed for the express purpose of deflowering mediaeval virgins. I sipped a glass of indifferent Côtes du Rhône, and tried to look as though I weren't out of my element as I stared at the pages of a recently published novel I'd heard contained descriptions of disfiguring facial injuries sustained by soldiers at the Battle of the Somme. The bar was so dimly lit I had to screw up my eyes to make out the words, and the music was throbbing so insistently I could barely process them anyway. I wondered how people managed to communicate in such an environment, and concluded they didn't, not really.

There was no sign of Maurice and Phoebe, and Nancy was late, of course. She was always late, which was why I'd brought the book. But this time the lateness dragged on till it became excessive, even by her standards. I watched numbly as people came into the bar, drank bottles of wine, ate three-course meals, paid their bills and left, until I was forced to admit, in a crescendo of rage that eventually bordered on pain, that Nancy had found something better to do than meet me as arranged. I'd been stood up.

The bar was now pulsating with late-night customers. I squeezed into the corner by the payphone and dialled Nancy's number, hanging up when I heard the answering machine start up. If she wasn't at home, and she wasn't here, where was she? I tried her mobile, but she'd switched it off.

'Cheer up,' said a man with a teddy-boy haircut who was waiting to use the phone. 'It may never happen.'

I told him it already had happened, and something in my face made him forget his phone call and move as far away from me as possible.

There was nothing to do but settle my tab and creep away, hoping no-one would notice that I was departing as I had arrived - alone.

Who was I kidding? Of course no-one had noticed. As usual, I'd been invisible.

Chapter 6
The Dog Kennel

The next morning I rang Verity Wilson and arranged to meet her later on in a low-ceilinged Soho dive called The Dog Kennel. Her choice of venue. The walls were plastered with posters promoting long-defunct bands overlaid by a spray-painted trelliswork of black and silver graffiti. It might have been considered 'edgy' in some quarters, but it made me think of bedrooms occupied by the sort of adolescents who fantasised about gunning down their classmates.

Wilson blended right in with her aubergine leather jacket and skirt, fishnets, and stilettos with six-inch heels. Her hair had been streaked and teased until it begged for mercy. I thought she looked like a man in drag, an impression not dispelled by a voice made husky from tar. She smoked constantly, and a steady draught from the nearby stairwell blew an unwavering stream directly into my eyes. The result was that tears streamed down my face, redistributing my mascara in a Rorschach pattern on my cheeks, but if Wilson noticed that I appeared to be weeping uncontrollably, she didn't remark on it. Perhaps she was used to her sources sobbing fit to bust as they sold out their loved ones for thirty pieces of silver.

I assuaged my feelings of guilt by assuring myself that I was selling myself out as well; this had been *my* exclusive, and my reasons for sharing it were complicated. The fact that I had no means of disseminating my story was a factor, but so was the conviction that what I was doing was as much for Nancy's benefit as for my own. There would come a time when she would realise I'd done the right thing. I just had to keep out of her way until that time came, and trust that in the meantime Verity Wilson wouldn't betray her source, and that Nancy wouldn't realise that I was the one who'd sold her out.

There was also, I have to admit, a pulsing kernel of resentment that my friend had left me stewing on my own all night in the Bar Chester.

And so Wilson and I sipped industrial-sized Bloody Marys through straws and screamed until we were hoarse to make ourselves heard above the deafening thrash metal booming from speakers the size of the World Trade Center. She placed her brushed chrome kidney-shaped microcassette recorder on the table between us - as if it were likely to pick up anything other than thrash - and said something I didn't catch. I shrugged and shook my head, exaggerating the gestures like a silent movie actor. She let out a visible sigh, as though it were my fault the music was so loud, and leant over to yell into my ear so shrilly I could feel the tympanic membrane quivering.

'Mystery blonde!' she yelled. 'Tell!'

I was already finding out, as Nancy had found out before me, that Verity Wilson wasn't one for surplus vocabulary.

'Redhead, not blonde!' I yelled back. 'We're best friends! I know everything about her! You want her name?'

Verity nodded enthusiastically.

'You've already met her!' I screamed at the top of my voice. 'It's Nancy! Nancy Loughlin!'

Wilson's eyes opened very wide. 'Her? *The* Nancy Loughlin?'

'The very same.'

'So these deaths *are* connected,' she said, eyes agleam in the Stygian gloom. 'Interesting.' Even over the music I could hear her knuckles crackling as she flexed her fingers, as though preparing to reach out and grab my every word. 'Go on,' she said. And so I told her everything. Not about my meeting with Jules Delgado, I was still keeping that to myself, but about all the attempts on Nancy's life, her audition, the exploding pregnancy test, the clinic. Especially the clinic. I tried to include my side of the story as well, but Wilson wasn't so interested in that.

'Maybe Nancy did it,' she said. 'Maybe she's the Soho Slasher.'

I could tell she had studied criminology at the school of Preposterous Thrillers with Unlikely Twist Endings, as Lars had called it. I shook my head. 'No way. She was drugged to her eyeballs. She was semi-naked, not a drop of blood anywhere on her.'

At the word 'naked', Wilson's eyebrows shot up.

'Semi-naked,' I repeated. 'Just a hospital gown.'

'So the father?'

'Might be her ex!' I shouted. 'They're always snogging in public, even though he's married to someone else and they have a baby and everything. It's not right. I think there's something a little sick about hanging around with someone you've broken up with, instead of...' Wilson yawned openly, as a reminder that she didn't give a fig what I thought. Her loss. If only she'd let me babble on, I would have ended up giving her Maurice's name, address and National Insurance number, which would have stood her in good stead later on.

'Nancy swears she didn't sleep with anyone!' I shouted.

Verity Wilson laughed. 'Ha ha! Virgin birth!'

'Christ, no!' I yelled. 'More like Strumpet Birth!'

This last comment coincided with a sudden lull in the music, though my brutalised eardrums continued to pulsate neurotically in time to the vanished rhythm. A youth with pink dreadlocks which had never been shampooed and a nose-stud resembling a suppurating boil stared at me dispassionately, as though he heard people shouting 'Strumpet birth!' all the time.

Wilson seemed perplexed. 'Not normal, tell you that.'

I had to get her to repeat the line three times before I could make sense of it. 'Of course it's not normal!' I shouted. A small piece of spittle flew out of my mouth and landed on her padded shoulder, but she didn't notice. Either that, or she was accustomed to being spat on. 'Normal pregnancies don't protect you from knife-wielding madmen!'

'Second Coming,' said Wilson.

I stared at her aghast. 'No! The Antichrist!'

She was looking uncomfortable, as though the Bloody Mary were giving her heartburn. 'Miracle baby either way.'

She looked down at the backs of her hands and once again muttered something I didn't catch.

'Say that again!' I shouted. My throat was raw. For a long moment, she stared at the cigarette in her hand without appearing to see it. I blinked back the tears and waited patiently, grateful for the lull and trying not to worry about what permanent damage the music might be doing to my hearing.

Then her features recomposed themselves into an expression that, were we still in a silent movie, would have been followed by the title card, I HAVE FINALLY MADE UP MY MIND TO CONFIDE IN YOU. She placed her mouth right up against the side of my head so that when she moved her lips, I could feel them tickling my left earlobe.

Later, when the lobe was no longer there to tickle, I would look back on this moment with something approaching nostalgia.

'Had a tumour. *In here.*' She pointed to her abdomen. Curiously, she was no longer having to shout to make herself heard. 'Now it's gone.'

Chapter 7
Under Siege

The dream was terrifying. I was playing for my life. I had all the letters for 'Beelzebub', but before I had a chance to place them on the board, an alarm bell began to peal, and I realised it didn't matter which tiles I had lined up - my opponents would almost certainly come back at me with 'oxazepam', 'quixotry' and 'gherkins'. I was almost relieved when the bells turned out to be the telephone. Still half asleep, I fell out of bed to answer it.

'Did I wake you?' asked Lars, knowing full well it was only six thirty, when all decent folk were still asleep.

'I was dreaming about playing Scrabble.'

'Against me?'

My opponents had in fact been a griffin, a sphinx and a minotaur, all side-eyeing me with murderous intent, but it seemed less complicated to tell Lars that yes, he'd been the other Scrabble player.

He laughed. 'You lead such an exciting inner life, Belinda.'

I wasn't equipped to deal with sarcasm this early in the morning, and began to explain that it had actually been quite scary since whoever lost the game would be decapitated. Luckily, the memory was already fading. I asked Lars where he was calling from, excited by the idea it was from his house, from right under his wife's nose...

'Office,' he said. 'Sorry it's so early, we had a

conference call from Hong Kong. But - oh my God, Lindy, have you seen the paper?'

Of course I hadn't seen it. Did I usually go out at six thirty in the morning to get the papers? A moment or two passed before my brain went from half-awake to fully alert in one seismic shift, and I realised what he was talking about. This was it, then. I'd gone and done it, and there was no going back. Though obviously I had to pretend not to know what he was talking about.

'Your friend Nancy.'

'What about her?'

'She's been outed as the mystery survivor of the Abortion Clinic Massacre.'

'Oh my God,' I said, trying to sound shocked.

He read out the headline. EXCLUSIVE! WE NAME BABY KILLER BLOODBATH REDHEAD. THE TERMINATION THAT WENT WRONG. IS MIRACLE BABY THE SON OF GOD?

'Whoah,' I said. 'Hyperbole. And how do they know it's a boy?'

'I'm surprised they don't mention you,' said Lars. 'I mean, you *were* there.'

This was good news. Verity Wilson had kept me out of it, as promised. One day, I would tell Nancy what I'd done, but not today. But I called her a few hours later, ready to commiserate. I had my lines all prepared, but was relieved when she didn't answer. I left a message on her machine. Now I would have plenty of time to decide exactly what to say when I saw her.

But the decision was no longer mine to make, because, just like that, she vanished, and without even saying goodbye.

*****

I wasn't the only one wrenched out of sleep by the telephone. Nancy's dreams were full of darkness and thunder and screaming, so it took her a while to realise the cacophony wasn't all in her head. By the time she'd rolled out of bed and reached the phone, the caller had hung up and the message counter was blinking. The entryphone was buzzing as well; on her way to the bathroom to empty her bladder she tipped the receiver off its hook to stop the noise. It wasn't the first time it had broken down; she had no doubt Mrs. Feaver would already be nagging the landlord to get it fixed. Mrs. Feaver did have her uses.

Nancy made a cup of tea and sat down with it next to the answering machine. The tape took so long to wind back she began to think it was broken. She pressed playback, and then stopped and fast-forwarded, dropping in and out at random, listening in growing disbelief to a babble of strange and frequently garbled messages. How on earth had she slept through all these? But the most recent message was a friendly voice she recognised: Maurice. She called him straight back.

'Nancy, sweetheart.' His tone was so grave she was filled with dread. Had someone else died?

'You haven't seen it?'

She could already feel a headache coming on. 'What time is it?'

'Ten thirty,' said Maurice. 'Oh baby, I am *so* sorry.'

She blew her nose on the bottom of her T-shirt, which already needed washing. 'For what?'

'For behaving like a heel last week.'

She thought back. 'I suppose you did, rather.'

'For God's sake, don't go outside,' he said, and she didn't think to ask why he would say that.

'I only just woke up,' she said.

'Want me to come round?'

'Yeah, sure. Give me half an hour. I need to put some clothes on.'

'No need to get dressed for my benefit,' he said before hanging up. She thought there had been a forced edge to his flirting. The phone started chirruping again, but this time she let it ring. Hunger was gnawing at her innards like a beaver and the fridge was empty again. She pulled on another, cleaner T-shirt and the sweatpants she sometimes wore to the gym. There was just enough time to nip out to the shop and stock up on Fudge Tub before Maurice arrived.

She went downstairs and opened the door and the morning exploded in her face.

Nancy flung up an arm, and a dozen flashguns popped again, capturing her in the classic don't-take-my-photo pose. She lowered the arm and peered through her fingers. The street was packed.

'Miss Loughlin, if you could just spare a moment...'

'This way, Nancy!'

'Over here!'

Her first instinct was to retreat into the building, but her stomach was rumbling like a small earthquake, and she still hadn't taken in what was happening. So instead of scuttling back to safety, she plunged straight into the crowd, not caring who or what she caught with her elbows, breathing through her mouth in an attempt to keep the stench of humanity at bay. As she pushed her way to the end of the street, she smelt alcohol and mouthwash and infidelity. The reporters came with her all the way, like a cloud of nagging insects.

'Nancy!'

'This way, please.'

'Who's the daddy?'

'Any idea who the killer is?'

A communal attempt to follow her into the newsagent's degenerated into an unseemly scuffle in the narrow doorway. The reporters, some now with bloodied noses, watched with unabashed curiosity as she stocked up on newspapers, cigarettes and Fudge Tubs, some of them itemising her purchases in their notebooks. They continued to bombard her with questions as she came out again and retraced her steps, never physically impeding her progress, but getting in her way just the same. By the time she made it back to her building, she was having to bite down on her lip to stop herself bursting into tears.

She was struggling to insert her key into the lock when Verity Wilson's voice sliced through the babble like a freshly sharpened steak knife. Ten people dead, Nancy. When are you going to tell us who the father is?'

'Nine,' said Nancy, thinking they might as well get *that* detail straight.

There was a ripple of callous laughter, but she finally managed to push the door open and slip inside, slamming it on the foot of a weaselly hack trying to slip in after her. There was a howl of pain. She began to shake with anger, and the howl went up an octave. She was still trembling as she reached her flat and double-locked the door. She flopped into the armchair with a toffee-flavoured Fudge Tub. She drew the newspaper on to her lap and at last allowed herself to read the headline:

EXCLUSIVE: WE NAME BABY KILLER
BLOODBATH REDHEAD!

And underneath, in smaller type, THE
TERMINATION THAT WENT WRONG. And there
it was - her name. An old mugshot she'd asked her agent
to throw out years ago. The street where she lived. A
photo of her building. An old picture of her mother in
one of her seventies sex comedies.

Someone had talked, but who? One of the
detectives? Someone at the hospital? Nancy clenched her
fists. Whoever it was, they'd be sorry. She quickly read
the story, which was even worse than expected. They'd
got it all, and they'd got it all wrong: her father's adultery,
her mother's drinking, her own stalled acting career and
part-time work as a tour guide. Quotes from anonymous
ex-boyfriends painted her as neurotic, promiscuous and
untalented, a self-centred sponger and dabbler in drugs,
practically a prostitute. Every detail of her life had been
dredged up, sneered at, and cruelly twisted, even down
to the fact that she'd just been rejected for a role in a
musical about Jack the Ripper, which - the paper didn't
lose the opportunity to remind its readers - was scarcely
a suitable subject for a mother-to-be.

Nancy read on, her sense of outrage mounting.
They made it sound as though she were obsessed with
serial killers. As though she were an attention-seeking
singleton trying to guilt-trip an absent father into
providing financial support for the baby, as well as
blackmail the local council into giving her a flat, never
mind that she had one already. There were insinuations
that the missing father was himself the Soho Slasher, and
had struck several times before, targeting any man who
had dared ogle the woman who was pregnant with his

child. Directly contradicting all that, the report had been rounded off with a lot of wild speculation about immaculate conceptions and virgin births in general, with accompanying anti-abortion quotes from assorted Irish clergymen.

Nancy finished the Fudge Tub, dropped the paper, and lit a cigarette. So this was it. Her fifteen minutes of fame had arrived, and now she didn't want it, not like this. The phone kept ringing so she unplugged it and paced up and down, chain-smoking. Where was Maurice? He should have been here by now. She turned to the television for distraction, only to find herself watching her own window as rolling news crews trained their cameras on the upper floors of the block. What the hell? Were they expecting her to throw herself out? She peeked out from between her curtains to look down at the flat where she'd seen the fat woman in the floral-print frock. The end of a telephoto lens peeked back at her.

She stomped into the bathroom, where the window was frosted, and curled up in a foetal position on the bathmat. It occurred to her that the foetus was probably curled up in the exact same position inside her. They were like nesting dolls.

*****

For a long time, she mistook the hammering at the door for angry pounding in her head, but eventually she pulled herself off the floor. A glance into the mirror showed her the bathmat had left a bouclé pattern imprinted on one side of her face. Why couldn't they leave her alone?

She approached the door as if it were a dangerous animal whose jaws might close on her head, and yelled, 'Fuck off!'

'Fuck off yourself!'

Relief swept over her. It was Maurice. She opened the door and he strode past her into the flat. 'Blimey, what a clusterfuck.'

'How did you get in?'

'Bumped into Tilly and Sam round the corner.'

'You didn't get torn to pieces?'

'I'm used to dodging press,' he said. As a demonstration, he pulled his hood up over his head, hunched his shoulders and growled, 'Fuck you, arseholes!'

For the first time that day she laughed. 'Ha! You do look like a meth addict!'

They went through into the darkened living-room. Maurice saw the drawn curtains and made a face. 'My poor darling, you can't live like this. You need to get out of here.'

Nancy sighed. 'Tell me about it.'

'You can't make life-changing decisions under this sort of pressure. I'm serious. You can't stay here with this circus going on. I'd invite you round to the loft but I don't suppose it would be much better there.'

'Where then?'

He'd already thought about it. 'Paris! Our place is empty at the moment.'

Nancy burst into tears. 'But I look so ugly.'

'You're not ugly, poppet.' Maurice patted her shoulder. 'Just expecting. When Phoebe was pregnant she was convinced she looked like Quasimodo.' He tried to ruffle Nancy's hair, but it was so greasy that strands of it stuck to his hand.

'If I try to leave they'll just follow me.'

'We'll see about that,' said Maurice, helping himself to one of her cigarettes. As he puffed on it distractedly, she could almost see a plan taking shape in his head. Finally he said, 'You're an actress. Why not *act* your way out? You could pretend to be my maiden aunt.'

Nancy was dubious. 'I don't have much experience with character roles.'

'Then this will be excellent training!'

They opened her wardrobe. Maurice homed in on a mushroom-coloured mackintosh that had belonged to her mother; Nancy had only hung on to it because it was a Mudway. 'This!' he said. 'And sensible shoes. Maiden aunts don't wear stilettos.'

'Maybe I'm a *sexy* maiden aunt,' said Nancy.

Maurice pointed at the Chaz Michaels on her feet. 'What if you have to run in those?'

Nancy reluctantly exchanged the heels for a pair of old trainers. The smell nearly made her gag, but she held her breath and slipped them on to her feet. She and Maurice agreed she would need to hide her hair. She experimented with a scarf, aiming for late-period Elizabeth Taylor rather than Irene Handl charlady, but finally settled for a brown velvet cloche. She tucked her hair out of sight and peered into the mirror. Fox into frump, in three easy stages. It was depressing to see how drab she looked.

'I can't go out looking like this.'

Maurice reminded her that she couldn't go out *unless* she looked like that. 'Where's your passport?'

'Church told me not to leave town.'

'And where is he now you're being harassed?

Anyway, not like you're fleeing to South America; you're only popping over to France. Couple of hours away. Takes longer to cross London in bad traffic.'

Nancy thought the passport was in one of the kitchen drawers. While Maurice went off to hunt for it, she started packing clothes into a suitcase. He came back with the passport and immediately vetoed the case. 'Too obvious.' He went back into the kitchen and returned with a couple of Priceway carriers. Nancy stuffed them full of garments and toiletries and studied her reflection sadly.

'Now I look like a bag lady.'

Maurice looked her over. He'd always fancied himself a film director; he'd just never got round to making any films. But now he had his own little scenario, complete with leading lady.

He was squinting at her, frowning. 'Something's missing.'

'My self-respect,' said Nancy.

Maurice's face lit up. 'Got it! I know just what we need! And I know just where to get it.'

Chapter 8
The Great Escape

Mrs. Feaver peered out over the security chain, and said, 'You've never shown any interest in walking him before,'

'It's a way of saying sorry for all the noise and inconvenience,' said Nancy. Out of the corner of her eye she glimpsed Maurice nodding approvingly at this spot of impro. Perhaps his plan was going to work after all.

Mrs. Feaver tilted her head, like a bird trying to get a better view. 'You look nice.'

While Nancy tried to work out whether or not she was being sarcastic, it was left to Maurice to charm the old lady into submission. Maurice could have charmed a cliff-face. He persuaded her to unhook the chain, and started flirting as though she were a giddy young thing and he was her swain. Mrs. Feaver giggled girlishly, and Nancy felt a pang of jealousy, but before she knew it she was being presented with one end of a leather leash. It felt soggy, as though the dog had been using it as a chewtoy. On the other end of the leash was Chip himself, writhing in outrage at the idea of being taken for a walk by his worst enemy. Nancy wanted to say, 'Good God,' but it came out as, 'Good dog.' She held the leash at arm's length so the animal couldn't get within nipping distance of her ankles.

'Doesn't like you much,' said Mrs. Feaver.

The dog was turning in angry circles, the leash twisting ever more tightly around Nancy's fingers until it threatened to cut off her circulation. She was wondering if all this fuss was worth it when Maurice squatted down to massage the beast behind its ears. Chip immediately stopped snarling and started wiping his nose against Maurice's hand, leaving it slick with doggy snot.

'You will look after him?' asked Mrs Feaver.

'We'll take good care of the little fellow,' said Maurice. He straightened up and picked up Nancy's bags. 'OK Nance, let's go.'

'You be careful now,' Mrs. Feaver said to the dog.

Chip scented the great outdoors and began to bound down the steps as fast as his stubby little legs would carry him. He was not a large animal, but he possessed the strength of a small tugboat. It was all Nancy could do to avoid being dragged headfirst down the stairs. There was a stack of mail waiting for her in the hallway. She stopped to sift through it.

'Sort that out later,' said Maurice, grabbing everything he could see with her name on it and thrusting the envelopes into one of the bags while Chip strained at the leash.

'Here we go,' said Maurice. He pulled his hood up, gave Nancy a broad smile of encouragement and opened the door.

What Nancy saw made her catch her breath. When she had gone out earlier there had been a dozen or so reporters, which had been bad enough. But now the throng had swollen to epic proportions, a multitude so large and unwieldy the police had closed the road to traffic. Nancy was annoyed they hadn't thought to check on how *she* was doing.

Beyond the immediate rabble, she could see vans bearing TV company logos, a coach, mounted police and

a hot-dog seller. Someone on the periphery of the mob
was strumming a guitar, and there were several
competing groups of hymn-singers. It was no longer just
cameras and microphones and cassette recorders; now it
was collapsible chairs and picnic hampers. It was dog-
collars and priestly robes, puffy red anoraks and black
leather jackets, twin-sets and tweeds, even a grey suit or
two. She tried to gauge whether any of the suit-wearers
posed a viable threat, but it was difficult to get a fix on
anything beyond the sea of upturned faces, all of them
directed at the upstairs windows.

Which was good, because it meant no-one was
looking at Maurice's maiden aunt as she stepped out of
the building.

Chip plunged straight into the thicket of legs, and
Nancy had no choice but to keep up. Maurice draped an
arm across her shoulders and, like a dutiful nephew,
began to usher her through the crowd. She was encircled
by a babble of excited voices, pushed and pulled by the
rise and fall of the swell, submerged in a rotten stink of
humanity. Was this what Chip was smelling? But at least
he was enjoying it, whereas she felt trapped by body
odour and tooth decay, by the stench of a hundred fry-
ups, bowls of milk-sodden cereal and slices of burnt
toast spread with Marmite. She detected painkillers,
whisky, a whiff of marijuana and a sprinkling of cocaine.
Many of the women seemed to be menstruating, and
there were a surprising number of nosebleeds. She even
sensed a couple of tumours nestling in nearby lungs and
bowels. As she pushed past, a jumble of disconnected
images poured into her head: a heated argument, some
children in a paddling pool, a boardroom somewhere at
the top of a skyscraper, a couple having sex...

Too much information. She dropped her gaze, and tried to empty her head. Hands brushed her raincoat, caught her arm as she tried to regulate Chip's progress through a canine heaven of odoriferous trouser-legs.

'Sir...'

'...I wonder if you'd mind, madam...'

'...neighbour?'

'...long have you known...'

'...just a few moments of your time...'

Maurice sensed her nervousness. 'Don't worry auntie,' he said. 'Give us some room here, will you.' Shielding Nancy as best he could, he shouldered his way forward, and the further they got from the front door, the more the crowd thinned out.

The open street beyond was theirs for the taking when Chip made a sudden lunge for freedom, jerking the leash out of Nancy's grip with a ferocity that almost took off two of her fingers. The force bumped her sideways against Maurice. The rim of her hat caught on one of his buttons. By the time she'd disentangled herself, Chip was racing around the corner. 'Oh fuckit,' she said. 'Mrs. Feaver will kill me.' And then her hat, already skewed like a rogue toupée, fell off. Strands of long red hair slowly unravelled.

Someone yelled, 'Hey, carrot-top!' and that was all it took.

'There she is!'

'Nancy!'

'That's her!'

'She's getting away!'

Maurice said, 'Run like hell.'

'But Chip...?' she said.

'Chip can look after himself.'

They ran. They made it around the corner, the pack snapping at their heels, pelting them with questions.

'This way, Nancy...'

'When did you lose your virginity?'

'When did you last go to church?'

Nancy had a stitch in her side. Surely it wasn't healthy for a pregnant woman to run so fast? Fortunately, their pursuers cannoned into a knot of Japanese businessmen bowing to each other on the pavement outside the sushi bar, enabling Nancy and Maurice to open up a lead. They reached Theobald's Road just as the lights were changing. Maurice stopped at the kerb, but as the throbbing line-up of vehicles surged forward in an oncoming wall of metal, Nancy grabbed his arm and pulled him across the road. There were several overlapping screeches of brakes, followed by a crunch of cars being backended.

'Are you insane?' yelled Maurice.

'You're safe with me!' said Nancy.

They turned into Lamb's Conduit Street. He pulled her sideways into a doorway and for a moment she thought he'd spotted some reporters and was pulling her out of sight. But then his fingers were tapping out a code on the keypad, and she realised they'd already reached the Minitours office.

Two floors up, she looked out of the window. About half a dozen of their erstwhile pursuers were drifting up and down the street, peering into coffee shops and hairdressers.

'Be careful,' said Maurice. 'They might see you.'

'They're gutter press,' Nancy said. 'It won't occur to them to look up.'

But as she gazed down, she spotted the fat woman from the flat above the sandwich bar, waddling past with a shopping bag. It looked like the same floral-print frock she'd been wearing the last time Nancy had seen her, except this one was a different colour. The sight made Nancy uneasy, though she couldn't put her finger on why; it was only natural the woman should be shopping here, only a few blocks away from where she lived. But it was enough to make her retreat from the window to the back of the room., where Maurice was hunched over his answering machine.

As he listened to his messages, she began to sift through her mail: some bills, a reminder to pay Equity dues, a demand for overdue rent, junk mail, a few hand-delivered begging letters, and an A4 envelope containing a comic book called *Revelation Man*. She dumped everything but the bills into the bin, then thought for a moment and dumped the bills as well. In all the excitement she'd left her cigarettes behind, so she perched on the edge of Maurice's desk and helped herself to one from his office stash.

'We made it!' she said. 'What now?'

Maurice, one ear still on his messages, was tapping on his computer keyboard. He took a credit card from the top drawer of his desk, and started entering details. 'That's done. Now just let me...' He stood up, slid his arms around her and kissed the back of her neck. It didn't mean anything. It never did. But a sudden rapping at the door made them leap away from each other.

Nancy went pale. 'They found us.'

'Who is it?' shouted Maurice.

'Who the fuck do you think?'

They both relaxed. It was Phoebe. She was

wearing low-slung trousers and a T-shirt with MEDIA TART picked out in sequins on the front. It was just skimpy enough to show off her skinny abdomen with its neatly pierced belly-button. Nancy felt self-conscious, torn between envy and the comforting thought that here was living proof you could give birth to an enormous bouncing infant (not for nothing had they called him Samson) and still end up with a stomach flatter than Norfolk.

'What are you doing?' she said to Maurice. 'You know we're supposed to be meeting Colin in forty minutes.'

'Yes of course,' said Maurice.

'You forgot, didn't you.'

Maurice grinned sheepishly. 'Just planning a jaunt for our girl-buddy here. Bit of a circus round at her place, so I said she could stay in Le Marais for a few days. Just till things calm down.'

Phoebe looked from him to Nancy and back again. She didn't need to be told what was going on. She already knew. It was a talent she had, instantly being able to judge a situation from all the different angles, and knowing instinctively what needed to be done.

'I'd better go change,' said Nancy.

'No, stay like that,' said Maurice. 'No-one ever looks a homeless person in the eye.' He checked his watch. 'Anyway, boarding in an hour.'

He handed Nancy some keys while Phoebe scribbled something on a sheet of paper. 'Here's the address, and the digicode, and this is Didier's number if you need anything.'

'She knows where it is,' said Maurice. 'She's been there.'

Phoebe didn't say anything out loud, but she threw Maurice a look that Nancy interpreted as, *Yes, but you know how scatty she is. She needs it written down.*

'Right,' said Maurice, patting his pockets. 'We need to get her to Waterloo.'

'Colin will go ballistic if we blow him out again.'

'Let him go ballistic!' said Maurice in the devil-may-care mode that Nancy always found so exciting, even though it could also be infuriating. 'He'll just have to wait. Anyway, we passed his name on to the Broughton-Thompsons, so he owes us.'

Nancy picked up one of the carrier bags, which immediately disgorged half of its contents through a breach in the side. Phoebe ran an incredulous eye over a grey pencil skirt, black Lycra dress and shocking pink strapless bra. 'Oh for heaven's sake, Nance, you don't have a clue, do you. You think you'll be able to wear these things in a month's time?' She looked hard at Nancy's figure. 'You think you can wear them *now*?'

While Nancy tried to shovel her belongings back into the ruptured bag, Phoebe opened a cupboard and dragged out a holdall, turning it upside-down so that one pair of unwashed shorts and two pairs of socks fell out. With brisk efficiency, she transferred the contents of Nancy's carriers into the empty holdall.

Nancy recognised the logo. 'I can't take that.'

'We got it free,' said Phoebe. 'There you go. Now you look less like a homeless person and more like an impoverished aristocrat who's managed to hang on to a few classic pieces.'

Maurice had slumped in a chair, apparently having exhausted his energy, but Phoebe took the lead now, smoothly as a runner being passed the baton in a relay race. She clapped her hands. 'Allons-y! Let's go!'

Maurice winked at Nancy as they clattered down the stairs. 'My wife,' he said. 'Likes to take control. You'd never guess she was half my age.'

'Stop exaggerating the age difference,' said Phoebe. 'It's an absurd affectation.'

'I'm old enough to be your grandfather,' said Maurice.

'Only if you started shagging at the age of six,' said Phoebe.

*****

Only when Phoebe's Citroën was barrelling along High Holborn did Nancy remember to check her purse. She was down to her last tenner. She touched Phoebe's shoulder. 'I need a cashpoint.'

They drew up outside a building society and sat there with the engine running while Nancy tapped out her bank code. Maddeningly, the screen responded with the message: CONSULT YOUR BRANCH. Worse, the machine refused to return her card. She pressed all the buttons in vain before kicking it in frustration and went back to the car.

'This is ridiculous. I *know* I'm not overdrawn.'

'Someone blocked your account,' said Phoebe.

'Dark forces at work,' said Maurice.

Phoebe nudged the car back into the flow of traffic. 'How much cash have you got on you?' she asked Maurice.

'Deposit for Colin. You *see?* I didn't forget.'

'Pay us back when you're rich and famous, Nance.'

Maurice half-turned to hand Nancy a fat envelope,

then pulled half a dozen notes out of his wallet and handed those over as well. 'Some francs to tide you over.'

Nancy opened her mouth to say something.

'Don't say a word,' said Phoebe. 'In any case, you have to keep on our good side because we've got plenty of compromising photos to blackmail you with.'

'What did I do to deserve this?' said Nancy.

'Very little,' said Phoebe. 'You're just lucky we like you.'

There was a minor disagreement when they reached Waterloo. Maurice wanted to see Nancy all the way to the gates, but Phoebe had started fretting about the architect again. Nancy assured them she could tackle this last stage on her own.

'Pick up your ticket over there,' said Maurice, pointing to the counters.

'There's an emergency stash of francs in the bathroom cabinet,' said Phoebe.

'Send us a postcard,' said Maurice.

'I will,' said Nancy.

And they drove off.

Chapter 9
The Battle of Waterloo

In the queue for the tickets she began to regret not having stocked up on Fudge Tubs. What did they even call them in France? Tonneau de Fudge? Grosse Fudge Bouffe? What if they didn't have them? What would she eat? Perhaps she could induce a miscarriage by swallowing vast quantities of oysters and sweetbreads, washed down with red wine. Her stomach contracted in revulsion.

The thing was, did she still *want* to get rid of it? She placed a conciliatory palm on her belly. *Looks as though we're stuck with each other. Sorry about the clinic, but you have to realise I was confused, and frightened. But that was still no reason for you to do what you did.* There was a small but significant spasm in her womb. As though whatever was in there had read her thoughts.

She collected her ticket. Phoebe's bag might have been chic, but it also seemed ergonomically designed to make her back ache, so she put it on a luggage trolley. She was wheeling the trolley towards the gates when the opaque glass doors on the other side slid open and she glimpsed a huddle of men at the security checkpoint. It was only for an instant, and then the doors slid shut again.

She stopped. The men had been wearing grey suits. She tried to persuade herself it was a party of businessmen on its way to Brussels. How could anyone have followed her to the station? She hadn't even known herself that she would be coming here.

But what if they *were* waiting for her? In that one instant, the welcoming prospect of a tranquil three-hour train journey had been tainted by the possibility of blood, and screaming, and death. The trip came crashing down around her like a collapsing building. *Can't I even take a few days off, for Christ's sake?*

Undecided as to whether or not to proceed, she paused for a cigarette. She thought smoking was probably banned in this part of the station, but there would just be enough time to squeeze in a couple of lungfuls before someone arrived to tick her off. She'd only just lit up when she sensed a presence behind her. She waited for the authoritative tap on her shoulder, but instead there was a soft muttering as three or four different voices, all with American accents, combined in whispered debate. They probably thought she couldn't hear them, but her super-senses were kicking in again.

'You assholes, you've got the wrong woman.'

'That's her.'

'That is *not* her.'

'*It is.* Goodman says so.'

'You said he lost her.'

'But we know what she looks like.'

'I can't trust you to do anything.'

'She was on the news!'

'It's her, Jules, I swear. Go ahead and ask.'

The tap on the shoulder finally came. 'Nancy Loughlin?'

She turned and blew smoke into the speaker's face, though he was shorter than expected, so most of it went over his head. His long black hair was pulled back into a ponytail. His eyes were hidden behind Ray-Bans. She wasn't surprised to see he wore a grey suit, as did the two men at his side; one gangly and young, the other thick-set, with an unnerving stare. But Ray-Ban's suit was visibly of a better quality. Bespoke, even.

'Definitely her,' said the gangly man.

'Give me a break,' said Nancy.

Ray-Ban turned back to her and his snarl turned into a smile so wide she glimpsed gold fillings. 'Too slow,' he said.

'Excuse me?'

'Smoking it to death will take too long. I'm sorry, but we must find a more efficient solution. And no more tricks.'

'How the fuck did you know I'd be here?'

'I had a dream,' he said.

'Of course you did,' said Nancy. The stench of garlic was so overpowering she had to clamp her free hand over the lower part of her face. The blend of smells was oddly familiar: a whiff of Cuban cigar, a suggestion of breath-mint, and a faint trace of raw steak; she tried to remember where she'd smelt that combination before.

'Feeling faint?'

This guy had to be the ringleader. He probably thought he was being charming, but she found him creepy. The way he was smiling, for example.

'I don't know what you hoped to accomplish by employing a stand-in. You might have known we'd find out. For God's sake, she didn't even *look* like you.'

Nancy stared at this crazy person, babbling nonsense. Ray-Ban tilted his head towards the exit. 'Come with us. Quickly. Before ComSec gets here.'

Idiots. They know what'll happen if they touch me. If they touch us.

So it was *us* now, she reflected.

She stood her ground. 'No way.'

'Lady, please. These are dangerous people. We need to talk about this.'

'We so do not. And please don't call me *lady*.' She didn't feel frightened - just weary. Why wouldn't they leave her alone?

'You *will* come with us,' said Ray-Ban, snapping his fingers several times, like one of the dancing gang-members from *West Side Story*. The other men in grey came out of nowhere, or perhaps they had been lurking behind her all along. All of a sudden she was being jostled by a bunch of them. A loudspeaker message announced that boarding was about to close. Nancy looked wistfully at the last handful of passengers making for the gates, and managed to catch the eye of a security officer. She mouthed the words, *This man is harassing me.* The officer came trotting over. 'Can I help?'

'Yeah.' Ray-Ban took off his sunglasses and fixed the official with a bloodshot stare. 'You can get the fuck out of here before I rip your fucking head off and shove it up your fucking ass.'

The security officer didn't blink. 'No problem, sir.' And he wheeled round and trotted back the way he'd come.

Had Nancy's ears played a trick on her? Had Ray-Ban *really* said that? It was as though she and the security guy had been tuned in to completely different frequencies. 'What do you mean, no problem?' she shouted at his retreating back, but he didn't turn. Ray-Ban replaced his sunglasses, exposing his gold fillings once again as he smiled in satisfaction at a job well done. She wondered if he'd just used some form of hypnosis. She dropped her cigarette and went through the desultory motions of grinding it out with her heel.

'Now listen. You're going to die. *All* these people will die unless you go away and leave me alone.'

'No-one will die,' said Ray-Ban, 'because no-one has any intention of hurting you. These guys may not be the brightest tools in the box, but they've learnt their lesson. We just want to go somewhere more comfortable to talk it over. It isn't safe for you here. You need to trust me.'

'Are you deaf? I'm not going with you.'

He shrugged and stepped away from her. Four of the men in grey stepped up. One was holding a syringe. She thought, oh *please*. She hated needles. *Hated* them. Did they really think she was going to let them stick *that* into her arm?

'It's OK,' Ray-Ban said in what was presumably his best reassuring manner, which of course wasn't very reassuring at all. 'This won't hurt you or baby. This stuff is *nice*...' Someone behind her suddenly reached around and pinned her arms to her sides. Another began to roll up the sleeve of her raincoat. He looked ridiculously young, and his grey suit was too big for him; it hung off him like a Sharpei's skin.

'You have got to be kidding,' she said, and the Sharpei's nose instantly began to bleed, splashing in flowery red drops on to the marble. She looked at the blood dispassionately, wondering when she'd stopped being affected by the sight of it. The young guy tried to act as though nothing was happening, but she could tell he was panicking. She tried to brush his hand away and a sudden jumbled impression of his existence burst into her head. His name was Larry Goodman, he was twenty-six years old and still a virgin, and over the years he'd harboured unclean thoughts about some of the little kids in his apartment block, though he hadn't yet acted on them.

Or was she imagining all that? Nancy recoiled as she felt herself invaded by his self-loathing and guilt, but deep inside her something clicked gently, like plastic cogs slotting gently into place. Her nerves were tingling, but in an unexpectedly pleasurable way. It was all starting to make sense. She *was* part of a team. *A team with superpowers.* She felt a rush of exhilaration.

'Don't say I didn't warn you, Larry,' she said. 'That *stuff* might not hurt us, but the *needle* will. Didn't anyone tell you that we don't like needles?'

He went pale. 'How do you know my name?'

Belinda had been right. It *was* all her. The groundwork had already been laid, and Nancy hadn't even been aware of it. She saw the slide-show, and smelled the burning before anyone else. She glanced down and saw that the bottom of Larry Goodman's trouser leg was smouldering. The trailing hem had come into contact with her discarded cigarette, which it seemed she hadn't stamped out as thoroughly as she'd thought.

She blinked slowly, like a cat.

As it is written, so shall it be done.

The cheap trouser fabric began to emit evil-looking fumes, and a small flicker of orange flame. Larry Goodman looked down, let out a yell, and started hopping up and down, flapping his arms like a chicken. The hand holding the syringe lashed out. The needle went straight into the eye of the man holding Nancy's other arm. The point broke off. That man's name was Lyndon Carter and once upon a time he'd tied a firework to a cat's tail, so Nancy didn't feel sorry for him when pinkish-white stuff started spurting out of his eyeball, like juice from a punctured lychee.

Larry Goodman tried to take his burning trousers off, but only succeeded in setting fire to his sleeve. Lyndon Carter was staggering around, screaming and clawing at his eye. Ray-Ban started to roar with laughter, his mouth showing more gold than a Tiffany's window display. 'Oh wow, you tell em, lady!'

She tried to see into his past, the way she'd dug into Goodman and Carter's, but he wasn't an open book like the others; all she got were some mixed-up impressions of cacti, and even those were cloaked in layers of obfuscation, like dusty velvet curtains blocking off a sunlit garden.

And now even Goodman and Carter's heads were hollow places, filled with nothing but screaming and pain and terror. The fourth man in grey barely had time to spit out the word, 'Witch!' before he stepped away from Nancy and fell backwards over her luggage trolley, cracking his skull so hard on the floor that the sound echoed around the forecourt. Still flat on his back, he started wriggling like a beetle and babbling words Nancy didn't recognise. She wondered if it was even a real language; more likely it was just his concussed brain giving off random noises.

Three down, two to go.

The fifth man had a gun in his hand, though he didn't look capable of pulling the trigger. He was staring aghast at his hopping, flapping colleagues. He looked back at her and said, 'Don't hurt me.' His name was Alvin Reese. Their eyes met and she began to feel sorry for him. Then there was a small, sharp noise like a walnut being cracked open, and he formed the word 'oh' with his mouth, the shape replicating a neat black hole that had suddenly appeared in his forehead. As Nancy stared at the hole in horror, it began to turn red and the man toppled sideways.

Now how did I do that?

There was shouting in the distance, and a smell in the air that reminded her of the Bonfire Nights of her childhood, before her parents had split up. But there was still work to be done. She steeled herself to deal with Ray-Ban. But he was no longer anywhere to be seen.

A member of the station staff let off a fire extinguisher, and a jet of white foam shot past her and knocked Larry Goodman to the floor. He struggled to get up, but two security guards were suddenly there, pushing him back; one started slapping at his burning legs with a jacket. Lyndon Carter was still shrieking and spinning in circles like an out-of-control sputnik. Three people were trying to get him to calm down and let them examine his punctured eyeball.

Nancy looked around at the bodies sprawled around her on the concourse and felt the last of her strength ebbing away. The bones in her legs turned to mush. A sharp pain bisected her head like a thin sheet of glass. *What have I done?*

Karl Petersen and the others had been freak accidents. If she *had* been responsible, it had been unconsciously, and indirectly. And she hadn't even been awake at the clinic. But what she had done to Larry Goodman and Lyndon Carter had felt almost premeditated. Self-defence, of course, but that didn't make her feel any better about it. Because, she realised, she had been *enjoying* it. For a few moments there, she had felt invulnerable, untouchable, all-powerful. Like a superheroine flexing her muscles.

She didn't feel like a superheroine now, though. Now she just felt mean. She suddenly felt very tired and lonely and in need of a shoulder to lean on. If only Maurice had come in to see her off. But Maurice had left and besides, he and Phoebe had things to do, architects to meet, lives to lead. She was on her own.

Or was she? As if in response to the unspoken question, there was a flutter in her lower abdomen.

Brisk movement caught her eye. She looked up to see the Fat Woman in the floral-print dress, striding across the concourse towards her, no longer clutching a shopping bag but a gun. Only now did Nancy understand that the hole in Alvin Reese's forehead hadn't been her work. She planted her feet apart and lowered her chin, ready to resist the newcomer.

'Whoa there, horsey,' the Fat Woman said in a surprisingly deep voice, and Nancy realised - how could she have been so stupid? - that the Fat Woman wasn't a woman at all. Up close, the unmistakable signs of five o'clock shadow were visible beneath the layers of pancake and powder.

'I need to sit down,' she said to no-one in particular, and did just that, right there on the blood-splattered floor, next to the sprawled body of the man who had fallen backwards over the luggage trolley. He'd stopped babbling, but his eyes were open, the pupils moving from side to side as though trying to find a way out of his head. One of his legs was twitching. *Look on the bright side*, she told herself. At least he wasn't dead. His head wasn't wrapped around the wheel of a bus, or crushed by a marble clock. Maybe she *was* getting better at this. Maybe she was learning to control it.

But how can you control something when you don't even know what you're doing?

'Thought you could do with a hand,' said the man formerly known as the Fat Woman. He prodded the twitching grey suit with the toe of one of his pink ballerina slippers and, once he'd ascertained the fallen man was no longer in any state to pose a threat, slipped the gun back into his padding. 'Let's get out of here before the rest of the troops arrive.'

Nancy stared at him blankly, a cold wave of déjà-vu washing over her. 'Leave me alone,' she said.

She expected shouting, coercion, strong-arm tactics, but to her surprise he squatted down next to her and said, 'You're free to go wherever you want, Nancy. You can even get on a train, any train, and we won't stop you. But I think you'll find it easier to come with us.'

Nancy laughed bitterly. 'That's what they all say.'

He was looking at her almost affectionately. 'And you're right to be suspicious. How can I convince you? What can we do for you? What could we offer that would persuade you to stay?'

This was unexpected. What *could* they offer? Nancy thought about it.

'Anything?'

'Anything. Just name it. Though putting an end to world hunger is currently beyond our means, alas, so no point in asking for that.'

'OK then,' said Nancy, raising her chin as the idea took hold. 'How about a job? I was up for a part the other day, and I didn't get it. But I'd be perfect for that role, I know I would. If you're serious about doing something for me, ask Les Six to cast me in his new play.'

The former fat woman chuckled. 'Les Six? You mean the Ripper musical?'

She didn't ask how he knew. Later, she would come to realise he knew everything, more or less.

'A role in a musical? That's all? As good as done.'

He gave her a mock salute, and she realised she'd sold herself too cheaply. She ought to have asked for the starring role in a big movie, or a contract with a major Hollywood studio.

He took her holdall. She got a strong whiff of him as he bent over her - a comforting cocktail of shaving foam and marmalade. She began to relax, despite her misgivings. It was as though someone had deliberately whipped up a comforting chemical man-smell to make her feel she was in safe hands, the way bakeries pumped the aroma of freshly baked bread into the street to attract customers. He beckoned her away from the trains, towards the exit. She glanced back and saw a clean-up operation swinging into gear: bodies loaded on to stretchers, officers in Balaclavas talking into radios, the public cordoned off behind yellow tape.

'I just wanted to take it easy for a few days,' she said, trotting behind him.

'You can take it easy at the house.'

'The house?'

He turned. 'The safe house, if you like. Rather a dramatic term for what is essentially an exclusive five-star hotel. I think you'll like it there. We have everything you need.'

Out of character but still in costume, he looked absurd, but no-one was laughing. In fact, everyone seemed to be treating him with deference; men in bulky black jackets nodded to him as they passed, uniformed police stood meekly aside, station staff gazed at him open-mouthed, as though they'd identified him as Supreme Station Master.

'I was going to Paris.'

The Fat Woman chuckled. 'Can't have you going over to the French,' he said, sticking his right thumb into the flesh beneath his chin and peeling a strip of rubber from his face as though it were a used suntan. 'You're our girl, not theirs. Jesus Christ, this stuff doesn't half itch.'

'Whose girl?' asked Nancy. 'Who *are* you?'

'Who am I?' He produced a dry wheezing that Nancy at first thought was a smoker's cough but eventually identified as laughter. 'You're not afraid of the big questions, are you.' The wheezing stopped. He was walking faster now, sloughing off thin strips of rubber, leaving a trail of artificial skin behind him. She had to scamper to keep up, and would have missed his reply if he hadn't turned back and held out a hand for her to shake. She shook it, wincing at the firmness of his grip. The impressions that flooded into her brain were very different from the kind she'd had from Larry Goodman and Lyndon Carter. These were full of blood and flame and death, but there was no guilt or indecision or self-loathing here.

She gasped and snatched her hand away. He nodded, as though he knew exactly what she'd seen. And had no problem with her seeing it.

'Stuart Milo Bull,' he said. 'At your service.'

PART THREE
WORMWOOD

Chapter 1
Walnutwood

The black Mercedes peeled smoothly out into York Road, leaving Waterloo behind them. Nancy turned to look out of the back window and saw a fleet of identical black vans converging on the service road they'd left behind.

'ComSec will take care of you,' said Bull.

Ah, so this was the famous ComSec. Nancy turned back to face the front. 'Commando Security, am I right?'

'Could be,' he chuckled.

Nancy was to learn this wheezy chuckling was Bull's way of deflecting questions he didn't feel like answering. She stared at the back of his thick neck until she was sure he could feel her eyes drilling into his flesh. He'd taken off the wig, but not the floral-print frock and the prosthetic padding. She began to understand why the windows were tinted.

'I guess you know all about me,' she said as they edged through traffic. He would have been able to see her in the rearview mirror, but for some reason preferred to twist his head round and look at her directly. Even though they were crawling along at a snail's pace, it made Nancy anxious. She wished he would keep his eyes on the road.

'I know you better than you know yourself, Nancy.' He started reciting biographical facts like a speaking clock. 'Father: Gregory James Loughlin, solicitor, dead, heart attack. Mother: Laura May Hamilton, former actress, alcoholic, currently residing in Tisbury, near Oxford, with seven cats, a tortoise and a rabbit.'

'The rabbit got run over,' said Nancy.

Bull made the dry, wheezing sound again. 'Oh, bad luck.' He droned on, and she stopped paying attention to this recitation of personal details, sinking into her own dark thoughts and only vaguely aware of the route the car was taking through central London. They crossed High Holborn, a short distance from her flat, but continued north. Past Euston, through Camden, up Haverstock Hill, and then eastward through a series of almost identical avenues, and she lost track, though guessed they were probably somewhere near Highgate. The houses were large and rather boring, inflated parodies of thirties suburbia, set back from the road behind huge gates and high walls, some topped by barbed wire, which only rarely permitted glimpses of overtended garden.

There was a burst of static from a dashboard speaker, and Bull said, 'Here we are', though she couldn't tell if he were talking to her or to someone who wasn't in the car. A set of gates swung open, and the Mercedes nosed its way into a wide gravel driveway to park alongside a dozen or so identical models. The gates shut behind them, blocking off her view of the road. There was no-one to be seen, yet Nancy could feel herself being watched.

'Welcome to Walnutwood,' said Bull. 'You'll probably end up calling it Wormwood, like everyone else.'

In the time it took Nancy to gather her

belongings, he was already out of the car and holding her door open. He took her holdall and she scrambled out and looked up at a large semi-detached house that didn't look anything like a hotel. Had that just been a ruse to lure her here? Bull handed her bag to a sharp-faced woman in a black trouser-suit who had materialised without a sound and was now staring at Nancy with unabashed curiosity.

'I'm going to hand you over to Miss Taylor. Excuse me, I need to slip into something more comfortable.' And he hurried away around the side of the house, leaving Miss Taylor to usher her through the front door.

The house only *looked* semi-detached. What appeared from the outside to be two separate homes conjoined at the hip had been knocked together into one vast interior which extended several levels above and below ground. Miss Taylor led her across a wide reception area, through a library, and across a dining-room into another hallway. The rooms were all spotless and deserted, like theatre sets waiting for the actors to appear. There was an strong smell of furniture polish. As they turned yet another unexpected corner, Nancy felt her sense of direction becoming scrambled; it was as though the layout had been designed as a labyrinth, full of random security doors to impede and confuse intruders. She tried to get a better look at the keycard Miss Taylor was holding against the electronic locks.

'Will I get one of those?'

'Of course,' said Miss Taylor. 'You're our guest, not a prisoner.'

They took a lift up to the third floor. 'What's on the other floors?'

'Offices,' said Miss Taylor. 'Medical suite. Staff quarters. There's a gym in the basement, and a swimming pool.'

'Am I the only guest?'

'For now.'

'And I can go anywhere I want?'

'Within reason,' said Miss Taylor. 'I don't suppose Mr. Cook would take kindly to you wandering through his bedroom when he's in the middle of watching one of his movies. You'll need to respect everyone's personal space, just as we'll be respecting yours. Anyway, your room is nicer than his.' She chuckled. 'Nicer than mine too. If I were you, I wouldn't want to leave it.'

*****

Miss Taylor was right. Nancy's room *was* nice. Very nice. There was a king-size bed, and a sofa, and footstools, and a writing desk, and a state-of-the-art plasma television twice the size of her own rented TV, no videos but a selection of DVDs still in their wrapping. She spotted *West Side Story*, which reminded her of Ray-Ban man. But already those flashing gold fillings seemed like a distant memory. She eyed the elaborate trelliswork over the window and saw it wasn't just decorative. Never in a million years would the men in grey be able to reach her in here. But what if there was a fire? How would she get out?

Miss Taylor seemed to read her thoughts. 'The window key's in *here*,' she said, pointing to a vase on the windowsill. 'In the event of an emergency, which isn't likely, you can unlock the lattice. There's a spare in the top drawer of your bedside cabinet. You're not...'

'Not a prisoner,' said Nancy. 'So you keep saying.'

Miss Taylor showed her how everything switched on and off, and said, 'I'll collect you when supper's ready. Now get some rest. You probably need it after today.'

'Mr. Bull told you what happened?' asked Nancy, trying to work out when this transfer of information might have taken place.

Miss Taylor smiled, which made her face look younger and less sharp. 'News travels fast around here. You're already a legend.'

Nancy was left on her own to examine her new toys. No-one she knew had a DVD player yet, though Phoebe had been talking about getting one. All her favourite films were present and correct: *Casablanca*, *The Wizard of Oz*, *Gone with the Wind*, along with a bunch of others she couldn't wait to watch again. They really had done their homework. She wasn't as enthused by the selection of books, mostly paperbacks with titles like *Zero to Midnight* or *Codename Quebec*. She would have to take a look around the library and find something else to read.

She found a stash of Marlboro and a minibar containing a full range of alcohol, and poured herself a whisky. Intending to unpack her holdall, she yanked open the wardrobe doors and found the interior already full of clothes, some with price-tags attached, everything several sizes too large. They were fussy and middle-aged, not her style. She was disappointed in the shoes as well: much too flat and sensible. Someone hadn't properly researched her taste in fashion, that was for sure.

Once she'd performed a thorough inspection of the bedroom and en suite, Nancy propped herself against a pile of pillows on the bed, and gazed in satisfaction at the crystal chandelier, the white china cherubs, and the marble mantelpiece. This was not just better than her flat, or Maurice and Phoebe's, it was better than Christmas.

Belinda would adore this, she thought. *It's so fucking tasteful.* She picked up the telephone on the bedside table, but before she'd even lifted her finger to dial a voice said, 'Hello, Nancy! Do you need something?'

'Can I have an outside line?'

'Sorry,' said the voice. 'In-house only.'

'No problem.' Nancy hung up and got out her mobile.

There was no signal. Not even a bar.

*****

'No, that's completely normal,' said Bull, when Nancy asked about it over supper. 'Outgoing calls are blocked.'

'A security measure,' said Miss Taylor.

'I thought I was a guest,' said Nancy.

'This isn't just about you. You know how easily calls can be traced?'

'My friends will be worried.'

'Your friends think you're on holiday.'

So they do, thought Nancy. 'What about emergencies? What if you need to call an ambulance?'

'You don't need to worry about that,' said Bull.

A large drop of blood welled up from one of his nostrils and plopped on to the tablecloth.

*****

There had been a token attempt to make the dining-room look like a miniature palm court, but the air was dry and the plants weren't getting enough light from the high windows, so the fronds were turning yellow. The round table was set for eight people, but there were only five present: Nancy, Miss Taylor and three men in identical navy-blue suits. Mr. Jones and Mr. Miller barely opened their mouths, but it wasn't until the third suit started talking that she realised it was Stuart Bull.

Without the prosthetics and foam rubber padding, he wasn't bad looking, albeit in an old-fashioned way - the sort of square-jawed handsomeness you saw on leading men in old black and white movies. Her mother would have adored him. In his forties, Nancy guessed, probably Oxbridge, unostentatiously athletic beneath the suit. Dark hair speckled with grey, broad shoulders, reliable face - the sort of person to whom you would readily entrust your life. If you noticed him, that is. It wasn't as though he would stand out from the crowd when he wasn't wearing a dress.

'Cheers,' he said, raising a glass of water. 'Grand to have you aboard, Miss Loughlin.'

Nancy wondered if she'd ever had a choice. She sipped her red wine, found it easy on the palate, and drained the glass, aware everyone else at the table was pretending not to stare. She set down the empty glass and transferred her attention to the plate in front of her. It was grim. She stared with mounting nausea at the sausages, overcooked broccoli, and lumpy mashed potato.

When Bull saw Nancy hadn't touched her knife and fork, he reached over and snatched the plate away so abruptly she thought he must be angry with her.

Without a word, he vanished through a set of swing-doors, leaving her staring at the table cloth while Miss Taylor and the two suits picked wordlessly at their food. For a few minutes, the only sound was the discreet clatter of cutlery on china, until finally Bull returned with a young man in white kitchen overalls. The young man was carrying a tray, which he set down in front of Nancy. On the tray were four varieties of Fudge Tub: banana, coconut, papaya, mango.

Miss Taylor's eyes widened, but she said nothing.

Bull sat down again, beaming at Nancy like a proud parent whose child had just graduated to solid food. 'Never let it be said we don't offer our guests the full gourmet dining experience.'

*****

Everyone tried not to notice the drop of blood on the tablecloth, but Miss Taylor's jaw clenched, and one of the suits shifted uncomfortably in his seat. Bull dabbed his nostrils with a napkin and carried on eating, calm as you like. *It's me doing that*, thought Nancy, though she still couldn't work out how she was triggering nosebleeds. She tore her attention away from Bull and redirected it at what was left of her Fudge Tub.

'How do you think EDEN tracked you down?' asked Bull.

'No, wait... What?'

'E.D.E.N. End of Days Event Nexus. Or End of Days Event Nucleus. Nucleus or Nexus, I'm not sure it matters; our friends in grey were just determined to give themselves a Biblical-sounding name.'

'What are they? Evangelists?' asked Nancy.

'Rogue branch of The Agency. Our American counterparts, if you like.'

'What do they want with me?'

Bull beamed. 'You're a walking weapon of mass destruction, Nancy. They can't afford to have you fall into the wrong hands.'

'Because I'm...? Oh, I see. I think.'

'Same reason we're protecting you. You're a British citizen, on British soil.'

'What are you? MI5? MI6?'

Bull chuckled. 'We're Civil Servants.'

'Why don't you deport these EDEN crazies?'

'We would if we could, but these guys are good. You heard about the assassination in Azerbaijan last year?'

'No.'

'You see? Proves how good they are.'

Nancy remembered the neat black hole in Alvin Reese's forehead. Reese hadn't been the first person Bull had killed, she was sure of it. He had been in a war; impressions she'd got just from shaking his hand had told her that much. But she had no idea *which* war. Or wars. Her touch-sense had indicated there might have been more than one.

'So ComSec doesn't... *assassinate* people?'

'That's not our brief.' He looked her straight in the eye. 'Though our adversaries would have you believe otherwise. There's a propaganda offensive going on here as well.'

'We operate to a strict moral code,' said Miss Taylor, smiling at Bull as though they were chatting about the weather. 'No-one here is above the law.'

But you carry guns, thought Nancy.

'We're part of an operation so deep-cover that even the cabinet is only barely aware of its existence,' said Bull. 'It was set up over a hundred years ago specifically to deal with cases such as yours. Wasn't ComSec back then, of course; that was a 1980s corporate makeover, new logo and so on. Most of our funding is private these days, so we always have to think of the bottom line.'

'What do you mean, cases such as mine?'

Bull was blotting his nose again. His napkin was covered with a recurring poppy motif. 'You think you're the first? Of course there have been others.'

Nancy felt herself go cold. 'Where are they?'

'Let's just say there have been some, uh, false alarms. Some unfortunate incidents. Jack the Ripper, for example. Well, that was...'

He interrupted himself and tilted his head. 'Well done, by the way.'

'What?'

'You're learning to control it. That's good. A few weeks ago, and I would have been bleeding out all over this table.'

*****

You're learning to control it. Over the next few days Nancy had plenty of time to think about what Bull had said. She decided it was time to explore her abilities - or at least test the extent of the powers to which she was somehow linked. But she had no intention of sharing her findings, least of all with Stuart Bull.

'This is going to be our little secret,' she said to herself, or maybe to whatever was growing inside her.

Chapter 2
Thirty Pieces of Furniture

As I watched the Holborn Harlot's break for freedom
on the news, I let out a howl of fury. The daring getaway
had been caught on camera more by accident than
design, since most of the lenses had been pointing
upwards, at Nancy's curtained windows. The footage
didn't show much more than the heaving scrum in front
of Natal Mansions. But when the fuzzy images were
slowed down and paused and replayed, you could just
about make out a flash of red hair, the back of
someone's hoodie, and a slow ripple effect in the crowd
as it dawned on them that the survivor of the Abortion
Clinic Massacre was giving them the slip.

I recognised that hoodie straightaway; Maurice
thought it made him look 'street' - which it might have
done had the street in question been Savile Row. But
despite the media's best efforts and pleas from Scotland
Yard for the 'mystery man' to come forward, Nancy's
escort had yet to be identified. I knew Maurice had
already been questioned by police and reporters, along
with everyone else in Nancy's vast social network. But
while some of the testimony from friends (almost
certainly now ex-friends) had been sensational and not
entirely flattering, Maurice knew how the game worked
and had deliberately confined himself to platitudes too
rambling to be edited down into audience-friendly
sound-bites: she was a reliable part-time employee and a

lovely person et cetera. He was so boring no-one could be bothered to press him further; they preferred juicy anecdotes from dashing actor types about the Bloomsbury Bimbo behaving like a feckless party girl, getting drunk and flashing her tits. Phoebe, I was glad to see, was also keeping a low profile; her column was as fatuous as ever, waffling on about ecologically sound nappies and rigorously avoiding any reference to her absent friend.

In the days that followed, the tabloids reported sightings of pregnant redheads in Plymouth and Scarborough, but with nothing to back up the speculation, the press eventually gave up and moved on to other news, such as a cat in Ebbw Vale which had learned how to tell the time, and a selection of root vegetables, dug up in Dorset, that were said to resemble members of the royal family. Nancy dropped off the map.

Or, if the postcards were anything to go by, she was busy exploring it. Several times a week, I would find one in my mailbox. The first two were tourist's-eye views of the Eiffel Tower and Nôtre-Dame. If only I'd stopped to think about it, this might have struck me as odd, because Nancy had been to Paris many times, and had got the whole sightseeing trip out of her system a long time ago.

Meanwhile, I tried to avoid crowds, made sure I always knew where the nearest exit was, and put distance between me and anyone who looked out of the ordinary. It was amazing how few ordinary people there were in London; it seemed thronged with freaky-looking folk wearing sunglasses after dark, or hopping around on crutches, or hiding their faces under hats or behind unfeasibly bushy beards. Sometimes I had the impression that the cast of an amateur theatrical production had been unleashed on to the streets and was wandering around in costume. But since no-one approached me directly, I began to relax. Maybe Delgado had followed Nancy to France. Or maybe the police were finally acting on my tip, so he'd gone to ground to avoid them.

I wanted to talk more about Delgado to Lars, but lately he'd been obliged to spend more time with his wife, who was so frequently poorly I began to suspect she was getting sick on purpose. 'Poor Eileen,' I said on the phone, trying not to sound bitter after he'd just broken it to me that he wasn't able to meet up after work as arranged. Eileen had an abscess that had made half of her face blow up, so Lars had to drive her to the dentist for emergency treatment.

'I hope she feels better soon,' I said, trying not to laugh at the mental image of his wife looking like The Elephant Woman.

'You're sweet,' said Lars.

He made it up to me two days later by calling unexpectedly to announced he'd be taking an extra-long lunch break.

'Excellent!' I said. 'Where shall we meet? The Five-Star?'

'Or we could cut the preliminaries and I could come straight round to your place,' he said. 'We might even be able to squeeze in a game of post-coital Scrabble before I have to get back to work.'

This pleased me no end, for I was beginning to enjoy our Scrabble sessions even more than the sex.

'My place it is,' I said. And so I spent the morning

fastidiously grooming in a way that would make it look as though I hadn't bothered, then tidying up the flat and concealing what little mayhem there was in the way of magazines and make-up. Unlike Nancy, I had never thrived on chaos.

It never crossed my mind that I should have hidden some of my recent acquisitions too.

'I say,' said Lars as soon as he walked in. 'If I didn't know better I'd say that was a Van Merkens.' He crouched down and ran his hand over the new rug, taking such evident pleasure in it that I blushed.

'Perhaps it is,' I said.

He rocked back on his heels and looked me straight in the eye. 'How on earth can you afford it?'

I should have known Lars, of all people, would know exactly how much a Van Merkens was worth. He had the most eclectic and unexpected range of useless knowledge out of anyone I'd ever met. Clearly we were soulmates, at least when it came to fixtures and fittings. I mumbled something about the autumn sales, hoping his useless knowledge wouldn't extend as far as the dates when shops slashed their prices. Christ, what had I been thinking? Just as well the sofa had yet to be delivered.

'Plus it's damaged,' I added.

Lars dipped his head to take a closer look at the hand-woven slub incorporating a decorative knotting technique first used by fifteenth century Abyssinian peasants. 'Doesn't show.' As he straightened up again, his gaze fell on something across the room. He whistled. 'New chairs as well? What on earth have you been up to, Belinda Pringle? Robbing the till at work?'

I let out a whoop of what sounded, even to my ears, like the fakest laughter ever. 'Picked them up in this really good secondhand furniture shop.' I crossed my fingers he wouldn't recognise the dining chairs as Lily Carver. 'They've got a lot of great pieces in at the moment. Someone with fabulous taste must have died recently.'

'You must give me the address,' said Lars.

I muttered something non-committal about digging it out for him, and made a mental note to keep him out of the kitchen, in case he spotted the forks. You had to say this for Lars - nothing got past him. I felt stirrings of pity for Eileen, imagining her tiptoeing in from unsanctioned shopping trips and having to conceal her purchases at the back of the wardrobe so that, one day, she could drag them out and exclaim in all honesty, 'What? *This* old thing? I've had it for *ages!*'

'You know...' began Lars, caressing the curve of one of the new chair backs. I steeled myself for some tough questioning, but he grinned. 'Taste like yours, Belinda, is wasted in a bookshop. You should have been an interior designer. You could have your own TV show, like Charlie Bingo-Stukeley or *Deco Deluxe*. You could call it *Lindy's Living Rooms*. Or *Salon Belinda*.'

Salon Belinda. I liked the sound of that.

And soon he was touching me the way he'd been touching the Lily Carver chair.

*****

Nancy sent me postcards from the Grand Canal, the Leaning Tower of Pisa and the window of a Viennese patisserie. The back of each card was filled with her slapdash handwriting - which in itself ought to have been a giveaway because Nancy's handwriting had never been consistent, even in its slapdashedness. The messages were variations on, 'Having a lovely time, wish you were here,' followed by a weather report: 'Nice and sunny' or 'Pouring with rain'. Not her style, but I was too blinkered by resentment to notice it.

All I knew was that she was going to have the baby abroad, not just a long way from the tabloid press and the men in grey, but a long way from *me*. I worried that by the time I caught up with her again, she would be carrying a mewling fait accompli, and some oily Eurotrash scribe she'd picked up on the road would be presenting himself in adorably broken English as her faithful Boswell.

But maybe, just maybe, I could scrape together enough money to join her on her travels, and she would be so relieved to see a familiar face she'd allow me back into her confidence, and then I would persuade her to return with me to London, and everything would be dandy.

There was one big flaw in this plan. I had no idea where she was. The postcards weren't much help; she was skipping from place to place, impossible to pin down. But I had one advantage over Verity Wilson and the rest of the press pack; I had recognised the back of Maurice's head. So when I spotted him and Phoebe lollygagging around in the Bar Bidoll one evening, I had no hesitation in reintroducing myself.

When I say 'spotted', what this actually meant was lurking in a corner of the Bar Bidoll every night for a week, eking out overpriced Beaujolais while keeping one eye on the door in the faint hope that Maurice or Phoebe would walk through it; Phoebe dropped its name into her column so often she made it sound as though they were regulars. But my patience was eventually rewarded; on a wet Tuesday night, just as I was on the point of giving up and going home, I sensed a faint swell of activity. There was extravagant air-kissing going on.

How they'd got through the door and all the way across the bar without my noticing I'll never know; I was feeling bleary by then, so maybe I'd nodded off over my Brouilly. But there they were, holding court from one of the mouse-grey nubuck banquettes, Phoebe's hair shimmering like a mahogany helmet and Maurice already wreathed in clouds of cigarette smoke. By the time I'd pushed my way over there, they were already thronged by supplicants eager for a piece of their social glamour.

I edged up to a spot just behind Maurice's shoulder and said, 'Hi.' The third time, he looked round and said 'hi' back. I took advantage of the moment by muscling past the skinny girl who'd been trying to monopolise him. There was an awkward pause that went on for so long I could feel my smile beginning to wilt.

'Belinda,' I said. He had that look of swivel-eyed panic that indicated he couldn't quite place me, so I helped him out. 'Nancy's friend.'

'Ah yes, Belinda.'

I got straight to the point. 'Heard from Nancy?'

He squinted at me. 'She's in Europe.'

'I know that. I've had postcards.'

'Us too,' said Maurice. 'Barcelona, Geneva...'

I felt a twinge of envy. 'I never got one from Geneva.'

'Oh well, maybe not Geneva. Somewhere with mountains and lakes.'

There was another pause before I said, 'I saw the

back of your head on the news.'

'Guilty as charged.' Maurice raised his hands in a jocular way, as if to say, *You've got me.* 'But honestly, I have no idea where she went after that.'

'She vanished in a puff of smoke?'

'You talking about Nancy Loughlin?' asked Skinny Girl.

'Mind your own beeswax,' I said.

Maurice winced and looked over to Phoebe for support, but she was deep in conversation with an earnest young man with a goatee, so he turned back to me and Skinny Girl. 'So... mmm… Melinda... Tania... What are you up to these days?' If only he'd been able to remember my name without prompting, we could have passed as the best of acquaintances.

Tania opened her mouth to say something, but I was quicker off the mark. 'Still at the bookshop,' I said, taking an almost sadistic delight in seeing Maurice's expression, which had once again turned to panic. *Bookshop? What bookshop?*

I stuck to my guns. 'Any idea when she's getting back?'

He shrugged. 'When the tabloids lose interest, I guess. You saw the rubbish they were printing.'

Phoebe dismissed Goatee Boy and leaned over to nuzzle Maurice's neck in a proprietary manner, as though she thought Skinny Girl and I might be hitting on him and needed a reminder that he was already taken.

'Did I hear you mention Nancy? Hi, Belinda. Hi, Tania.'

'Hi,' I said, feeling a warm rush of satisfaction that at least my literary rival knew my name, even if her husband didn't. I repositioned myself so that Tania was definitively cut out of the conversation. After a moment or two, she gave up and drifted away.

'Not like Nancy to not call,' I said, though actually it was exactly like her.

'She's leading a nomadic existence,' said Phoebe.

'You haven't spoken?' I asked.

Maurice and Phoebe exchanged a glance. Fleeting though it was, it told me they knew more than they were letting on. 'Just postcards,' said Maurice, not looking me in the eye.

'You'll like this, Belinda,' said Phoebe, who knew exactly how to distract me. 'We just had a Finnish sink installed in the laundry room.'

She was right. I did like it. 'What make?'

'Salomaa. Not sure how you pronounce that.' I wasn't sure either.

'Goat willow!' said Maurice.

'I didn't know you even had a laundry room,' I said.

'Used to be a cloakroom,' said Phoebe. 'But now it's a cloakroom *and* a laundry room, combined.'

I felt like being sarcastic, but in truth I was fascinated, and envious. If only I'd had a spare cloakroom lying around, I too could have converted it into a laundry room.

'Salomaa's sourcing and craftsmanship are impeccable,' I said. 'Did you get rectangular or round? Inset or mounted? I bet it smells good when it's full of hot water. I'd give anything to see it in situ.'

'Pop round anytime!' Maurice said in that airy way he had.

Phoebe shot him what might have been interpreted as a dirty look, but her next words belied this: 'You're always welcome.'

I smiled and said, 'When?'

Phoebe seemed momentarily disconcerted, but rallied well and got out her diary, a big battered leather thing bristling with multi-coloured post-its. I surveyed her handwriting, upside-down, and was pleased to see it wasn't as elegant as mine. It was spikier, and messier. Though the longer I looked, the more I had a nagging sense that, ill-formed as it was, the effect was somehow more stylish. I was left feeling mildly anxious.

'Supper on Thursday?' said Phoebe.

I was pencilled in for the late shift, but it would be easy enough to bully Alain or Elspeth into swapping. No way was I going to pass up an invitation to inspect the Pflums' new sink.

Phoebe nudged Maurice. 'Another one of those, perhaps?'

'Why not? What are you drinking, Melissa?'

'For God's sake, Maurice, it's *Belinda*,' said Phoebe. 'I swear,' she said to me, 'he'll be forgetting his own name soon. Smoked too much grass in his teens.'

'I'll have what you're having,' I said, which was how I ended up with a disgusting concoction called a Blue Fairy, which made me violently ill. So while Phoebe and Maurice and their chums exchanged bons mots and celebrated the good life, I was stuck on my knees in the ladies' toilet, throwing up and knowing no more about Nancy's whereabouts than at the start of the evening.

But at least I didn't come away from the Bar Bidoll empty-handed. I'd scored an invitation to Planet Pflum.

Chapter 3
The Pickle Factory

Bull announced the big news over breakfast.

'Your agent called.'

'Anthony? How?' Nancy still hadn't found an outside line, but was pretending not to be perturbed by it.

'You've been offered the leading role in Les Six's new production.' He raised his coffee cup. 'Congratulations!'

'Congratulations, Nancy!' said Miss Taylor, raising her glass of orange juice.

Nancy felt so elated she forgot about the phone problem. *Yes!* At last something good had happened. It was about time.

'When do I start?'

'They're having a read-through tomorrow,' said Bull. 'Jones and Miller will take you there. Do them good to be exposed to a bit of culture.'

Mr. Jones and Mr. Miller exchanged long-suffering looks.

*****

On Tuesday morning, Mr. Jones drove the Mercedes with Mr. Miller riding shotgun and Nancy in the back. The first time the car stopped at lights, she idly tried the door and wasn't surprised to find it locked.

Mr. Jones, watching in the rearview mirror, said, 'For your protection.'

'Just curious,' she said. 'I wasn't going to run away.'

'We're more concerned about someone climbing in,' said Mr. Miller.

She supposed he had a point, but didn't see why she needed to be escorted all the way into the rehearsal as well. 'You could wait for me outside.'

'Just following orders,' said Mr. Miller.

So she played along, and a routine was established. Mr. Jones set them down on Clerkenwell Green by a door marked The Pickle Factory, which was being guarded by a burly man in a leather jacket. Mr. Miller would take her inside, where Mr. Jones would later join them until just before the end of the rehearsal, when he would leave to collect the car and bring it round to the door again, so it was waiting at the kerb when they emerged.

Nancy knew exactly where she was. Clerkenwell Green was only a few blocks away from the Pflums' loft; she was tempted to ask if they could stop off there on the way home so she could pop in and surprise them, but dismissed the idea. The less contact Mr. Jones and Mr. Miller had with her friends, the better. They knew too much about her as it was. She would surprise Maurice and Phoebe later, when she'd found a way to give her security detail the slip.

*****

On the first morning, Nancy went up to Les Six and quietly thanked him. He peered at her over the top of his spectacles and said, 'Ah yes, the girl who kicked me in the gonads,' loudly enough for everyone else to hear.

'I am *so sorry*.'

He lowered his voice. 'You realise I didn't have a choice?'

Nancy held his gaze. 'I promise you won't regret it.'

Six's eyes dropped to her stomach. 'Is it going to be a problem?'

'Not at all,' said Nancy, who had worked out the run would be over long before her due date.

'Let's hope you don't go into labour on stage!' boomed Rod Carpenter, whose ears had been flapping.

'We had to move the booking to accommodate you,' said Six.

Nancy wondered what kind of offer ComSec had made that he hadn't been able to refuse.

*****

First read-throughs were always nerve-racking, but this one was especially so. It was the first time since her audition that Nancy had even glanced at a script. By the time she arrived, the others had already selected their seats at the table and were busily reaffirming the common bond they'd forged in previous get-togethers, before Syrie Holt had met with her unfortunate mishap and the production had been put on hold.

Nancy took the last available seat; she had to shift her chair to look past Lucy Welbeck, who was blocking her view of the others. Worse, she was stuck at the wrong end of the table, in amongst the ingenues and also-rans, with all the important decisions taking place at the other end, where the dominant personalities were already making their mark. Rod Carpenter, still obsessed with shedding his lowbrow comic past, had established himself as unofficial father figure, though it was clear the real movers and shakers were Jasper Andrews, a former stand-up comedian quietly carving out a name for himself as a serious actor and soon-to-be-published novelist, and Jet Coleman, who'd just landed the small but showy role of Saint-Just in an action-packed mini-series about the French Revolution.

Carlotta, naturally, had inserted herself between them and was already flirting with both, though Nancy already suspected she was sleeping with Six. Nancy wished she were sitting next to him and Dougal. But instead she was sandwiched between mousy Lucy, who giggled at just about anything that anyone said, and ethereal, neurotic Emma Harris, who mostly kept her mouth shut but whose sleeves, Nancy noted, were not quite long enough to conceal the hesitation marks on her wrists. The useful thing about Emma, though, was that she smoked almost as much as Nancy, so the two of them sat there, puffing away, deaf to Wally Winters's complaints about them polluting his airspace, and trying to ignore Bunty Mackay's tiresome attempts to make everything about her.

They started the read-through, much to Rod's annoyance. 'How many times do we have to do this?'

'This is for Nancy,' said Six. 'And you'll see I've made some changes for her benefit.'

'Yeah, like who are those guys?' asked Dougal, as Mr. Miller came in from having parked the car and took his place next to Mr. Jones, already sitting back to the wall behind Nancy. Everyone turned to stare at the men in the navy-blue suits. Mr. Miller's mouth twitched. Mr.

Jones pretended to look at his newspaper. The suits were so well-cut they almost concealed the bulges around the armpits. Nancy had once dated an actor who'd been cast as a minor hoodlum in a low-budget British gangster film and who'd insisted on keeping his holster on at all times, even in bed. But this was the first time she'd kept company with men carrying real guns, and despite her qualms she couldn't help but find it thrilling. Mr. Jones and Mr. Miller discouraged attempts to engage them in conversation, but this just made them all the more fascinating to Jet - who seemed to be studying their behaviour in preparation for the day he'd be cast as 'bodyguard' - and Dougal, who'd always had a weakness for strong silent types.

It didn't take long for Nancy to find that the other actors hated her. It wasn't personal, but they felt duty-bound to loathe her out of loyalty to Carlotta, who'd been Syrie Holt's understudy and couldn't understand why she was still languishing in the lesser role of Annie Chapman instead of promoted to top billing. Nancy heard several members of the company had visited Holt in hospital, and that she was sitting up in bed and swearing, so her life didn't seem to be in danger, at least. Apparently, she'd fallen down some stairs and now both legs were in plaster. Nancy wanted to find out which stairs, and who had been present when she'd fallen down them, but her curiosity was interpreted as schadenfreude, so she backed off.

Another reason for the hate (she learned from Bunty, the mumsy ex-soap star who was playing the Ripper's first victim and who didn't let her dislike of Nancy stop her passing on all the gossip) was because the other actors thought she was a kept woman who couldn't step out of the house without two of her keeper's lackeys in tow. In a sense, they were right. She *was* a kept woman. They were just wrong in assuming her keeper was one of the musical's backers.

Towards the end of the day, when Mr. Jones had left to fetch the car and Mr. Miller appeared to be on the point of nodding off, Nancy touched Lucy's arm and whispered, 'Can I borrow your phone?'

'Didn't you know? They're not allowed.'

'Whose idea was that?' asked Nancy.

'Sixy can't stand mobiles going off while he's talking. Hits the roof.'

'Is that so.' Nancy wondered if ComSec's offer to Six had included a rider about phones.

*****

The other actors hated her even more when they realised she wasn't a very good singer. Certainly no better than Carlotta, and nowhere near the same league as Lucy, the girl with the golden voice who was playing Third Victim. At her first musical try-out, Nancy noticed some of her fellow cast-members covering their ears. She knew she wasn't *that* bad, but again, there was no point in taking it personally.

Les Six sighed and said, 'We can work around it.'

'What d'you know, could've sworn this was a musical,' said Harry Bones, the semi-legendary jazz musician who had written the score and who was now playing the world's first black Montague Druitt. He was lounging at the side of the stage, stretching out his tightly-trousered legs and smoking a spliff. Even on the other side of the room, the unmistakable whiff of burning grass was making Nancy feel giddy.

'We can farm out verses from her big solo so she doesn't have to carry it all by herself,' said Six. 'Or she could do it Sprechstimme.'

'Like hell she could,' said Harry.

Carlotta put her hand up. 'I know the lyrics.'

'Of course you do.' Six smiled. 'But I'm afraid that by this stage you've already been eviscerated.'

'You could change the order,' said Carlotta. 'Or I could be one of the walking corpses.'

'Don't worry, Nancy,' said Six. 'We'll work it out.'

Nancy wasn't worried. She knew she could go deaf, dumb, blind and develop a disfiguring skin disease, and still no-one would take this role away from her. ComSec would see to that. But it didn't mean she wasn't going to give it her best shot. She would show them what she was capable of.

Carlotta was scowling at her. Nancy smiled back, amicably. *I own you, bitch*, she thought. *I own all of you. All I have to do is say the word, and you'll be falling downstairs before you know it.*

*****

The most tiresome part of staying at Wormwood was the morning check-up - or the Daily Probe, as she began to call it. Every day, Dr. Smith took her blood pressure and asked for a urine sample, and never once cracked a smile, not even when she presented him with three and a half jars. He had white hair and even whiter skin, like a basement-dweller, and only his bushy black eyebrows and piercing blue eyes stopped him looking like an albino. There was something unnatural about his perfect enunciation; no natural-born Englishman would ever speak English with such precision. If he'd been around during the Third Reich, Nancy thought, he would have been a death-camp doctor, for sure. As it was, he probably spent his spare time vivisecting small animals. She wasn't entirely comfortable with him being her obstetrician.

Some of the tests were fun: pressing buttons in a soundproof booth or spotting coloured dots on a video screen. But then one day Dr. Smith produced a needle the size of the Eiffel Tower and approached her like a lion tamer approaching the lion with a chair. She didn't have to say anything, just shook her head, gave him a small nosebleed, and he retreated, put the needle away and didn't try anything like that again.

But the other tests continued. They were for her own good, she was told, though she didn't understand what IQ scores or inkblot tests (she lied, saying 'bunch of flowers' when it had quite clearly been an eagle tearing a mouse to pieces with its beak) had to do with her being pregnant. And then there were the scans; Dr. Smith assured her they were perfectly safe, and she concluded he was right; if they'd been harmful, the Shrimp would have lashed out. The thought reminded her of what had happened at the clinic, which put her in a low mood for the rest of the day.

But the Daily Probe was the price she had to pay for the rest, which she had to admit wasn't bad. Her room was cleaned and tidied every day except Sunday. The supply of cigarettes was replenished daily, as were the bottles in the mini-bar. Clothes were picked up from where she'd left them on the floor or draped over the furniture, then laundered and returned wrapped in plastic or in neatly ironed piles.

There was usually time for a swim after rehearsal, or a yoga and meditation session with Miss Green. These were a lot more fun than Dr. Smith's tests, not least because Miss Green was chattier than anyone else - which was how Nancy learnt that hatchet-faced Miss Taylor was embroiled in a clandestine affair with Mr. Miller, and that Mr. Cook, the chef, was saving up for a sex-change.

'These are made-up names, right?' asked Nancy. 'I mean, a chef called Mr. Cook? Come *on.*'

Miss Green swore they were real.

To fill the empty hours, she browsed the library and came away with armfuls of books. For the first time in her life, Nancy found herself reading for fun. She read English classics, and then some French and Russian ones. She read popular science, and history, and a bit of philosophy. She even sped through *Zero to Midnight* and *Codename Quebec*, which were about rugged special forces being dispatched to Africa or the Middle East, where they slaughtered a lot of foreigners and restored order to the British Empire. She didn't enjoy them much, but she suspected they might provide her with some insight into the mindset of her hosts.

*****

'So tell me about it,' Bull said over dinner that night. 'Jack the Ripper, right? You're one of the working girls?'

'I'm the heroine,' said Nancy, toying with a spoonful of banana-flavoured Fudge Tub as though it were a dainty cocktail canapé.

'Don't all the women die?' frowned Bull.

'Les Six thought that was too downbeat,' said Nancy. 'He rewrote it so Maggie Crook avenges her friends by killing the murderers.'

Bull shook his head as if to say, *whatever next?*

'So who's the villain this time?'

Nancy explained Six had a new theory about the Ripper's identity, though she'd flicked through some books and watched a couple of movies as part of her tour preparation, and knew Six's idea wasn't as original as he thought. In his version, the murders ascribed to the Ripper were the actions of a cabal comprising Lord Salisbury the Prime Minister, Prince Albert Victor the Duke of Clarence, Sir William Gull the surgeon, Montague John Druitt the barrister, Walter Sickert the painter, Harry Dam the reporter, George Lusk the president of the Whitechapel Vigilante Committee and Inspector Frederick Abberline - all of them acting in cahoots. In the penultimate musical number members of the patriarchy linked arms and literally danced over the corpses of their female victims, which by that time - as per stage instructions - had been substituted by dummies filled with stage blood.

'Well, that certainly sounds interesting,' said Bull. 'I hope you'll get me a ticket for opening night.'

'Me too,' said Miss Taylor.

Nancy said 'Sure,' but had already decided she didn't want the entire staff of Wormwood gawping at her from the front row, and possibly trying to muscle in on the post-performance party as well.

*****

Phoebe had been right. Just looking at the garments

she'd brought from home made Nancy burst out laughing. It wasn't long before she had to switch to the clothes she'd found in the wardrobe. All those baggy sacks and shift dresses? Well, they fitted her now. They were well made, and clearly expensive, but they weren't to her taste at all: too many ruffles and bows and furbelows, somebody's misconceived notion of femininity. But it wasn't likely she'd be going shopping for clothes any time soon, so she wore what was provided. At least her friends weren't around to see her dolled up like one of *The Golden Girls*. She would never have lived it down. As it was, the other actors thought her taste in clothes was strange, though they couldn't decide if it was retro or avant-garde.

'Did you choose this?' she asked Miss Taylor one day, twirling round so that the full skirt swung out.

'Good lord, no,' said Miss Taylor. 'You have Bull to blame for that. He supervised the acquisition of the wardrobe.'

Nancy stopped twirling. 'You mean he..?'

'He selected your clothes, yes.'

Chapter 4
Planet Pflum

Two days before supper at the Pflums, I fell in love. The object of my desire was an Antonius Block dining table, sighted after dark in the window of Cromarty and Cosbeck. It might have been hewn from a single mighty redwood felled by magic woodcutters in the Fairy Forest, though had more likely been chopped down by chainsaws somewhere in Southern California. If you peered closely enough into its grain, I fancied, you could see Spanish Jesuits trying to convert Native Americans to Christianity.

But this love was doomed to be unrequited. Because I couldn't afford it. I went home and sweated over my bank statement and regretted having frittered away so much of my windfall on what had once seemed like essential items - a notebook bound in faux ponyskin, a 1930s Nahum Whitley fountain-pen with a clip in the shape of an ostrich, a vintage Janos Rukh hot water bottle cover trimmed with ironic pom-poms. If only I'd been able to resist those temptations, I might have been able to stretch to the table. And what about my plan to fly out and join Nancy? I needed to hold some money in reserve for that.

I had to face facts. I had sold Nancy's story too cheaply. The thrill of the windfall had gone to my head and I'd behaved like a giddy spendthrift instead of the sensible shopper I normally was. Surely it couldn't end like this. Perhaps I could dredge up some juicy detail to rekindle media interest in my missing friend. How about that time she'd snorted cocaine in the House of Commons bar? Or the wedding reception where she'd shagged the groom in the kitchen? The problem was, I couldn't be sure she'd ever confided in anyone else about these misdeeds. The trick would be in selecting titbits that couldn't possibly be traced back to me.

In any case, I didn't trust Verity Wilson. I'd left messages on her voice-mail, but she'd never rung back. I felt soiled and resentful. She'd only been pretending to be my friend, and she hadn't even done that very well.

It wasn't just cash-flow problems that were putting me in a foul mood. Eileen's health had got worse. I wondered if she'd guessed about me and this was her way of fighting back, or if she just sensed Lars slipping away from her. Like so many men, he was oddly naïve when it came to women's health problems. It never occurred to him his wife might be falling ill on purpose, in an attempt to reclaim his attention.

This time it was a lump in her breast. 'I'll try and get away next week,' he said. 'But she doesn't drive, so I'm having to ferry her around to specialists. She doesn't have a lot of friends, Belinda. She isn't self-sufficient like you.'

'That's OK, I understand,' I said, gritting my teeth. Self-sufficient? Only because some of us didn't have the luxury of choice.

We exchanged bland pleasantries before he said, 'I love you,' and rang off, as though in a hurry to get back to his wife's lump. Once upon a time, those three little words might have given me a thrill, but I'd heard them so often, and from the lips of so many liars, that I knew exactly how little they were worth.

*****

'*That girl!*' said Lisa Kramer. 'I've never met anyone so hungry to taste every new experience life can throw at her.'

This didn't sound much like Nancy to me, but everyone around the table thought they knew her better than I did. For the first time, I didn't have Nancy to act as a buffer between me and the Pflums; Phoebe's invitation had been extended to me alone, not as a plus-one. I surveyed the other guests, wishing I felt more at ease in their company. They all had enviable jobs, and even more enviable family or old school ties that had got them those jobs. Lisa Kramer was one of Phoebe's editors, and married to Jenson McCabe, who had inherited a small publishing company which now published his wife's ghastly chick-lit novels. Nevertheless I persuaded him to give me one of his business cards. I wasn't going to pass up an opportunity like this.

'Ha ha, I'd better be nice to you,' he said when Phoebe told him I worked in a bookshop. 'You're in the front line of the book wars. The personal interface with our readers!'

'I'm also a writer,' I said. He nodded politely, but before I could elaborate, his wife barged in to brag about her latest sales figures. I made a mental note to hide her books at the back of the shelves as soon as I got to the shop in the morning.

On the other side of the table sat Arwen Gates, one of Maurice's cousins and an illustrator whose twee 'feminist' cartoons were a regular feature of the paper that published Phoebe's column. She'd brought her current girlfriend, an undernourished jewellery designer called Marnie Cardew whose father had once made a record that had once got to Number Seven in the hit parade, and apparently that was all it took to get her mentioned in the diary pages with sickening regularity, even if readers were never quite sure who she was, or what she did, though I noticed she was incapable of opening her mouth without trying to flog her overpriced bijoux.

We were seated around the big oak table Maurice's parents had had shipped from Sweden at vast expense and which only rekindled my desire for the Antonius Block. I was delighted to see my Spud Williams candelabra planted in the middle, though only ten minutes into the evening Maurice said, 'Let's move this, shall we,' and shifted it to the floor.

I asked, 'You don't think it looks better on the table?'

'Of course it looks better on the table,' said Phoebe, 'but maybe not during dinner. It's a bit awkward having to peer around it while we're talking.'

I thought a certain amount of awkward peering was an acceptable price to pay for a display of such impeccable craftsmanship, but refrained from saying so.

The sixth guest was an affected loafer called Tenebris Shaw, who was introduced to me as a 'poet', though he apparently passed his time frittering away his late father's fortune on extended holidays in the south of France. When I asked why he was called Tenebris, he rolled his eyes as though I'd said something foolish.

What a shower, I thought. If this was the cream of

the nation's intelligentsia, it might not be such a bad thing for End of Days to wipe us all off the face of the earth.

*****

It didn't take long for the conversation to turn to Nancy. Everyone except Marnie and Tenebris had met her. Everyone liked her, and thought she was a bit mad. Trust Nancy to go and get herself mixed up in something like this. Nancy this, Nancy that. What a girl! No-one seemed concerned that she might have *died*, that *I* might have died. They listened politely as I gave them a gore-lite résumé of the carnage at the clinic, but reacted as though this were the sort of thing that happened every day, just another outrageous chapter in the continuing soap opera of Nancy's life.

'Doesn't anyone know who the father is?' asked Lisa.

'Satan is his father,' I said, and everyone laughed. Then, as though I'd never opened my mouth, they spent the next fifteen minutes trying to guess the identity of the foetus's sire, proposing and rejecting all the suspects I'd already thought of and mentioning several I'd never heard of. My friend was a bit of a good-time girl, that was for sure, but I felt obliged to stick up for her.

'Nancy says she didn't have sex.'

Several people chuckled. 'Nancy's always having sex,' said Lisa.

It was Phoebe's turn to bristle. 'Not always.' She glanced at Maurice, who was staring at Arwen's sparkly lipstick as if mesmerised. 'We're not all lucky enough to find our soulmates at the first attempt.'

'It's brave of her to go through with it,' said Marnie. 'I must point her in the direction of my Lone Goddess collection.'

'She has no choice,' I said.

'It's a woman's right to choose,' said Tenebris, as though I'd said something politically incorrect.

'She could still get an abortion,' said Lisa.

'Surely too late now.'

'Maybe she's changed her mind,' I said.

'You could be right,' said Maurice.

'I'd love to hear her side of it,' said Lisa.

'I could tell you that,' I said, but once again everyone ignored me and I began to feel like part of the furniture.

'Isabella ran into her in Milan,' said Arwen.

'I overdosed in Verona once and they poured milk down my throat,' said Tenebris.

'I worry about her,' I said.

'Me too,' said Phoebe, smiling at me so warmly that for a few seconds I thought it might be nice to be *her* best friend, instead of Nancy's.

'Isabella's talking bollocks, as usual,' said Maurice. Phoebe fluttered her fingers in a warning gesture, but he carried on regardless. 'She never went further than Le Marais.'

'Your place?' asked Jenson.

Phoebe sighed and gave in. 'Yes.'

This triggered a flurry of Paris-related anecdotes which I barely heard because I was drowning in a tsunami of envy. So much for the postcards, presumably part of some vast and elaborate joke I was too feeble-minded to grasp - Nancy had been in Paris all along! If only I'd know earlier I could have gone over to join her.

Whenever I went to Paris I ended up in cheap flophouses near the Gare du Nord, whereas the Pflums' pied-à-terre in Le Marais had old beams propping up the ceiling, and a view across the rooftops, and the smell of freshly baked croissants drifting in from the neighbouring boulangerie. I knew this not because I'd been there, but because I'd once been present when Phoebe had described it to a pretentious would-be film-maker called Erwin Demple. She'd rounded off the description with, 'So do let us know if you're ever going to Paris and need somewhere to crash,' which was rich considering she'd known Demple all of ten minutes, whereas by then I must have met her, oh, a dozen times, and no such invitation had ever been extended to me.

I continued to stew in my own envy as Maurice entertained the table with the story of how he and Phoebe had helped Nancy dodge the press, which only confirmed my suspicions that Phoebe Pflum had now entered the game. She had contacts in all the right places. She knew editors and publishers. And even more crucially, they knew her. So my heart was in my mouth when I said, 'So you'll be writing about Nancy in your column?'

'Heavens, no!' She sounded genuinely shocked. 'I never write about *friends*.'

'Tell that to Gary Johnson,' said Arwen. 'You always have to watch what you say around him, or it ends up in one of his stupid novels.'

'I suppose she might want to tell her side of it one day,' said Phoebe. 'I'll be there for her then.'

'Let me know when that happens,' said Jenson, all but licking his chops and getting out his chequebook.

I don't suppose Phoebe was aware that she'd just

thrown down a gauntlet. Now it was a three-way race between me and her and Verity Wilson...

I was so lost in my thoughts that when Maurice dropped the bombshell, I almost missed it.

'I thought you said she was in Paris,' said Arwen.

'Not any more.' Once again I noticed Phoebe signalling with her hand.

I laughed weakly, trying to camouflage my distress. 'Since when?'

'We haven't actually *seen* her,' said Phoebe, trying to play it down. 'Maurice spoke to her on the phone.'

'So where is she?' I demanded. I knew Nancy hadn't gone home. I'd never returned her keys, so had popped round to her flat several times to check for signs of recent activity. I hadn't found any.

'Top secret!' said Maurice. We all turned to stare at him, trying to work out what he meant.

'I guess the police have to keep an eye on her till they catch the Clinic Killer,' said Jenson.

'If they do ever do,' said Arwen. 'It'll probably end up as one of those unsolved mysteries.'

'I wonder why she didn't call me,' I said.

'Probably busy with rehearsals,' said Maurice.

My mouth fell open. Mr. and Mrs. Pflum were full of revelations this evening. Rehearsals? What rehearsals? I wasn't the only one who wanted to know.

'Les Six's latest,' said Maurice.

'That Jack the Ripper musical?' I said, eager to show I had an inside track. 'But she didn't get it!'

'Sixy changed his mind,' said Lisa.

'Of course he did,' said her husband.

'You can't *buy* that sort of publicity,' said Lisa.

'Where did you hear this?' I asked, wondering why

I was last to know.

'You just need to know how to listen, Melinda,' said Jenson. 'The tom-toms are played very close to the forest floor.'

'Sixy always did know which side his bread is buttered on,' said Lisa.

'I bumped into him and Ally Dixon in the Rue Bar last week,' said Marnie. 'She ordered some of my Lapis Lazuli earstuds for her shop.'

Tenebris snorted with laughter. 'Les Six? You mean Leslie Lambert? He was in my year at Magdalen. Talentless clown. I buggered him once.'

'Somebody must know where they're rehearsing this thing, this *play*,' I said.

'I'm sure the tabloids will get wind of it sooner or later,' said Maurice. 'And then the whole circus will start up again. Poor Nancy.'

'Nonsense. She's enjoying the attention,' said Tenebris. 'It's what actors crave.'

'It's the wrong sort of attention,' said Phoebe.

'There *is* no wrong sort,' said Tenebris, who clearly had experience in this area.

'But she didn't say where she is?' I persisted.

'It's some sort of protective custody,' said Phoebe.

'How do you know she hasn't been kidnapped?'

'Nah,' said Maurice. 'She's keeping a low profile, and I don't blame her. She doesn't want any of us getting harassed. It happened to my dad after Robina's suicide, cameras shoved in his face all day, and it's no joke.'

He started talking about his father, and the conversation moved on to one of his dad's film-maker friends, who had just dumped his wife of thirty years for a teenage waitress.

I stopped listening and sat there fuming. Nancy was back in town, and hadn't even bothered to call me.

*****

After dinner, when the candelabra had been restored to its rightful position on the table and we had adjourned to the U-shaped arrangement of sofas on the other side of the room, and because I grew tired of conversations about over-privileged wastrels who were forging careers out of being the sons and daughters of Z-list celebrities, I started shuffling through the stack of magazines on one of the end tables. Which is how I stumbled across the comic, which stood out like a tumour amid the how-to-have-a-glossy-lifestyle manuals to which Phoebe and Maurice normally subscribed.

For want of anything better to do, I started flicking through its garishly coloured pages. The crime-fighting superhero was also known as Anti-Antichrist. He had long black hair and wore Ray-Bans and a natty grey suit, and on one page he appeared to be simultaneously wrestling a dragon and quoting from the Book of Revelation. A horrible suspicion came over me. I closed the comic and looked more carefully at the cover. The author's name was Jules Delgado.

Just when I thought I'd got shot of him! A vision of hammered Chihuahua heads swam into my head, and all the moisture drained from my mouth.

'Whose is this?' I gasped, no louder than a couple of corduroy trouser legs rubbing together. Unsurprisingly, no-one heard. I swallowed and tried again, more loudly. 'Hey, where did you get this comic?'

This time my voice penetrated Phoebe's bubble,

and she looked over. 'That's Maurice's.'

Maurice, who'd been good-naturedly fending off Tenebris's amorous advances, looked up at the sound of his name. 'Nothing to do with me. Somebody left it at the office.'

'Can I borrow it?'

'You can *have* it, Melinda.'

'I think it was always meant for me anyway,' I said, but he'd already turned back to Tenebris.

Chapter 5
The Kick Inside

Nancy asked if her friends still thought she was in Paris. Bull shrugged and said he supposed so.

'Shouldn't I tell them I'm here now? They'll be worried.'

'Better not. Jules Delgado's still at large, and I bet *he'd* love to know where you are.'

He was like a parent threatening a disobedient child with the bogeyman, dropping Delgado's name into the conversation whenever Nancy made noises about making contact with her old life. But she wasn't a child, and Delgado didn't frighten her.

'I got away from him at Waterloo.'

'With our help,' Bull reminded her. 'He's not the sort who gives up easily. Nasty piece of work.'

'I can look after myself.'

'You don't know what he's capable of. Remember the clinic.'

'I think about that every day!' she said. She hadn't mentioned her conviction that the deaths at the Faraday had been her fault, or the fault of whatever was inside her - not because she still felt guilty about it, which she did, but because she had an uneasy feeling he would find it exciting, and would insist on subjecting her to even more testing.

'What makes you think it was him?'

'M.O. You know that greaseball's speciality?'

'No, but I guess you're going to tell me.'

'Decapitations. Likes to leave heads on gateposts. Thinks it makes his handiwork look like the cartels.'

'You've spoken to him?'

'He was interrogated by Special Ops in ninety-one, and again in ninety-eight.'

'And you think he wants to leave *my* head on a gatepost?'

'We're here to make sure he doesn't,' said Bull.

'All right, I get it, he's a bad man, ' said Nancy, wrapping her arms protectively around her stomach. It was true she hadn't wanted to go with Delgado when he'd accosted her at Waterloo Station, but he'd struck her as more deluded and arrogant than dangerous. Bull, now: *he* was dangerous, and the more he smiled, the warier she became.

But neither Bull nor Delgado were any match for what was inside her, she was confident of that.

*****

Despite Les Six's no-phone edict, she decided one day to try and sneak her mobile into The Pickle Factory. But when she searched her room for it, it was nowhere to be found. She wondered whether to challenge Bull about it, but decided it was better to pretend she hadn't noticed its absence.

Later that day, she spotted Emma Harris sneakily tapping out a text message beneath the table.

'Can I borrow that for a sec?'

'No!' said Emma. 'Sixy will confiscate it.'

'I'll take it into the loo,' said Nancy, and Emma grudgingly surrendered the phone. Nancy excused herself, locked herself into a toilet cubicle, and called Maurice's office.

'Nance! We were starting to worry. Where *are* you?'

'Back in town,' said Nancy, who couldn't be bothered to explain that she'd never been away, especially after all the trouble he and Phoebe had gone to. All that could wait.

'Are you OK? Where *are* you?'

'Hey, remember that musical? Well, I got the role after all!' She'd been longing to share this news with someone other than the ComSec staff.

'Felicitations!'

There was knocking at the toilet door, and Mr. Miller called, 'Miss Loughlin? Are you in there?'

Nancy lowered her voice. 'Listen, I have to go,' she said. 'I'm in rehearsal and this isn't my phone. Can't tell you just yet where I'm staying, it's all very hush hush, but I'll call again soon.'

As she emerged from the toilets, Mr. Miller looked at her suspiciously. Nancy glared back. 'Not even going to let me pee in peace? You do realise I have to empty my bladder a lot?'

He looked embarrassed. 'You were gone for so long we started to worry.'

'No, I wasn't,' said Nancy. 'It was hardly any time at all.'

She stalked back into the rehearsal room, letting Mr. Miller feel the full force of her disdain by way of a trickle of nasal blood.

Emma gave her a sly look as she returned the phone. 'Called your secret lover?'

'Sort of,' said Nancy.

But the next day, when she tried to borrow the phone again, Emma made a face and shook her head.

'No signal. It's a dead spot.'

'It wasn't yesterday,' said Nancy.

Emma shrugged. 'Maybe Sixy installed a jamming device overnight. Who knows?'

Nancy surreptitiously tried Bunty's phone, and then Dougal's, but it was the same story each time: no signal. After passing Dougal's mobile back to him, she noticed Mr. Jones watching them. He slowly shook his head at her.

ComSec had got wind of her call to Maurice, she knew it. This tight security was getting on her nerves. She knew she could walk away whenever she wanted, but Mr. Jones and Mr. Miller would almost certainly try to stop her, and they had guns. She wasn't worried for herself, but she didn't want anyone else getting caught in the crossfire. If she did decide to make a break for it, she would have to time it very carefully.

There was also the consideration that it had been ComSec that had got her the part. And if she did walk out on them, they might take it away from her, out of spite. She didn't just want this role, she *needed* it. She was having the time of her life, and she had no intention of going back to being an out-of-work actress, cobbling rent together by helping Maurice with his tour groups, a has-been before she'd even begun.

And even if she did leave Wormwood, where would she go? The idea of finding herself once again under siege in her tiny Holborn flat made her feel panicky. Didn't she have everything she needed at the safe house? Everything except freedom of movement, and that she could reclaim whenever she felt like it. Not just yet, though. Maybe it would be best to give birth there under proper medical supervision, with the press and the men from EDEN kept safely at bay, and then afterwards she and the baby could leave at their leisure.

But leave to what? She considered this carefully. If everything went to plan she would have at least one theatrical triumph under her belt by then. And it *would* be a triumph, she had never felt more confident of anything in her life. So she would be a single mother *and* an actress. *Ripped!* would lead to bigger and better roles, maybe even movies. Perhaps she could share Phoebe and Maurice's childminders, or persuade her mother to lay off the sauce and behave like a proper grandma instead of Blanche DuBois. And hadn't Belinda already volunteered her services as a babysitter, several times?

Nancy felt bad about Belinda. She could be a pain at times, but she'd always been a good and loyal friend. It had taken her years and a lot of counselling to get over Croydon, and the last thing she'd needed after what had happened there was to stumble headlong into the carnage at the Faraday Clinic. Nancy felt terrible about that. She wished she hadn't got Belinda mixed up in this mess. She would have to work out some way of making it up to her.

*****

'This is serious,' said Bull, but his mouth was twitching, as though he were trying not to smile. 'Try to remember.'

She had just got back from rehearsal and had been looking forward to a nap before supper when he'd asked her to step into the drawing-room. The rehearsal hadn't gone well. She'd forgotten her lines several times, and on each occasion Carlotta had chipped in before she could get them out.

Stay zen, thought Nancy. *Think banana.* Miss Green had helped her come up with a mantra: *banana coconut papaya mango.* She repeated it to herself in times of stress, and it really did calm her down. Losing her temper could have serious consequences, and much as she disliked Carlotta, she didn't wish her physical harm. Well, nothing permanent. Then, too, the essential truths of her character were still eluding her. Who *was* Maggie Crook? What motivated her? What was it about her that made her a survivor, while the others died? Who had made her pregnant, and what had happened to him? She began to construct Maggie's back story in her head. In some respects it was not unlike her own, except that Maggie, being a streetwalker, had very definitely had sex.

The drawing-room was full of overstuffed armchairs. Nancy kicked off her shoes and arranged herself on the sofa, propped against by cushions, feet up on the armrest. Bull stayed standing. Even at a distance of six feet, she could smell the whisky on his breath. She hadn't known him start this early before. He was sweating more than usual, too. She could smell it.

'Have you told me everything, Nancy?'

'Of course,' said Nancy. As usual, she was lying; she'd left out most of what happened in rehearsal, but had no doubt Bull would hear it anyway from Mr. Jones or Mr. Miller. But she never told him what she got up to in her own time - the careful testing of her abilities, talking to the foetus, compiling mental lists of things she needed to watch out for, the caution and the calculation, the planning. She was careful, in Bull's presence, to always appear more airheaded than she really was.

Bull's mouth twitched again. 'Something happened last night.'

Nancy's brain stopped ticking over and snapped to attention. 'I didn't hear anything.'

'I know,' said Bull. 'You were sound asleep.'

'How would you know that?' Nancy locked her door at night. She didn't like the idea of anyone sneaking into her room to look at her as she slept, least of all Bull.

'I was just checking. Someone tried to break in.'

'Who?'

'Delgado's men.' Bull scratched his ear, trying to keep things casual. 'Three of them died.'

She couldn't help herself; she sat up straight and stared at him, aghast. 'You mean you killed them?'

Bull spread his arms. 'Electric fence.'

'Is that even legal?'

'Plenty of warning signs. We can't help it if intruders choose to ignore them. We managed to save a fourth bloke, but he swallowed his tongue.'

Christ almighty, she thought. 'Accidentally or on purpose?'

Bull shook his head again. 'We just wanted to know how they knew you were here.'

Nancy felt revulsion. Once again, it seemed her active participation wasn't required for a slaughter to take place.

Bull looked stern. 'You'd tell me if anyone tried to contact you, wouldn't you?'

Nancy lit a cigarette. 'Of course I would!'

'Not a single one of those goons gets close enough to touch you,' said Bull, chewing his lip. 'And yet they keep on coming...'

His voice died away and he stared past her

shoulder into space. Nancy sat and smoked and waited patiently. She didn't like to disturb him when he drifted off like that. She had a hunch that anyone who took him by surprise risked being karate-chopped to death.

Eventually, he shook his head, as though clearing fog out of his synapses, and asked, 'What do you do to them, Nancy?'

'I wish I knew.'

She didn't tell him that when Mr. Cook had slipped on a boiled potato and dropped the plates he'd been carrying, that had been their doing, hers and the Shrimp's. Or that when Mr. Jones had been distracted by a sudden burst of ear-splitting music from the car radio and slammed the door on his fingers it hadn't been an accident. Or that when Miss Green had got a mild electric shock when she'd tried to turn up the sound system in the exercise room, it was because her bare feet had come into contact with some water Nancy had spilled earlier. It hadn't been a *bad* shock, no more than a tingle, and she'd never intended to hurt Miss Green. It was just practice. But she didn't want Bull knowing about any of this. The less he knew, the better.

For a few seconds, he looked like a man preoccupied with exceedingly weighty matters of life and death, like someone calculating the precise number of bombs required to wipe out a city the size of Dresden. Then, quite unexpectedly, he smiled. 'Whatever you do,' he said, 'it's pretty impressive. But then you're pretty impressive all round, aren't you?'

'I'm really rather ordinary,' said Nancy.

'I've seen what you can do. Chiltern Street, for example.'

'Chiltern Street?' Nancy tilted her head. 'I haven't

been there since...' She tried to work it out. How many months had passed since the Faraday Clinic? It seemed aeons ago now, something that had happened in another lifetime. She remembered his fat woman disguise and felt uneasy. 'You were watching?'

'Watching *over* you. Watching - and waiting to step in if something went wrong.' Bull let out one of his wheezy chuckles. 'That poor bloke you clobbered with the clock. I didn't see that one coming. Neither did he, of course.'

'Out of interest, when did you start following me?'

He dodged the question. 'Just as well you're on *our* side, or we'd be in deep shit. Have you ever tried, you know, experimenting? Trying to channel it?'

Nancy shook her head. 'I wouldn't know where to start.'

'Maybe we could help you there. We could bring in a parapsychologist, someone with practical experience.'

'I'd rather you didn't. Dr. Smith's tests are bad enough.'

'You should think about it,' said Bull. 'It might be useful to have some measure of control when you go into labour.'

*****

Dr. Smith winced as Nancy stubbed out one cigarette and almost immediately lit another. She was stretched out on the examination table like an odalisque on a chaise-longue. An odalisque with a swollen stomach, draped in green.

She placed mental bets as to how long it would

take for him to start complaining. It didn't take long.

'I wish you wouldn't do that,' he sighed. 'It's bad for baby.'

Nancy chortled. She'd been smoking so much even her laughter sounded hard-boiled. 'Nothing is bad for *this* baby.'

Dr. Smith made a huffing noise. 'You're responsible for this,' he said, pointing at the monitor.

What Nancy had originally thought of as a shrimp now bore more resemblance to a tiny kitten. As she eyed it dubiously, she felt a small, convulsive movement inside her and glimpsed a corresponding twitch on the screen. 'It moved!' She balanced her cigarette on the edge of the table and flattened both palms against her stomach, awaiting further activity.

'You see,' crowed Dr. Smith. 'Baby doesn't like the smoke.'

The movement stopped. Disappointed, Nancy picked up her cigarette and took another drag. The kitten kicked out again. Nancy kept smoking steadily, staring intently at the screen, observing every twitch and flutter.

'You're wrong,' she said. 'Kitty loves it when I smoke.'

Dr. Smith scowled, but couldn't deny that the electronic image did indeed appear to be dancing.

'Interesting,' he said, scribbling something on his clipboard. 'Clearly you're beginning to bond.'

'Is it a boy or a girl?'

Dr. Smith adjusted his spectacles and hunched forward until his nose was a few centimetres from the screen. He peered back at her over his shoulder. His face was blurry, as though a giant had picked him up by the scruff of his neck and given him a good shaking. Nancy felt a cold hand work its way into her chest and wrap its icy fingers around her heart. She thought she heard him mutter, 'Let's just hope it's a baby.'

'There's something wrong with the foetus, isn't there.'

But *of course* there was something wrong with the foetus. Hadn't there always been something wrong with it? The way it had implanted itself inside her, for example. She stubbed her cigarette out into a stainless steel bowl.

'Nothing to worry about.' Dr. Smith was now looking decidedly worried. 'Everything seems to be in place.'

If the purpose of a bedside manner was to put patients at their ease, then his was rotten.

*****

'Green suits you,' said Bull, cocking his head like a terrier as she walked into dinner. 'It's the colour of... mystery.'

'The colour of seasickness,' said Nancy.

He poured her a glass of wine. It was just the two of them at table.

'Where is everyone?'

'I gave them the evening off,' said Bull. Then he asked, 'How many weeks is it?'

'Dr. Smith said twenty-five.'

'But...?'

'I think he's wrong. Can't I see a female doctor? Or a midwife? I don't like Dr. Smith very much.'

'He has a lot of experience,' said Bull.

'Not with pregnancies like mine. I'd find it easier

to talk to a female doctor. Dr. Smith's people skills are not great.'

Bull smiled. 'That's true.'

'He makes me nervous.'

Bull's smile disappeared. 'We can't have that. Your welfare is our priority, of course.'

'So you keep telling me,' said Nancy.

'Leave it to me,' said Bull. 'I'll see what I can do.'

Chapter 6
Revelation Man

The Anti-Antichrist, also known as Revelation Man, wore trousers so snug they might as well have been tights. The flowing black hair and Ray-Bans indicated the artist had based their character design on the writer, but had tactfully given him longer legs and broader shoulders. I thought it a misstep on their part to dress him in a T-shirt bearing the letters AA, but otherwise the artwork was nicely done.

I started reading *Revelation Man* with trepidation, prepared to encounter all manner of mutilated lapdog sex, but it turned out to be reassuringly kink-free. Demons were infiltrating the world and assuming enticing disguises to corrupt gullible mortals by tempting them with money, power and sex. Geryon, one of hell's dragons, disguised himself as a baseball star whose loyal following turned their backs on God to worship The Diamond. Kobal's image was beamed out to the nation every day in the bubbly blonde form of a TV chat-show hostess whose fans chanted her name while she humiliated honest guests, while Baal had adopted the persona of a charismatic but depraved Hollywood actor with a sideline in fake environmental causes, and Beelzebub was running for President on a liberal ticket, the only crack in his glamorous alter ego the halo of flies that were forever buzzing around his beautiful face.

Guided by premonitory dreams, the Anti-Antichrist hunted them down, one by one, and tore off their masks in public, exposing the reptilian hideousness beneath to astonished onlookers before beating them up in displays of superpowered fisticuffs and ZAP! POW! KERRUNCH! effects and sending them scurrying back to Hell with their tails, literally, between their legs.

It was absurd, repetitive (oh yawn, yet *another* person in a position of power and influence turns out to be a demon!) but presumably reassuring to readers who believed truth, justice and the American way would always come out on top.

I took *Revelation Man* into the shop and showed it to Alain. He started flicking through with interest, but it didn't take long for enthusiasm to wane.

'This is shite,' he said.

I felt deflated. I'd found the comic diverting, though it probably helped that I was already familiar with the names of the demons and their special characteristics.

I asked, 'Have you ever come across this writer before?'

Alain checked the credits. 'Nah. You do realise this is some sort of fundamentalist Republican pro-America propaganda? You know there's a whole Christian-backed film industry churning out bad movies about the Apocalypse and the Antichrist? Probably the same crew. Trying to get in with the kids. But it's reactionary junk.' He grinned at me. 'I thought you'd left all that behind you.'

'This isn't the same thing!' The words came out more vehemently than intended.

'Do you want to talk about it?'

'About what?'

'Well, you know.' Alain shrugged. 'Everything that's going on in your life. I haven't seen your fancy man in here lately. Have you two broken up?'

'Not that I'm aware of,' I snapped. For a moment, I was tempted to tell him what I knew about the author of the comic, but before I could start he'd launched into one of his monologues.

'Let me show you some good stuff. Have you read *The Creep*? Right up your street, Belinda. What about *The Evil Spinsters*? That's brilliant, really subversive. Or *Baku the Nightmare Eater*...' And he was off, and I zoned out.

*****

Two days later, I was manning the till when someone slapped a copy of *Natural Disasters and Their Consequences* down on the counter, harder than was necessary. I looked up and there he was, Revelation Man himself, an I HEART LONDON badge pinned to his charcoal grey lapel. My heart did a triple-flip.

Jules Delgado smiled pleasantly, and said, 'I could strangle you.'

My mouth opened and closed several times before I managed to say, 'It's not my fault you jumped to conclusions.'

'You were in her apartment.'

'So were you.' The cash-desk was between us, but I kept my hand in my jacket pocket and whispered, 'I have a knife.' I didn't have a knife, just a bus-pass. There were a dozen customers in the shop, some browsing within arm's reach, so I didn't think he was going to strangle me in such a public place. Not that being surrounded by witnesses had ever stopped any of the men in grey launching themselves at Nancy.

Alain came up behind me. 'You all right? You want me to kick him out?'

Clearly my body language - crouched behind the cash register, eyes narrowed, groping for the scissors - was conveying the message that I considered myself in deadly peril. I asked Alain if he could postpone his lunch break and stick around for a bit. He nodded and, apparently having misheard, immediately disappeared into the office. I watched in mute shock as the door closed behind him.

'Relax,' said Delgado. 'You're more use to me alive, *Belinda Pringle*. You see? I know your real name.'

'I never pretended it was anything else.'

I didn't relax, but unclenched a bit and removed my hand from my pocket. Delgado was smiling, but I didn't trust him. He put his elbows on the counter and leant towards me.

'That's close enough,' I said.

'I don't bite.'

'No, you get other people to do it for you. Like at the clinic. Thank you *so much* for giving me nightmares for the rest of my life.'

He tilted his head. 'How so?'

'One doctor, one nurse and one anaesthetist,' I said, thinking it sounded like the start of a smutty music hall joke.

'The Baby Killer Bloodbath?'

'You didn't have to *kill* them!'

'Why would I do that?'

'Why would you want to hammer Chihuahua heads into your mother's eye sockets?'

I sensed a rustling nearby. Several browsers were trying not to eavesdrop. I could see another customer hanging back, wanting to pay for his book, but reluctant to interrupt such a chummy tête-à-tête.

'I was yanking your chain, Pringle,' Delgado said. 'I love dogs. Anyway a Chihuahua would never fit into a human eye socket.'

'But its *head*,' I said, sounding more anguished than I'd intended.

He burst out laughing. 'Not even a head. Have you ever even *seen* a Chihuahua? Even the teacup variety isn't *that* tiny. I spun you a yarn, and you fell for it.'

I felt stupid. All these weeks of lurid imaginings, and I'd been grossed out for nothing.

'Why would you *do* that?'

'I don't know, Pringle. Maybe your face. It's just begging to be bamboozled.'

'Hey, *I'm* not the one who mistook me for Nancy.'

He snapped his fingers. 'Touché! I like your spirit. But I'll tell you this, I was nowhere near the clinic when that shit went down. That's not my style, Pringle. I'm disappointed... *deeply* disappointed you thought it was. Why would I want to interrupt a procedure that would have solved all our problems?'

I squinted at him sceptically. 'Then who...?'

He shrugged. 'Suicide?'

That didn't seem likely. I tried to think back to that black hole of horror, but the attempt nearly made me retch. I swayed, and had to grab the counter to keep my balance.

'Steady on,' said Delgado, taking a step back.

'I'm sorry, it's just...'

I realised I'd erected such a heavy mental block

around the events at the clinic that any further attempt to circumvent it would likely result in a great deal of physical unpleasantness.

Delgado was peering at me curiously. 'You OK there, Pringle?'

First Alain, now Delgado: all the wrong people were concerned for my wellbeing. Where was Lars when I needed him?

'Excuse me,' said the customer with the book. 'Can I just... nip in here and pay for this?'

I took his money, rang up the sale and bagged the purchase. The buyer snatched it up and darted away as though he thought I might projectile-vomit over him. I took advantage of the pause to gather my wits and take a sip of water from the bottle I kept on the shelf under the cash-desk.

'How did you find me anyway?'

'Saw you in a dream. You were surrounded by books.'

I snorted. 'That could have been anywhere.'

'It wasn't hard. We have resources.'

'By *we* you mean...?'

'The Agency.'

My interest was piqued. 'You're with a publishing group?'

He sighed. 'Also known as The Company.'

I fixed him with my hardest stare, trying to work out if he were pulling my leg again. 'I'm not going to tell you where Nancy is.'

'Honey, you don't *know* where she is. But maybe we could pool our resources.'

'If you really were with an agency, you wouldn't need my help. But what's the point? You know you can't touch her anyway.'

Delgado laughed again, showing the gold in his teeth. 'Plan B,' he said. 'There is always a Plan B. Sometimes a Plan C as well. There's an established protocol for dealing with cases such as this.'

'Cases such as...? There's more than one?'

'You surely don't think the Antichrist would put all his eggs in one basket? Or, you know, sperm. Of course Nancy isn't the first.'

I gawped at him. It had never occurred to me that my friend's situation might not be unique. 'What happened to the others?'

He shook his head so ruefully I wished I'd never asked. 'Passed on, mostly. Some by their own hand.'

I breathed out, slowly. 'I'm guessing your publishing company mopped up the rest.'

'I wouldn't put it like that.'

'How *would* you put it?'

'Let's just say the unborn children weren't equipped with the same level of awareness as Nancy's. It hasn't always been easy to distinguish between genuine misunderstandings and authentic cases which hadn't learnt how to defend themselves. Regrettable, of course, but better to err on the side of caution than sit back and twiddle our thumbs while the human race faces extinction.'

I wished Alain were there to hear this. 'You murdered them!'

'No! There have been... accidents. Several survived and we're monitoring their progress.'

'You mean you've got them stashed in a bunker under the Nevada Desert.'

He shook his head again. 'You still don't

understand. If even one of these pregnancies is allowed to come to term, we may as well say hello to the Four Horsemen.'

'Hello, Conquest!' I said. 'Hi there War, Famine, Death, how's it hanging?'

He looked at me sideways. 'Maybe not literally.'

Strange as it may seem, Delgado was winning me over; he was using his smile a lot, and staring directly into my eyes. How could I ever have taken that gruesome monologue seriously? No wonder it had freaked me out - he'd been *trying* to spook me.

'So what are you going to do now?' I asked him.

'I was thinking the Natural History Museum. I hear they have a real dinosaur.'

'No, what are you going to do about *Nancy?*'

'We watch and we wait.'

'For what?'

He grinned, showing his gold crowns. 'We are not the only players in this game. Sooner or later, someone will make a move.'

'I am not a player!'

He grinned again. 'Oh, but you are, Pringle. You're a *very important* player. I don't think you realise how important you are. You're Nancy's friend, right?'

'Best friend,' I said. 'I'm the only person she really trusts.' That might have been a slight exaggeration, but I didn't see the harm in it. I was talking myself up. How could I have known it would come back to bite me on the bum?

'Then you're important,' said Delgado.

The truth dawned. 'You already know where she is. But you can't get to her.'

'No-one can get to her.'

'Why not? Is she locked up in the Tower of London?'

'I just love your crazy Beefeaters! And how about those ravens?' Delgado grinned like a big kid, and gave me a mock salute as he turned towards the exit. 'Till the next time, Pringle. And don't do anything dumb. We're watching you.'

'No, wait,' I said. But he was gone.

On cue, Alain emerged from the office. I scolded him for having left me at the mercy of my visitor, but without much conviction. The encounter with Delgado hadn't gone as horribly as I'd feared. He hadn't tried to strangle me. And if he'd found out where Nancy was hiding, then I didn't see why I couldn't do the same.

Alain shook his head in disbelief. 'First Clark Kent, now this creepy male model.'

'He's not creepy,' I said.

'How do you do it, Belinda? I had no idea you were such a dude magnet.'

'I'm not,' I said, but couldn't help smiling. Lars may have been neglecting me, but perhaps Delgado could fill that man-shaped gap in my life. Just as long as he didn't start telling freaky stories again.

It was only later, when I'd gone to bed and was lying there, trying and failing to fall asleep, that I started thinking about the clinic massacre again - not the gory details so much as the big picture. If Delgado hadn't done it, who had? Or maybe it *had* been him, even if I couldn't work out what his motive might have been. I tried to dig back into my memory for clues, but all I came up with were early warning signals. DANGER! DO NOT PASS THIS POINT UNLESS YOU WANT TO VOMIT UP YOUR ENTRAILS.

*****

I called up Les Six's agent to ask where they were rehearsing the Jack the Ripper musical. I was kept on hold for ten minutes, then passed from one extension to another before someone finally told me I was wasting my time. I would just have to get in touch with Six some other way. I remembered Marnie Cardew saying she'd seen him in the Rue Bar, which seemed as good a place as any to start.

I found a picture of Six in the arts diary pages of the *Evening Dribbler;* the camera had been focused on his companion's cleavage, so his face was blurred, but I reasoned there couldn't be *that* many bald men in the Rue Bar at any given moment. And so I sat there night after night, quaffing overpriced Beaujolais. I was beginning to think it was a waste of time and money when I finally spotted what I'd been looking for: light from the ceiling spots bouncing off a shiny scalp as its owner wove his way through the rabble.

Les Six! No mistaking him. He was accompanied by a brunette so far out of his league she had to be an actress who wanted a role in his play. I switched from Beaujolais to mineral water and manoeuvred myself into a better vantage point. Les and his companion guzzled champagne and nuzzled each other's ears till two in the morning, when they staggered outside to get a taxi. While the brunette was struggling to clamber into the back without exposing her crotch, Les Six dipped his head at the driver's window. I managed to saunter past just in time to hear an address.

Which was how I ended up in Chepstow Villas at

eight-thirty in the morning, in a cab parked just down the road from Six's digs, squirming with anxiety as the counter racked up an increasingly alarming sum and the driver kept threatening to drive off because he didn't want to get a ticket. I promised to pay it if he did, but he didn't seem reassured. After one hour and twenty minutes of fractious bargaining, I saw Six and the brunette emerge and climb into a Skoda. We followed them across London to Clerkenwell Green. It cost me a small fortune in fare, but I was counting on my scoop to reimburse me many times over.

*****

It was an old industrial building, repurposed to serve Clerkenwell's hip new demographic. The brass plate on the wall was engraved with the words, 'The Pickle Factory'. Blocking the door was a beefy guy in a battered leather jacket.

'So this is where we're rehearsing,' I said.

Leather Jacket nodded, but not to me. I looked back over my shoulder and saw he'd been signalling to a car on the far side of the green. 'What's up?'

'Jack the Ripper?'

'No Jack the Ripper here,' said Leather Jacket. His voice was so basso profondo I could feel it rumbling up through my feet.

'Of course there's no Jack the Ripper *here*,' I said. 'It's a *play*.'

Someone came up behind me and apologised as he squeezed past. The face was vaguely familiar, the complexion ruddy. Without a word, Leather Jacket opened the door and Redface vanished inside. The door swung shut again, though not before I'd glimpsed the bottom of a staircase.

Belatedly, I realised where I'd seen the face before. 'Oh my God, that's Rod Carpenter!' I said, trying to follow him inside, but Leather Jacket had wedged himself in the doorway again.

'Run along now.'

Being told to 'run along', as though I were some sort of troublesome street urchin, made my blood boil. 'I'm the historical adviser! Les Six will give you hell when he hears you wouldn't let me in!'

'Tell you what,' said Leather Jacket. 'Give us your name and number, and if I ever meet someone called... What was it? El Sixo? I'll tell him you swung by.'

He extracted a small black notebook and Biro from one of his pockets and handed them to me. The notebook felt soft and moist, as though it had been thoroughly kneaded. The inside was filled with indecipherable scribble and doodles of big-breasted women; on the first free page I could find I printed GABRIELLE DE ROSPIN and the phone number of the bookshop, and handed it back, with no real hope the number would ever find its way to Six. Why hadn't I accosted him in the Rue Bar when I'd had the chance? Oh yes, because he and the hot brunette had had eyes only for each other and I couldn't think of any reason why he might want to transfer his attention to the likes of me. My lack of self-esteem would be the death of me yet.

But at least now I knew where he was to be found, and that Rod Carpenter was in the play. I was due at the shop, but all I had to do was swing past the Pickle Factory later on, or the next day, and check out the rest of the cast as they arrived or left. I felt impatient, but hopeful. I was getting closer to Nancy, I could feel it.

*****

I rearranged my schedule, quashed the usual complaints from Elspeth and Howard that I was wrecking their social lives, and asked Alain if I could borrow his Beetle, with its handy Islington parking permit. He agreed in exchange for a blow-job which I had no intention of ever giving him, and I knew he knew that.

'You're lucky I fancy you,' he said with the sort of insouciance that only someone who didn't fancy me could have summoned.

'Luck has nothing to do with it,' I said. 'I'm just highly skilled at manipulating people.'

Alain snorted with derisive laughter, making three of the browsers in the comic book section look round defensively. 'Keep telling yourself that, darling.'

Sometimes I found myself wishing Alain were more dynamic. We got along well enough, but his lack of ambition was off-putting. Alain actually *enjoyed* working in the bookshop and couldn't imagine doing anything else. 'It's not like manual labour,' he said. 'Plus I'm surrounded by books all day. What's not to like?'

'You've never felt the urge to, you know, actually *write* one?'

He looked at me as though I were mentally defective. 'What would I write about? Working here? You think anyone wants to read about working in a bookshop?'

'It doesn't have to be set in a bookshop. You could write about superheroes.'

He laughed. 'I'll leave the creativity to you, Belinda. How's your magnum opus?'

'Coming along,' I said. 'One day soon you'll be inviting me back to sign copies.'

*****

It was raining as I parked on the far side of the green, armed with binoculars and a bagful of Viennoiserie. I'd munched my way through several croissants before I spotted Jasper Andrews, whom I knew from his appearances on TV panel shows. He rolled up with a mousy girl he'd obviously spent the night with. I wondered if she were in the play too, or just a groupie. I opened my journal and started a neat list.

09h47: Leather Jacket in position
10h03: Jasper Andrews + Miss Mouse
10h06: Les Six + Rue Bar brunette
10h07: Busty girl in brown leather jacket
10h11: Creepy old man in a fedora, looks like he should be playing Dracula
10h17: Skinny black guy with ponytail
10h18: Rod Carpenter

And so on. The other arrivals included a mumsy woman whose face looked familiar, an ethereal waif with crimped blonde hair, and a poseur in a paisley cravat.

At 10h35, just as I was starting to think Nancy would never show, a black Mercedes with tinted windows drew up. Two rugby players in suits got out and checked the perimeter, or whatever it was those types do - not very thoroughly, as it turned out, as neither of them noticed me. Maybe they just weren't expecting a threat in a Beetle, or maybe I was wrapped in my cloak of invisibility again.

Then one of them opened the back door and Nancy climbed out. One of the rugby players offered her his arm; it took effort for her to straighten up. He held an umbrella over her head for the dozen or so steps she had to take between the car and the door. There was no hiding it now; she was definitely pregnant. She was wearing a pale blue linen dress and matching coat, not her usual style at all; she looked like an elegant throwback to another era, Jackie Kennedy stepping out for a lunch date. But there was another difference I spied through the binoculars: her face. She looked more, I don't know, *intrepid*. Like a glamorous explorer embarking on an expedition into uncharted territory. The thought of her setting out without me gave me a hollowed-out feeling in my abdomen.

Leather Jacket opened the door and she went in. Rugby Player Number One climbed back into the driver's seat of the Mercedes and drove off. Rugby Player Number Two stopped to say a few words to Leather Jacket before following Nancy into the building, and the door closed behind him.

I had mixed feelings. I'd expected Nancy to be a mess. I'd assumed she would need my help, but the Nancy I'd seen had been in control; her burly escorts were there to do her bidding, and not the other way round. I wondered if she'd become the mistress of a wealthy crime lord. There was no indication that she was being held against her will, unless she was suffering from Stockholm Syndrome and had bonded with her captors. What could I possibly offer that she wasn't already getting from whoever was providing her with food, shelter and security?

There was one late arrival: a lanky, intense type who looked dishevelled and out of breath, probably because he'd been running. Leather Jacket let him in and took a good look around before locking the door and taking up position in front of it again.

*****

Subject to shifts at work and Alain's willingness to let me dictate the staff timetable, I staked out the Pickle Factory, on and off, for nearly a fortnight - sometimes in the morning, sometimes the end of the the afternoon. One morning no-one turned up at all. I ate a lot of croissants that day. Another time, everyone turned up except Nancy. But otherwise, I would watch as she climbed in or out of the Mercedes, each time looking as though she'd raided another outfit from Doris Day's wardrobe. But her face was radiant, and her hair was lustrous again. I guessed the vomiting phase was over.

Where was she staying? I already knew she hadn't returned to Natal Mansions. On my last visit I'd fiddled around for ages, trying to unlock the door, until a bearded man flung it open and told me to fuck off, the previous tenant had moved out, he was fed up with being pestered and had changed the lock. A couple of times I tried to tail the Mercedes, but I was too cautious a driver to be much good at following cars in the London traffic. The first time they got away from me in Haringey, the second time Tufnell Park. From what I saw of the route, they changed it every day, as if they suspected someone might try to follow them, though I don't think they ever spotted me.

*****

Delgado kept coming into the shop. I still trusted him about as much as I would have trusted a poisonous snake, but he no longer seemed threatening; in fact I almost came to look on him as a friend whose visits added a touch of colour to the dull routine. He didn't always make direct contact, but sometimes I'd see him ostentatiously pretending to peruse *Ding an Sich for Dummies* or *The Secret History of Cheese*, as though he thought that might amuse me. (It did.) Once I spotted him perched on a kick-stool in the children's section with *A Child's Guide to the Cosmos* open on his knees. He caught me looking and waved, and I waved back.

'That guy really likes you,' said Alain.

'He's waiting to get me on my own so he can kill me,' I said.

Alain sniggered. 'You really know how to pick them. How's Mr. Universe, by the way?'

'He's in Shanghai,' I said, though I was no longer sure if this were so. I hadn't heard from Lars since we'd spent a rollicking evening in the wine bar, mispronouncing lines from his Mandarin phrasebook - and I didn't think business trips lasted *that* long. I wondered if he'd dumped me and was too lily-livered to say so to my face. But a part of me had been expecting something like this to happen ever since we'd first got together. After all, what did I have to offer apart from no-strings sex and a Scrabble board?

Delgado didn't strike me as a Scrabble person. Whenever we talked, he would steer the subject into geopolitics, trying to make me see the bigger picture, but I would zone out and start thinking about biscuits, or ponies. Once he showed me a set of postcards of British kings and queens he'd bought from the National Gallery gift shop, and was shocked when I told him I was a republican. He was no more my type than Lars had been, but at least he had a creative streak, even if it was currently being misdirected. When I told him I'd read *Revelation Man*, he tried to act casual, but I could see he was pleased. 'What did you think?'

'Not really a comic, is it,' I said. 'More like Fundamentalist pro-America propaganda in graphic novel form.'

I couldn't see his eyes because of the sunglasses, but his mouth twitched as though he were trying not to let it crumple, and I regretted my harshness. He was probably a stone-cold killer, or, at the very least, some sort of evil spymaster, but now here I was, worrying in case I'd hurt his feelings. I tried to think of something positive to say. 'I thought the evil chat show hostess was cool.'

He brightened up, or his mouth did. 'You did? I think she's cool too. How about Beelzebub? Too on the nose?'

At least we had one interest in common. We started nattering away about his demons. Drawing on my extensive knowledge of the subject, I gave him tips for future volumes, as well as the names of some minor entities I thought he might find useful. He nodded enthusiastically and made a note of Dagon, Mulciber and Urakabarameel as subjects for further research. Anyone eavesdropping would have assumed we were the best of chums.

274

*****

It was while I was staking out the Pickle Factory that Verity Wilson suddenly went from playing hard to get to someone I couldn't get off my back, not just finally returning my calls but bombarding me with unsolicited ones. It might have had something to do with my having bragged that I was seeing Nancy again. Which wasn't a lie, technically.

I decided to ask for more money this time, and maybe a co-credit. I still wanted my real name kept out of it, but maybe I could persuade Wilson to take 'Gabrielle de Rospin' under her wing, as an apprentice.

'So you don't actually know where she is,' said Wilson, already looking bored.

'I do, kind of,' I said.

'Not spoken?'

'She has bodyguards.'

Wilson looked interested again. 'Oh yes? Why?'

'I guess so she doesn't get attacked by any more men in grey.'

'Ah yes, the grey suit guys,' said Wilson, looking sceptical again. 'Ever seen one?'

This time we weren't in the Dog Kennel but the Sheep Dip, though there wasn't a lot to choose between them; just another godforsaken dive where the air had been replaced by cigarette smoke, and the sound set to 7.5 on the Richter Scale. This time I'd known better than to wear mascara. It didn't stop my eyes from watering, but at least I didn't end up with black streaks all down my face.

I told her I hadn't actually *seen* any of the regular

men in grey. But pride impelled me to divulge that I had met their leader, that I was in fact *friends* with him. Wilson stroked her chin thoughtfully, as though she thought there might be the beginnings of a beard sprouting there.

'Really? And can I touch him?'

Touch him? Did she mean *get in touch* with him? Or did she want to jab him with her finger, maybe to confirm he wasn't a figment of my imagination? I already regretted having brought Delgado's name up. He'd been my secret weapon, one I ought to have kept to myself, but now I'd let the cat out of the bag and it was running around miaowing and impossible to stuff back in.

'He's not an easy man to touch,' I said.

'Maybe reward,' she said, eyeing me slyly.

A glowing vision of the Antonius Block dining table floated into my head like the holy hallucination of a redwood relic, and I said, 'I guess I might be able to fix up a meeting.'

*****

Whereas Verity Wilson favoured basement dives, Jules Delgado preferred to drink as near to the clouds as possible, which is why the three of us ended up in The Penthouse Bar in Park Lane.

'So this is London,' he said, gazing out of the huge window at the lights laid out below in a series of mystical configurations that no modern architect could have been aware of. Though I wasn't sure how much of the view Delgado could actually see, because though it was dark outside and the lighting in the bar was fashionably dim, he was still wearing his Ray-Bans.

'See my place from here,' said Wilson, pointing east. 'Lights on, nobody home.'

I started to feel dizzy, so turned my back on the window to face my drinking companions, who seemed to be getting along like a house on fire. He was sipping mineral water with a twist of lemon and a dash of bitters, Wilson was halfway through her second Mojito, and I'd plumped for a Chocolate Martini. It wasn't a smart choice; after only a couple of sips it wasn't just the view that was making my head spin.

'I saw you with your brothers in a dream,' Delgado said to Wilson, removing his sunglasses so she could get a good look at his orange nebulae. 'You were emitting a heavenly aura, like a seraph.' I tried not to snigger, but Wilson was gazing back at him, rapt.

I butted into their mutual admiration society. 'Where's your photographer friend?' I'd thought the plan had been for Clive Mengers to get some pictures of Delgado to add verisimilitude to our story. I was calling it 'our story' now, though Wilson had yet to give any sign she was willing to collaborate.

'Bognor Regis, taking photos of marmots.'

'But why?' We were talking about what looked set to be the biggest story of her career, and her photographer was off taking pictures of critters.

'Cute animals in demand,' she said. 'Offset the misery.'

I huffed. 'There'll be more money in Nancy's story.'

Wilson gave me an accusing look. 'Might, if we knew where she was.'

Delgado looked at her with fresh interest. 'What would you give?'

'What you want?' And there passed between them another look of complicity from which I was excluded.

'I know where she is,' I said, trying to reclaim the floor.

'So spill,' said Wilson, offering Delgado a cigarette. He shook his head and brought out one of his noxious cigars. The sudden cloud of smoke made me cough as I told them about the rehearsals, making sure not to divulge the location.

'Surrounded by people?' asked Wilson.

'Surrounded by *actors*,' I said. Delgado listened politely as I babbled about Rod Carpenter and Jasper Andrews and the woman I had finally identified as Bunty Mackay - names that would have been meaningless to anyone not weaned on British TV.

And then he calmly trumped me. 'I know where she goes at night.'

Wilson promptly lost interest in my rollcall of minor celebrity and turned her back on me.

'How do you know?' I demanded, furious he hadn't told me earlier.

'We have a contact at the Hutch,' said Delgado.

'You never told me that!'

He winked. 'It's secret.'

'The spooks have her?' said Wilson.

'Not exactly. Outfit called ComSec. Independent operators, privately funded.' He shook his head in disgust. 'No accountability, none at all; three of our guys got fried and they just covered it up.'

I wasn't sure what he meant, and neither - judging by her expression - did Wilson. He noticed her bafflement and added, 'Electrocuted.'

'I told you!' I said. 'Nancy's untouchable.'

Delgado shook his head. 'Electric fence.'

'Where?' asked Wilson.

'Billionaire Boulevard full of tunnelled-out basements. Whole street heaving with private security, but this place makes them look like amateurs. Cameras, dogs, fences, the whole enchilada. We've been calling it the Corleone Compound.'

'But Nancy could walk away any time she wants, and they wouldn't be able to stop her,' I said.

'Maybe she doesn't want to.'

'Why wouldn't she?' My voice had shot up a couple of octaves. The idea that Nancy was free to come and go as she pleased, yet still couldn't be bothered to get in touch with me, was more than I could bear. I preferred to think she was being held against her will.

'Comfort? Security?' said Wilson. 'Not having to deal with the world? We did a piece on the Alhambra Whistleblower last year; said was like luxury hotel he never wanted to leave.' Out of the corner of my eye, I saw her shift her chair closer to Delgado's. Her fingers brushed his arm. He pretended not to notice. 'Won press award for that,' she added, fluttering her lashes.

'We need to get a message to Nancy,' said Delgado. 'Let her know she's not as safe as she thinks.'

'So she'll step outside the fence and you can get another shot at her?' I sneered.

Delgado shook his head again. 'We want to work *with* Nancy, not against her. Those people taking care of her? They're dangerous.'

'Nancy can take care of herself,' I said. 'Anyone tries to harm her, they're toast.'

Delgado pointed his sunglasses at me. 'They have no intention of harming the *baby*. They'll keep the *baby* safe.'

Wilson gasped. 'So as soon it's born...?'

Delgado nodded. 'There'll no longer have any reason to keep the mother around.'

'So they'll let her go then?' I said brightly.

Delgado and Wilson looked at me as though I'd said something incredibly stupid.

'What?' I said.

Chapter 7
Fan Mail

While they were all waiting for Bones to come back from the bathroom, Jet Coleman drew Nancy to one side. He was the touchy-feely type, always hugging, so neither she nor anyone else thought it odd when he snuggled up to her and whispered in her ear. People were pretending not to look at them. She felt strangely turned on.

'Fan mail,' he whispered. 'Not from me, though I *am* your biggest fan.' He pressed a scrap of folded paper into her palm. 'Hot dude last night,' he murmured before disentangling himself.

Nancy closed her hand around the paper, and stole a glance at Mr. Jones, who was on the other side of the room, pretending to flick through *Aloha!* Ever vigilant, he sensed her attention on him and looked up. She waved. He raised an eyebrow and went back to pretending to look at the magazine.

Using her script as a shield, she unfolded the message.

WATCH OUT NANCY ~~THE'RE~~ *THEYRE GOING TO KILL YOU. DONT WORRY WELL GET YOU OUT OF THEYRE. THE SECRET PASSWORD IS* ~~CHIWAHWAH~~ ~~CHEWAWA~~ *CHIHUAHUA. BP. PS DESTORY THIS.*

Nancy lit a cigarette with a match, then discreetly held

the tip of the flame to the edge of the paper and ground out the smouldering remains in the ashtray.

BP? There was only one BP she could think of. Belinda Pringle! But the messy scrawl hadn't been anything like Belinda's handwriting. Belinda never made spelling mistakes. Maybe she had dictated it, and the note had been written by someone else. But who?

*****

That night, Nancy lay awake and fretted about the secret message. She'd memorised the contents, but wished she hadn't been so quick to burn it. Perhaps there had been clues that she'd missed. Or might it be a trap set by ComSec to make her tip her hand?

'Chihuahua,' she whispered, rolling the word around her mouth. 'Chihuahua...' She vaguely recalled someone talking about Chihuahuas in the recent past, but couldn't remember who.

Finally, she gave up trying to sleep, and studied her script. She knew all her lines now, but Jasper liked to improvise. She suspected it was a deliberate ploy to throw her off balance, and started thinking up strategies to turn his own impro against him. *And if those fail, I could always give him a nosebleed.* The wickedness of the thought make her chuckle softly. Of course she would never give anyone a nosebleed *deliberately*, but that didn't mean she was never tempted to make Jack Banner fall over, just to wipe that snooty expression off his face, or to give Carlotta her period early.

It was two in the morning. Normally she was asleep by now, but Kitty was more skittish than usual. Nancy lit a cigarette. Her first intake of smoke was rewarded by the usual reaction in her belly. But this time, the activity continued even after she'd smoked the cigarette all the way down and stubbed it out. It felt as though a small but perfectly formed footballer were trying to kick its way out of her, but this was more violent than usual. Each kick was making her her flinch. Was this normal? Surely she couldn't be going into labour already? Her hand hovered over the bedside telephone. She'd been told to call Miss Taylor at the slightest hint of anything unusual.

But instinct stopped her from picking up the receiver. Instead, she stood up and began to pace up and down. The kicking didn't stop, but she noticed a pattern emerging. Whenever she walked towards the door, the kicking died down. But as soon as she turned away from it, it started up again. She turned back towards the door. Blessed peace.

You want to go for a stroll? Is that what you want, you little fucker?

She drifted out on to the landing, a big-bellied wraith in a floaty white nightgown, wafting through patches of moonlight. Prodded along the hallway, in fits and starts, she padded on bare feet which left slight traces on the wooden floor - impressions so faint that within seconds of her passing they'd disappeared, like footprints washed away by the tide. Apart from the ticking of a clock and the faint fluttering of a moth, the air was still. She smelt antiseptic beneath the omnipresent furniture polish; she'd complained about the smelliness of some of the household products they'd been using, and they'd been replaced with other, less malodorous ones, but the stink of polish was still disagreeable. There was no sound from Miss Taylor's bedroom, along the hallway, but, as usual, Nancy had the sensation of being watched. She couldn't actually *see* any cameras, and Bull and Miss Taylor had vehemently denied their existence, but she had no doubt they were there. She wondered who was watching her now. She waved at the wall, just in case. *Hey, nothing to see here. Just going for a stroll.* Nothing was stirring. She wasn't fooled, though. Mr. Jones and Mr. Miller and Mr. Carter, or others like them, were somewhere, listening, always on alert, making sure no-one could slip through the protective net. She thought about the message again. Maybe it wasn't what was *outside* the net she ought to be concerned about. Maybe Jules Delgado was the least of her worries.

She passed the lift, which would have made too much noise, and paused at the top of the staircase until another flurry of kicks nudged her down to the floor below. On the second floor landing, her ears picked up a murmur of voices from the medical suite. What was Death-Camp Doctor up to at this hour? The door was propped open, so she slipped inside. The consulting room was deserted; the voices were coming from the inner office. She floated towards the sound.

'Of course it's fashionable, but many mothers choose not to, and in fact, there are innumerable advantages to bottle-feeding.' She wasn't surprised to hear Dr. Smith, and she recognised the other voice as soon as the speaker opened his mouth.

'The chief one being that the presence of the mother isn't required,' said Bull.

'There you have it.'

Nancy suddenly felt an urge to sit down, but the nearest chair was on the other side of the room. She leant against the wall and prayed her legs wouldn't give way.

'We're running out of time,' said Bull.

'Foetuses have been known to survive from as little as twenty weeks,' said Dr. Smith. 'But any normal baby delivered so prematurely would be dangerously underweight, at risk from infection. At the very least it would have to be kept in an incubator, possibly for several months.'

'But we're not talking about a normal baby, are we, Doc?' Nancy could almost hear the slow grin spreading across Bull's face. 'We're not even talking about a *baby*, in the generally accepted sense of the term. We're talking about a creature with such an overwhelming ability to survive that anyone who approaches it with harmful intent is instantly spifflicated.'

There was a pause. Nancy's breathing was so loud in her own ears she thought the men would surely hear it. Bull spoke again: 'I don't think such a creature would need respiratory support, do you?'

There was a short, sharp report which might have been somebody clapping his hands together.

'So long as you understand I won't be present at the delivery. It's in my contract. Taylor or Wilson can look after it. I daresay there's less of a risk at this stage, but after what happened at the Faraday...'

'Let the girls do the hazardous work, of course. Don't worry, Doc, we'll keep you clear of the danger zone.'

Bull sounded affable, though Nancy thought she detected an undercurrent of contempt.

'We need to take the initiative before things fall apart,' said Dr. Smith. 'I don't care for her attitude at all.

She's much too independent, and you should restrict her access to the library; she could be picking up ideas.'

'Isn't that what libraries are for?'

'And you need to run another mole-hunt. These leaks could compromise everything we've achieved.'

'Ain't no tattletale in my department, I can promise you that. But I agree, the sooner we can implement the transfer of funds so we can cancel the cheque, the better. If she makes up her mind to leave, there's no guarantee we'll be able to hold her.'

The switch to banking terminology threw Nancy for a loop. She'd always thought Bull looked a bit like a bank manager, but now he was even starting to talk like one.

'You should stop her going out and seeing those *people*,' said Dr. Smith. 'I told you it would be a mistake to let her come and go as she pleases.'

'You forget who we're dealing with,' said Bull, and Nancy thought she could detect admiration in his voice. Or maybe this was just wishful thinking on her part; despite her mistrust of Bull, she found herself wanting his approval and realised belatedly this had probably been his strategy all along. He'd been presenting himself as a father figure, no doubt knowing all about how useless her real father had been in that respect.

'That play is the reason she agreed to come her in the first place. If we tried to take it away from her, who knows how she might react? Would you want to take the risk? No, I didn't think so. You've never seen her in action, have you, Doc? Take my word for it, you don't want to get on her bad side.'

There was a pause, and then he added, 'But we do need a completion date.'

Nancy could almost hear the abacus clicking in Dr. Smith's brain. At last he delivered his verdict. 'Three weeks should give us time to prepare.'

'Make that four,' said Bull. 'Let her have her first night. Let's aim for the thirty-first, in fact. Be a nice way to usher in the new century.'

'The longer we put it off, the more dangerous she'll be,' said Dr. Smith.

'The longer we put it off the more *pregnant* she'll be,' said Bull, 'and that can only be to our advantage.'

This time, there was definitely a note of contempt in his voice as he added, 'Wipe your nose, Doc.'

*****

Nancy wasn't sure how she got back to her room. She lay on the bed, chewing at what had once been, thanks to Miss Green's administrations, perfectly manicured nails. Kitty had quietened down, but Nancy's mind was in turmoil. It had taken less than twenty minutes for her world to crumble. All those plans she'd been making, all her hopes for the play, all that calculation and caution - it had all been for nothing. BP's note had been right; she was in danger here. Bull and Dr. Smith had no intention of allowing her to run this show. Four weeks. *Four weeks.* Much too early; she would be nowhere near the due date. They were going to induce labour. Or maybe they would slice her open and go straight in.

What had she expected? A pat on the back and a bouquet of roses? They couldn't touch her while she was pregnant, that much she knew. But what about *after* the birth? She and Kitty would no longer be a team; they'd be two separate entities. What if Kitty was whisked away from her as soon as she was born, with no time for them to bond? No, wait, hadn't they *already* been bonding for the last few months? But would that be enough?

They think I'm expendable, thought Nancy. Could ComSec really make her disappear, just like that? Wouldn't Les Six kick up a fuss if he had to replace yet another leading lady? And wouldn't her friends alert the police if she went missing? Oh that's right, they all thought she was in Paris, or doing the Grand Tour of Europe. And in her one phone call to Maurice, her only chance to ask for help, she'd told him she was fine. Now it would be ages before anyone started wondering what had happened to her, and by then it would be too late. Carlotta would step into the starring role with a pussycat grin on her face, life would go on, and no-one would give a damn. She could already see the headlines. BABY KILLER BLOODBATH ACTRESS VANISHES WITHOUT TRACE. Then maybe, a few weeks later, 'I KILLED THEM ALL!' CRACKED ACTRESS CONFESSES TO CLINIC MASSACRE IN SUICIDE NOTE BEFORE TAKING FATAL PLUNGE OFF BRIDGE. It wouldn't be so difficult to arrange, not for someone like Bull. They'd cover it up the way they'd covered up the deaths of the men in grey and the intruders on the electric fence.

She ought to have known better. Never trust a man who reminded you of one of the male models on the cover of a vintage knitting pattern.

She felt Kitty lash out, and a packet of cigarettes. fell off the bedside table. Just as well no-one was in range. She took a deep breath, letting the air fill her lungs, as Miss Green had taught her, and expelling it slowly, slowly, slowly as she could.

Banana coconut papaya mango
It worked. It calmed them both down.
Bull could go to hell. They could all go to hell.
She and Kitty would send them there, if necessary.

*****

At breakfast, the Fudge Tub tasted sour on her tongue.
'Rehearsal today?' Bull asked over his cornflakes.
Miss Taylor was there too, drinking cup after cup of
black coffee and occasionally taking tiny bites out of a
slowly diminishing square of toast.

'Actually I was thinking of going home,' said
Nancy. 'I'm not feeling too great.'

As soon as the words were out of her mouth she
realised it was the wrong thing to say. Bull's expression
didn't change. Miss Taylor set her toast down, and said,
'If you're unwell then it would be better to stay here,
under our supervision.'

'I'm fed up with being supervised,' said Nancy. 'I
just want to go home.'

Bull was all concern. 'Why don't you go upstairs
and lie down? I'll contact Mr. Six and tell him you're
feeling under the weather today.' He smiled, but the
warmth didn't extend to his eyes. 'Perhaps you've been
overdoing it.'

Something must have shown on her face, because
his smile faded. 'Would you like us to contact your
mother? Or your stepbrother? We know how to get hold
of them.'

Of course you do, thought Nancy. 'I'd rather you
didn't drag them into this.'

'Maurice and Phoebe Pflum, then? And what's the

name of their baby? Oh yes, Samson. They don't live so very far away. We could have them here like *that*.' He snapped his fingers, so violently it made her jump.

The room felt chilly. Only now did Nancy realise she really did feel unwell. Not nauseous, but fuzzy and abstracted, as though the Fudge Tub had been spiked with something that was making it hard for her to focus. There were things she needed to think seriously about, but each time she tried, they kept skittering away, like antic field mice.

'I think I will just go and lie down for a bit,' she said, getting up from the breakfast table. For a moment she though she was going to lose her balance, but managed to regain it without anyone noticing. Or so she hoped. She moved towards the door.

'Oh, and Nancy,' said Bull.

'What?' she said without turning round.

'Best not to go wandering around after dark,' he said. 'The lads are still jumpy after the other night.'

*****

Upstairs, she curled up fully-dressed beneath the duvet and was on the point of dozing off when Miss Taylor materialised by her bedside like a bad fairy, and insisted on taking her temperature. She had a mild fever.

'I'll ask Dr. Smith to take a look at you,' said Miss Taylor.

The very mention of Death-Camp Doctor made Nancy feel worse. 'Oh no, not Smith,' she groaned.

'Shall I see if Dr. Wilson has arrived?'

Nancy nodded. She hadn't yet met the new doctor, but he couldn't be worse than Smith. Miss Taylor permitted herself a rare smile, trying to convey sisterly solidarity, but all it did was remind Nancy of a shark. On her way out of the room she tripped over one of Nancy's discarded shoes and broke a finger nail on the door jamb.

'Sorry about that,' Nancy muttered under her breath.

Left on her own again, she tried one of Miss Green's breathing exercises, but after five minutes of trying to get to the island, she could still feel her heart pounding wildly. Why not just walk out of Wormwood right now? They couldn't stop her, but the way Bull had casually dropped the names of her family and friends into the conversation gave her the chills. How far was he prepared to go? As far as necessary, judging by the conversation she'd overheard.

Wormwood had softened her up, dammit. It was a refuge, where she felt protected from all the bothersome idiots who'd been making her life intolerable. She'd almost forgotten what it was like to make her own decisions or buy her own Fudge Tubs. But her room didn't seem as wonderful as once it had. Now it seemed full of hidden traps. She stared at the chandelier, wondering which of the dozens of glass droplets contained cameras or microphones. And the cherubs were in terrible taste, she could see that now. Everything here was fussy and twee, as if to provide hundreds of places where snooping devices could be concealed. Even if she managed to locate one or two, she couldn't possibly find them all.

She looked down at her swollen body; she was a prize heifer who'd failed to notice she was being fattened up for the slaughter. She had to face it: the safe house was about as safe as a jerry-built crazy cottage full of trapdoors in a dodgy carnival run by grifters who routinely flouted Health and Safety standards.

*****

'How you feeling?' asked Dr. Wilson as she crossed to the bed, white coat flapping unbuttoned, as though she'd only just pulled it on over the rust-coloured bouclé jacket and surprisingly short skirt. Nancy watched uneasily as she approached; she'd imagined a female doctor would be more sympathetic, but there was something so undoctorly about the way this woman moved that it didn't inspire confidence. A downward glance showed why: Dr. Wilson was balanced precariously on a pair of red stiletto slingbacks. Nancy stared at them in a bewildering mixture of consternation and raw desire until she was finally ordered to open her mouth and say *ah*.

Nancy locked her jaw open, and almost choked as Dr. Wilson thrust a mini-flashlight halfway down her throat. The doctor's face was partially obscured by heavy spectacle frames, but Nancy had a vivid, out-of-focus vision of bright red lipstick and heavily powdered skin, backed up by mental impressions of smoke-filled bars and lines of white powder. *Doctors*, thought Nancy. *They're the worst.* The smell of Miss Dior was so overpowering it was making her head swim. She gasped for breath and pushed the flashlight out of the way.

It was the perfume that did it. Nancy was swept into the recent past as efficiently as if she'd been riding in a time machine. 'My God,' she said.

Verity Wilson laid a finger across her patient's lips

and narrowed her eyes into warning slits. 'Chihuahua,' she whispered. *'Chihuahua.'* Then, more loudly, 'Nothing serious. Probably stress.' She fished a small jotting pad out of her pocket and scribbled on it with a stubby pencil that looked as though it had been nicked from Ikea.

Nancy couldn't believe it. *It was all this woman's fault.* This was the person who had splashed her name all over the front pages, who had told so many lies about her, who had made her life a misery. It was Verity Wilson's fault she had been forced to flee, Verity Wilson's fault she had ended up in ComSec's clutches. And now she had the nerve to barge in here and order her around. Nancy fixed her with her most contemptuous glare, but Wilson simply tilted her notepad so Nancy could read what she'd written.

Room probably bugged.

'You don't say,' said Nancy. She took a deep breath and forced herself to simmer down; she had to keep cool and think hard. Maybe Wilson was her ticket out of here. Perhaps they could do a trade; her story in return for the newspaper's protection. She decided to play along.

'I do hope it's not German Measles.' She leant towards Wilson and whispered into her ear: 'They want to cut me open.' Then, more loudly, 'I don't know how you pronounce this, but I'm worried I might have it.' She reached for the pad and scribbled, *They're planning to kill me.*

When Wilson read what Nancy had written, her eyes lit up like a Las Vegas fruit machine. 'Highly unlikely,' she said out loud as she scrawled on the pad. 'The people who work here have been checked very thoroughly for germs.'

Her bedside manner didn't strike Nancy as terribly credible, but Wilson grabbing her wrist and pretending to feel her pulse gave her another chance to glance at the notepad.

Meet tomorrow night, kitchen 3am. Transport + lodging arranged. In return u give me exclusive rights to yr story.

'Done,' said Nancy.

Wilson straightened up. 'Just another of those pesky hot flushes,' she said loudly. 'You pregnant women get them all the time.'

'I thought that was the menopause,' said Nancy.

Wilson glared as though she'd said a dirty word.

'Don't forget now,' she said, tearing the used sheet off the notepad and crumpling it into a tiny ball which she stuffed deep into the pocket of her white coat. Nancy found herself worrying about what Wilson would do with the coat when her shift was up. Surely she wouldn't be so stupid as to leave it lying around with that scrunched-up message in the pocket?

'Get some sleep, drink plenty of water, and I'll give you another once-over in a couple of days.' She winked at Nancy. 'And try to cut down on cigarettes and alcohol. They're bad for your arteries.'

'What if Dr. Smith...?' began Nancy.

A thin-lipped smile. Another narrowing of the eyes.

'Women's problems,' said Wilson. 'He couldn't possibly understand. You leave old Smithy to me.'

Chapter 8
The Crackle Glaze Amphora

Once again Verity Wilson had managed to home in on the loudest bar in town. This time it was a heavy metal pub called The Stuck Pig, where I was the only customer without visible tattoos or pierced extremities. Even Verity had multiple eyelets punched through the gristle of her ears, and a blue-black smudge etched into the junction between her left thumb and forefinger; possibly a Chinese character, but now so blurred by age it looked as though she'd been using a leaky fountain pen.

'Could you say that again?' I leant closer and tried to read her lips, which were coated with sticky pink gloss which caught the light as they moved.

'Need your help.'

I felt a thrill of triumph. She was ready to collaborate! I reached for my bag, and said, 'Would you like to see what I've got so far?'

Wilson wrinkled her nose, as though a wasp had landed on it. 'Come again?'

I pulled the journal out of my bag and slapped it down on the table with a satisfying thump. Wilson reacted as though it were a mashed hedgehog I'd scooped off the road. 'What is this?'

'You'll find everything you need in there,' I said.

She opened the journal cautiously, and turned the first few pages, looking at them open-mouthed, eyes flicking from side to side. 'It's not typed.'

I waited for her to compliment me on my handwriting, but instead she retracted her chin and said, 'Fucking kidding me.'

This wasn't proceeding as expected. 'You said you needed my help.'

She gave me one of her *duh* expressions. 'Getting Nancy out of house before they cut her open. Tomorrow night. No time to read *diary*.'

The way she said *diary* made me feel two inches tall. I slid the journal back into my bag and tried to pretend I'd never got it out, but inside I was seething. *It wasn't a diary! It was a journal!* More pertinently, it was a detailed day by day description of events relating to Nancy. The inside story! It was more truthful than anything Verity Wilson had ever written. What kind of collaboration was this anyway? How *dared* she talk to me like that?

But all I said was, 'What house?'

Wilson rolled her eyes. 'Corleone compound.' She fished a notepad and pencil out of her bag and sketched a series of lines. At first I thought she was doodling, then the lines started to connect and I saw it was a floorplan. 'Ground floor,' she said. 'Entrance, library, dining-room, kitchen.' She jabbed at it with her finger. 'Meeting Nancy kitchen tomorrow night, three am.'

'How do *you* know where the kitchen is?' I stared at her open-mouthed.

'So scared.' I took it she meant Nancy was scared. Verity Wilson didn't look scared at all.

'Nancy can come and go as she pleases,' I reminded her. 'She doesn't need our help.'

Wilson lowered her head and gave me an accusing look from under her eyebrows. 'Not sure you realise dealing with here.' As usual it took me a while to work out what she'd said, and even longer to decipher what she said next. Apparently, she had already infiltrated the compound disguised as a doctor. I looked at her blonde streaks, rust-coloured bouclé jacket and skirt so short it was technically more of a pelmet, and found it hard to accept she could even pass for a New Age quack, let alone any sort of responsible physician. The scepticism must have showed on my face, because she told me her son was at medical school and had given her a crash-course in the jargon.

I had to rewind. Verity Wilson had a *son?*

'Nancy needs free. Child needs free.'

'Nancy can look after herself,' I said. A fuzzy plan was already forming in my brain. I would persuade Wilson that Nancy didn't need our help after all, then nip into this hellhole and spirit her away on my own, before the reporter knew what had hit her. All I needed was the address, and finding a way of turning off the electric fence that had killed three people.

'Not so simple,' said Verity. 'Alone, frightened, not knowing who to trust.'

'Trust's a hard thing to come by these days,' I said, taking another swig of the disgusting rum cocktail she'd bullied me into ordering

'Let Nancy know she's not alone.'

Words couldn't begin to convey how cynical this made me feel. Wilson was acting like the world's biggest altruist, when it was clear that she was only in it for the scoop. She added a dotted line to the floorplan, then sketched in a couple of long, straight lines, and an arrow leading to a small rectangle.

I pointed to the rectangle. 'What the fuck's that? A

garden shed?'

'Wheel man.'

I spluttered. 'Oh yeah, and where do we get one of those?'

'Jules will steal a car,' she said.

Now it was my turn to say 'You're joking. Jules is a maniac.'

She chuckled. 'Nah, pussycat.'

Something in the way she said *pussycat* made it obvious she and Delgado had been sleeping together.

Fucking kidding me. The ground was falling away from under my feet. Wilson was muscling in on *everything*, including all the men in my life. I decided I might as well introduce her to Lars, so she could sleep with him too. And Alain. Hey, why not? This was not going the way I'd anticipated. This had been as much my story as Nancy's, and now I'd been bundled off to the sidelines once again. It reminded me of school hockey practice, where I would spend the entire period running up and down the wing, occasionally getting glimpses through the freezing mist of the other twenty-one players obliviously passing the ball to one another on the far side of the field.

Wilson extracted a card from her purse. I thought she was preparing to pay for the drinks, but no. 'Open sesame!' she said, swiping it diagonally through the air several times, as though a keycard functioned in the same way as a musketeer's sword..

'So what do you need me for anyway?' I scowled.

Wilson looked at me as though I were a halfwit. 'Girl can't stay my place.'

'Why not?' *You've got the rest of this caper sewn up.*

She gave me that *duh* look again. 'My children.' She

explained she was the mother of not just the medical student, but twin girls in their late teens. It was like sharing a house with students, she said. In fact, she was the only one who *wasn't* a student.

'Gobbler sorting out secret digs for Nancy, but not ready for couple of days. Till then she needs to be with people she trusts. Me, you.'

I looked at her sharply. 'Have you said anything to her about me? About, you know, me telling you all that stuff about her?'

She returned the look, keenly, over the top of her Caipirinha, and in that instant I saw I'd been underestimating her.

'Don't worry,' she said. 'I won't tell on you. Not yet, anyway.' And she grinned.

*****

That night and all the next day, I did a lot of brooding, and as I brooded, my fury mounted until I could barely contain it. Verity Wilson was planning to blackmail me. Maybe not straightaway, maybe not tomorrow or the next day, but as soon as I'd outlived my usefulness she would threaten to spill the beans. Because we both knew that if ever Nancy heard the truth, she would show me the red card and Verity would be left with the hockey field all to herself. It wasn't fair. Not after all the work I'd done.

At the shop, poor Alain bore the brunt of my wrath.

'What's up with you?' he asked after I'd bawled him out for putting *The Zombie Apocalypse Survival Manual* in non-fiction. 'Got out of bed on the wrong side this morning?'

'Sorry Alain, I'm a bit on edge.'

'If you ask me you're *over* it,' he said and then added, more kindly, 'I'm always here for you, you know.'

I looked at his honest, earnest face, and said, choosing my words carefully, 'What if you'd done something unforgivable to someone, only they didn't realise it, but now someone else was threatening to tell on you? What would you do?'

Alain looked interested. 'Blackmail, you mean?'

'Not exactly. Well, sort of.'

'That's easy,' Alain said cheerily. 'Kill the blackmailer. Problem solved.'

I laughed, a little hysterically. 'Isn't that a bit extreme?'

'You mean that fellow who comes in here? What did he do? Throw you over?'

'Just a story I'm writing.'

'Ah, your famous writing,' said Alain. 'So when will we see your name on the bestsellers shelf?'

'Sooner than you think,' I said. 'I just need an ending.'

'That's easy,' said Alain. 'The zombies take over and everyone dies.'

I suppose Alain might have unwittingly planted the seed in my head. But you could never call what happened premeditated. If I'd had time to think it through, I would never have made such a mess of the bathroom.

*****

Verity Wilson rolled up at the Bunterberg towards

midnight. I could tell she'd already been drinking, but she didn't turn down my offer of a large gin and tonic. I had one as well and watched helplessly as she embarked on the arduous task of filling my flat with evil-smelling cigarette smoke. 'Nice place you've got here,' she said, heels clacking on the parquet as she stalked around my living-room, peering into every corner and strewing ash everywhere.

'It's OK,' I said. 'Though of course it's really a one-person flat. I don't know how Nancy's going to fit in. I hope she's stopped smoking.'

'Won't be for long,' said Verity Wilson, pretending not to notice my hint about the smoking. 'Maybe can swing some arrangement tomorrow. Gobbler's owners have shares in Ritz. Maybe get her suite there.'

'And me?' I asked, imagining Nancy and Verity Wilson clinking champagne glasses in a luxury hotel bar while I was left outside, peering through the window like a starving orphan eyeing a display of continental pastries.

'Sure we can work it out,' Verity Wilson smiled. 'Do deal.'

'What kind of deal?'

'Money?'

'How about you just let me help you with the story? We can share syndication proceeds.'

Verity Wilson did a double-take. 'Come again?'

'It makes sense.'

She looked puzzled. 'You're not the story.'

'I was at the clinic.'

'Sure you were,' said Verity. 'But you're not the one hatching Baby Jesus in your womb. Why would anyone be interested in you?'

'It's not Jesus, it's the Antichrist!' I found myself

short of breath. 'Didn't you read *any* of the stuff I sent you?'

'What stuff?' She had the air of a Great White Hunter being distracted by a mosquito when he wanted to get on with the serious business of tracking rogue elephants.

'You know. By Gabrielle de Rospin?'

'Gabrielle de...?'

'Rospin.'

'Who?'

'My pen-name. How many times do I have to tell you?' Though when I thought back, I couldn't actually remember having mentioned Gabrielle to her. Maybe I had, maybe I hadn't. I wasn't sure about anything any more.

Verity Wilson searched for something to say. She finally came out with, 'But handwriting...'

'I'm not interested in cheap word processors, but if this comes off I can maybe afford a Toorop.'

Light dawned, not very brightly, in her eyes. She was eyeing me oddly. 'All that scribble... You?'

Jesus. How many times did I have to say it? 'Gabrielle de Rospin is my pseudonym.'

'Is your...' And she exploded into raucous laughter. 'Oh, I'm sorry. It's just that...'

'What?'

'Thought was some nutter.'

A finger of suspicion scratched the edge of my consciousness. 'Did you even *read* any of the pieces I sent?'

'Sure I did.'

'Well?'

Verity Wilson put down her glass and looked me

straight in the eye, and for once didn't seem to be mangling any of her words. Though I began to wish she had.

'Sure I read them. I read the choicest parts out loud, to everyone in the office. For a laugh. We get a lot of fruitcakes writing in, handwritten stream-of-consciousness bollocks. They have no idea at all. Needs editing. Needs rewriting. Only with your stuff, Belinda, there was nothing to rewrite. One hundred per cent drivel. The unsavoury nose-pickings of a delusional mind. Forgive me, Belinda, but you really should stick to the day job. Where is it you work? In a shop?'

I hadn't planned to hit her. And particularly not with my crackle glaze celadon amphora. Luckily it didn't break. Verity Wilson's head wasn't so fortunate; one of the handles swiped her across the temple, leaving a broad furrow which rapidly started filling up with red. Her eyes opened very wide, and I was still stuttering an apology as she crumpled face down on to the rug. I managed to get a newspaper under her head before the furrow overflowed. It was all very neat. She might have been illustrating the headline underneath her: NHS CRISIS: PATIENTS AT RISK IN AMBULANCE STRIKE.

She was in no condition to go and fetch Nancy, that much was obvious. I would just have to go in her place.

Chapter 9
Palace of Ice

Dr. Wilson's visit left Nancy bubbling over with excitement, but she was careful not to show it. She lay on her bed all afternoon, dipping in and out of *Dangerous Liaisons* and listening to the distant noises of the house: footsteps, doors slamming, Classic FM, two people (Miss Taylor and Mr. Miller?) murmuring obscene endearments to each other. She turned on the television, but found herself gazing blankly at rolling news about hospital closures and a fresh outbreak of toxic jellyfish. Her mind churned like a waste disposal unit, chewing up the same information over and over again, stirring it round and round until her thinking was reduced to mush.

Banana coconut papaya mango

She tried to relax by closing her eyes and visiting the island. For a while, she could almost smell the salty breeze, the coconut suntan oil, and the rich aroma of wild orchids. Then the sun went cold. She opened her eyes. She was still on the beach, but the sky was no longer blue. Now it was a threatening purple, swollen to bursting with tropical storm. Thunder rumbled like the growling of a giant predator stalking through the jungle towards her, toppling palm trees as it came. *This isn't meant to happen*, she told herself, struggling to regain control. A new odour wafted past her nostrils. The smell of burning meat. Something was being barbecued on the other side of the trees. Nancy sat up on the bed. The island vanished, leaving nothing but the sounds and smells of the safe house. Only now it felt less like a five-star hotel and more like a high-security asylum, with herself a dangerous inmate who needed to be watched round the clock.

Miss Taylor looked in to see how she was feeling, and a short while later Bull popped his head around the door, but she pretended to be asleep until they went away and left her alone. The knowledge that they had opened her door, even though she had locked it from the inside, was not reassuring.

*****

The next day she acted as though everything were back to normal, though it required constant vigilance to keep up the pretence. The rehearsal went badly; she repeatedly flubbed her lines, but she had other things on her mind, such as the best way to walk out of Wormwood without getting anybody killed. She just hoped Verity Wilson realised what she'd let herself in for.

Dinner passed without incident, with only small talk from Miss Taylor to distract her. Bull was absent, which was a relief. She felt on edge as it was, and the last thing she needed was another of his attempts to winkle out what she was thinking and feeling. Having to keep smiling back at him was exhausting when all she wanted was to tell him to go to hell.

She ate her Fudge Tub as normal, exchanged desultory platitudes with Miss Taylor and, as soon as it seemed polite, slipped back up to her room. As the evening wore on, she listened to the house shutting down around her. Doors slammed. Keypads were tapped. Voices and footsteps receded. Somewhere on a distant planet, car engines coughed. Time slowed to a crawl. No matter how many times she looked at her bedside clock, the minute hand refused to speed up. She closed the blinds and drew the curtains across, leaving the room in darkness, but by now she knew how to feel her way around. She loaded a bag with anything she thought might come in useful: a corkscrew, scissors, sewing-kit, cigarettes, lighter, the small amount of cash she'd never had a chance to spend... And then sat back on the bed, and waited.

At last it was twenty to three. She got up, felt her way across to the wardrobe, and changed into the disgusting old trainers she'd brought with her from Natal Mansions. They looked odd with the dress, but they were comfortable, and she would be able to run in them, if it came to that. Still groping her way through the darkness, she heaped pillows into a mound that, in torchlight, could be mistaken for her slumbering body. Then she picked up the bag, quietly unlocked her door and slipped out into the corridor. By now, she knew exactly which floorboards creaked and steered clear of them as she crept down the stairs to the ground floor, sticking to the shadows as she crossed the dining-room. She had no doubt there were hidden cameras in here too, and anyone diligently peering at the security monitors would have spotted her, but she was counting on no-one inspecting any of the unlit rooms too closely.

In the kitchen, orange light spilled through the high window across the quarry-tiled floor. Apart from her own ragged breathing, the only sound was the rickety hum of the big fridge. It was colder here than on the upper floors. Her hands felt icy. She began to regret not having put on a coat, though it would have been harder to explain away if she'd run into someone on the way down. She switched on one of the gas hobs and warmed her hands in the rising heat from the flame.

Two minutes to three. She stared mesmerised by the faint flickering of the digital clock on the oven, and before she knew it another eight minutes had slipped past without her even noticing. Wilson was late. Had something gone wrong? Had someone at ComSec found that scrap of paper? They might have her arrested, or worse. The woman was either colossally brave or colossally stupid, maybe both. Exclusive rights to her story was the least Nancy could offer in return. She could just imagine the headlines. SECRET GOVERNMENT DEPARTMENT EXPOSED! CAESAREAN SCANDAL OF MINISTRY FOR MOTHERS-TO-BE! DEATH-CAMP DOCTOR CONVICTED OF CRIMES AGAINST HUMANITY!

Ten past. She'd been primed and ready to rock, and now a gigantic cloud of anti-climax was hovering over her head. Could she get out of this place on her own? Nancy realised to her shame she didn't know how. She already knew her keycard didn't work on the front door, because she'd tried it, but the door had always been opened for her when she needed to get to rehearsals. Getting outside had never been an issue - until now. The windows in the kitchen were too high, and too narrow, but could she unlock one of the grilles in the dining-room? But they were almost certainly rigged with alarms, and she wasn't sure she was up to anything that might involve clambering, or jumping, or squeezing through tight spaces. And that was before she had to deal with the electric fence.

She decided to give it another five minutes, but her mouth was already parched with disappointment. She filled a glass with water and sipped at it, staring at the glowing green numerals of the oven clock as she considered her options. Returning to bed and then carrying on as normal felt like the coward's way out.

Her ears picked up a faint sound and she tensed so abruptly that water slopped out of the glass and over her hand. The glass began to slide through her fingers, but just in time she adjusted her grip and quietly set it down on the worktop. Footsteps? A long way away, but coming closer. She tried to analyse the sound. This was not the tippety-tap of stilettos; it was a stealthy, crêpe-soled, slightly squeaky creep. Someone was trying not to make a noise. She found herself hoping it was Wilson, who'd swapped her heels for more practical prowling footwear, but she knew the hope was a forlorn one.

The footsteps were drawing closer. Now they were coming from the dining-room, cutting off her obvious escape route. But she stayed calm; she already had an excuse prepared. Everyone knew pregnant women had cravings that were not to be denied. She crossed to the big fridge. There were no cappuccino-flavoured Fudge Tubs in her room, so she had popped down to the kitchen for one. Her being dressed was a minor detail she was sure she could explain away. She pulled the fridge door open and stood blinking, dazzled by the light flooding out of it.

As her vision cleared, what she saw in the fridge made her want to shut the door again so she could go back to bed and dismiss all this as a bad dream. But it was impossible to tear herself away, so she continued to stand in the pool of light, blinking stupidly, trying to make sense of what was in front of her. It couldn't have been more than a second or two, but time was playing tricks again and it felt as though she'd been standing there for hours when she heard Bull say, 'Oh my God.'

He was right behind her. She hadn't heard him creep those last few yards, because her mind was now on other things. She was grateful he couldn't see her face; she didn't want him thinking she was frightened. But she had stared directly into the eyes of the Medusa, and had turned to stone.

The last thing she'd expected to see in the refrigerator was Verity Wilson's head, wedged between three dozen free-range eggs and a two-litre container of milk. The eyes were wide open, so that for one brief deluded moment it was as though Verity were actually hiding in there, waiting to leap out and surprise her. But her skin had the deathly pallor of frozen pastry, and her neck ended in a silvery-dark puddle on a plate. A few drops of blood had splashed on to the waxy paper wrapped around the large Brie on the shelf beneath.

Never mix meat with dairy.

The sight was blotted out as something clamped itself over her eyes. A hand, smelling of single malt and carnation-scented soap. Bull had always been a stickler for hygiene.

'You don't want to look at that,' he said. She let herself be turned around as he kicked the fridge door shut behind them. 'Back to bed, now.' He lifted his hand away. He wasn't wearing a suit, but sweatpants and a navy blue windbreaker. She'd never seen him so casually dressed.

'Didn't see that coming,' she said with a nervous laugh.

'I'm so sorry,' said Bull. He bent closer now, whispering into her ear. 'Someone slipped up. I'll have their guts for garters.' He laid an arm across her shoulders and began to steer her in the direction of the dining-room. 'I'll get you something to help you sleep.'

'No.' She dug her heels in. 'I want to go home.'

Bull turned her around again, like an ice-dancer spinning a compliant partner. His hand still rested on her shoulder as he stared into her face, apparently searching for something. His fingers were deceptively light; she could sense, rather than feel, the enormous power behind them.

No, she thought, *I'm not having this.*

Like someone getting a small electric shock from a metal doorknob, he snatched his hand away and wafted it to and fro, as if he thought the night air might cool it down. Nancy watched dispassionately as a thin line of blood spilled like fine red thread from his left nostril.

'I'm grateful for everything you and ComSec have done,' she said. 'It's just...' Her voice died away. She didn't know what to say. *I have no intention of sticking around here till you give me an overdose, or push me downstairs, or put a bullet in my brain?*

'Not easy maintaining objectivity in such circumstances,' he said, wiping his nose on one of his sleeves.

She nodded, without knowing precisely what he meant by 'such circumstances'. Best to humour him. He was looking at her eagerly, like a suitor on a first date. 'I've been meaning to talk to you for some time.'

'We talk to each other every day.'

Nancy took a couple of steps backwards, but he immediately closed the gap.

'You don't tell me everything,' he said.

'I tell you all you need to know.'

'It would be a shame to break up the team. We have so much in common.'

'Such as?'

'We're both actors. You saw my fat lady.'

'Yes, I did.'

'She's not my only character,' he said. 'They're a motley bunch, but all pretty convincing, if I say so myself. I take them out into the field from time to time, to put them through their paces.'

'Which character are you playing now?'

Something solid checked Nancy's progress. She had backed up against one of the worktops.

'This is me,' he said. His stealthy approach was oppressive. Nancy tried not to look directly at him, sensing he might be capable of hypnotising her, like a vampire. She turned her head, searching for something, anything, to give her an advantage. Her gaze fell on the magnetic knife-rack. As she stared at it, it wobbled and two of the smaller blades clattered on to the worktop. She tried to get a mental grip on one of them, but nothing happened. She felt panic flare up, but pushed it back down again. She had to stay calm.

'I've been watching you,' said Bull. 'The way you walk, the way you sink into a chair, exhausted at the end of a long hard day. But oh so gracefully. You know all about carrying that extra weight.'

Oh, for heaven's sake, did he think she was *stupid?* Yes, he probably did. Wasn't that what she'd been trying to make him think for this past month?

'Talking of extra weight,' she said. 'What happens after the birth?'

'Easily shed. Diet and exercise.'

'No, I mean what about me? *I'm* the extra weight. You think I'm dispensable.'

He looked bewildered, then shocked. 'No! Why would you think that?'

There no longer seemed any point in obfuscating. 'I heard you talking to Dr. Smith.'

'Oh, *that!* I knew you were there; I know *you*, Nancy. I left the door open on purpose; I wanted you to hear what Smith was planning. I can have him dismissed, you know, like *that!*' He snapped his fingers, but the sound was dull. 'Smith's the dispensable one. You need never see him again. Say the word, and he's gone.'

'Gone? Like Verity Wilson?'

Even in the half-light, she could tell his face had turned as grey as the sky over her fantasy island. 'You don't think.... Oh Christ, you do. Listen, I've done some terrible things, but nothing to...'

'Who was it then?'

He stared at her. 'Jules Delgado, of course! This has his fingerprints all over it, the sick bastard. We picked him up half an hour ago... But too late to stop... this.'

She didn't drop her guard. 'How did he get in?'

'Contact on the inside.'

'Who?'

'That's what we've been trying to find out. You'd be surprised what people will do for money. People you trust, people who say they're your friends.'

She stared at him. 'So tell me, what *will* happen to me afterwards?'

'What would you *like* to happen?' He licked his lips, put one hand up, felt the wetness trickling from his nose, and started fishing in his pocket for a handkerchief.

'There's kitchen towel over there,' said Nancy. 'But you need to let me leave.'

'I can't do that.'

'You've seen what I can do.' Once again, Nancy tried to shift the knife with her mind. This time it didn't even twitch. All that practising in secret, and the best she could manage was a small nosebleed.

Unexpectedly, Bull broke into a smile, but there was blood on his teeth now, so the results were ghoulish. 'I would never hurt you, Nancy. Never! But you're all alone, and frightened, and you need someone to look after you. A child needs a father as well as a mother. You can't do this on your own. Let me help.'

She felt her skin erupt into goose pimples. 'You're telling me you want to be its *father?*'

'A partnership. We already have a connection, can't you feel it?'

She spoke carefully. 'We would still have a *connection*, as you call it, if I were somewhere else, somewhere outside. And I just don't feel comfortable here any longer.'

He showed her the palms of his hands, as if to prove there was nothing concealed there. 'OK then. First thing in the morning I'll arrange for Jones to take you home.'

'Not in the morning,' said Nancy. *'Now!'* She was sure he had no intention of letting her go anywhere. If she were to return to her room, there would be no leaving it again. She didn't know how, but he would find some way of trapping her in it. He would let people die to keep her there, if necessary.

Bull shook his head. 'If you leave now, they'd come after you.'

She thrust her chin out. 'I don't care.'

'You're upset. It's understandable.' He pulled a mobile phone out of his pocket and flipped it open.

'Stop that,' said Nancy.

He pressed a key.

'I said, *stop it.*' The harshness of her own voice surprised her.

Bull paused and looked up at her in frank amusement. But his finger was still poised over the keypad.

'Put it away,' she said.

Reluctantly, he slid the phone back into his pocket and wiped his nose on his sleeve. 'Truth is, you're not like any of the others. I didn't expect any of this to happen.'

'What others?'

'I've come to care for you in ways that aren't entirely... professional.'

Nancy felt sick. 'Oh yes?'

'You're special. Not just because of what's inside you, but because of how you've embraced it, how you're no longer struggling against it. You've accepted your destiny.'

'What makes you think that?'

'There's a serenity to you. I think that's probably why...' He hesitated, almost bashful.

'Yes?' said Nancy.

'I can't stop thinking about you.'

Before Nancy could even snort in derision, they

were interrupted by shrill beeping. Bull whipped round like a samurai swivelling to face a sneaky foe. Kitty kicked out, and Nancy had just time enough to identify the noise as the electronic timer on the cooker before she saw Bull's left foot come down into the small puddle of water that had earlier slopped out of her glass.

As it is written, so shall it be done.

Everything had already been mapped out, and now she couldn't stop it even if she wanted to; the slide-show of her life flashed in front of her again, speeding through the past before slowing down to show his heel coming down in the water and skidding several inches. He didn't go down, but lost his balance, and in trying to regain it bumped against the vegetable rack. A single King Edward potato bounced in slow motion across the stainless steel worktop like one of Dr. Barnes Wallis's bombs, then, towards the end of its trajectory, abruptly sped up and cannoned into a stack of linen napkins, spilling them sideways. The top one unfurled lazily across the gas hob Nancy thought she'd switched off. But she'd turned the knob the wrong way; not off, but low, so low the flame was barely visible. The fabric immediately began to smoulder.

Bull saw what was happening, chuckled in delight, and calmly reached across to yank the napkin away just as the bud of flame began to creep along one edge. In a single fluid movement, he turned on the cold tap and plunged the burning fabric into the gushing water. Nancy stared open-mouthed. Whatever Kitty had mapped out, it hadn't worked.

'I knew it,' he said. 'You *have* been practising.' And with his wet hand he reached across to turn the gas off. The instant his fingers came into contact with the controls there was a soft blue flash and a sizzling noise. At first he didn't react, and she assumed he was unscathed, but then her nostrils caught a whiff of barbecue, like the smell of burning on the other side of her fantasy island, and there was smoke coming out of his collar and his fingers seemed glued to the switch.

Kitty had been thinking outside the box.

'You see what happens when you try to make us do things we don't want to do?' said Nancy.

The sizzling died away. Bull wrenched his hand away from the switch with a force that left him tottering. He opened his mouth to say something, but all that emerged was a gasp of smoke. At least he was still standing, she thought, before she saw he was collapsing on the inside, like a building in which the basement had been dynamited. The lights were going off, one by one. She watched dispassionately as he sank to his knees. But he was smiling again, a creepily indulgent smile, like a martyr confronted by a shimmering vision of the deity.

'That was extraordinary,' he whispered. 'I felt... It was like...'

'Sorry,' she said, not feeling sorry at all. She coughed, almost choking on the smell of burnt meat. 'Soon as I get out of here I'll call an ambulance.'

Bull's lips were still moving. She made out the word *no*, or it might have been *oh*. He ground his teeth together and managed to squeeze out a coherent sentence. 'You silly goose, I'm on your side...'

'What?' said Nancy. He was bullshitting again.

'...told was going to be a closely monitored pregnancy... But our paymasters decided... Why I brought Wilson in...'

She tensed. 'What do you mean you brought

Wilson in?'

He tried to switch on his smile again, but the muscles in his face were no longer working properly, and his mouth twisted into a grimace. 'Should never have brought you here... You need to get out while you still can... And Nancy...'

'Fuck's sake,' Nancy said.

'Good luck with the play. Whatever happens, I made sure they can't take that away from you...'

He tried to say something else, but now the only noise coming out of his mouth was a faint gargling. His eyes were clouding over. He groped for his jacket pocket, and she tensed, thinking he was looking for his mobile again, maybe even a gun. Instead, he drew out his keycard and, with immense effort, pressed it into her palm. His features lost their definition. The circuits were shutting down. His breathing became increasingly laboured, then stopped altogether. She grabbed his wrist and dug her thumb into it, searching for a pulse. Nothing. Had he really been on her side all along? Why the hell hadn't he *told* her? She squeezed his wrist, willing him to recover just enough to explain, but the sudden chirruping of the mobile in his pocket made her let go of his hand and his knuckles smacked against the floor.

The ringtone cut off abruptly. Had it been a signal? Mr. Jones, she thought, or Mr. Carter or Mr. Miller or one of the other goons. They would come looking for her now. She could feel Kitty kicking frantically inside her. She had no choice but to get out before they caught her standing over the body. Only when she was halfway across the dining-room did she realise she'd been holding her breath for so long the lack of air was making her dizzy. She exhaled and drew oxygen into her lungs with a long shuddering inhalation that was almost a sob. All those hours of practice, and still she was a walking time-bomb. She'd never intended to *kill* Bull. What would they do now? Send tanks?

There was a commotion from somewhere over her head. Someone ran across the floor. A door slammed. Shouting. They were looking for her, of course.

She steadied herself and gripped Bull's keycard tightly. Time to get out of Dodge.

*****

She used Bull's keycard to open the door and then the gates, and walked as far as Hampstead High Street, where she hailed a cab.

Of course, it wasn't that simple. Of course they tried to stop her, but past and present merged in her head once again, and Mr. Jones got midsectioned by a pipe, which passed most of the way through him. Or rather, Nancy inadvertently brushed against a car, which set off an alarm, which startled a passing biker, who skidded and drove into the side of a badly parked van so that the string holding its doors closed snapped and sent a bunch of pipes cascading out. She was sorry about Mr. Jones; she hadn't felt any personal animosity towards him, and he'd just been doing his job; maybe he could still be patched up. She didn't see what happened to Mr. Miller, but as her taxi did a U-turn she could hear someone screaming and thought it might have been him.

So she left Wormwood behind and headed home, shivering and exhausted, as though returning from a party that had stretched on for forty days and nights. She took advantage of the journey to steady her breathing.

Banana coconut papaya mango

The driver eyed her in the mirror and said, 'Not gonna pop that out in here, are you?'

Was it that obvious? She assured him the baby wasn't due for another three months.

The street outside Natal Mansions was deserted. No reporters, no men in grey and the only fat lady in the vicinity was her. But what had she been expecting? A welcome committee? It was four thirty in the morning, and the press had long since forgotten about her. She didn't think ComSec would forget, but she and Kitty had given them a kicking. They would need to regroup and hold meetings and decide how to deal with her. She thought back to what Bull had said. Had he really been on her side? She wanted to trust his words, but the image of Verity Wilson's head floated into her mind and she had to bite her lip to stop herself from crying out. Bull's shock had seemed the equal of her own, but what if it had been faked? He'd said himself he was an actor.

*****

She hauled herself up the five flights to her flat, pausing on each landing to recover her breath. On the fifth floor she fiddled with the keys for several minutes before realising the lock had been changed. She kicked the door petulantly. What was the point of having superpowers if things like this happened? She ought to have foreseen it; she'd had plenty of time to consider all the possibilities, but this one had never occurred to her. She'd already been late with the rent, and her bank account had been blocked. She ought to have been better prepared. Where the hell was she supposed to go now, with no phone or credit card? She had enough cash for a hotel, but what then?

She began to trudge downstairs, running through a mental list of friends she could call on, but as she reached the fourth floor, the door to number ten flew open and Mrs. Feaver stood there in a quilted bathrobe and foam-rubber rollers, framed in her doorway like resurrected Jesus appearing to a cringing disciple.

Nancy felt a stab of guilt. She would rather have confronted Stuart Milo Bull, ComSec and EDEN all at once than face the elderly neighbour whose dog she had lost. How could she have been so thoughtless? She hadn't even sent an apology. She ought to have asked ComSec to find a replacement Jack Russell.

She began stammering excuses while Mrs. Feaver stared at her with a face stony as an Easter Island statue. After several ice ages had passed, the old bat must have judged Nancy had suffered enough, because she bobbed down behind the door. When she turned back, her arms were wrapped around a scrawny bundle of snarling brown and white fur.

'Poor Chip. Baby was hit by a bicycle, but I got him back, no thanks to you. A nice old sea captain found the little possum crouched by the road with a wounded paw. Luckily my address was on his collar.'

Sea-captain? *Sea-captain?* Nancy rolled her eyes. Was there really a Captain Birdseye roaming the streets of Holborn, rescuing lost dogs? Or had it been Bull in another of his ridiculous disguises? She stared hard at Mrs. Feaver, half-expecting the old lady to peel off a rubber face and reveal herself as an agent of ComSec.

Mrs Feaver did nothing of the kind. Instead, she

said, 'I have something for you. Hold Chip.' Before
Nancy knew what was happening, the mutt had been
thrust into her arms. The animal squirmed like an eel,
trying to wriggle free, but Nancy wasn't going to make
the same mistake twice; braving the gusts of meaty
breath, she clung on for dear life. Just as Chip was trying
to pour himself beneath one of her arms, Mrs. Feaver
reappeared, carrying a cardboard box bearing the legend
CHEESE TOASTIES.

'This is yours,' she said.

Nancy peered into the carton and recognised a
pair of blue mules with sequin trim, her answering
machine and a packet of Sobranie Black Russian.

'Lots more back there,' said Mrs. Feaver, setting
the box down at Nancy's feet and reclaiming her dog.
'Landlord wanted to put your belongings out on the
street, but I said I'd look after them. Didn't know you'd
be gone so long, or I mightn't have been so quick to
offer.'

'I appreciate it, thank you.' Nancy was touched.

'Give me your new address and I'll send them on,'
said Mrs. Feaver.

Nancy hadn't the faintest idea where she was
headed. 'I'll pop back for them.'

Mrs. Feaver's gaze fell on the packet of Sobranie,
and her face took on a pained expression. Nancy
guessed what she was going to say before she'd even
opened her mouth. 'You shouldn't be smoking, not...'

'...in my condition,' finished Nancy. 'Mrs. Feaver,
you have *no idea* what my condition is.'

Mrs. Feaver puffed herself up like a peahen, and
said, 'I have more idea than you'll ever know.' For a
fleeting instant, the querulous hag faded away and was

replaced by another woman, one with an incident-packed and possibly even scandalous past. For the first time, Nancy wondered how long Mrs. Feaver had lived in Natal Mansions. And what had happened to Mr. Feaver? She had a fleeting impression of slow dancing, and dull brown offices, and uniforms, and a child, and laughter, and a hospital ward and weeping, and a funeral.

Mrs. Feaver narrowed her eyes. 'Is that blood?'

Nancy glanced down at the stain on her sleeve. 'Spaghetti sauce.'

'Where are you off to at this hour?'

Nancy couldn't think of what to say. Mrs. Feaver sighed, and said, 'You'd better sleep on the sofa.'

She stood to one side, giving Nancy a clearer view of the hallway with its clashing patterns. The flat exuded a not unpleasant aroma of moth balls and lavender, as though it had been spritzed in Old Lady Home Fragrance.

'Come in then. You don't want to be wandering the streets at night.'

'Very kind of you,' said Nancy.

'Just for tonight.'

There were more clashing patterns in the living-room, and a framed print of dogs playing cricket on a village green. The sofa was too short, and upholstered in a slithery floral fabric, but no sooner had Nancy kicked off her trainers and put her feet up then she was fast asleep.

She dreamt about Verity Wilson's head on display in a palace of ice. The eyes blinked open, and the mouth, after several abortive attempts to speak, formed the words. 'This is all your fault.'

PART FOUR
BRIMSTONE

Chapter 1
The Morning After

I stayed up all night, cleaning blood off the bathroom walls. Let's face it, the big rescue hadn't gone as planned. Parts of the fiasco were mercifully obscured by the jagged black holes in my memory, but the fragments I could remember were a nightmare and it didn't help that my head was throbbing like an injured extremity in a Looney Tunes cartoon. On the back, where I'd banged it against the bathtub, was a lump the size of a soft-boiled egg. I couldn't stop poking at it, fascinated by its spongelike qualities, which only made it hurt more. I ran out of Doliban and had to raid the First Aid kit in the staffroom.

I'd rolled up late for work with wet hair and skin scrubbed raw, looking like Nightmare Life-in-Death from *The Rime of the Ancient Mariner*. After an initial show of concern, Alain ticked me off for spending too much time in the True Crime section, leaving him to do all the unpacking. And it was true that, when Nancy came to find me, I was staring mesmerised at a photo in *Practical Homicide Investigation* showing a corpse covered in Rice Krispies that on closer inspection turned out to be maggots.

'Belinda?'

I looked up and let out a squeak of surprise. She was clutching a cardboard box brimming with shoes and magazines and cigarettes, but my attention was caught by what she was wearing: a ladylike green dress with a full skirt, pussycat bow at the neck, and a rust-coloured stain on the sleeve. The stain made me feel sick all over again.

After the catastrophic events of the previous evening, Nancy was the last person I'd been expecting to see. My first thought was: *What did I tell you?* I'd *known* she hadn't needed our help to get out! My second was that she had shrunk, till I glanced down and saw she was wearing trainers instead of her usual heels. My third was that all those Fudge Tubs were starting to show.

'Wow, you've put on weight,' I said.

She grimaced. 'Nice to see you too.'

All of a sudden I felt dizzy and had to prop myself up against the counter.

'You OK?' She reached out to hold me up but the instant her hand touched me a look of bewilderment crossed her face and she snatched it back as though my arm had been red hot.

'What the..?'

She knows, I thought. Then told myself that was impossible. She couldn't possibly know.

'Are you *sure* you're OK?'

'Pulled an all-nighter,' I said. 'Feel like shit.'

'I didn't get much sleep either,' she said. 'Fucking awful night.'

Jesus, couldn't she even let me win at that?

'Thank you for the postcards,' I said, and she winced.

'Can I stay at your place? Just a couple of nights, till I sort myself out.' She launched into a long-winded account about having been locked out of her flat in Natal Mansions, and I had to pretend I hadn't known about that already.

After my late arrival, I couldn't see Alain agreeing to my skipping off work early again, so I reluctantly gave Nancy my keys and told her to make herself at home till I got back. I was worried about what her supersensitive sense of smell might pick up in my flat, and particularly in the area of the walk-in wardrobe, but she didn't leave me with much choice. It was either give her the keys, or turn her out into the street where she would be a sitting duck for government agents or men in grey or reporters. Worse, she might end up going to stay with my rival. I felt gratified that in her hour of need she'd elected to come to me rather than Phoebe and Maurice. Only later did it occur to me it was because she hadn't wanted to put them in danger. She had placed their safety above mine. All right, so they had a baby, but I didn't see why that should have made my life any less worth preserving.

'I won't smoke,' she said.

'No, that's OK,' I said. 'Smoke as much as you like.'

She looked taken aback. 'You sure?'

I prodded the packet of Black Russian. The stinkier the better. 'Not a problem.'

*****

I'd steeled myself for awkward questions relating to my recent acquisitions on the home furnishing front, but there was no need. Nancy wouldn't have known a St. Malo armchair from a stuffed llama. She knew smells, though. She was an expert in those. As soon as she opened the front door, the stench hit her with such force that she almost passed out.

Christ, what *was* that? Room freshener? Rotten meat? It wasn't like OCD-adjacent Belinda to forget to put out her rubbish. But instead of hunting for the source of the smell, Nancy chose to obliterate it, by lighting the first of many, many Sobranies.

That afternoon she swept through my place like a hurricane, leaving devastation in her wake. She took a long hot bath, apparently having no problems with the smelliness of my eye-watering expensive Smulky crystals since she used up half the jar. While wallowing in the aromatic soup, she flicked through a mint copy of the arts and crafts issue of Isme, which I surmised she must have dropped into the bathwater since I later found most of the pages glued together.

And then she got dressed in clean clothes. In *my* clothes. In a Riza Niro ribbed top which, by the time I saw it only a few hours later, had already been stretched into a sort of shapeless mediaeval peasant smock. She put her dress through the hottest cycle of my washing-machine, leaving most of my white underwear dyed green, wolfed down two of the Fudge Tubs she'd picked up on the way home, and retrieved her antediluvian answering machine from the Cheese Toasties carton. She pressed play, but the machine was clogged with mangled tape. Patiently, she began to disentangle it, winding up the slack with a Biro.

She was still untangling when I got home. I'd been expecting to smell cigarettes, but even so, the wall of evil-smelling fog that greeted me when I opened the door made me reel in dismay. It was a wonder she hadn't set off the smoke alarm. Later, I checked to see if it was still working, and found that at some point the battery had run down. Evidently the cheeping of the trapped bird I'd spent so long trying to find hadn't been a trapped bird after all.

She saw my face. 'Too much? Sorry, I'll open a window.'

'No!' I said quickly. 'Not a problem, honestly. Oh. Is that... oh my God... My Riza Niro!'

'Your what?'

'Never mind,' I said. 'Tea?'

I brewed a pot of Lapsang Souchong and Nancy gave me an abridged account of everything that had happened to her since she'd made her Great Escape from Natal Mansions. As she described the Battle of Waterloo and Stuart Milo Bull and Wormwood and Les Six's Jack the Ripper musical, I was able to confirm in close-up that my distant impressions of her outside the Pickle Factory had been on the money. She really had changed, and it wasn't just the weight; she had acquired, I don't know, *gravitas*. Pregnancy had been teaching her things; even her manner of speaking hinted at a determination and resourcefulness I'd never glimpsed before.

I got straight to the point. 'Why didn't you call me?'

'I told you, no outside lines.'

'You could have called from the Pickle Factory.'

'It's a dead spot.'

'You called Maurice!'

'Only once,' she said. 'Then they blocked the signal.'

Yeah, right. If she'd really *wanted* to call, she would have found a way. So many excuses, but I could see there was no point in pursuing it further.

'It's good that Les Six changed his mind,' I said,

marvelling at how things had turned out. Hadn't I always known this pregnancy was special? I felt vindicated. Selling her story to Verity Wilson hadn't just been for my own short-term gain; now it was getting her work.

'When did we last see each other?' she asked.

'We arranged to meet at the Bar Chester on the evening of Monday the twenty-fifth of October, but you stood me up.'

'Did I? Sorry about that. I was fighting for my life.'

'No, that was later...' I began, but gave up. What did it matter?

'By the way, thanks for the tip-off,' she said. 'I owe you one.'

I was about to ask, 'What tip-off?' when she thoughtfully added a description of the note she thought I'd sent. 'You probably saved my life,' she said, and then paused, frowning, cogs turning. 'How did you know where to find me?'

'I called up Les Six's people.' Which wasn't a lie, technically. Of course I wasn't going to admit I'd spent days staking out the Pickle Factory and spying on her through binoculars.

She looked at me curiously. 'How did you know what ComSec was planning? And how did you know about ComSec anyway?'

It was probably too late to confess I'd been hobnobbing with the guy who'd tried to kidnap her at Waterloo Station. I certainly couldn't let her know that while she'd been cooped up with a cabal of professional killers I'd been sipping Chocolate Martinis with Jules Delgado in the Penthouse Bar. 'I think you mentioned them after the clinic, and then Maurice said something,' I said vaguely. 'Did I tell you they invited me round to see their Finnish sink?'

Unlike me, Nancy wasn't easily distracted by Finnish sinks. 'It wasn't your usual handwriting.'

I told her I'd written the note in a hurry. In the dark. With a horrible pen. I nearly said I'd injured my hand as well, but judged I'd already gone far enough and, as usual, began to regret not having told the truth in the first place. Why had I even lied? Luckily, as usual, Nancy found her own story more interesting than mine. She went on to tell me how she'd eavesdropped on Dr. Smith and Bull, and how Verity Wilson had pretended to be a doctor and set up the escape. But then, just as she was on the point of describing what had happened next, she clammed up and sat there with a weird expression on her face. I detected sadness in it, and resignation, and resolution, but there was something else I couldn't pinpoint.

'Then what happened?' I already knew Wilson hadn't turned up to meet her, but I'd been hoping Nancy could fill in some of the gaping holes. Like, what had I done with Verity Wilson's head?

Nancy's eyes had opened wide, but she wasn't focusing on anything. 'Look,' she said at last. 'I'd rather not talk about that just now. There's still a lot I need to process. I don't know who's telling the truth any more.'

'I always tell the truth,' I said, a bit too quickly.

'I know *you* do,' said Nancy. 'You tell the truth even when you think you're lying, Belinda.'

'Yeah,' I said, trying to work out what she'd meant by *that.*

She returned to rewinding her tape, which looked scrunched beyond redemption, a bit like my memory. But finally she wrangled it into a playable state, more or less, and slotted it into my cassette deck. Every so often the sound wobbled, but each time the tape rallied gamely and trundled on its way.

The recordings dated back to the end of October, and at least one of the voices seemed to be coming from beyond the grave. It sent a chill through both of us, though of course I had to pretend I didn't recognise Wilson's throaty rasp. She wasn't the only reporter who'd left messages, but she'd been the most persistent, and her voice punctuated the others like an eerie refrain. Several times she mentioned a 'source' as in, 'We already have a source, Nancy; we just want to hear your side.' I waited, heart in mouth, for her to name that 'source', but she never did. I looked over at Nancy, hoping my relief wasn't too obvious, but she was frowning at the cassette player so hard that her eyebrows were practically meeting in the middle, Frida Kahlo-style.

Among the other callers was Detective Inspector Church, with a series of tetchy requests for Nancy to contact him. ('He doesn't sound happy, does he? But he washed his hands of me, so what does he expect?') My voice was in there too, issuing an invitation to birthday drinks; this time she did glance at me, sheepishly. ('I'm so sorry, Belinda. You know I'm bad at dates.') There were some relentlessly jolly calls from Maurice, a few deceptively casual inquiries from Phoebe, who was obviously trying to gather information, and some slurred rambling we both knew was from Nancy's mother, and more wrong numbers than was normal, and Bible quotations and people trying to sell her life insurance, and at least half a dozen callers who said nothing at all, though we could hear them breathing heavily down the line.

And then there was Clive Mengers, trying to fix up a portrait session. He sounded as though he'd been drinking, and the clarity of his words wasn't improved by the wobble on the tape, but it occurred to me that Wilson might have shared compromising information with him, so I jotted down his number while Nancy wasn't looking.

The messages came to an end, which was presumably when her landlord had unplugged the machine and shoved it into a cardboard box with the rest of her stuff. Nancy rewound and started listening to the tape all over again, as though she thought she might have overlooked a vital clue.

I got bored and adjourned to the bathroom to mop up the small flood she'd left there, but after a few minutes she called me back; my cassette deck had stopped working. I opened it and found it jammed with a soldered wad of brown spaghetti. I plucked at the lump, but this time the tape was beyond saving and so, by the looks of it, was my machine. Hurricane Nancy had struck again.

Chapter 2
Everest

I arranged to meet Clive Mengers on Friday night. Even if he hadn't been carrying his camera case, I would have recognised him. He stood out from the modish Soho crowd like a suppurating opposable digit in a fistful of flawless phalanges. He was sitting at a counter by the window, unshaven, chain-smoking and so twitchy I guessed he'd already swallowed half a dozen espressos. He might once have been good-looking, but his boyish features were puffy, like a dissipated cherub's. As each new customer entered the coffee bar, his head moved in jerky little movements, like a chicken's, giving the newcomer the once-over before retreating behind the tabloid he was so obviously not reading. MARTINE'S JELLYFISH ORDEAL! was plastered across the front page, over BLACK THURSDAY: MARKET PLUNGES TO RECORD LOW and A PLAGUE OF FORGETTING: THE NEW FLU?

I decided to play it cool. I ordered a double macchiato and spent the next ten minutes observing him, confident he'd never notice me. There were advantages to being the Invisible Girl. When I finally went up to introduce myself, he nodded convulsively, trying to gulp down another mouthful of coffee at the same time. 'You're... er...'

'Gabrielle de Rospin,' I said, to forestall any embarrassment. I'd already given this name on the phone, but hadn't expected him to remember it. In the flesh, he didn't look capable of remembering anything much. It was heartening to meet someone whose powers of recollection were probably even worse than mine.

He squinted sceptically. 'French?'

'Sort of.' We shook hands, and I worked my buttocks up on to the moulded plastic seat of the stool next to his, which was cunningly designed to make anyone under six foot feel like a chubby-legged infant.

'So you've seen Verity?' said Mengers.

'Not *seen*,' I said, confident he wouldn't be able to get his facts straight. 'We just spoke on the phone.'

'When?'

I hummed and hawed. 'Last week?'

He showed no interest in my fudged answer, which was a blessing, and stared at his feet. 'She hasn't put in for expenses, which is not like her. Why did you phone her, again?'

'*She* phoned *me*,' I said. 'I sent her something I'd written, and she really liked it.'

He gave me a *don't waste my time* look and got to his feet.

'Wait!' I forgot about playing it cool and pawed at his arm. 'Another espresso?' Additional caffeine was the last thing Mengers needed, but I wasn't about to let him slip out of my clutches so easily. I wasn't sure how useful a puffy-looking paparazzo would be to my career, but I did know he'd be needing a new writing partner, even if he didn't realise it yet. Maybe it would be easier to sell articles to the press if they already had photos attached.

Clive Mengers paused in mid-departure and looked at his watch. 'Something stronger, perhaps.'

He didn't usually drink this much, he assured me unconvincingly, but he was worried about Verity. His hand, as he lit another cigarette, was shaking, but otherwise the booze seemed to be neutralising the caffeine.

Wilson had never said it, but I'd assumed she and Mengers had slept together. I soon gathered from his ramblings their relationship had been more of a mentor-protégé thing. Wilson, who'd been in the newspaper business since the days of hot metal, had taken him under her wing as soon as he'd stepped off the train from Wolverhampton with his portfolio and a certificate in media studies. For no reason other than an apparently altruistic desire to foster a young person's career, she'd told him to bin the certificate and had used her network of contacts to help him snag his first commission for one of the Sunday magazines - portraits of the capital's hottest young chefs. The pictures, especially the one of cuisine's latest enfants terribles pretending to urinate into his own soup, had caused a stir, and he'd never looked back.

He'd never forgotten he owed it all to Wilson. So when she'd fallen on hard times - editors preferred Oxbridge graduates with photogenic bylines to hard-bitten hackettes with heavy cocaine habits - he'd returned the favour. It had been his pictures that helped flog her article about the glamorous folk she'd met in rehab, and now she was back in the saddle. The piece she was putting together about Nancy was all set to be her biggest scoop so far. Book publishers had expressed interest. A couple of Hollywood studios had already inquired about film rights.

I felt a flutter of panic. 'She didn't mention Hollywood to me.'

Mengers looked baffled. 'Why should she?'

'I know Nancy better than anyone.'

Mengers snickered politely. 'Nobody knows more about their subject than Verity. When she gets her teeth into something, that woman is relentless. She's a terrier.'

No, I thought, she was a *bitch*. She'd been stealing my story. The thought made me feel slightly better about what had happened to her. But only slightly. While Mengers drank his way through a succession of very large brandies, all bankrolled by me, he regaled me with Verity's life story, followed by the life stories of Henri Cartier-Bresson and Robert Capa. When he dissolved into sentimental tears for the third time, I realised I was dealing with a hopeless lush. I tried hard not to be embarrassed, which wasn't easy since his monologue was now featuring words like *fuck*, *cocksucker* and *cunt* with monotonous regularity. Other customers cast exasperated glances in our direction. I could feel my face flushing pink, and pretended we weren't together, though the fact he was sitting next to me might have given the game away.

What I ought to have done was make my excuses and leave. Mengers was so far gone I doubt he would have noticed. But an optimistic part of me was clinging to the hope that he might yet help me realise my dearest hopes and dreams. Also, I was a bit drunk. Not as ratfaced as he was, but I'd necked a few, to keep him company. And so, like an idiot, I stayed.

When finally it became clear that if we didn't leave soon, the staff were going to throw us out, I asked

Mengers for his address. He was in mid effing flow and gave no sign of having heard, so I patted him down, extracted a wallet from one of his pockets, rifled through the receipts until I found one with his address on it, and led him outside, where I hailed a taxi to take us to Ladbroke Grove.

*****

I'd never intended to sleep with Clive Mengers, though it wasn't so much *sleeping* as a mutual loss of consciousness. We went back to his flat and chugged a lot of beer and half a bottle of cheap brandy until I began to feel almost as drunk as he was, and then... The memory, once again, was a little hazy, but we groped each other, and of course he couldn't get it up, not even when I tried to give it the kiss of life, so we thrashed around for a while in a sweaty, non-penetrative fashion before passing out.

At around four in the morning, I was shaken out of my stupor by an earth tremor. In North Kensington, yet! I leapt out of bed and braced myself against the doorframe, which according to my doomsday survival manual was the place least likely to collapse in the event of seismic activity. Only then did I look back at the bed and see it hadn't been an earthquake but Mengers snoring, which was making the bed vibrate like a sex-aid in a Hong Kong love hotel. I pulled on my clothes and wandered through to the living-room. I could tell from the number of empty bottles that we'd been drinking like demons, while the overflowing ashtray and stinkiness of my Selma Jacobson sweatshirt testified to Mengers's chain-smoking.

I was feeling surprisingly hale for one who had

drunk so much, but knew from experience there was a hangover lurking around the corner, waiting to leap out and mug me. Swaying gently, surveying the wreckage of the room and wondering whether it mightn't be a smart idea to strike out for home while I was still capable of standing, I noticed a small red light flickering in the corner of the room, and remembered why I was there.

Mengers's computer was in hibernation mode. I sat in his revolving chair and pressed a key, and the screen-saver sprang into action. The screen was filled with small babies crawling hither and thither, mouths opening and closing, pudgy little limbs working like mad as they tried to break out of their confines with the single-mindedness of P.O.W.s from *The Colditz Story*. I was cooing over the babies when a giant foot suddenly descended out of nowhere and stomped on them, again and again, until every last infant had been crushed to a bloody pulp. Then the babies were miraculously resurrected, and the cycle began all over again.

Reluctantly I tore my addled gaze away from the carnage and began to explore Mengers's inbox, which is how I discovered he knew more about me than I'd realised - probably more than even *he* realised, since it was unlikely he'd got round to cross-referencing his mail. He still thought he'd gone to bed with Gabrielle de Rospin, but I found several references to 'BP', 'Pringle' and 'Belly-Ache'. When I'd finished reading Verity Wilson's emails, including the one in which she'd announced the time and place of her last meeting with me, I carefully deleted them. Then I deleted every email in which Nancy's name was mentioned, usually in some laughably erroneous context. They'd even blamed her for the fluctuations in the stock market and the plague of jellyfish.

I rocked gently from side to side, debating what to do, and must have lulled myself into a light doze. In my half-waking state I dreamt about Verity Wilson's family, who - to judge by what Mengers had said - didn't sound like the sort of people you'd want to mess with. Besides the medical student son and the two teenage daughters, there were two brothers who'd been professional boxers and a third who seemed to be some sort of debt-collector, all of them in thrall to a formidable matriarch called Vera who sounded as though she would have given Violet Kray a run for her money. Verity had started out as Vera too, but as soon as she'd landed her first magazine column, in an early 1970s teenage monthly called *Chicklet*, she'd changed her name.

'This was going to be her big break,' the debt-collecting brother said in my half-dream. 'Or one of them, anyway. Verity has had a few breaks in her time.' He gazed intently into his beer, as though it might hold the key to his sister's whereabouts. 'I was really fond of her, you know.'

And I saw it wasn't the debt-collecting brother after all. It was Mengers. He looked up from his beer, and his eyes opened wide, as though he was only now seeing me as I really was. 'My god,' he said. 'I should have guessed. You're not Gabrielle de Rospin at all! You're the...' Then his mouth filled up with blood, and I shivered and woke up to find myself still hunched in Mengers's revolving chair. The computer had long since gone to sleep, as had the foot tucked beneath me.

Outside, it was still dark. Inside, I was still drunk, so I postponed setting out for home and gulped down several glasses of water before curling up on the sofa beneath a moth-eaten tartan blanket. Eventually I drifted off, to be woken again by a crash that sent me leaping off the sofa in alarm. After peeping out through the front door, I identified the noise as having been connected to a pile of mail on the doormat of the communal hallway. I lay down again, but now the hangover was kicking in, and a couple of workmen were working on the inside of my head with a pneumatic drill. After ten minutes of head-banging agony, I realised they weren't imaginary at all, but real workmen with a real drill, ploughing up the street outside.

Now feeling like death, I hobbled into the bathroom to empty my bladder, and afterwards hugged the lavatory bowl for a while, gazing into the discoloured porcelain, before staggering back into the kitchen to cobble together a cup a tea. The milk in the fridge had lumps in it. The only mugs I could find were encrusted with tree-rings of ancient tannin and needed sterilising, but I had to make do with a rinse and wipe down. I gulped down scalding tea and was about to leave when it struck me I should say goodbye to my host, if only to establish the groundwork for further collaboration. I poured him some tea, opened the bedroom door and slipped into the penumbra.

Nancy, with her olfactory superpowers, would have parsed the tell-tale odours at an earlier stage, but my sinuses were still bunged up with secondhand cigarette smoke, so it was only now that the stench hit me. It smelled like a single man's bedroom, a blend of fermented night breath and unwashed socks, but with a sickly-sweet undertow. Mengers gave no sign of being awake. Gingerly, I picked my way across the room towards the bed, holding the mug out like a placatory offering. Halfway there, my ears picked up the buzzing of a solitary fly. I was concentrating so hard on not spilling the tea it never occurred to me that anything might be amiss. How could anything have been wrong? Hadn't I been in that same bed myself only a few hours earlier? Everything had been fine then.

How would you know anyway? You were still drunk as a skunk.

I was vaguely aware of the mug slopping some of its contents on to the bedroom carpet, but couldn't spare the energy to adjust my grip, because my attention was now directed towards the bed. The light filtering through the drawn curtains (brown striped polycotton) was murky and discoloured, but it was enough. The duvet cover had already been dark, but now it was darker in some places more than others. And those darker places were glistening, because they were not just dark, but wet. The fly stopped buzzing. Maybe it hadn't been a fly after all, maybe it had been the distant sound of the drill, filtered through fifty layers of mental cotton wool. In the silence that followed, I watched and listened, but there was no movement beneath the duvet. Not even breathing.

'Clive?' I watched and listened some more, feeling every hair on the back of my neck standing on end and doing a Mexican Wave, and then I lent forward and prodded the shape on the bed with the rim of the mug. There was a small but significant squelching. At first I thought Mengers must have pulled the bedclothes right up over his head. Then I saw he hadn't. The reason I couldn't see his head was because there was no head to see.

Oh fuck no, I thought. *Not again.* The mug slipped

from my fingers and rolled off the bed and bounced over the carpet, and what was left of the tea splashed my ankles. *If you can keep your head when all about you are losing theirs...*

I didn't see much point in investigating further. Mengers was very obviously beyond help, so I turned my back on the bed and slipped out of there sharpish. In the hallway, I felt a cold draught and found the front door ajar. I remembered closing it after looking out at the pile of mail, but had I locked it again? I tried to strongarm my thoughts into some sort of order.

At some point, probably while I'd been dozing on the sofa, someone had crept into the flat and murdered Clive Mengers. I locked the door, and went back into the living-room and my knees suddenly gave way and I sat down heavily on the sofa as I realised what a narrow escape I'd had. What if Mengers's snoring *hadn't* woken me? What if I'd been asleep in that same bed when the killer had snuck in and hacked his head off? They would have cut mine off too! I could feel my heart racing.

What was I supposed to do now? Go to the police? *Please.* They'd want to know what I'd been doing in Mengers's flat, and then they'd start asking questions about Wilson, and then they'd search my flat, and then... And Nancy was there, and... No, the trail had to stop here. I put my head in my hands.

On the other hand, what if *no-one* had snuck in? What if the murderer had been here all along? *What if it had been me?* What if, while I'd been asleep, Gabrielle de Rospin had emerged from my head and dispatched him, the way she'd dispatched Verity Wilson? It was farfetched, but not nearly as farfetched as what had been happening to Nancy these past few months. I preferred to pin the blame on crazy fundamentalist hitmen, though since I'd got to know Jules Delgado, he didn't seem as crazy as I'd originally thought. On the *other* other hand, I hadn't seen him since the weekend and he *had* been sleeping with Wilson, so maybe he'd found out what I'd done to her, and this was his warped idea of revenge...

Or perhaps I was grasping at straws. Just thinking about the movements, sights and sounds relating to act of detaching someone's head from their body made me feel ill. *I* wasn't capable of that, but Gabrielle was another matter. Gabrielle de Rospin was a crazy witch, an evil id who was acting out my subconscious desires, including the systematic elimination of my rivals. I'd seen it in films. I tried to think back to the part where I had subconsciously wished Clive Mengers dead, and failed. Then again, subconscious desires *were* subconscious, so maybe I didn't realise I had them. I wondered if Phoebe was in danger too, and whether I ought to be warning her.

I'd somehow got blood all over me, and spent twenty minutes sponging it off so I wouldn't frighten commuters on the way home. Then I spent a further twenty minutes wiping down all the surfaces I'd touched before it occurred to me my DNA would be all over Clive Mengers's sheets, and possibly over what remained of Clive Mengers as well. So unless I wanted to start doing laundry, I didn't have much choice in the matter. Trying not to look too closely at what was on the bed, I poured the rest of the brandy over it, lit a cigarette with his Zippo, took a couple of clumsy puffs to make sure it was going nicely, and left it smouldering on the pillow.

Everyone knew you should never smoke in bed. Especially when you'd had a lot to drink.

I pocketed the Zippo, because it was a design classic and I was loath to let it go to waste. By the time I left, smoke was beginning to drift out of the bedroom. Out in the communal hallway, I cleared the pile of mail from the doormat and saw from one of the envelopes that Mengers's full name was - or had been - Clive Everest Mengers. *Everest.* A name full of soaring hope: the end of rationing, a new dawn, the promise of future peaks to be assailed, albeit with a leg-up from a couple of Sherpas. It was that silly little detail, more than anything, that made me want to cry.

Then I realised I'd left my fingerprints all over the mail as well, so I had to carry it away with me to dump in a litter-bin next to a hamburger restaurant on Euston Road.

Chapter 3
Ginger Nuts

Nancy was furious. I'd stayed out all night, and hadn't phoned her. 'I thought something had happened to you!'

I spun a convoluted yarn about a boozy reunion of Croydon survivors and a sofabed in Shepherd's Bush. She wanted to know more, but I blew her off with an excuse about needing to take a nap before my afternoon shift, and she bought it. It started off as another lie, but no sooner had I laid my aching bones on the bed she hadn't bothered to make, I fell into a deep and dreamless sleep.

For the next few days I grabbed every newspaper I could find, including locals and freebies, and studied each item and photographic byline so thoroughly that even Nancy, self-absorbed as she was, noticed my seemingly voracious appetite for news.

'So what's going on in the world?'

'Nothing much,' I said, which as far as I was concerned was the truth. I'd found Verity Wilson's name attached to a story about a gang of graffiti artists who'd been painting giant penises on walls across London, but that was all. The only mention of Clive Mengers was as a byline under a photograph of two otters wearing top hats. I couldn't find any items, even tiny ones, about missing journalists, or house fires in West London, and the only discovery of a corpse was that of an official from the water board who had committed suicide in his car. After a while, I started wondering if I'd imagined the whole thing. I'd been very, very drunk, and after that I'd been very, very hungover. Maybe what I'd seen in Mengers's bedroom had been a flashback to the clinic. I was suffering from Post Traumatic Stress Disorder. Yes, that was it. If there was nothing in the papers, then it couldn't possibly have happened.

I wondered, hopefully, if maybe I'd imagined what had happened to Verity Wilson as well. I decided to act as though this were so. That way, the nightmares wouldn't be so disturbing.

*****

After a two day break, Nancy felt sufficiently recovered to go back to rehearsals. During the taxi ride she kept her eyes peeled for men in suits - grey or navy blue, they were all enemies now - but arrived without suspicious sightings. If there were people watching her, they were doing it discreetly. She wasn't so naïve to think ComSec had forgotten about her, but maybe the mayhem she'd triggered had convinced them to keep their distance.

On her first day back, she approached Les Six.

'Have you heard anything from the people who got me this job?'

He frowned at her. 'What do you mean?'

'No-one's been putting any... pressure on you? They haven't told you to replace me?'

He looked offended. 'I'm running this show. No-one tells *me* what to do.'

'I know, I just wondered if...'

'What are you implying?'

'Nothing,' said Nancy. 'Nothing. I'm just glad you

changed your mind about me.'

His face softened. 'You know what? So am I. Holt was a has-been anyway. You're going to be great.' He smiled and squeezed her hand.

At long last the other actors, even Carlotta, seemed to have accepted her as the star of the show, and their initial animosity had been replaced by varying degrees of affection and solicitude. She was one of them now. The absence of Mr. Jones and Mr. Miller didn't go unremarked, but Dougal was the only one to ask where they'd got to, probably because he'd developed a crush on Mr. Jones. Nancy told Dougal she had no idea where Mr. Jones had gone or how to get hold of him, and tried not to think about him sitting in the road with a pipe through his torso.

*****

Having to share my flat wasn't all bad. We watched TV together, and I did Nancy's nails, and she did my hair, and I enjoyed her wicked impressions of the Wormwood staff, who sounded like a barrel of laughs. I didn't like to point out that she'd left several of them dead or bleeding.

On Sunday morning, Nancy picked up the last of her boxes from Mrs. Feaver and ferried them to the Bunterberg by taxi. By the time I got back from work, they were stacked along the hallway and against most of one wall of the bedroom, virtually sealing off the walk-in wardrobe. This suited me fine; apart from the obvious considerations, I didn't want her borrowing any more of my clothes. She was already stretching my eye-watering expensive Sonny Wortzik pyjama bottoms out of shape.

Just the sight of them straining over her pregnant belly made my innards churn with anxiety.

'How long do you think you might be staying?' I asked, watching in horrified fascination as the build-up of ash on her latest cigarette grew longer. 'I mean, so I can plan around it.'

She was examining a script and didn't reply, so I tried again. 'Those pyjama bottoms look tight. Wouldn't you prefer something a little more comfortable?'

Nancy looked up at last. 'These are fine,' she said, patting her stomach. 'Nice and stretchy.'

'That's what I'm afraid of.'

'Would you like to touch it?'

'What? Oh, I see. OK, why not.'

I stretched out a hand and laid it flat against the Sonny Wortzik. Nancy's face twitched and she seemed to tense up, then closed her eyes and made a visible effort to relax.

'I can't feel anything. Except you're fatter.'

'You think?'

'Ow!' I jerked my hand back and stared at it. It was like pins and needles in my fingers.

Nancy opened her eyes and chuckled indulgently, as though her foetus had just done something adorable.

'You felt that?'

I asked if I could try again, and this time didn't snatch my hand away when the tingling started. I tried to follow Nancy's example by breathing slowly and evenly. The pins and needles sensation spread to my wrist and up my arm. It felt as though I were being scanned, perhaps even tested for suitability to join a secret society. The sensation wasn't entirely unpleasant. In fact, I could see how it might become quite addictive.

'What the hell have you got in there?'

'A little footballer,' she said. 'Just letting us know she's alive and well.'

'She? They confirmed it's a girl?'

'I don't think they know, to be honest.'

I wanted to say, *Let's hope it's not a jackal, or a billy-goat,* but desisted. It probably wouldn't be smart to remind a expectant mother that it would be a miracle if her baby turned out to be human, especially if that expectant mother could give you a nosebleed.

'We're bonding!' I said.

'I wouldn't go that far.' Nancy tenderly removed my hand, and I tried not to notice the look of revulsion that passed across her face again as she touched me. Her words were gentle though. 'Bedtime, I think. You don't want to be asleep on the sofa when they arrive.'

The word 'bedtime' made me yawn before I even realised what she'd said. 'When who arrives?'

'You won't even know we've been here.'

I couldn't make my lips form the obvious question, but she continued anyway. 'Factory's getting rewired, so we're rehearsing here. Just a few of us.'

I found my voice. '*Who's us?*'

'Just this once. You don't even have to stick around. Though'd be great if you could pop out in the morning and get some more milk. And biscuits. They like chocolate digestives or Jaffa Cakes. And some of them take sugar.'

I was too dumbfounded to object, and there was a part of me that was excited. Actors! *In my flat!* And so, next morning, I obediently trotted out to replenish milk and sugar supplies, though I drew the line at Chocolate Digestives or Jaffa Cakes. They'd have Ginger Nuts or nothing. But if Nancy thought I was going to leave a bunch of unattended thespians unsupervised to go impro all over my flat and its hard-earned contents, she had another think coming. I knew what these people were like. I knew Nancy, didn't I? It would be crumbs down the back of the sofa before you knew it. I told Nancy I was going to sit in on the rehearsal, and she couldn't very well say no.

*****

And so I met the cast of *Ripped!* Or some of them. They were rejigging a scene that hadn't been working, and since it involved a chorus of zombie prostitutes I wasn't surprised. They weren't rehearsing the chorus now, though, but some dialogue; just as well since the size of my flat didn't lend itself to full-blown zombie action.

Even on my own territory, I felt like a ghost at the banquet; no-one took much notice of me apart from Jet Coleman, who was so absurdly good-looking and so complimentary about my taste in furnishing I unfurled like a flower in his company, thinking perhaps he was working up towards inviting me on a hot date. Later, Nancy told me he was like this with everyone.

Carlotta Reese I recognised instantly as Les Six's companion from the Rue Bar - a skinny-ribbed harpy with silky raven hair, the sort of woman who systematically antagonises the female half of the human race but makes up for it by ladling concentrated pheromone, like maple syrup, all over the male half. Up close she seemed less of a knockout, more of a plastic bimbo whose forehead had acquired a Mekon-like smoothness from having had so much Botox pumped into it. I felt proud of Nancy for stealing the leading role away from this alien creature, especially when she sneered at the plate of Ginger Nuts as though they weren't good enough for her ladyship.

Les Six, on the other hand, turned out to be a sweetie. For an egomaniac who had managed to coerce a couple of dozen grown-ups into acting out his adolescent fantasies in public, he was surprisingly self-deprecating, though I didn't care much for his habit of referring to himself in the third person. And I did have problems with his precious play, which I could tell by listening to a few lines of dialogue was utter bilge. Just because I liked hanging out with writers and artists didn't mean I didn't have standards.

Six's people skills were impressive though, as I watched him covertly reassign more dialogue to Nancy while reassuring the others that yes, they had a handle on their characters, they were sensitive and talented human beings and this was all set to be their breakthrough role, because after *Ripped!* the offers would start pouring in. After *Ripped!* they would all be household names.

He was right. After the press show their names would go down in theatre history, or what was left of it. But not quite in the way they'd imagined.

*****

Nancy was nervous about the climax of the musical: a big fight scene in which members of the Jack the Ripper killer-collective attacked Maggie Crook en masse, only for her to turn the tables on them. It had originally been scripted as a few basic self-defence moves, but that was before Six had been to see a new science fiction movie in which the combatants flew through the air and practised a sort of weightless kung-fu. He'd set his heart on Maggie and her assailants locking horns in similar fashion. 'If Peter Pan can do it,' said Six, 'so can we.'

He'd had to lower his sights when the Stage Manager had deemed it inadvisable for a pregnant woman to be trussed into a harness and hoisted into the air, so Les had had to settle for hiring a choreographer to create a flamboyant dance routine that supposedly mimicked the actions of oriental martial arts. Even so, the scene was making Nancy anxious.

The day after the Bunterberg rehearsal I came home from work to find her sunk in gloom, chain-smoking as usual, and staring at the wall. You could almost see the dark cloud around her head, and it wasn't just the smoke from her cigarettes. Still gazing at the wall, she said, 'I want you to tell me the truth, Belinda,' and I thought *uh-oh*, because in my experience, people who told you they wanted to hear the truth rarely thought kindly of you when you gave it to them.

She turned around and I saw her mascara was smeared. When my mascara smeared, I looked like a panda that had been punched in the face, but Nancy managed to appear smoky and dolorous, like a Pre-Raphaelite model who'd been tippling too much laudanum. She looked me straight in the eye, and asked, 'Am I good, Belinda?'

Whoah. I hadn't been expecting this. I considered the question and its implications very carefully before responding with, 'Everyone's a sinner, Nancy.'

She sighed. 'No, I meant as an *actor*.'

Ah, so we were talking career. The talent thing. Guessing the truth was the last thing she wanted to hear,

I said, 'You're great!' It wasn't a lie, exactly. She did have talent, though I'm not sure it was for acting per se.

She shook her head sadly. 'I'm holding something back.'

'You are?'

'We've been blocking out fight moves. Oh, we've been through them before, many times, but I was never really trying. Until today, when I decided to go for broke. I was really authentic, Belinda. Those emotions were *real.*'

'And?'

'Nothing happened.'

'What did you expect?'

'A small accident. But... nothing. He didn't even get a nosebleed.'

I looked at her curiously. She'd mentioned trying to control her superpowers, but this was the first I'd heard about her deliberately using them as a weapon.

'You sound disappointed.'

'Well, of course I'm glad Rod's not hurt. But, Belinda...' She ground the remains of her cigarette out into a Provençal malachite vide-poche she'd adopted as an ashtray. 'If what I'm doing as an actress is truthful, if what I'm emoting is *from the heart*, then surely something should have happened to him? A migraine, fit of sneezing or something? Nothing serious, nothing that couldn't be patched up. But nothing happened at all!

'I see what you're getting at,' I said, slowly cottoning on. 'It's that Method thing, isn't it. You think you have to feel it for real.'

She nodded, and a single tear slid down her cheek.

'Obviously you've never heard the story about Dustin Hoffman and Laurence Olivier when they were filming *Marathon Man*,' I said, and she shook her head. So I told her how Hoffman had stayed up for three nights on the trot to prepare for a scene in which his character hadn't slept, and how Olivier had said to him, 'But my dear boy - why don't you just try *acting* it?'

'Probably apocryphal,' I said. 'Hoffman says he was just dancing the night away at Studio 54. But you see, acting doesn't have to be real, sometimes you just have to *pretend*. Simple as that.'

Nancy laughed, though I could see she wasn't entirely convinced.

'Besides,' I said, 'imagine how messy it would get if someone got hurt at every performance. They'd have to keep replacing the actors.'

'You're right,' she said. 'It wouldn't be practical!'

'By the way, you sounded terrific in rehearsal yesterday.'

She brightened up. 'Really?'

And I realised this was all she'd needed to hear, after all.

*****

What else is there to say about life with Nancy? Everything revolved around her, but nothing had changed there - she'd *always* been the centre of attention, even at school. I was always tidying up after her, like a lady-in-waiting; what little attention she'd ever paid to housework had disappeared altogether since her stay at Wormwood, where they'd spoiled her rotten.

But I'd almost forgotten *why* they'd spoiled her till the Saturday we went out to buy a new tape deck to replace the one she'd buggered up. We were halfway up

Tottenham Court Road when she stopped and clutched my arm. 'Look at that,' she whispered. She pointed across the road. I stared blindly. 'No,' she said. '*Look!*'

All I could see was a branch of BabyCare.

'Come on,' she said, pulling me off the pavement and straight into the traffic. My scream of terror was drowned out by the screeching of brakes.

'Don't forget some of us aren't superhuman,' I gasped as by some miracle we reached the opposite kerb unscathed.

'Sorry,' she said, but didn't sound it. I was still trembling as she pulled me into the shop. The sounds of the outside world were instantly cut off; it was unnaturally hushed in there, like a church, though there must have been more than a dozen other pregnant women wandering up and down the aisles.

'Just a quick look,' Nancy insisted with a deceptively casual air that reminded me of a junkie claiming that although she sometimes used heroin for fun, it wasn't something she actually *craved*. She fell into a trance and began to drift up and down the aisles with the other women, staring enraptured at rows of disposable nappies and elfin trainers, bibs and potties and buggies. I was left feeling awkward by the door, wanting to explain that this wasn't really my scene, that I was only here because my pregnant friend had hauled me inside. But when it became apparent that Nancy wasn't in a hurry to leave, I stomped after her, looking pointedly at my watch. 'I have work,' I reminded her.

'Yes,' she said, smiling at the assistant who was hovering nearby.

The atmosphere of hushed pastel reverence was bringing me out in goose pimples. Somebody, surely, would spot me for the imposter I was, and then they'd all point and, maybe, pelt me to death with small tins of apple sauce. I was sidling back towards the door when I spotted a fellow interloper lurking behind a display of high-chairs. Someone else who didn't belong here. I nodded in solidarity, but he bobbed down behind a display of dummies. Only when he was out of sight did I recall he'd been wearing a grey suit.

I shuffled back to where Nancy was stroking a tiny white sock, entranced, as though it were a puppy. She turned to me and asked, 'Do you think I should take up knitting?'

'Nance,' I said, touching her elbow.

Something in my voice caught her attention. She replaced the sock and followed my gaze towards the dummy display. There was no sign of Grey Suit now, but I felt her stiffen. 'Don't even think about it,' she said in a quiet voice that carried all the way across the shop, so that other customers glanced up in surprise at having their reveries disturbed. The assistant to whom she'd been talking, a bright-looking girl with cleverly concealed acne and a badge informing us her name was Deirdre, quickly assessed the situation. Her benign expression hardened. 'Is that guy bothering you?'

Grey Suit reappeared, sauntering past a nearby stack of tricycles. He looked even more out of place than I felt. When he spotted Nancy he stopped sauntering and wavered, hand hovering over his trouser pocket like a cowboy preparing to draw his pistol. Nancy tutted and shook her head, but whether at Deirdre or Grey Suit I couldn't tell. Then her eyes opened very wide and she let out a little gasp and tottered against a pile of teddy-bears. As though we'd rehearsed the move a hundred times, Deirdre and I grabbed her arms and kept her upright.

Nancy reached out and touched a plush teddy-bear, and said, *'So shall it be done,'* this time speaking so softly that Deirdre and I were the only ones to hear it.

The hairs on the back of my neck were once again rising to the occasion. At last I was seeing with my own eyes what she could do. The touch had been delicate, and only a few of the bears fell off the back of the pile, but it was enough to trigger a mini-avalanche of baby sneakers, which in turn overloaded a shelf crammed with economy-sized containers of cotton-buds. The end of the shelf fell to the ground, and on its way down knocked against the pedal of a tricycle halfway up the stack. The swivelling pedal propelled the vehicle forward off the pile, and it landed on Grey Suit's head.

I rubbed my eyes, trying to absorb what I'd just seen. Deirdre advanced towards Grey Suit, but he looked more shaken than hurt, and extricated himself before she got there. Then he was up and out of the shop as though being chased by demons, an expression of starkest terror on his face. Through the window, I saw him haring down the street, careening into other pedestrians like a pinball.

Deirdre came back to check on Nancy. She lowered her voice, as though imparting a dirty little secret. 'You wouldn't believe the number of creeps we get in here.'

'Tell me about it,' said Nancy.

I'd lost all interest in tape decks. There was an lingering electric current in the air which made me nervous. All it needed was a spark, I sensed, and the whole place would go up in flames. When we got outside, Nancy lent against a wall while I flapped my arms, trying to flag down one of the cabs that seemed to be methodically ignoring me.

'That was amazing,' I said.

'I thought they'd given up,' she sighed. She lit a cigarette and sucked in the smoke as if recharging her internal batteries. The tension drained out of the air, and I relaxed slightly. After a couple of puffs, she stamped out the rest of the cigarette and made a small movement with her hand and a taxi immediately drew up next to us. She clambered into the back. I noticed she didn't bother to belt herself in.

We didn't talk much on the ride. Nancy was sunk in her own thoughts, while I was trying not to punch the air in triumph. I'd finally seen her in action, and it had been terrifying, but I was filled with an exhilaration that kept me afloat all through the rest of the day at the bookshop. I was prepared to bet Phoebe had never witnessed anything like it! I'd stolen a march on my rival.

*****

Later, when I got home from work and poured us each a glass of Morgon, I asked Nancy how it worked. 'Do you wiggle your nose, like Samantha on *Bewitched*?'

She laughed. 'I *wish*.'

'What does it feel like?'

She pondered for a while, then attempted to describe the process. 'It's like everything goes into slow motion while all the elements are laid out in front of me, like a slide-show; I just have to select the correct ones and... rearrange them in my head.'

I looked at her doubtfully. 'Like a Picture Editor?'

'More like a series of flashbacks. It feels as if they're going on for ages, but it only lasts a split-second.'

'How do you know which flashbacks are the right ones?'

'I don't. Or I didn't to begin with. But I had help.' She patted her bump. 'And we've developed more of a rapport. Now it's more like good cop, bad cop, and I'm the good one; I try to make sure it doesn't get out of hand.' Her face darkened. 'Like it did at the clinic, when I was out of it.'

Oh yes, the clinic. My mood plummeted. 'You still think that was you?'

'Wasn't my fault, but I feel responsible.'

I didn't want to talk about what had happened the clinic either, because I wasn't so sure it had all been Nancy's doing, not after what had happened to Wilson and Mengers.

'What about the nosebleeds? I don't understand how you do that. It's not like you're going around stuffing Fudge Tub spoons up people's nostrils.'

She shook her head. 'No idea. Might have something to do with changes in atmospheric pressure. You know, the way dogs start barking just before an earthquake. Or maybe there isn't a scientific explanation. I don't think what's happening to me can be explained scientifically, or even pseudo-scientifically. You know, psychokinesis, precognition, things like that.'

Blimey, she *had* been reading. This was definitely not the old scatterbrained Nancy I knew and loved. I wasn't sure what I thought about New Model Nancy. All I knew was I had to treat her with kid gloves. So of course I threw caution to the winds and asked, 'Can you show me something now?'

She glowered. 'It's not a party trick, Belinda.' The glare softened. 'Though actually, I am getting quite good at it. Watch!' She nodded towards the table. Nothing happened for half a minute, but then her eyes seemed to fix on something in the distance, just as they had in BabyCare, and she exhaled and said, '*There.*'

I looked back at the table and saw the ashtray rocking. The ashtray which had started life as a Provençal malachite vide-poche. The ashtray into which she had been grinding out cigarette butts for the past half hour. 'No, not that...' I said, but too late. The repurposed vide-poche tumbled off the edge of the table, strewing its contents all over the Van Merkens.

'Oh, *well done.*'

'Sorry. I didn't mean for it to actually fall off. That was the result of me stubbing a cigarette out a few minutes ago, but I must have miscalculated.'

'So you can read the future,' I said crossly, trying to pick fag ends out of the rug.

'No, I just provide ingredients, mostly without being aware of it.'

'What do you do if you want to, you know, *kill* people?'

She looked shocked.

'Sorry,' I said, 'I'm just trying to...'

'I never wanted to kill anyone.' She started fluttering her eyelids rapidly, and I finally saw she was blinking back tears. 'We just move things.'

'Like Carrie?'

'Nothing like that. Small stuff.'

I felt a pain in my sinuses and decided it was time to distract her so my nose wouldn't start bleeding. 'Thought of any names yet?' How about Damien?'

Nancy gave me a look. 'It's a girl.'

'Well then, Lilith,' I said. 'Belladonna? Morticia? Maleficent?'

Nancy relaxed and joined in. 'Astarte. Isis. Medusa. Gorgonzola.'

'Christabel. Clytemnestra. Lucrezia. Messalina...' I ran out of evil girls' names.

'Actually she's already got a name. Kitty.'

'Short for Katharine?'

'Just Kitty.'

*****

Those were the good times, but after two weeks of us being cooped up together, I was starting to find Nancy's presence intolerable. My flat wasn't big enough for two people, especially when one of them was heavily pregnant. I hadn't realised just how disaster-prone she was till I noticed rings on the table where she'd forgotten to use a coaster, or brutal creases furrowing the hitherto virginal spines of my favourite Penguin Classics. She was ploughing through Tolstoy and Stendhal and thick tomes on architecture, typography and the principles of design as though they were Janet and John readers.

I resented her sleeping in my bed, which left me permanently camped on the Egon Spengler sofa that hadn't been looking or smelling quite so fresh since she'd spilled whisky over it. *My* whisky, of course: my best McTarry single malt, which she loutishly diluted with Cola or - on one memorably gruesome occasion - coconut-flavoured Fudge Tub. She also depleted my supplies of gin, cognac, vodka - even the bottle of Orloff that nobody would touch because it gave off an odour like decaying flesh (though the red and black label was a design landmark, which is why I'd bought it). She had a maddening habit of leaving just a quarter-inch of liquor at the bottom of each bottle so she couldn't be accused of having finished any of them.

And I worried, all the time, about the walk-in wardrobe in my bedroom, which in my fevered imagination had morphed into a cosmic black hole. If the door were to be opened even a fraction, it would rip a gigantic hole in the fabric of reality and suck everything into it. Each time I went into the bedroom, the smell seemed worse. Even the miasma of Sobranie and cheap perfume barely masked the whiff of rotting flesh. It was even worse than the Orloff.

Chapter 4
The Split

Everything was going to turn out all right in the end. I truly believed that. And even if it didn't, there were ways of forcing it. I'd always had a soft spot for that version of Cinderella in which one of the Ugly Sisters sliced off part of her foot so she could squeeze it into the glass slipper. There's pragmatism for you. Showed remarkable initiative, I'd always thought, as well as a willingness to sacrifice minor body parts. It wasn't her fault the Prince found her out. I suppose he must have spotted the blood through the glass.

On the other hand, wasn't there a version of the story in which the slipper was made of fur, not glass? In which case, the Ugly Sister might have got away with it and married the Prince after all. Or maybe there never was any slipper, and it was all a metaphor. Maybe he was trying out the size of her vagina, or something.

*****

A few days after the BabyCare incident, Nancy offered me a lift to work in her taxi. I soon regretted having taken her up on it; she ordered the to driver take such a roundabout route that I ended up ten minutes late.

'What's wrong with Rosebery Avenue?' I asked as we negotiated the one-way system beneath Holborn Viaduct.

'Too obvious,' said Nancy.

'Do you do this every time you go to rehearsal?'

'Pretty much. I guess it's a habit now. Can't be too careful.'

'You think ComSec is still following you?'

Instead of answering, she asked, 'What time do you finish work?'

I thought she was going to suggest meeting up for a drink, and told her eight, as usual.

'See you half eight, then,' she said as I climbed out.

*****

Shortly before seven o'clock, Lars came into the shop. I was still vexed at not having heard from him since the trip to Shanghai. I punished him by ignoring him, but he followed me around like a puppy as I unpacked a carton of travel books and placed them on the shelves.

Eventually his lugubrious loitering got on my nerves, so I turned to face him and said, 'Well, look who's here,' with as much sarcasm as I could muster.

'I'm sorry, I should have called.'

He seemed thinner, and there were purplish shadows around his eyes. In fact, he didn't look well at all.

'You've lost weight,' I said.

He lowered his voice. 'Fucking Mumbai. Been in the bathroom ever since.'

I pounced on the discrepancy. 'You said it was Shanghai!'

He sighed, as though I were being unreasonable. 'Shanghai was *last* month,' he said. 'I only got back from Mumbai last week. Anyway, these cities are all the same when you're on business. You don't get time to look around.'

'You could have sent me a postcard from the hotel.'

His lower lip trembled. 'Look, the reason I haven't called... Eileen isn't doing so well.'

He was on the verge of tears; I didn't want him making a scene in the shop, so didn't press him further. Maybe I'd been wrong about Eileen. Maybe she wasn't faking it.

'The chemo is really taking it out of her, and my Delhi Belly isn't helping.'

'Be careful. You don't want to infect her if she's already poorly.'

He studied the floor. 'I don't think she's going to make it, Lindy.'

'I'm sorry,' I said. I wasn't lying; I was sorry we couldn't return to our early days of carefree carousing without having to worry about his wife.

I tracked down Alain and asked if I could get off work early. It was the third time I'd made the same request that week, so he wasn't pleased.

'Go on then. Make him suffer for dumping you.'

'He hasn't dumped me.'

Alain rolled his eyes heavenward. 'You're so gullible sometimes, Belinda. You shouldn't let these guys take advantage of you like this.'

'I'm not' I said, annoyed. 'His wife's really sick.'

'Oh, *right*,' said Alain. 'Don't tell me. She doesn't understand him, and they haven't had sex for years.'

This annoyed me all the more since Lars had indeed said something very much like it at the start of our relationship. 'People don't *always* do things for selfish reasons,' I said, turning my back on him in disgust and returning to my erstwhile lover, who was now dejectedly flicking through the pages of *How To Photograph Your Dog*. I remembered how he'd encouraged me to talk when I'd so desperately needed someone to confide in, decided the least I could do was return the favour, and suggested we go for a drink.

'But no sex and Scrabble tonight, I'm afraid. I've got a friend sleeping over.' I silently cursed Nancy, whose presence at the Bunterberg looked set to ruin my love life as well as my clothes.

Lars looked as crestfallen as a schoolboy whose tadpoles had been nicked. 'But I want you so badly.'

'Sssh,' I said, pretending to be embarrassed, but casting sidelong glances at nearby customers, hoping they'd overheard. Yes! Inside my boring bookshop assistant exterior beat the heart of a passionate love goddess!

We went to the Bar Tholomew, which was thronged with City boys and their mobile phones, all going off at once. At one stage we had the theme from *The Godfather* vying with *Orpheus in the Underworld* and *In the Hall of the Mountain King*.

Lars cocked his ear at this last one. 'That's Eileen's favourite. She wants it played at her funeral.'

It didn't strike me as very funereal, but who was I argue with an ailing wife's musical choices?

'But I'd rather not talk about Eileen. It's just *us* here, you and me. How *are* you, Lindy? You've lost weight too.'

This perked me up, though I should have realised the past few weeks hadn't just warped my psyche, but had changed my physical appearance as well. The problem was, I didn't want Lars knowing who my mystery guest was, because I knew he'd start begging to come back and meet her. So with both Eileen and Nancy off the menu, our talk became disjointed and uneasy.

I prattled on, trying to fill the pauses between ringtones with dramatic monologues about plagues of flying ants and the approaching Millennium. Lars assured me that when he yawned, it was because he was tired and not because he was bored. But the wine loosened my tongue, and I might have ended up mentioning Nancy once or twice, and I think Delgado might have crept into the conversation as well, but mostly I just talked about myself and my living-room furniture and the bookshop, being sure to leave out all the parts about my alter ego being a crazy mass murderer.

Afterwards, my recollections of the latter part of the evening were a little vague, but one thing I definitely remembered was Lars holding my face and peering into my eyes and saying, 'I know it's been hard for you, and I'm sorry. I have to look out for Eileen - she's my wife, and I owe her that - but if you ever need me, Lindy, remember you can count on me. You can call me any time at all, day or night.'

I became quite maudlin in my gratitude, even though I knew this was bullshit. Lars hadn't even given me his home number - probably thought I'd drunk-dial Eileen behind his back - and whenever I left messages on his mobile service, he was never in a hurry to ring back. Such were the drawbacks of dating a married man, and I'd always accepted them.

But then Lars could say what he liked because I

was drinking much faster than he was, even if he did seem to be outdoing me on the pork scratchings front. And despite my laudable aim to provide him with a sympathetic ear, I ended up doing most of the talking as well. I might even have babbled something about Nancy's stay at Wormwood, fortunately not coherently enough to stir his curiosity. But then I made the mistake of accusing Lars of being obsessed with her.

'That's so unfair!' he said. 'You were the one who brought her up.'

'She's paranoid,' I said. 'Always looking over her shoulder, thinking she's being followed.' I described the roundabout route our taxi had taken earlier that day.

'I wouldn't worry,' he said. 'Pregnant women always go a little nuts. When Eileen was expecting, she thought *everyone* was out to get her. Including me!'

Just because I was drunk didn't mean I was stupid. His words jangled a warning bell in my head, but it took me a few minutes to work out why, by which time we were already talking about something else.

'I thought you didn't have children.'

I waited for him to stutter a lame excuse, but he gazed at me with an expression so grief-stricken it hurt to look at it.

'Oh, Lindy. I wasn't going to tell you, but she... *we*... We had a miscarriage.' He stared down into his wine. 'You remember I said she had to go into hospital?'

Of course I remembered. Eileen's medical history was etched on to my brain. It was an explanation that might have mollified a lesser mistress, but not me, because I also remembered him swearing that he and Eileen hadn't had sex for years. So how could she have got pregnant in the first place? Unless it was some sort of Immaculate Conception, of course, like Nancy's.

'So I guess you'd better get back to her, be supportive and all that,' I said.

So you can have sex with her again, you lying bastard.

We were interrupted by the barman ringing last orders. I leapt to my feet, albeit a little woozily. All that red wine was taking its toll on my balance, though the keeping-tabs-on-what-Lars-had-said-about-Eileen part of my brain had been functioning efficiently enough. Lars grabbed my arm and said, 'I'll see you home.'

I shook him off angrily. 'I can manage.' But I grudgingly allowed him to escort me as far as the bus-stop, by which time I'd forgotten what I was supposed to be sulking about and we fell to snogging like a couple of randy teenagers, tongues down each other's throats. For the sake of public decency, it was probably as well the bus arrived when it did.

'Give my love to Eileen!' I called as I left him standing there forlornly.

On the way home, one or two passengers cast glances in my direction, but I don't remember my behaviour being anything out of the ordinary, and if I lurched on my way to a seat, it was only because the bus was lurching too. So I only really and truly realised how smashed I was when I found myself jiggling up and down in front of my front door, trying to open it and keep control of my bursting bladder at the same time. After much fumbling and jiggling and hopping, I finally accomplished the task by scrunching up one eye and poking the key into the lock like an elderly rake forcing his flaccid member into an unwilling maidservant.

The door swung open. Despite my need for the lavatory, I paused on the threshold. The flat was in darkness. Perhaps Nancy had gone to bed early, but when I flicked the switch it stayed dark. I flicked it another couple of times, to ensure I'd flicked it properly. Still dark.

This ought to have put me on my guard, but I started groping my way along the hallway and sliced my knee open on the corrugated edge of one of Nancy's boxes, which she'd left with the flap sticking out. And then I looked up and caught sight of a dark shape framed in the kitchen doorway, and my bladder finally gave up the struggle - not out of fear, but from the realisation that it didn't much matter if I wet myself since I was doomed anyway.

The shape growled like a bear as it bore down on me. I tried to back away, but going into reverse was too complicated a manoeuvre. It was enough to stop me going forward though, which was fortunate because there was an ominous creaking, followed by a muffled thump, and I only narrowly avoided tripping over a shoe and impaling myself on the Rand Hobart coat-rack which had finally fallen off the wall, exactly as I'd been expecting from the moment my houseguest had started overloading it with extra coats and bags.

Then I realised, too late to preserve any remaining dignity, that the shape advancing towards me wasn't a bear, but Nancy. Her face loomed forward out of the shadow, so twisted with fury that when she reached out and switched on the kitchen light she looked like some mythological goddess of revenge. At the same time she seemed to recognise me too, because I heard a hiss of air escaping from her lungs as she shrank from Incredible Hulk back into a pregnant woman.

'You idiot! I could have killed you!'

'Gotta go,' I said, squelching up the hall to the bathroom.

Even after I'd cleaned myself up and changed into Gerry Jeffers pyjamas, Nancy was still simmering with slow-burning rage. She followed me around like a silent rebuke as I filled a bucket with hot water, added a splash of disinfectant, and began to mop up the puddle I'd left on the stone tiling. At least it hadn't been the Van Merkens, not that it would have made much difference now that cigarette ash and crushed ginger nut had been trampled into the pile.

'You gave me a fright,' I said, scrubbing away cheerfully. I had no intention of letting her know how badly I'd been scared.

'You said eight thirty.'

'I did?'

She paused, as though testing the air. 'And you stink of cheap red wine. You're so drunk you pissed yourself.'

'It wasn't *that* cheap.'

She leant towards me, nostrils quivering. '*And* you've been kissing someone. Your Scandinavian fancy man. I can smell his fashionable shaving-foam!'

'He's not my fancy man.'

Her voice went up an octave. 'For Chrissake, Belinda, I thought something had happened to you!'

I should have found her concern for me touching, but all I did was yell back, 'Who the fuck died and made you my mother?'

Her lower lip quivered. 'Who died? *Who died?* Apart from *Verity Wilson?*'

I froze. She turned her back on me and went into the living-room and I heard the metallic *click* of Clive

Mengers's Zippo as she lit a cigarette. I left the bucket and followed her and listened in mounting dismay as she finally told me what had happened in the kitchen the night she'd got out of Wormwood.

At last I'd found out what had happened to Wilson's head. I started feeling sick. I couldn't actually *remember* having put it in a fridge, but there was little doubt this had been Gabrielle de Rospin's doing. In a way, it had been quite smart of her, trying to pin the blame on Jules Delgado. My Mrs. Hyde knew what she was doing, all right. Maybe I needed to let her off the leash more often.

'You have no idea what these people are capable of,' Nancy said icily.

'I know what Gabrielle can do,' I said, trying to out-ice her.

She did a double-take. 'Who the fuck is Gabrielle?'

'You don't want to meet *her*,' I said. 'She's a maniac.'

'You're right, I don't want to meet her, I've got enough maniacs on my plate already. But, Belinda...'

'What?'

'I don't like to think of you stumbling around on your own, drunk and vulnerable.'

I'd calmed down a bit, but this set me off again. 'I can look after myself!'

She fixed me with a pitying stare that annoyed me even more. 'I'm not sure you can.'

Her voice was filled with so much compassion it made me feel even sicker than I felt already. I preferred it when she was angry and giving me nosebleeds.

'You haven't been yourself, Belinda, not since I moved in here, and I've getting some dark, dark signals off you. I've been meaning to say something for some time now. Maybe you should talk to someone.'

'I talk to lots of people! Alain, and Lars, and Elspeth...'

'I mean get professional help.'

The nerve! I tried to respond with a barb of drunken wit but all that came out was incoherent spluttering, so instead I got up and headed for the drinks cupboard, where I found an eight of an inch of whisky, about a quarter-inch of gin but no tonic, and just under an inch of Calvados.

'*I'm* the one who needs help? I'm not the alcoholic around here.'

I divided what remained of the Calvados between two shot glasses, where the measures didn't look so stingy, and handed her one. She swallowed it in one gulp and reached for her Sobranie. I flinched, but it wasn't just the smoking. Her misdeeds were too many to count. She'd finished all the toilet paper and forgotten to tell me so I didn't find out until it was too late. She'd left the top off the toothpaste tube so its contents had squirted all over me. Worst of all was when she'd dyed her hair, though to judge by the state of the bathroom only a small amount of dye had made it as far as her head, and I couldn't for the life of me work out why she'd had to leave her mark on so many towels, which she'd left piled on the floor in a mushy grey heap. Black didn't even suit her. Red hair had always been one of Nancy's biggest assets. Black made her look like a witch.

I could have whinged about any of these things. But it ended up being the cigarettes.

'I know you don't give a shit about the baby's lungs, but what about mine?'

She lit up and sat down. 'You want me to leave? Just say the word.'

'I didn't mean it like that.'

How had I ended up on the defensive? Nancy was already disappearing into the bedroom; I followed and found her throwing things into a bag. My things. And my bag. But I already regretted having shot my mouth off.

'You can't go now. Let's talk about it in the morning.'

'I am so out of here.'

'Come and sit down.'

'No, I really *am* out of here. You're always complaining about my cigarettes, but your flat really stinks, you know? Like something crawled under your bed and died. I don't think I can stand it another day.' She stuck her chin out. 'And that ponky air-freshener doesn't help.'

'Muscade de Venise by Mary Gibson!' I was outraged. 'Thirty quid a pop!'

It was Nancy's turn to be outraged. 'Thirty quid for a fucking *candle*? You really are out of your gourd.'

I felt undermined, as though she were chipping away at the foundations of my belief system. 'You have to get on a waiting list for a Mary Gibson.'

Nancy snorted. 'Queuing for a candle? Dumbest thing I ever heard.'

That's because you don't have a clue about what's really important in this life, I wanted to say, but didn't. Nancy was on her way out of the door anyway. I wanted to plead with her, but just asked, 'Where will you go?'

She said, 'I'll send a cab for my stuff,' and closed the door behind her.

She never did send a cab. The next day I looked through her boxes, in case there was something I could purloin as compensation for the damage she'd done to my furniture. But there was nothing of value. No books, no clothes, no interesting stationery; just old magazines, eyebrow pencils and a pink plastic case containing a cracked dental retainer - leftover pieces of a life she had already left behind.

Chapter 5
Mimosa and Croissants

It was raining again. Nancy hauled herself to the top deck of the night bus, where despite the no smoking rule she lit a Black Russian. Cigarettes were the nails holding her together. Take them away, and she would collapse into a sobbing heap. She was already regretting having walked out. Belinda couldn't be expected to understand the responsibility pressing down on her shoulders, the nagging guilt, the worry her friends might be used as leverage or bargaining chips to make her fall into line. She and Kitty could take care of themselves, but there had to be limits. What if ComSec sent troops, squadrons, battalions? She couldn't possibly kill them all, even if she wanted to.

The other passengers were a mixed bunch of shift-workers, drunks and smartly dressed bumpkins on their way home from the West End. But the only one who dared complain about the smoking was a whiskery old duffer in an itchy-looking tweed jacket which stank of incontinent Labradors. Nancy stuck out her chin and told him to fuck off back to the farm. His face flushed purple and he shrank back into his seat, humiliated. He reminded her of her granddad, his haemorrhoids were playing up, and she'd dented his ego, which was one of the few things the poor old sod had left. She turned to apologise, but he avoided her gaze.

She didn't stop smoking even when the conductor

came up to collect her fare. He wrinkled his nose, but didn't say anything. It might have had something to do with her expression. She knew it was fierce, and made no attempt to soften it.

As the bus crawled eastward, she gazed out of the window. Who were all those people out there? They were all drunk and shrieking hysterically, oblivious as to what was really happening in the world. Or perhaps this was just their way of coping with it. Nancy looked down at them enviously. Everyone was out on the town, and here she was, stuck with a big belly and inching ever closer towards the day of reckoning.

She patted her tummy and whispered, 'Mummy loves you. Please try not to destroy the world.'

The bus turned into a street not far from Natal Mansions. She waited for a few stops, then got off and went into the Push Bar, where she ordered a Dry Martini and was chatted up by a magazine editor who was too drunk in the half-light to see she was seven months gone. In between Martinis, she slipped out to the pay phone by the toilets. Twice she got the babysitter, but on the third attempt Phoebe picked up.

'Nancy!' said Phoebe. 'How *are* you?'

Nancy opened her mouth to explain her current predicament, before realising she was too tired for anything more complicated than, 'Pheebs, I need somewhere to crash.'

*****

Any misgivings Nancy might have had about imposing on the Pflums disappeared as soon as she stepped into their apartment. Phoebe and Maurice welcomed her with open arms, saw immediately she was too tired to talk, and tucked her up in their spare room, where she sank into a deep and dreamless sleep. In the morning she was greeted by freshly ground coffee and a full range of Fudge Tub. They never once complained about her Sobranie habit, and indeed the smoke seemed to disperse miraculously, leaving the loft smelling pleasantly of mimosa and croissants.

The three of them sat around reading the papers as watery sunlight streamed through the industrial-size windows.

'Jellyfish again,' said Maurice.

'It's just a distraction,' said Phoebe. 'Saves the government from having to address the real issues.'

'Which are what?'

Before Phoebe could answer, Nancy chipped in.

'Bad rulers, civil discord, war, drought, famine, plague, comets, sudden deaths of prominent persons and an all-round increase in general sinfulness!'

Phoebe and Maurice stared at her. 'Blimey, where'd you read that?' he asked.

'Belinda says these are End Times.'

Phoebe looked stern. 'She's exaggerating.'

'Who's Belinda?' asked Maurice.

Nancy wished she had called them earlier. The sense that she might be putting them in danger had receded; she felt safe here, safer than at Wormwood or the Bunterberg. Maurice and Phoebe were delighted to have her as a guest and, unlike Belinda, had enough space to swing a couple of dozen cats. The guest bedroom was smaller than her room at Wormwood, but had its own en suite, and she felt at home. Maurice and Phoebe told her she was welcome to stay for as long as she liked, even after the birth, if necessary.

They still seemed to think it was a normal pregnancy and, because she didn't want them worrying, she inserted a few harmless fibs into her account of what had happened since they'd dropped her off at the Eurostar Terminal. She know if Phoebe got wind of what was really going on, she would want to launch a full investigation, and after what had happened to Verity Wilson, Nancy couldn't let that happen. The less they knew about ComSec, the better. And so The Battle of Waterloo had never taken place, and yes, she *had* spent a week in Le Marais, here are your keys back, and thank you very much for the loan of l'appartement. The stay at Wormwood was transformed into a couple of weeks in protective custody, followed by house-sitting for friends of friends who were performing at an arts festival in New Zealand, followed by a couple of increasingly disagreeable weeks at the Bunterberg. Unlike Belinda, Phoebe and Maurice didn't seem at all offended that she hadn't called them. It didn't seem strange to them that she'd wanted to concentrate on the play.

Meanwhile, her nesting instincts were kicking in. That first weekend, she taught herself to crochet and knit, and turned out a lopsided blanket and an acceptable pair of bootees before embarking on what the pattern called a 'matinee jacket', but which she concluded was simply a small cardigan. When she wasn't attending rehearsals, which by now had moved from the Pickle Factory to Carlo's Place, she stayed at home and crocheted.

Phoebe and Maurice, for their part, were thrilled to have an in-house babysitter. Till now, Nancy had looked on Samson as another one of Phoebe's designer gadgets, one that produced more sounds and smells than the others. But it was hard not to warm to the little critter and his lopsided smile, the unbounded joy with which he kicked his little cot, the tuft of hair that reminded her of Tintin, the awestruck way he would gaze at the exotic bird mobile slowly revolving above his head. Sometimes, when neither Phoebe nor Maurice were around, Nancy made it revolve faster. It was worth it just to hear Samson's happy chuckling. To judge by the joyful kicking inside her, Kitty could hear it too.

*****

'Your friend called again,' said Maurice. 'Whatsername, Melissa.'

He and Phoebe were dining on snapper and steamed vegetables. Nancy, as usual, was tucking into a colourful array of Fudge Tub.

Phoebe looked pained. 'Why are you so crap at names? It's *Belinda*.'

'I'm dyslexic,' Maurice said with a shrug.

'What did she want?' asked Phoebe.

'What do you think?'

'What did you say?' asked Nancy.

'I told her you were fine. Was that right?'

'Poor Belinda. I shouldn't have left her like that. She was in an awful state.'

'Ask her round,' said Phoebe. 'You can invite anyone you like. *La nostra casa è la tua casa* and all that.'

'I think she needs space,' said Nancy, who knew putting Belinda in the same room as Maurice and Phoebe would be asking for trouble. Belinda's odd behaviour would almost certainly worry them, and she was bound to blurt out something about Wormwood. 'She's probably relieved to see the back of me.'

'Au contraire,' said Maurice. 'She sounded desperate to talk to you.'

'That flat is so tiny,' said Nancy, 'and I... I mean *we... We* did take up a lot of room.'

'She's a strange girl,' said Phoebe. 'Said some crazy stuff on the phone the other day.'

'She didn't like me borrowing her clothes.'

Phoebe burst out laughing. 'I'm not surprised!' Look at you!

'Let me get this straight,' said Maurice. 'Melinda... sorry, *Belinda*... She's the one who likes cats?'

'That's Jilly,' said Phoebe. 'Belinda's the bookshop one. The one with good taste. *Scary* good taste. She came to dinner, for heaven's sake. You know, last time we had Lisa and Jenson over? She gave us that candelabra, the one you said looked like a flayed moose head.'

Maurice shook his head. 'Still can't place her.'

'I give up,' said Phoebe. 'I do hope this isn't early onset dementia. I have no intention of spoon-feeding you as well as Samson.'

'It was saintly of her, putting up with me for as long as she did,' said Nancy. 'Put the kibosh on her love life.'

'Belinda has a love life?' Phoebe sounded surprised. 'What's he like? It *is* a he?'

'I told her she could bring him back and I would sleep on the sofa, but she didn't seem keen on the idea.'

'She didn't want you meeting him in case he fell in love with you.' Maurice was joking, but Nancy squirmed in embarrassment, remembering when she'd slept with a boy Belinda had fancied. As far as she knew, Belinda had never found out about it, but the memory still made her uncomfortable.

'She hasn't been herself since the clinic.'

'That's understandable,' said Maurice.

'You need to look after yourself,' said Phoebe. 'You can't start worrying about needy friends.'

'Maybe that's why she has the cats,' said Maurice.

'I worry about *you*,' said Phoebe.

*****

On Christmas Day, Maurice's cousin Arwen came round with her girlfriend and a small dog called Frederick, and everyone pulled crackers, played Charades and Trivial Pursuit, drank too much, and presented each other with small gifts. Nancy hadn't felt up to braving the Christmas shopping crowds, but she'd made it as far as the wool shop and had crocheted scarves or shawls for everyone.

Phoebe cooked goose, and, to Nancy's surprise, she found herself eating a slice, with vegetables, and without once throwing up. She even managed to keep some Christmas Pudding down.

The Fudge Tub phase was over at last.

Chapter 6
The World of Pain

The morning after Nancy left I awoke with a brain even more scrambled than usual, and a heart full of crippling guilt. Like some sanctimonious Victorian patriarch, I'd driven my pregnant friend out into the rain. I was a horrible person. It would serve me right if she drowned herself in the river, or caught pneumonia, or decided never to speak to me again and share her story with someone else. Phoebe, for example.

I had a pretty good idea of where she'd gone. I phoned the Pflums, and said, 'I know she's there.'

'She's not up yet,' said Phoebe.

I tried not to sound too desperate. 'Can I talk to her?'

'I'll get her to call you.'

'I've been meaning to call you anyway,' I said. 'You should watch your back.'

'Excuse me?'

'Be very careful.'

'Of what?'

I could hardly say *my evil id*, so I said, 'I've got a stalker. She's obsessed with me, copies the way I dress and everything, but Phoebe, *it isn't me*. You need to watch out for her; she might be dangerous.'

There was a silence that went on for so long I thought we'd got cut off. 'Hello?'

'Have you been to the police?' asked Phoebe.

'They're not interested,' I said.

'Who did you speak to? Do you want me to have a word with them? I did a feature on stalking last year.'

'No, no, it's all right.' I realised I'd gone too far. 'Probably nothing to worry about. She's been pestering some of my friends, is all. Just be careful.'

'I will,' said Phoebe, sounding sceptical.

I hung up, thinking that at least I had *tried* to do my duty as a conscientious citizen. And it's true I sensed some subconscious urges simmering inside me. The idea of Nancy cooped up with my rival, drinking too much fine wine and sharing every detail of her experiences made my stomach contract in anguish. Worse, I had brought this on myself; I had driven my friend away, and now I would just have to deal with the consequences.

At least now I was in a position to restore my flat to its former impeccable state. The sofa and rugs and paperbacks would never again be immaculate, but I threw myself into housework as if it were the one thing standing between me and the abyss, and - thanks to another trip to Mary Gibson - managed to replace the odour of stale tobacco with the more civilised aromas of Myrtille Compôte and Roulade de Frangipane.

But there was still that other malodorous undercurrent to deal with, and now Nancy was gone I no longer had an excuse to postpone it. I would have to open the walk-in wardrobe and face the horror and find some way of getting rid of it permanently. I was counting on the canal to provide a solution. But would I be able to lug a headless corpse all the way out of my building, around the corner and up the road to the towpath without anyone noticing? Or would I first have to cut it up into more manageable pieces? This was not an agreeable prospect, but it would have to be done, so I screwed my courage to the sticking-place and made preparations. It required expeditions to several different hardware stores in my lunch hour, since I thought it safer not to make all my purchases at the same outlet.

And so on Friday evening, after work, I drew the curtains across all the windows, pushed Nancy's cartons and the chest of drawers aside, and spread plastic sheeting all over every surface of the bedroom. I slipped into disposable overalls and, anticipating the smell inside the cupboard wasn't going to be Attar of Roses, strapped a dust-mask to the lower part of my face. The finishing touch was a pair of lightly powdered latex gloves. I stared into the mirror at what looked like an early responder at a hazchem crisis, and struck a few action poses. Perhaps, after the apocalypse, this would be everyday attire.

Finally, when I couldn't put it off any longer. I tore myself away from my reflection and opened the cupboard door. Flanked by my emergency stash of tinned tuna and bottled water, the trunk stared back at me. Only now did I remember it was locked, but where had I put the key? My memories of that evening were so confused it was impossible to retrace my steps in any orderly fashion, but eventually I fell back on logic. Where would I have hidden a key I didn't want anyone to find? In plain sight, of course. Amid all the others on my Plotka key ring. And yes, there it was. I prised it off the ring, inserted it into the lock, gritted my teeth and lifted the lid, all set to vomit or faint or both at once.

The trunk was empty.

My legs gave way and I sank to the floor. What the hell? Had I already disposed of the corpse and then forgotten about it? I should probably have been relieved at having one less thing to worry about, but instead I felt lightheaded and out of control.

Numbly, I stripped off the overalls and sat down with my journal to make a list of Things I Couldn't Remember:

1) The unpleasantness at the clinic. I remembered the results, which would have been impossible to forget without undergoing some sort of lobotomy. But not how I had achieved them.

2) Cutting off Verity Wilson's head, wrapping it up and taking it all the way across town, presumably on public transport or in a taxi. Then infiltrating a heavily-guarded building, somehow finding where the kitchen was, and placing the head in a fridge for Nancy to find.

3) Disposing of Verity Wilson's headless corpse, which I could have sworn I'd wrapped in clingfilm and left in the trunk.

4) Killing Clive Mengers, cutting off *his* head, and leaving it... God knows where. I had no idea where I'd put that. Maybe in another fridge somewhere.

5) Presumably I had at some point gone back and disposed of Clive Mengers's corpse as well, since I had yet to find any reports of his death. Nor had I read anything about mysterious house fires in west London.

Clearly Gabrielle de Rospin had gained sentience and was merrily slaughtering people and then disposing of all the evidence behind my back. What did that make me? A sociopath? Psychopath? Norman Bates? What if I went to the police and confessed? Would they even believe me? I chewed at what was left of my fingernails.

At work the next day, I gravitated towards the

Psychology section.

*****

It was the worst Christmas of my life. I dutifully visited my grandmother at the nursing home. She might have been pleased with the book I gave her, but it was hard to tell; at least, I thought, the nursing home staff could read the poems out loud to their patients, if they were so inclined. I went for drinks with Alain and Elspeth and Howard, and got drunk and told them all about Gabrielle de Rospin, but they were drunk too so they didn't take me seriously, though I did spot Elspeth making a face at Alain, which confirmed my suspicion they'd been sleeping together. We all gave each other gifts, which when we'd unwrapped them turned out to be books.

I made up for all the time I'd been taking off by filling in for everyone's shifts right up to six o'clock on Christmas Eve, when the shop closed for the holiday, the only time of year it was ever shut. I borrowed *The Beginner's Guide to Paranoid Schizophrenia* and *I'm Not the Only One Here: How to Spot a Split Personality* to take home and pore over, and on Christmas Day pigged out on foie gras, and went for a long walk along the canal and got soaked, because of course it was bucketing down with rain again; the papers had said it was shaping up to be the wettest December since records began.

And I finally got to talk to Nancy, to wish her a Merry Christmas. She was friendly but distant, and the hubbub of laughter and clinking glasses in the background made me uncomfortably aware of my own empty flat. I rang off feeling so depressed I had to watch three hours of Christmas specials on TV, just to hear the voices. The bottle of Gigondas was pretty good, though.

Since Nancy had left, I'd carried on scouring the press for information about severed heads, headless corpses or missing journalists, without results. But three days after Christmas Day, during a lull while manning the till at work, I started leafing through a newspaper Elspeth had left under the counter, and my attention was caught by the picture of a witchy-looking woman in the arts pages. She looked maddeningly familiar, but several disorientating moments passed before I realised it was Nancy, with her black hair.

The accompanying article was an interview with Les Six, whose radical new meisterwerk was about to be exposed to the critics. The writer of the piece - someone called Lionel Stiffkey - seemed keen to convey how unimpressed he was by the leading actress, especially since the play had been restructured to allow for her delicate condition. Stiffkey kept referring to her as 'Pregnant Nancy' as though 'Pregnant' were her first name, though since the picture was a head shot, you couldn't even see her bump.

Something else I'd forgotten, then. The press preview of *Ripped!* was due to take place the following evening. I rang the box office at Carlo's Place from the phone in the staffroom, and told the woman who answered that I wrote for *The Catholic Chronicle*. Perhaps the choice of publication was a mistake; I should have said *Theatres R Us* or *Pregnancy Periodical*. But I was too late - they were all out of press passes. Well then, I said, I would like to *buy* a ticket. The woman told me tough, the preview was sold out, and tickets for the following week were selling like hot cakes so I would need to pull my finger out. I told her I was Nancy's best friend.

'In which case I'm sure she'll be happy to give you one of her comps.'

I hung up, fuming, and turned to find Alain had been standing in the doorway, listening in.

'*The Catholic Chronicle*, eh. Where did that come from?'

'Just trying to get a ticket to see my friend's show.'

'Maybe if you didn't shout at them they'd sell you one.'

'I wasn't shouting,' I said.

*****

I lay awake half the night, mulling over ways of sneaking in to Carlo's Place. Could I pretend to be a stagehand? It was a matter of some urgency: this was an important occasion for Nancy, and as her official biographer I needed to witness it. Perhaps I could delegate the task to Gabrielle de Rospin? She seemed to be the most efficient part of my personality and would undoubtedly be able to score a ticket, even if it meant leaving a trail of horribly mangled corpses in her wake.

'Gabrielle,' I whispered experimentally, staring wide-eyed at the ceiling. 'Are you there?'

No response. But what did I expect? That I would be able to *talk* to my alter ego?

'Please get me a ticket to Nancy's show,' I whispered, and closed my eyes, and managed to drift into a light sleep for a couple of hours. But when the alarm went off I found myself in exactly the same position on the bed, with nothing to indicate that Gabrielle de Rospin had occupied my slumbering body, got up and got dressed and gone out to raid the box-office at Carlo's Place. What was the point of an evil alter ego if she refused to perform simple tasks? Maybe all she was good for was murder.

I arrived at the shop twitching and bleary-eyed.

Alain noticed. 'Burning the candle at both ends again?'

'There is no candle,' I said. 'Or at least not the sort you can burn at both ends.' I gave him a comprehensive description of how Mary Gibson wax came in little glass jars so exquisite that you wanted to keep them even when the candles themselves were all burnt down.

Alain was staring at me with a weird expression I'd been noticing a lot lately, and which made me wonder if he were ill. 'You need a holiday, Belinda.' But when I told him I was slipping off for an early lunch he grumbled.

'Please *please* fill in for me,' I begged.

'Another I.O.U.?'

'If you must,' I said.

'One of these days I'll collect,' said Alain.

And so I sloped off to Lou's Café. I ordered a cup of vile instant coffee and was poring over the new edition of *A Gazetteer of Oro-Facial Diseases* when I sensed someone peering into my face as though they'd spotted a squamous cell carcinoma there. For a moment I thought it was Alain, come to haul me back to the shop, but then I caught a whiff of garlic.

'Oh, it's you,' I said, pushing back the wave of panic that threatened to engulf me.

'Yeeow,' said Jules Delgado, gesturing at my book as he settled into the empty seat next to me. 'Looks nasty.'

'I thought you'd buggered off back to America.'

He chuckled at my quaint English argot. 'Your Queen invited me to stay.'

'Yeah right.' I could just picture Delgado regaling members of the royal family with stories about his carnal relations with decapitated corgis. 'Buckingham Palace?'

'Pentonville.'

I tried to remember which of the royal residences this was, until it finally clicked. 'Oh my god, they put you in *prison?*'

'Trumped up charge,' he said. 'There I was, sitting in a stolen car, minding my own business...'

'Why on earth did they let you out again?'

'My lawyers can be very persuasive.'

'I'm surprised you weren't deported.' I checked my watch pointedly and started to get up. 'Sorry, gotta go.'

'Enough of this small talk,' he said, and grabbed my wrist and yanked me back down into my seat. I let out a small yelp, but the sound was swallowed up by the rattling of crockery.

Delgado put his mouth to my ear and whispered, *'Are you going?'*

I tried to scrape my chair away from him, but there wasn't room. 'Yes, if you'll let me.'

'To see Nancy.'

'I don't have a ticket.'

He took hold of my chin and turned my head so I had no choice but to look straight into his eyes, which for once weren't hidden behind Ray-Bans. The orange nebula seemed to have spread; the brown I remembered once seeing there had all but disappeared.

'The last time I saw her, she was on her way to see *you.*' And I realised he wasn't talking about Nancy any

392

more.

'Verity Wilson? She never arrived.'

He studied my face. 'She left a message saying she was about to knock on your door.'

I looked straight back at him and said, 'I stayed up all night for her,' which wasn't a lie. 'I thought she must have changed her mind.'

'That was the last I heard from her.'

'Maybe she was kidnapped,' I suggested. 'Have you been to the police?'

His laughter was halfway to a snarl. 'I've had enough of your English cops to last me a lifetime. They knew exactly where to find me, too. Almost as though they were acting on a tip.' He glared at me meaningfully.

'Well, I'm sorry, I have no idea where Verity Wilson is.' Again, this wasn't a lie.

'You know where your friend Nancy is, though?'

'I think so, yes,' I said, relieved he was finally changing the subject. 'She *is* my best friend.'

'I need to get a message to her.'

'OK,' I said. 'I'll pass it on.'

'It's outside, in the van.'

'Just tell me what it is. You can jot it down, if you like.' I started hunting in my bag for a pen, but he grabbed my wrist again.

'This'll only take a second.' He stood up, pulling me with him.

'I have to pay for my bagel.'

Delgado slapped a fiver on the table. 'Make it snappy. I'm parked on a double yellow line.'

I looked at the money. 'That's too much.'

He shrugged. 'What can I say? I'm a generous tipper.'

'I have to get back to work.'

'This'll only take a minute.' Using coercion rather than brute force, he was steering me towards the door, and no-one in the café was even seeing it. We were out of the door. This wasn't good. I needed time to think.

'Wait...'

'Over here,' said Delgado, piloting me towards to a white van parked at the kerb with its hazard lights flashing. Sitting in the driver's seat was a fresh-faced youth who hardly looked old enough to have a licence.

They had got to be kidding. Did Delgado expect me to get in the van? Did he think I was born yesterday?

'No, I don't think so.'

'Won't take a second,' Delgado said. 'I'll get that message for you, and then you can get back to your horrible picture book.'

He let go of my wrist, and for some reason this made me relax. So instead of backing away as he rolled the side-door open, I took a step forward. The back of the van was full of decorating equipment: I could see paint cans and a stepladder, even a couple of decorators. But the odd thing was, they weren't wearing paint-splattered overalls, or even old jeans and sweatshirts. They were wearing suits. Grey ones.

I'll admit I was a little slow on the uptake. I should have turned on my heels and run like hell, but I was still trying to make sense of what I was seeing when Delgado grabbed my wrist again and, in one swift movement, pushed the sleeve of my sweater all the way up past the elbow.

'Hey watch it,' I said. 'This is Fluff Phillips and she costs an ahhh...'

And then I said 'Ow!' because something stung my

arm. At first I thought it was an insect, then I spotted the syringe, which looked exactly like the ones littering the banks of the canal. 'That *hurt*!' I said, outraged, but my voice was already sounding peculiar, and I decided it was time to take some sort of defensive action, maybe even scream. This wasn't a dark alley after midnight. This was Islington in broad daylight. We were surrounded by passers-by. Surely someone had seen the syringe? Surely someone would see I was being kidnapped? I tried to shriek, but it came out sounding like the squawk of someone whose toes had just been trodden on, and no-one took any notice, no-one at all. Just another of the drawbacks of being invisible.

I had just enough time to worry about the sort of diseases you could pick up from shared needles, and my last impressions before I passed out were of being bundled into the back of the van, and the smell of paint mixed with something else, something that bore me back to a long-lost era of grazed elbows and scuffed knees and the school nurse's office.

But as it turned out, the needle wasn't shared, and Jules had no intention of infecting me with anything. Which was why, when he did what he did while I was out for the count, he didn't stint on the antibiotics.

*****

At first, I didn't feel like opening my eyes. I was more comfortable with them closed. The land of darkness was warm and welcoming and limitless. Opening my eyes, I sensed, would only usher me into a harsh new world of pain.

When I considered it, though, the world of pain

was already busily annexing new territory in my brain. Skirmishing parties were even now staging lightning raids well beyond the frontiers, where they were building camp-fires to roast sausages in those parts of my head which by rights should have been out of bounds to the passport-holders of suffering. They hadn't got as far as pitching their tents there, but I was aware I had only to open my eyes for them to start hammering in the pegs.

So of course I felt compelled to open my eyes, just to find out how bad it could be. I was promptly greeted by a throbbing from the left side of my skull, as though my head had been forced into a tightly crocheted helmet four sizes too small.

Where was I? Because this sure as heck wasn't midway between Military History and Mind and Body.

I flexed my limbs in exploratory fashion and counted all eight apparently functioning properly before remembering there were only supposed to be four. Whatever they'd given me, it was working, because apart from the throbbing and the extra limbs, I felt fine. Still fuzzy around the edges and not fully compos mentis, and I couldn't actually remember the last time my mentis had been compos anyway, but not gibbering with fear either. I felt a bit like you do when you're drinking, but just before you've drunk too much - uninhibited and effortlessly witty, just teetering on the edge of that stage of intoxication in which you forget words such as 'cat' and 'table' and confess to your alter ego having murdered five people.

I was sitting on a moulded plastic chair, the only piece of furniture in a room that took minimalism to extremes. At first I thought I must have misplaced an entire day, because the sky on the other side of the big window was dark. Then I noticed the darkness was unnatural, the sort of overripe purple-grey of something about to burst and disgorge... what? Nothing as commonplace as rain, that was for sure. Probably a shower of venomous toads or smouldering body parts.

According to my watch it was mid-afternoon. I'd lost three hours. As yet unaware time wasn't all I'd lost, I tottered to my feet and lurched over to the door and tried the handle, but it was locked. I looped back to examine the window at closer quarters, mainly by leaning against it and sliding down. It was the sort of double-glazing that would be impossible to penetrate without power tools. A long way below, I could see a goods yard, disused warehouses, a small segment of brown canal. I couldn't make out any people, but there were a few black dots; I thought about trying to attract their attention before realising they were specks on the glass. I tried to wipe them off, but they were on the outside. Behind them, silhouetted against the glowering sky, were a set of gasometers and the gothic towers of St. Pancras.

At least now I knew where I was, more or less. Had the window been on the other side of the building I could probably have spotted the top of the Bunterberg. But I might as well have been living in Kansas for all the good it was doing me now. As I flopped back on to the chair, Lars's words floated into my head, 'Call me any time.' How I wished he were here now. For the first time in my life I regretted not having a mobile, though my kidnappers would probably have confiscated it anyway, like my bag, which was nowhere to be seen.

My head began to spin, so I closed my eyes. I might have nodded off, except it was at this point the pain stopped ticking over in neutral and stepped into gear. It was acute, not to be denied, and it was coming from my left ear.

Or where the left ear had been, as I discovered when I tried to touch it.

*****

Eventually a weasel-faced man in grey opened the door in response to my yelling. I tried to barge past, but he easily blocked the doorway and handed me a small bottle of mineral water and a packet of Panokil Extra Strength. I told him to let me out. He didn't reply, but I gathered from his expression the painkillers were as much for his benefit as mine. Realising noise was power, I began to shriek again, and he shut the door in my face. But it was liberating, letting rip like that. A shame I hadn't been able to do it earlier, when I was being dragged into the van.

Ah yes, the van. It was coming back to me now.

By the time Delgado came in, about ten minutes later, I'd screamed so much my throat was hoarse.

Chapter 7
Earless in Islington

I stared at Jules Delgado in distaste, wondering how I'd ever found him good-looking. Whatever goggles I'd been wearing throughout our earlier encounters were off now. The greasy hair and leer gave him the air of a low-rent gigolo. He stood against the window with his arms folded, a grey shape even darker than the grey sky behind him. His suit was very nicely cut, though. I had to give him that. And grey. This season's colour. *Hue du jour.* The phrase had a nice ring to it. It was only when he squinted at me like a pirate wondering why his parrot had been swapped for a pigeon that I realised I'd spoken out loud.

'What?'

'Oh! Oh my God, look over there!' I cried, pointing out of the window. When he turned to look, I made a dash for the door and tried the handle again. This time it opened! But instead of flinging myself through it, I pulled up on the threshold. In the adjoining room were gathered a dozen or so men in grey suits. They seemed unfeasibly young; I might have been looking at an unusually formal-looking youth club from the fifties. Some were eating sandwiches or drinking cups of coffee. Three of them were huddled around a radio, listening to some kind of sporting event. Another was rehearsing conjuring tricks with a magic wand and a white rabbit. Thinking back on it later, this last detail was odd, but at the time it seemed no odder than anything else that had been happening.

As one, they turned their heads and gazed at me inquiringly. There were too many of them to deal with, so I closed the door and returned to my plastic chair. Delgado was still wearing a perplexed expression. I was resolving to keep him off balance when a searing spasm of pain from the side of my head made me recoil like a badminton spectator being thwacked in the face by the shuttlecock. Gingerly, I explored the soggy dressing with my fingers, and winced again. This time the pain was dull, but it lasted longer.

'Leave it alone and it should heal up nicely,' said Delgado.

'I thought you were my friend!'

He looked apologetic. 'You'll still be able to hear, though maybe not quite as well. The outer part of the ear simply functions as a sort of trumpet.'

I leapt to my feet, sending the plastic chair flying. 'What have you done with my outer part? Give it back!' The words emerged as a bloodcurdling screech, like a witch's curse.

'We no longer have it, I'm afraid.' Delgado sighed and stepped back, as though he feared I would make his manhood shrivel up and drop off. If only I'd had Nancy's powers I would have made it my top priority.

He righted the chair and said, in a mild tone, 'Stop yelling or we cut off the other one.'

This made me giggle. *Earless in Islington.* Whatever he'd injected me with, it had left me in a peculiarly buoyant mood somewhat at odds with my situation. He'd probably expected me to be whimpering with fear by now, grovelling on my knees, begging for mercy.

Well, he'd picked the wrong cookie. I'd once read about someone fending off muggers by reciting a Dada poem. All I could come up with were nursery rhymes, but I sang one anyway.

'Twinkle twinkle little star, How I wonder where you are.' I sang this to the tune of *Baa Baa Black Sheep*, but I'd never been the best singer in the world so it might have been hard to tell. 'Up above the world so high, like a tea tray in the sky.'

Delgado's mouth dropped open so far I could see his gold fillings, and then he cracked. 'Shut up! Shut up!' He had to shout to make himself heard above the din I was making.

I stopped singing, not because I'd been told to, but because I couldn't remember the next line. Something about Lucy in the Sky with Diamonds? While I was inwardly debating this question - though for all I knew I might have been talking out loud again - Jules approached and patted me on the shoulder, as though I were a crazed mare that required gentling.

'Oh boy, maybe we gave you too much of that stuff. Can you remember your name?'

'Belinda Rose Pringle,' I said.

'You know who I am?'

'You're the plonker who cut off my ear.' I could see he wasn't sure about the word *plonker*. I wasn't sure about it either; it wasn't part of my everyday vocabulary.

'Do you know why?'

I racked my brains. 'Something to do with Nancy?' It had to be. Everything was about Nancy.

'Bingo. Understand this, Pringle. This is about Nancy, not you. So if you play your cards right you can walk out of here with most of your extremities intact.'

I imitated the klaxon of a TV quiz show buzzer and said, 'Wrong answer!' Why was no-one ever interested in *me*? I stuck my chin out. 'It *might* be about me. You don't know me at all.'

'You're Nancy's best friend. Isn't that what you keep saying?' Delgado looked uncomfortable. 'Look, we thought if we sent her something of yours, she might be open to negotiation, maybe even give up the baby to keep you safe. If that doesn't work, we can cut off one of your fingers and send that.'

I tried to follow this logic, and failed. Why would Nancy care how many fingers or ears I lost? OK, I didn't think she'd be thrilled about it, but I couldn't imagine her placing my wellbeing above that of her unborn child. Pelting her with assorted body parts wouldn't make the blindest bit of difference.

'Something of mine? You're making it sound as though you sent her a monogrammed handkerchief. *You cut off my bloody ear!*'

He sighed. 'No need to go on about it. I'm told they make good prosthetics now.'

'Does your agency know what you're up to?'

Delgado snorted. 'Those clowns? *Please*. Give me some credit.' He patted me on the shoulder again, but distractedly, as though his attention had already moved into the next room. He turned towards the door. I saw he was about to walk away, and I would be shut in that room till I died of starvation or managed to attract the attention of a passing helicopter or the world ended - whichever came first.

'I know what happened to Verity Wilson,' I said, and he stopped. He didn't turn back, but I saw his shoulders stiffen.

A plan was forming in my head.

'I promise I'll tell you,' I said. 'But first you have to do something for me.'

'You're not in a position to make deals.'

'How do you know? You don't even know what you're up against.'

He turned. 'The Antichrist comes in many guises.'

'What makes you so sure it's the Antichrist? How do you know it's not the new Jesus?'

He looked like someone wrestling with mental trigonometry. 'You think Jesus would drop chunks of marble on people's heads?'

'His father did worse than that.'

'And why would he choose someone like Nancy when he has all the virgins in the Bible Belt to choose from?'

'Nancy's a temporary vessel. I'm thinking God has someone else in mind to do the heavy lifting later on.'

'Like who?'

He was humouring me now. I didn't care.

'Like me! I've already bonded with the baby. I'll be responsible for its spiritual upbringing.'

I hadn't considered this before, but now it struck me as an excellent plan. When I'd felt the baby kicking in Nancy's belly, there really had been some sort of psychic connection between us. And it was obvious the child would need looking after in ways my friend wouldn't be able to provide, always supposing she survived the birth itself, which I had no doubt was going to be difficult. I'd scored 97% in my last R.E. exam, so I was qualified.

'I'm more than Nancy's friend,' I said. 'I'm John the Baptist.' I remembered too late what had happened to him and quickly corrected myself. 'A John the Baptist who doesn't get his head cut off.'

'We read the signs,' said Delgado. But he didn't sound so cocky now.

'Signs?' I ran through the list again. 'Bad rulers, civil discord, war, drought, famine, plague, comets and jellyfish in the water supply blah blah blah. When *haven't* we had all that stuff?'

Jules scratched his left ear and I felt a pang of envy. I would never be able to scratch mine again. I felt tears pricking at my eyes.

'We just want to talk to her,' he said.

'Good luck with that.'

'She'll listen when she knows what I have to say.'

'No she won't. As soon as she sees you she'll make your eyeballs explode.' I didn't know if Nancy could make eyeballs explode, but I was sure she was capable of making them bleed, at the very least. I paused for dramatic effect, and added, 'But maybe there *is* a weakness in her defences.'

Delgado squinted at me. 'What?'

'That's for me to know and you to find out.'

He lost patience and slapped my face. 'Stop playing the coquette. It doesn't suit you.'

My head was already hurting so much that the blow barely registered, but I slapped him back anyway. And then, incredibly, his manner changed, as if violence were the only language he understood, and he was all smiles and charm. Or what he thought passed for charm. From my angle, it was as though a snake-oil salesman had decided to offer me a discount.

Next thing I knew, he was striding to the door and snapping his fingers, and there were comings and goings, and the minimal furnishings were supplemented by another plastic chair and a folding table. One of the men in grey set down a wooden tray bearing a cafetière, and two cups, a plate of Danish pastries and a pile of paper napkins.

'I'll have milk,' I said. 'Plus I'd like my bag back.'

Delgado looked at me for a few seconds as though deciding whether or not to knock my block off, then returned to the door and opened it a crack and said something to whoever was on the other side. Moments later, another man in grey trotted in, my distressed Delphine Garnier slung over one of his shoulders, and set down a creamer in the shape of a cow.

'A proper English teatime!' said Delgado. 'Let's talk over a *cuppa*.'

Ignoring his lamentable attempt at a Cockney accent, I stroked the rim of the tray. 'Hey, this is a Pellonpaa. Hewn from a single piece of weathered birch. Though of course this is the mass-produced version.' Delgado frowned as though my words were a cypher he was unable to crack, and pushed the plunger on the cafetière down with more force than was required, so that coffee slopped over the top. I started to dab at the spillage with a napkin.

'Never mind that,' he said. 'I want to ask you something.' He reached into my bag, on the floor by his side of the table where the flunky had left it, and pulled out a tan leather case. My heart leapt as I spotted an old friend. My Apocalypse Kit!

'You are one crazy bitch,' he said, unzipping it. 'What is this shit?'

'It's for emergencies, because you never know...' I began, and then tailed off, because he was unfolding my Étripouille. There were rust-coloured stains on the blade. I guessed they weren't rust, though.

'You bastard!' I said. 'You sliced my ear off with my own knife...'

A look of horror passed across his face. 'No! Why would you even *think* that? We used a surgeon's scalpel with a sterilised blade. And Perez has medical training.' He peered into the case. 'It's a mess in here. Somebody used this knife, but not today. Not for a while. It's all dried, see?'

He looked at me and his expression changed, slowly and painfully, as though his veins were slowly filling up with small air bubbles. 'You've been walking around with this all the time? With all this DNA and everything? Oh boy, you *are* crazy!' He picked up a napkin and carefully started to wipe the blade.

'I can do that.' I held out my hand for the knife but Delgado shook his head.

'You think I'm a dummy? '

'It wasn't me. It was Gabrielle de Rospin.'

'Who's he?'

'*She.*' Whatever they'd injected me with was beginning to wear off, and I began to shiver. 'She's my alter ego.'

'What the fuck?'

'Like Jekyll and Hyde. I'm Jekyll, she's Hyde. She kills anyone who gets in my way.'

He threw back his head and roared with laughter. 'Listen lady, I've met some killers in my time, and you're not one of them.'

I felt insulted. 'But you haven't met Gabrielle. She's not like me. She's dangerous.'

'Let me get this straight. You've got a demon inside you who takes over and kills people? You've been watching too many bad movies, Pringle.'

'Not a demon. An alter ego!'

My extra limbs had disappeared, leaving me with just the regular four, but each one felt like a roll of carpet. And my eyelids were drooping. All I wanted was to go home and stretch out on my Savaard Nite-Bliss and sleep this madness off. I'd as good as confessed to Delgado, and even he didn't believe me. I would have to commit murder right in front of him. Maybe Gabrielle could murder *him*. I forced my eyes wide open and tried to summon the sort of homicidal rage that would enable me to snatch the knife from his grasp and... And then what? Cut his throat?' No, the very idea of cutting someone's throat made me queasy with terror.

'Are you OK?' he asked. 'You look like you've got heartburn.'

Wearily I said, 'Maybe we can come to some arrangement. About Nancy, I mean.'

*****

When I'd finished telling Jules what he needed to know, there was a difference in the way he was looking at me. It wasn't admiration, exactly, but there seemed to be a little less contempt in his expression.

'You're smarter than I thought, Pringle,' he said. 'But let's see how smart you really are. You're coming with us.'

'You said you'd let me go!'

'Someone needs to keep an eye on you,' he said. 'To make sure you don't do anything you might regret. You're not yourself.'

I yelled, 'I just told you I wasn't!' and threw

another screaming fit and declared I had no intention of going anywhere with him, but especially not with my head wrapped in bloodstained bandages like a creature out of a Hammer horror movie. Delgado didn't know what Hammer horror movies were and refused to take no for an answer, even when I attempted to explain. But I finally got him to agree to a quid pro quo. If he wasn't going to let me go, he would have to do something for me.

He refolded the knife and slid it into his pocket, but at least he returned my bag. I did what I could with lipstick and concealer. But there were some things that just couldn't be covered up.

Chapter 8
Agonistes

We didn't have far to go, but they made me travel in the back of the van, as though they were ashamed of me. The suspension wasn't too good back there; I clung to a strap and tried not to throw up as we bumped over what felt like an unploughed field full of boulders. My only compensation was that Kaprisky, the man in grey assigned to sit in the back and keep an eye on me, looked just as ill as I felt.

If Phoebe was surprised to hear my voice at her entryphone, she hid it well. But she was shocked when she opened the door.

'Belinda! What have you done to your head?'

Her eyes shifted toward the men behind me and a hard look came over her face and she tried to slam the door on us. Too late! Arbogast had already stuck his foot out. Delgado and Kaprisky barrelled past me into the flat as though I weren't even there. Phoebe backed down the hallway. 'What's going on?'

'Where's Nancy?' I asked, bringing up the rear.

'At the theatre, I guess.' She was so cool. Acting as though her home hadn't just been invaded by three complete strangers. Instead of flapping, she looked pointedly at her watch. 'Babysitter's arriving any second.'

'You don't need one,' I said.

'The curtain goes up at eight.'

'Yes, and I'll there when it does,' I said. 'But I'm

afraid you and Maurice won't. Where is he, anyway?'

'Look, I don't...'

Delgado took over. 'We have a proposition.'

Phoebe's eyes narrowed. 'Who the fuck are you? Get out of my house.'

I said, 'Let's go into the lounge.'

'What's got into you, Belinda?' Phoebe's eyes narrowed. 'It *is* Belinda, isn't it? Is this what you meant by having a stalker? Well, I know it's you, and I don't have time for this shit.'

'Then you will make time!' I yelled. Phoebe flinched, but so did Delgado, while Arbogast and Kaprisky exchanged glances. I was rather enjoying this new demonstrative me, the one who refused to fade into the wallpaper. I savoured the taste of power as we traipsed through to the Pflums' vast living-room. Kaprisky, who looked as though he should have been forking hay on his daddy's farm, stood by the window and started playing with the potted aloe on the ledge. Arbogast positioned himself in front of the exit in case Phoebe decided to make a break for it, but I knew she'd never dream of leaving without Samson, who had to be around here somewhere. Probably the nursery. I'd seen it on one of my visits; they'd painted it yellow and even though it was the smallest of their three bedrooms it was still almost as big as my flat.

My eye was drawn to the items on the big oak table: a fruit bowl the size of a satellite dish, a yellow legal pad and pen, and a cup of half-drunk tea. I wandered around to the other side, trying to read what Phoebe had been writing on the pad. Maybe her latest column? But there was something missing from this cosy domestic scene, and I finally worked out what it was.

'Where's the candelabra?'

'The what?' Phoebe was staring in alarm at Delgado, who was pulling books off the shelf, flicking through the pages and then dropping them on the floor.

'The candelabra. Where is it?'

'We're having it cleaned.'

'Didn't need cleaning. Where is it really?'

She tore her attention away from Delgado's casual vandalism and met my gaze. 'Storage room in the basement.'

'Why?'

'For safekeeping.'

'Safekeeping?' I echoed.

Phoebe sighed and gave up the pretence. 'You can't honestly think we'd want to live with that monstrosity? It's like a load of glued-together body parts. You want us to have nightmares?'

I couldn't believe what I was hearing with my one remaining ear. 'But it's a Spud Williams!'

'What's Spud Williams?' asked Delgado, tossing aside a couple of hardbacks.

'It might have gone down well at a Borgia family supper where everyone ends up poisoning each other,' said Phoebe. 'But that's not us.'

I groped for words. 'You had it on the table last time I was here.'

'Because we knew you were coming! We didn't want to hurt your feelings, Belinda. But now I'm wondering if you have any feelings to hurt. You've gone too far, barging in like this. Who are these goons?'

'I'm not a goon,' said Delgado.

'We want to see Nancy,' I said.

'She's not here, I told you. She's probably doing voice exercises or knee-bends or whatever it is actors do to warm up. Look, if you like that fucking candelabra so much why not keep it? It never went with our decor anyway. I'll go and get it, shall I?'

'It's too big for my flat!' I was finding it hard to judge volume via my one fully functional ear, but I could tell by the way Phoebe winced that I was shouting again. 'We can't all afford to live in aircraft hangars like you!'

From behind one of the doors to my right came a thin wail, like a malnourished car alarm. Phoebe looked panicked. 'Now look what you've done! You'd better get out before Maurice comes back.' She made a move towards the door to Samson's room.

Delgado cocked an eyebrow at me. 'What do you want to happen here?'

'I want their tickets.'

Phoebe spun round on the threshold. 'What?'

'Sit down, Pheebs,' I said.

'Don't call me Pheebs.'

'Shut up and sit down!' I shouted.

'I would do as she says,' Delgado said. He directed a forefinger at his head, and rotated it.

Phoebe rounded on him. 'What have you done to her?'

'Don't ask me,' said Delgado. 'She was like this when I met her.' He bent forward to whisper something into Phoebe's ear. She looked bewildered and shook her head. The wailing from the next room was getting on my nerves.

'You're not going to Nancy's play,' I said, trying to reclaim their attention.

'She's expecting us.'

'She doesn't give a fig whether you're there or not.' More wailing. I needed it to stop.

'That's not true,' said Phoebe. But there was doubt in her eyes, as well as fear. Had she too begun to suspect that Nancy was growing away from us, leaving us all behind? 'But if it means that much to you, Belinda, fine, we'll stay at home. Just let me go and see to Samson.'

'Yeah, shut that brat up,' said Arbogast. 'That noise is getting on my...'

Delgado whipped his head round and Arbogast stopped in mid-sentence and looked sheepish. Phoebe moved back towards the door.

'No, wait,' I said. Everyone turned to look at me. 'Let *me* see to Samson.'

Phoebe said, 'No!' but I ignored her and headed for the door.

'Oh boy,' said Delgado, coming after me. Phoebe tried to follow as well, but Kaprisky grabbed her arm. She tried to pull away, but he held on tight.

'Don't you dare touch him!' she shouted.

'Take a chill pill, Philippa.' I didn't know what she thought I was going to do, but as I went through into Samson's room, I decided I rather liked being regarded as a loose cannon.

As I reached Samson's cot, Delgado came up behind me. 'Noisy little bastard, isn't he,' he said, beaming down at the red-faced wriggling bundle. He stuck out a finger and Samson immediately stopped bawling and seized it with both hands. I stuck my hand into my bag, feeling around for my Apocalypse Kit, and unzipped it. I could feel the package containing the space blanket, and the Bar-F matchbook, and the packet of Doliban... But there was something missing.

'Looking for this?' asked Delgado. With his free hand he was holding my knife. Too late, I remembered he hadn't put it back into the bag.

'Give me that,' I said.

'What do you want it for?'

'What do you think?' I tried to brazen it out, but the truth was I really didn't know why I wanted it. Maybe I just wanted to restore it to its designated place in the kit. I had no intention of sticking it into anyone, least of all the baby. At least I didn't *think* I had. With all the blood I had on my hands already, what difference would another one make? Might as well go all the way.

He smiled. 'Because if you're thinking of doing something you can't take back, I would advise against it.'

'You do stuff like that all the time.'

Delgado shrugged. 'This isn't you, Pringle. You just happen to have gotten caught up in something big. Doesn't mean you have to sink to our level.'

My eyes prickled with tears. 'Bit late now. I've already killed five people.'

He snorted. 'Are you nuts?'

'It's not the sort of thing you forget,' I said, though obviously it was, in my case. 'If it wasn't me, who was it?'

Delgado looked at me searchingly, and I looked away because there was sympathy in his gaze, and I couldn't bear that, not from him. I wiped my eyes with my sleeve.

'Ask yourself who had something to gain,' he said. The baby chuckled and tightened its grip, bringing its little feet up as though it wanted to fasten its toes around the finger too.

'Gabrielle de Rospin,' I said, extracting a used paper tissue from my pocket and trying to blow my nose on it.

'Oh yeah, your evil twin. The one you have no control over.'

'No. I don't know. Maybe.' The tissue disintegrated in my hand. I dropped what remained of it on the floor, spotted a packet of Baby Wipes and used one of them to finish blowing my nose.

'You want to know what I think?' said Delgado, who still seemed to be paying more attention to Samson than to me. 'I think someone's been messing with you, Pringle. Someone very sick in the head.'

'*I'm* the one who's sick!'

'I won't disagree with you there. But you're a special kind of sick, Pringle. Not sick like that.'

I longed to believe him, and he was still looking at me with an odd expression that made me wish we'd met in other circumstances. And I was dying to get it off my chest. So I took a deep breath and finally confessed to him what I'd done to Verity Wilson.

*****

No sooner had I hit her with my crackle glaze celadon amphora than I began to regret my rash action. What now? I couldn't leave her bleeding all over my rug. And she was going to be *so* pissed off at me when she came to, maybe even have me arrested or something. I would just have to convince her she'd tripped and fallen; maybe caught one of her heels in the Van Merkens, plus she hadn't been facing me full-on, so maybe she wouldn't have seen me lashing out with the vase.

PATIENTS AT RISK IN AMBULANCE STRIKE. The newspaper was in danger of becoming sodden, so I wrapped an old pashmina around her head to soak up the blood. The best move, I decided, would be to move her into the bathroom, where I could splash cold water on her face to bring her round. But mainly I wanted to move her there because all the surfaces were washable. She was heavy - but not when you compared her, say, to the Egon Spengler sofa, which I had lugged around the room several times before settling on the best place for it. After much tugging (from me) and groaning (from both of us) I managed to get her in a kneeling position with her head over the bath and the blood trickling down the plughole, though to my relief there didn't seem to be as much of it now. I paused to catch my breath and she turned her head and mumbled something.

'Not to worry,' I said. 'We'll have you back on your feet in no time.'

She murmured something else and started coughing and clawing at her throat, so I unbuttoned her collar and turned the cold tap on. Next thing I knew the tub was filling with pinkish water and the more I tried to rinse the cut, the pinker the water became.

After that I'm not entirely sure what happened, because it was here that things started to get messed up. I reached out to take a towel, but as soon as my hand came into contact with the rail there was a small detonation in my head, followed by a shockwave of pain, and the bathroom floor came up to meet me.

By the time everything swam back into focus, it was too late, and I'd done something I couldn't take back. Or Gabrielle had done it while I'd been unconscious. My bathroom was all-white, but now there was a lot of red in it. It was just like the clinic. And once again my memory was a cloudy collage of impressions, none of which made sense. Wilson was still slumped over the side of the bath. It was only after I'd struggled to my feet and splashed my face with cold water from the basin that I saw there was a lot more blood in the bath. And on the floor. And on the walls. Only it was no longer coming from the gash on Wilson's head, because her head wasn't there any more.

I threw up into the toilet. After I'd wiped my mouth, I became aware I was kneeling on something. I thought maybe the bathmat had got rucked up, but when I looked down, I saw my Hirschmüller Santoku with full-tang handle, which I'd last seen in the kitchen knife-block. Clearly I'd been mishandling it; the blade was nicked in several places.

I sat with my back against the wall and tried to breathe. So my berserker id had got loose and done all the stabby hacky slashy things my subconscious had apparently always wanted to do. I'd unleashed my inner beast, like a psychopath in a horror movie; I tried to think back to all the videos my ex had made me watch so I could pin the blame one of those, but I couldn't recollect a scenario quite like this one. For a while there, in the red bathroom, I wondered if I might actually be a werewolf. But it wasn't a full moon, and there wasn't any blood around my mouth, which was a small mercy. At least I hadn't *eaten* the head.

Hauling myself to my feet and staggering around like a drunken robot, I checked the cupboards, in the wardrobe and under the bed. I checked the kitchen. I even staggered out to the dustbin area and checked the rubbish sacks. There was a lot of sordid refuse there, none of it mine, but no sign of Wilson's head. I couldn't for the life of me remember what Gabrielle had done with it. My eyelids were drooping and I wanted nothing more than just to go to bed and sleep it off, but the idea of waking up to that carnage was more than I could bear, so I stayed up most of the night scrubbing and bleaching and getting everything back to normal. Everything except my brain, which I now realised was seriously askew.

Back to normal. Or as normal as things could be when there was a headless corpse in my bathroom.

Thank you so much, *Gabrielle. You couldn't have disposed of the body as well as the head?*

I'd seen enough blood for now, and what was left of my strength was ebbing fast. So I wrapped what remained of Verity Wilson in yards of shrink-wrap so she ended up looking like an Egyptian mummy past its sell-by date, and crammed her into my leather steamer trunk, which I locked and shoved to the back of the walk-in wardrobe. I was a little anxious about the smell, but it was here that my collection of Mary Gibson candles came in handy. Thirty quid a pop, but worth every penny.

As it turned out, it was just as well I didn't put off cleaning the bathroom, because that was the day Nancy came to stay.

*****

'So you see, it was an accident,' I said. 'Most of it.'

Delgado was still so intent on keeping Samson amused that I couldn't be sure he'd been listening, but when he straightened up and looked at me, his mouth was set in a grim line. He was angry, but careful to direct that anger away from the baby. Towards me.

'That was no accident.'

'I'm sorry,' I said. 'I blacked out.'

'How do you think that happened?'

'The heated towel rail wasn't properly earthed?'

He laughed, though I didn't think it was a laughing matter. 'You think it was an electric shock?'

'My hands were wet.'

He exhaled wearily, as though trying not to lose his patience. 'For Christ's sake, Pringle. Someone socked you.'

'Excuse me?'

'They cold-cocked you.'

'I think I would have noticed.'

He rolled his eyes. 'Not if they came up behind you. Punch to the back of the head, or a small cosh. No wonder your brains are addled.'

'But...' I tried to process this, and failed.

'They knew what they were doing,' he said. 'As I said before, someone is messing with you.'

I couldn't work out what was worse: going into a fugue state where I was evil and and killed people, or being so lame I'd allowed someone to hoodwink me into thinking that. 'Who would do that?' I glared at him, almost annoyed that he'd ruptured my nightmarish fantasy of turning into a cold-blooded Terminator. 'Did you...?'

'No!' said Delgado. 'You think I'm a sick bastard?'

'You cut my fucking ear off,' I said.

*****

I trailed him back into the living room where Phoebe

was awaiting our return, her face almost as ashen as mine felt.

'Baby's fine,' Delgado assured her. 'I'm good with kids. I'm a terrific dad. The best.'

Phoebe made a sound in her throat and rushed into the nursery.

'You have kids?' I asked, shocked. He and Verity Wilson had certainly made a pair. I recalled how well they'd got on in the Penthouse Bar, and for the first time felt bad about the way their relationship had ended. I wondered if they'd talked about their children to each other. 'I'm sorry about Verity.'

He shrugged. 'Barely knew her.' He seemed subdued, all the same.

'Have we finished here?' asked Kaprisky.

'Shut the fuck up,' said Delgado.

I kept reminding myself I probably hadn't killed Wilson, though had yet to fully embrace Delgado's theory about my having been knocked unconscious. How could I trust a person who'd cut off my ear? Everyone else seemed to be messing with my brain, so why not him?

After a few minutes, Phoebe emerged, looking calmer, but there was a quaver in her voice when she said, 'You need to leave. All of you. Right now.'

'Just give us the tickets,' said Delgado.

'Have the fucking things!' Phoebe crossed to a part of the bookshelves he hadn't got round to vandalising. 'Here!' She picked up an envelope and threw it at us. It fluttered to the floor.

Delgado picked it up. 'You'll thank me later,' he said.

'Why would I thank *you*?'

Delgado smiled mysteriously. 'You'll read about it in the papers tomorrow.'

'What?' As we turned to leave, she was already reaching for her cell phone, but Arbogast plucked it from her hands and, ignoring her yelp of indignation, handed it to Delgado, who dropped it into my bag. Kaprisky strode over to the landline socket, yanked the cable out and crushed the plug beneath his heel.

'Better if you don't call Malcolm,' I said.

Phoebe frowned. 'Who's Malcolm?'

'Silly me,' I said. 'I meant *Maurice*. Just be thankful he's not here. He would have done something stupid. Not too bright, is he. Can't even remember my name.'

Phoebe glared at me. 'You're not welcome here, Belinda. You'll never be welcome here. Consider yourself persona non grata. Same goes for your fucking stalker.'

'Suits me, *Phyllis*,' I said, still pissed off about the candelabra.

Chapter 9
Ripped

Kaprisky and Arbogast were less than enthusiastic about having to escort Delgado and me to the theatre. From the back of the van, where Kaprisky was again keeping an eye on me, I could hear Delgado and Arbogast arguing in the front. Arbogast wanted to go back to HQ and watch a boxing match on the sports channel, but Delgado was having none of it.

'I need you to watch her. You saw how she is.'

Kaprisky glowered at me as though it were all my fault. Which I suppose it was, in a way.

We spent twenty minutes looking for somewhere to park, and rolled up at Carlo's Place just before eight. The place was already packed to the rafters. There were only two tickets in Phoebe's envelope, and four of us, so Delgado waved a fistful of hundred dollar bills in the ticket tearer's face. After a pause in which she appeared to be mentally calculating the exchange rate, she started negotiations with a middle-aged couple seated on the nearest bench. They weren't in a hurry to move, but the ticket tearer must have said a magic word because all of a sudden they were falling over themselves to get out of there. Or maybe they just caught sight of Delgado's gangsta teeth and my bloodstained bandages. Either way, it left enough space for the four of us to squeeze into the vacated space.

I wanted to sit nearest the exit, in case I had to

make a quick getaway, but found myself sandwiched between Delgado and Kaprisky. Arbogast, on the other side of Delgado, was straining at the bit, apparently all for storming the stage before the actors had even appeared, but Delgado held him back. 'If what Pringle says is true, we need to bide our time.'

'Of course it's true,' I said, though wasn't entirely sure what he was referring to. What on earth had I told him, other than how I'd bashed Verity Wilson over the head with a vase?

Arbogast looked anguished. 'You actually expect us to sit through this abomination?' I couldn't tell whether he was judging it on artistic or religious grounds.

'Duty,' said Delgado. He turned to me and winked. 'You have no idea what it's like, having to party with these rubes.' He patted me amicably on the shoulder and I bit my lip, hoping no-one would think I had actually chosen to go on a date with this greaseball. On the other hand, people were probably wondering why the greaseball was on a date with someone who looked as though she'd just undergone brain surgery at the hands of a drunken quack played by Peter Lorre. I'd been given the last of the Morphetamine, but the effects were already wearing off, leaving me feeling like a deflated balloon. At least the pain would stop me falling asleep.

I swivelled in my seat, trying to spot a familiar face. The media were salivating in anticipation of Nancy's first public appearance in months, so it wasn't just theatre buffs and critics in the audience but news reporters, gossip columnists, diarists and minor celebs. At least I'd made sure Phoebe wouldn't be among them. It was almost a glittering occasion, and a crying shame

Les Six's meisterwerk wouldn't be worthy of the attention, unless he'd completely rewritten it since the Bunterberg rehearsal. The air conditioning hadn't been designed to cope with a full house; I scanned the crowd, trying to spot notepads or cameras, but all I could see were row upon row of programmes being used as makeshift fans, trying to summon a faint breeze from the stagnant atmosphere. Most of the spectators were casually dressed, but I spotted a sprinkling of suits, a cluster of Chinese tourists, and a fat lady in a floral-print dress who looked as though she ought to have been at *The Mousetrap*. There were even people sitting on the steps, in the aisles. I began to fret about fire safety arrangements.

Delgado chuckled and rubbed his hands together. They squeaked faintly, as though they'd been lightly doused in oil. 'So what kind of a play is this? Shakespeare?'

'I told you, it's a musical about Jack the Ripper.'

'Jack the Ripper,' he echoed. 'Jacko the Ripster. Jack O' Ripperoony...'

I gazed at him in amazement. How could it be possible? 'You've never heard of Jack the Ripper? Do you even know what a musical is?'

Delgado, who'd been in a frisky mood since we'd left Phoebe's flat, started humming *Surrey with the Fringe on Top*, and only stopped when Arbogast begged him to shut up.

'You wait,' I said. 'Going to be a lot of singing before Nancy appears.'

At seventeen minutes past eight, the houselights dimmed and the show began.

*****

There was no denying the breadth of Les Six's vision, but he would have had problems squeezing it into the Colosseum, let alone into an intimate fringe venue not much bigger than Phoebe and Maurice's living-room.

It started like *Oliver!* and got steadily worse. The stage was thronged with flower girls and knife grinders, pimps, slumming toffs and a bunch of grubby-faced urchins played by brats from the local showbiz school, who performed cartwheels and cheekily picked a pocket or two before being ushered off to bed so the rest of the company could get on with the X-rated material.

And then the singing started.

Some say we're way below
The very lowest of the low
That the East End is the kind of place
Where the gentlefolk don't go

It's the pits, it's shit, it's underlit
Your throat's at risk of being slit
In the city of dreadful night

The company belted the song out so enthusiastically that our benches vibrated, the singers' pathologically cheerful demeanour a startling contrast to the downbeat lyrics and gloomy electronic backing. The discrepancy was probably intended as ironic, but I could feel the audience cringing.

Then the hookers took over. Trust Les Six to create a full complement of meaningful roles for women in low-cut blouses. There was a collective gasp as they stepped up to bat; Six had obviously found Nancy's condition inspiring, because all the other actresses in *Ripped!* were now padded out to simulate pregnancy and were waddling around as though well into their third trimesters. Still no sign of Nancy herself, though.

The padding had other uses too, as the first murder demonstrated. It took place just after Bunty Mackay had belted out:

> *Going down on my knees*
> *In the mud and the sleaze*
> *The future's not bright*
> *In fact it's shite*
> *In the city of dreadful night*

At the words 'The future's not bright,' the stage area darkened and a cloaked figure emerged from the shadows. As Mackay reached the climax of her song, the figure slid a large knife into her fake belly, releasing a steaming torrent of animal entrails. It was at this point that the first walk-outs occurred.

I heard Jules chuckling to himself. 'This is sick.' It's true it wasn't *The Sound of Music*, but, incredibly, he seemed to be enjoying the spectacle. Unlike Arbogast and Kaprisky, who were staring wheyfaced at the stage as though their testicles were being twisted into monkey fists. I wondered how long I had to endure this hell and squinted at the photocopied programme, only to find a Writer's Statement in which Les Six explained why he didn't believe in diluting the intensity of his stagecraft with unnecessary concessions to the bourgeois pleasures of gin, tonic and visiting the cloakroom. As soon as I realised there wasn't going to be an interval, and that this torture was going to go on and on without respite until everyone was dead, including me, the side of my head began to throb so insistently that at first I thought it was part of the electronic drone that was passing itself off as a score. As the characters on stage posed and pontificated, and despite the persistent thrumming of my absent outer ear, or maybe even because of it, I felt sleep tiptoeing up on me, until finally it arrived and I nodded off.

I couldn't judge how long I dozed, but I was woken by the sudden jerk of my own head dropping forward. I rubbed my eyes. Nothing much had changed. On stage, the hookers were still whinging about their rotten lot in life. The audience was rustling impatiently. People were either falling asleep, like me, or squirming on their unyielding wooden benches like bored schoolchildren waiting for the end-of-period bell.

> *Poor Annie Chapman didn't stand a chance*
> *All she wanted to do was sing and dance*
> *But to masculine eyes she was worse than nada*
> *So they sliced her up and cut out her bladder*

As Elizabeth Stride, Catherine Eddowes and Mary Jane Kelly consorted with sinister-looking gentlemen and one by one succumbed to their gruesome fates, as Inspector Abberline shiftily demonstrated his incompetence, as the stage area was covered by piles of steaming offal which had to be removed by stagehands dressed as street-sweepers, the audience grew restless, their interest roused only intermittently by incidents such as Carlotta Reese's bodice popping open in mid-murder. And for some reason they loved everything about Dougal

Metcalf, egging him on to new extremes of camp posturing and improvised asides, as though they thought this was a panto and he was playing Widow Twankey.

But the animal entrails lost their novelty value, and presently the continuing trickle of punters heading for the exit seemed spurred less by outrage than by the stench emanating from the stage. We were able to spread out a bit on our bench, which was no longer as tightly packed. I craned my neck, trying to work out how many people had walked out, and saw Les Six leaning against the exit just behind me. I overheard him murmuring to the man next to him, 'The day no-one walks out on one of my productions will be the day I'm finally embraced by the stinking status quo.'

Who the hell talks like that? I thought, trying to remember why I'd ever found him so affable.

At long last, Nancy made her entrance, and there was a shift in the atmosphere, like a mass intake of breath. Alongside me, Delgado sat up straight. He wasn't the only one; the remaining spectators were all sitting up and taking notice, and some of those who'd been heading for the exit changed their minds and returned to their seats. This was what they'd been waiting for. *Nancy!*

She began to sing in a voice that was thin and high, but not altogether unpleasing.

> *Do-gooders call us ne'er-do-well*
> *Condemn us to a living hell*
> *But what they never seem to see*
> *Is at least we're livin' free*
> *Livin' free ooh ooh livin' free*

My first reaction was surprise. After all the fake

pregnancies Six had paraded before us, not only did Nancy's look real, but she had got a whole lot bigger since I'd last seen her. She was plumped up like an overripe pumpkin, ready to burst. And she was no longer looking witchy, but energised and full of vim, like a goddess of fecundity. Her black hair gleamed like a raven's wing. The limelight suited her.

But what was now obvious was something I hadn't predicted: she really did have star quality. Her singing and acting were mediocre, at best, but it didn't matter - nourished by the attention, or perhaps by her third trimester, she was giving off a subliminal glow, like radioactive cereal. There was no denying the fact: she had *it*. All she'd needed to get noticed had been preternatural impregnation, people trying to kill her, and merciless hounding by the tabloid press. The audience stopped fidgeting. As the scene continued, Six's awful dialogue suddenly seemed full of possibility. She was selling it. She was really selling it.

Nancy's arrival gave the play a second wind, though it was arguable as to whether it had ever had a first one. But as she went through the motions on stage, we couldn't tear our eyes away. She truly was Six's secret weapon. The action around her trundled on, no less nonsensical than before, but nobody minded now. This was what we had come to see. This was grand theatre, and we were all along for the ride.

After a while, it became apparent that the play was approaching its climax. The shadows lengthened, and Maggie Crook was in deadly peril. Delgado tapped me on the shoulder, and leaned across so he could whisper into my good ear, 'Would you say the big fight is coming up?'

'I guess so,' I said.

He started rummaging in one of his trouser pockets. For a dreadful moment I thought he was masturbating, and avoided looking directly at him, just in case. But the next thing I knew, he said, 'This is my cue,' in a stage whisper and dipped his head to say something into my swaddled ear. By the time I worked out what it was, he'd gone.

Wish me luck, Pringle.

From his point of view, knowing what he knew about Nancy, what he was about to attempt was heroic, even if he believed what I'd told him. He knew what had happened to Petersen, Bidlack, Koslo and the others, yet still he went for it. He honestly believed he was saving the world.

What I'd told him. It all came back in a sickening rush. Had I really told him how he might be able to penetrate Nancy's defences? What had I been thinking? This was the worst thing I'd done, worse than selling her story to Verity Wilson. I'd totally betrayed my friend, and now if she were killed it would be all my fault. No, this wouldn't do, it wouldn't do at all. I tried to follow him into the aisle, but Arbogast's arm came down like a barrier at the entrance to a car-park, pinning me in my seat.

Delgado slipped stealthily, a dark shadow, down the steps towards the stage until I lost sight of him, and Arbogast slid into the vacated space so that now I was flanked by men in grey, both staring in stony silence at the spectacle unfolding in front of us. There was nothing to be done, so I let my attention swing back to Nancy as the lighting dimmed even further, and the spaces at the edge of the stage area filled with shadowy figures,

430

whiskered phantoms I recognised as Inspector Abberline, the Duke of Clarence, Montague Druitt, Sir William Gull, Harry Dam and the President of the Whitechapel Vigilante Committee, whose name had slipped my mind.

I was probably the only person in the audience, apart from maybe Les Six and the stage manager, who would have noticed a seventh male figure on the stage, one who wasn't supposed to be there. What Delgado lacked in stature and whiskers, he made up for in other ways. Like the knife he was carrying, not a folding one like my Étripouille, but a fixed-blade Bowie I hadn't seen before.

But they were all carrying knives, so what difference did another one make?

I glanced back at Six to see how he was reacting. He was staring at the stage, mouthing something. Maybe counting heads. Had he noticed Delgado? Did he even care? I decided to have a word with him and tried to get up, but I'd barely lifted my backside off the bench before Arbogast thrust his arm out again. And so I stared at the stage, mesmerised, but not by the play. As the throbbing from my side of my head grew more intense, so fragments of my drugged-up afternoon kept coming back to haunt me. I'd told Delgado that Nancy wouldn't hurt anyone so long as she was *acting*. Ah yes, I'd been trying to impress him with my insider knowledge, trying to hold his attention, like Scheherazade, so he wouldn't have me put down. I'd been trying to save my own skin.

So there was Nancy on the stage, singing her heart out, surrounded by shadows with knives. But at least one of those knives wasn't a prop with a retractable blade. I shrank down on the bench as far as I could go. I didn't want to see what happened next, but I couldn't look away. Whatever happened, it was going to be bad.

The kung-fu fight began. This was the big set-piece. It was Nancy against the rest of them, kicking and punching with the sound designer adding crunchy audio effects. The audience watched stupefied. Even Delgado seemed unsure what to make of it as the actors around him launched themselves, one by one, at Nancy, only to stagger back, vanquished by her superior martial artistry and covered in stage blood. It was just like the fight scenes in action movies: if only her assailants had ganged up to attack her en masse, they would have defeated her easily, but instead they presented themselves to her one at a time, so she had no trouble picking them off.

The ZAP! POW! KERRUNCH! sound effects reminded me of something, and I finally worked out it was: Delgado's *Revelation Man* comic. But each deafening report only aggravated the throbbing in my head, which was threatening to split my skull in two, so it was probably to put an end to that, more than anything more selfless, that impelled me to do what I did next.

Without considering the consequences, I lurched to my feet and, shoving aside Kaprisky and Arbogast's attempts to pull me back down, yelled, *'Nancy! Look behind you!'*

I'd had a lot of yelling practice that afternoon, so my voice sliced through the theatre. Everyone around me turned to stare, saw my blood-soaked bandage and shrank back, assuming I was part of the show. They shrank back even more when I yelled, *'The knife is real!'*

I couldn't tell if she recognised my voice or if she'd made out the words, but her head whipped round and she blinked rapidly into the lights. Then she froze into a statue, and for a few seconds her mind seemed to be somewhere else. Was she watching one of her mental slide-shows? Then she came back from wherever it was she'd been, and smiled into the void, and like some sort of M.C. announced to the audience, *'As it is written, so shall it be done.'*

The people around me were already fidgeting nervously. Was the action going to move up here into the audience? Would they get pelted with fake blood and pigs' entrails? Would they be *humiliated in public?* Arbogast and Kaprisky were looking as panicked as JFK's bodyguards on Elm Street. I reached a decision and grabbed my bag. Arbogast's arm shot out again, but this time I ducked beneath it and forced my way past. My bandage caught on one of the buttons on his cuff and as I followed Delgado's route down to the stage it started unravelling behind me. From somewhere behind me I heard Six exclaim, 'Bloody hell! Genius!' Impossible to tell if he was referring to his own work or the impromptu amendments now being made to it.

Nancy was still squinting into the audience, shading her eyes from the glare. Something was happening, she didn't know what, but it was enough to make her step out of character. So when Prince Albert Victor - otherwise known as Jasper Andrews - launched himself at her back as choreographed, knife at the ready, she was caught off-guard.

And that was all it took.

*****

The downward rake was so steep I found myself taking

the last few steps too fast. Unable to stop, I hurtled headlong on to the stage just as the last of the bandage unravelled and, with one last regretful tug, parted company with the drying blood which was now the only thing gluing it to the side of my head. There was a shocked gasp from the audience as the sticky mess underneath was laid bare. But no-one was walking out now. The spectacle had become deliciously unpredictable, and now I was a part of it.

My fall was broken by something soft, which turned out to be Jasper. It was my turn to squint at Nancy, who was now looming above me. She bent down as far as her vast belly would allow and I felt her cool fingers probing the part of my head that was still throbbing away like an idling engine. She leant closer and whispered into my one remaining ear, 'So it's yours.'

'What?' It didn't help my already shaky grasp on reality that I seemed to be hearing everything in mono, but I was keenly aware of hundreds of pairs of eyes fixed on me. They could see me but I couldn't see them. I felt horribly exposed. Was this what it was like to be an actor?

'Don't worry about me,' I said to Nancy. 'I'm fine.' I nodded at her, when I should have been shaking my head. *Insensitive cow,* I thought. *Can't she see I'm in agony?* I tried to shield my eyes from the glare until I seemed to be looking out at a sea of masks against a painted backdrop. I heard someone behind me exclaim, 'Good Lord, it's the Ginger Nut girl!' before I was seized by the armpits and dragged to the side of the stage. The audience applauded madly.

I'd lost sight of Delgado. There were so many actors on stage that he'd easily been able to mingle, and no-one in the audience had thought it strange that one of the performers should be dressed in a contemporary grey suit instead of Victorian period costume. They simply assumed he was another part of the ongoing all-male conspiracy and an integral part of the artistic statement. So I didn't spot him until it was too late. And neither did Nancy, whose attention was still on me.

Almost affectionately, he hooked his arm around her shoulders and stuck his Bowie into her left flank.

'I'm so sorry,' he said. 'But we don't have a choice.'

Nancy's eyes opened wide in surprise, and she cried, 'There's *always* a choice!' There was a murmur of appreciation from the audience. This was terrific acting.

Too soon, I thought numbly. This was no way for our friendship to end.

The two of them stood there, locked in their embrace for what seemed an eternity, Delgado hanging on to the hilt as though he was never going to let go, his face inches from hers. He was grinning again, so broadly I began to doubt it really was a grin at all. Then he gave the knife a vicious twist and tugged it back towards him. It took an immense effort, as though he were dragging a drinking straw through quick-setting concrete, and he was forced to use both hands.

Nancy's eyes closed, and she swayed, and I thought she was going to collapse. No, I thought she was *dying*. I thought I was dying, too. My heart stopped, literally. I felt it cease to beat, though the blood continued to pulse in my one remaining ear, like waves pounding against the walls of a cave. I'd never meant for it to come to this. Someone, somewhere, was bound to blame it all on me.

And then Nancy opened her eyes, and my heart

stuttered and restarted. *Saved.* I clearly saw her, Delgado and the knife. But there was something missing from this tableau, and, in my confused state, it took me several moments to work out what it was.

Blood. Of course. He'd stuck a knife into her, but she wasn't bleeding. As if she'd read my thoughts, Nancy reached behind her back and undid something. Her fake belly swung aside like a stiff apron, the knife firmly embedded in it. I'd thought earlier that she'd got a lot bigger, and so she had. Les Six, it seemed, hadn't been satisfied with her actual bulk. He'd taken one look at the fake pregnancies lined up in rehearsal and realised Nancy would need to be padded out to match them. He couldn't possibly have his one authentic pregnancy shown up by the faux versions.

Delgado was wearing the dazed expression of a gambler who had just placed everything he owned on red and watched it come up black. *Padding.* How could he have anticipated that?

'Damn,' he said and began to weep tears of blood.

I had no idea what kind of groundwork had been laid to trigger what happened next - whether it was a change in atmospheric pressure, or psychokinesis, or a pre-existing condition prodded into overdrive. Delgado tried to say something else, but the blood that had started seeping from all his facial orifices at once was getting in the way and made him splutter. It was coming out of his ears too, I noted dispassionately. Lucky old him. At least he still had two ears for it to come out of.

He didn't live long after that. It was more spectacular than anything I'd seen in any of the medical textbooks. I watched in astonishment as his eyes bulged until they burst out of his sockets (*There! hadn't I warned him she would make his eyeballs explode?)* and then he was screaming and clutching his head, as if trying to hold something in, but it was too big to be contained, and there was a *crack* and globs of greyish stuff went flying in all directions, as though someone had smashed their fist down into a bowl of porridge. I realised now this was all part of the show. Grand Guignol. The Theatre of Cruelty, with state-of-the-art effects. None of it seemed real. But the audience was lapping it up. Someone yelled, 'Go, Nancy!'

Only Jet Coleman and Rod Carpenter had remained in character. Jack Banner and Wally Winters were yelling at the top of their voices, but you couldn't make sense of the words. Dougal Metcalf, as always, was camping it up, while Harry Bones was chuckling ruefully to himself, as though it were all a bad acid flashback. Meanwhile, Jasper Andrews was lying in a pool of his own blood, crying for his mother. Determined not to be left out now it was degenerating into a free-for-all, Carlotta Reese galloped back on stage, fake belly removed and stays flapping. When a small grey gobbet hit her on the cheek, she stopped to wipe it off, examined what was on her finger and exclaimed, 'Oh, gross!'

Jules Delgado was still standing, but it was hard to see how, when the top part of his head was looking as though he'd walked into the rotor blade of a helicopter. Nancy was still staring at him with a blankness that filled me with dread. I sensed it would have been better for all of us if she'd been showing some emotion. I knew it wasn't over, not by a long chalk. She was an earthquake waiting to happen. I steeled myself. Here it was. The Big One. And here was I, right at the epicentre.

There was a hollow booming in my one remaining ear. Maybe I was going deaf, which would be a mercy since I wouldn't be able to hear the end of the world when it happened.

Nancy let out a big, shuddering sigh and looked down. There was a damp stain on her skirt, and a corresponding puddle at her feet. I was pleased to see I wasn't the only one who responded to stress by wetting herself, but despite the hundreds of pairs of eyes fixed on her, she didn't seem in the least bit embarrassed. Instead, her gaze roved around the stage area, passing over the other actors, one by one, before finally coming to rest on me again.

'Hey Belinda, it's happening.'

'It most certainly is,' I said.

'I mean it's *time*, Belinda. It's coming.'

This was it, then? The end of the world?

What was left of Delgado collapsed into a deliquescent heap, as though his bones had been dissolved. It was at that moment Dudley Walker decided to bring up the house lights. I stared dazed as the audience leapt to their feet and applauded wildly. There were loud cheers and some whistling. Nancy looked bewildered, as though she'd forgotten she was being observed, but Dougal and Rod seized her by the arms and tipped her forward into a shallow bow. The other actors joined in uncertainly, all except Jasper, who was definitively indisposed, and Harry, who had got out his tobacco tin and was now lolling in the wings, rolling a submarine-sized joint. The applause continued, even as some of the spectators stood up and began to clog the aisles, jostling other early leavers to get out and catch their trains. Their progress was checked by a swarm of latecomers, some in uniform. I spotted a red face I recognised as Church. Someone behind him was waving frantically, trying to catch Nancy's attention: it was Maurice, with Phoebe, who still looked royally pissed off. I felt a surge of jubilation, even though I knew we were all going to die. She was too late! She'd missed it! I had won!

Church and his men were battling to get down to the stage, but there were so many theatregoers surging in the opposite direction it was gridlock. Only one man managed to elbow his way through the crowd and run on to the stage, where he punched the air repeatedly, trying to rekindle the dwindling applause. Les Six. He capered like a jester, blowing kisses at the audience before grabbing Nancy by the hand. Only when she failed to twirl triumphantly alongside him did he really look at her.

'Shit a brick,' he said. 'You're early.'

Nancy had lost her fierceness. 'It hurts.'

Lucy and Dougal were now sprawled stylishly across the front benches, talking intently to a grey-haired man in a wine-coloured smoking jacket. Two women clambered through the lower section of the audience and rushed over to kneel next to Jasper. One of them unbuttoned his shirt and began to massage his chest.

Six looked around in wonderment before coming to a decision. The comedy was over; now the drama had begun.

'Let's go,' he said to Nancy, springing into action as though he were a proud father-to-be and not the writer of a musical which would never again live up to its sensational premiere. 'Can you walk?'

Nancy nodded. 'Just about.' He wrapped his arm

around her shoulders and began to usher her off the stage.

Rod blocked his path. 'What about Jasper?'

Carlotta rematerialised next to him and started tugging at Six's arm. 'What about the party?' Blood was trickling from her nostrils. She wasn't the only one with a nosebleed; all around us, people felt wetness on their philtra, clamped hands to their faces and rooted frantically in pockets for tissues to stem the flow.

'What about me?' I said, dragging myself to my feet.

Six, unconcerned about the blood trickling out of his own nose, ignored the actors and looked straight at me. 'What about you?'

'I need plastic surgery.'

He smiled nastily. 'I'll second that.'

'Get that bitch out of here.' Carlotta's voice was muffled by the arm she'd mashed against the lower part of her face.

'Bite me, Carlotta,' said Six.

'Shouldn't we be getting to a hospital?' I was desperate to to escape before one of these stupid actors rubbed Nancy up the wrong way and the roof caved in. She needed a midwife; I needed painkillers, and a surgeon.

Six jerked his head at me. 'Come on then if you're coming. Shake a leg.'

He led us through an unmarked exit, leaving Phoebe and Maurice and Church and the uniforms trapped in the maelstrom of milling humanity.

*****

Well, the drive was a nightmare. As soon as we got outside there was a drumroll of thunder, and Niagara Falls began to rain down on us. Only a few streetlamps appeared to be functioning; all the traffic lights seemed to be out. The gloom was crisscrossed by chaotic beams from headlights, while the torrential rain turned the windscreen into an impressionistic blur which rearranged itself each time the wipers passed over it.

Nancy flopped about on the backseat of Six's Skoda. Whenever the cramps took her, she'd forget her breathing exercises and start screaming and thrashing around like a small fishing boat in a storm. Strapped into the front passenger seat, I was yelling too. It felt as though someone had stripped the skin from the side of my head with a potato-peeler. I couldn't stop prodding what remained of the ear root, which twanged back into place each time with a gust of raw pain, worse than any toothache. Our discordant wailing reverberated in my one remaining ear like competing fire alarms.

'Shut the fuck up,' Six said in a reasonable voice, fat drops of blood splashing on to his knees as he drove. He made occasional attempts to stem the flow with his sleeve, but mostly ignored it to concentrate on the street ahead, peering through the rain at an obstacle course of bad driving in which the highway code seemed to have given way to untrammelled road rage.

'What the fuck is going on?' he asked.

'End of the word,' I gasped. Delgado had been right.

'More likely a power cut,' he said. We slowed to a crawl, stopping and starting as cars tried to negotiate unregulated junctions and opportunistic motorists tried to weave in and out between the other vehicles but only succeeded in blocking the road even more. Nancy's breathing exercises broke down again and her screaming took over. I gave up trying to compete and let my own weeping subside to weak snivelling as I pulled out my Apocalypse Kit and tried to patch up the side of my head with sticking-plasters.

Six glanced sideways at the green and purple dinosaurs and said, 'Where the fuck do you think you are? Jurassic Park?'

Halfway down Farringdon Road, just as I thought Nancy's shrieking would rupture my eardrum, I realised the noise wasn't coming from her but from a small armada of emergency vehicles, blue lights flashing in vain as they tried to nose through the traffic behind us. Some of the more conscientious drivers tried to edge out of their way, but there was nowhere for them to go.

One of the cop cars finally scraped through and drew level with us. I looked across and saw Church gesturing frantically out of his window. 'Pull over!' he yelled.

'No time!' Six shouted back. I marvelled at his calm; he didn't seem fazed by all the fluid leaking out of him.

'Pull over!' Church yelled again, looking as though he was about to have a cardiac arrest, but now it was his turn to start wiping his nose. He stared at the back of his hand, surprised. There was blood on my hands too, but I couldn't tell if it was coming from my nose or my ear.

'You see?' shouted Six. We have to get her to hospital.'

Church's face went the colour of putty. He got out a mobile phone and started yelling into it. Nancy stopped screaming for a few seconds and glanced out of the window and said, 'Oh God,' and there was a screech of brakes and a crunch of chrome as half a dozen cars in front of us piled into each other, not violently enough to do serious damage, but enough to open a narrow gap. Les accelerated into it. Behind us, the traffic immediately closed back up and sealed off our route, like the Red Sea cutting off pursuing Egyptians.

The blood was collecting in the lobeless hollow of my ear like rainwater in the bell of a flower, soaking the plasters and coursing steadily down my neck, drenching the neckline of my Fluff Phillips, now looking as though it had gone ten rounds against a heavyweight boxer.

'She's making me bleed,' I complained.

'Welcome to the party, pal!' sniffed Six, trying to clear his nasal passages as though he were suffering from a heavy cold. The sound of him snorting back blood made me feel sicker than ever.

'I'm going to throw up.'

'Go ahead and barf,' he said. 'I'm not stopping this car for love or money.'

We sped past an archway I belatedly recognised as the entrance to St. Bart's. 'You missed it!'

'We're not going there,' said Six. 'Didn't you hear? Their A & E got closed down last week.'

Beyond Smithfield, the streets were less clogged, but Six only managed to get through by mounting pavements and ignoring one-way signs. I looked back and saw a cluster of flashing blue lights, but a long way behind us. We had the edge. Six mounted another pavement.

'Ow!' I said as my head banged against the window. 'Ow!'

Nancy trumped my snivelling with an extra-big

wail. 'Oh Christ, it hurts!'

'Nearly there,' said Six. 'Then we'll find you some drugs.'

'Where? Where are we going?'

'St. Cuthbert's,' said Six. 'Came here last year for my colonoscopy.' He turned into a side road, and then into another, and then we were crossing a car park. We had no trouble finding a space, which should in itself have tipped us off that it wasn't business as usual.

'Not this fucking place again!' wailed Nancy.

'I think this is a staff car park,' I said, face pressed against my window. Something was wrong. I opened the door and saw what it was. Apart from a car covered in graffiti and a van which had had its wheels removed, the car park was empty.

'There's nobody here,' I said.

'Nonsense,' said Six, throwing his door open. 'Of course there's someone here.'

But the only sign of life was a bedraggled black cat scurrying beneath a car to escape the rain.

'They've shut it down! Take us back to Bart's.'

Nancy started to scream again. 'It's coming!'

'You hear that?' said Six. 'We'd better get her inside.'

'But what..'

'Shut up and give me a hand,' he said, opening Nancy's door.

Don't ask me how we got her across the car park. It was like trying to steer a large blancmange. The downpour was so heavy the drains had given up trying to cope and we found ourselves ankle-deep in swirling water. I kept babbling it was pointless; Six insisted we press on, even though there was so much blood leaking from his eyes that without the rain to wash it away he would have been blinded. I felt a ray of hope as the automatic doors slid open and we stepped through into a brightly lit reception area, only for it to be snuffed out as we saw it was deserted. Spray-painted across the wall in fluorescent green were the words, THE JUEWS ARE THE MEN WHO WILL NOT BE BLAMED FOR NOTHING and a crude drawing of a giant phallus.

The power was still on, though, which was something. Six pressed a button for the lift. 'Let's get her to a bed.' When the door opened I walked Nancy inside, but he hung back and said, 'I'll go and find someone.'

'Who?' I asked, though *How?* would have been nearer the mark. Six didn't look in any state to walk. I lowered my voice. 'Don't leave me alone with her.'

'Hello! I can hear you,' said Nancy. 'I'll try to calm down.' She took a deep breath. The bleeding from my ear didn't stop, but it did seem to coagulate a little. I pressed the button for OBSTETRICS & GYNAECOLOGY and tried to keep her upright, but she was still wobbling in all directions at once, while I wasn't exactly a pillar of stability myself.

'Wait,' I said as the door began to slide shut. 'How long does labour go on for?'

'No idea.' Six's voice floated through the diminishing gap. 'Could be days. I know that my...'

His voice was cut off as the door slid shut. The lift juddered and began to move upwards.

'Days?' I squawked. '*Days?*'

What had I let myself in for? Nancy sagged again, and I just managed to stop her slithering all the way to the floor. I knew that if she collapsed all the way down, I'd never be able to pick her up again, not on my own.

The lift came to a stop and the door opened on to a large landing and another reception area. It was as deserted as the downstairs one, but at least I spotted a sort of gurney and managed to manoeuvre Nancy on to it. I pushed her along a corridor and through the first open door I came to, into what looked like an examination room from which all the equipment had been stripped out, leaving only a couple of rickety chairs and a metal-framed bed with a broken leg. I propped up the leg with one of the chairs and tipped Nancy off the gurney and on to the mattress. Whoever had spray-painted the graffiti downstairs had been in here too, and scrawled O HAVE YOU SEEN THE DEVLE WITH HIS MIKERSCOPE AND SCALPUL across the wall.

'How are you doing?' I asked.

'How do you think?' she snapped, and then added, 'Oh God, I'm sorry, Belinda. Just give me a minute... ' She breathed steadily in and out a few times. 'There, that's better.'

'I thought it was coming.'

'I thought so too,' she said. 'But not long now, I can feel it.'

I left her for a few minutes while I went out to case the joint. Further along the corridor I found a bunch of sheets and some grungy old pillows in a linen trolley. They were crumpled and stained, but I didn't think it mattered.

When I got back to Nancy she was moaning again. 'Oh Jesus, no-one told me it would hurt like this.'

Sounding a lot calmer than I felt, I said, 'Try to relax.'

She yelled so loudly into my remaining ear I could feel the tympanic membrane twanging like a guitar string: 'How can I relax when I feel like I'm shitting a melon?'

I was still wondering how best to respond when she revised upwards. 'No, I'm *shitting a planet!*'

'Let's hope it's not Jupiter,' I said.

Which is where we came in.

Chapter 10
The Babylon Mantra

'BABYLON SCORPION WORMWOOD
BRIMSTONE BABYLON SCORPION
WORMWOOD BRIMSTONE'

Nancy is chanting like a zombie priestess and I'm scared. I'm even more scared when she breaks off and starts laughing. How can she laugh at a time like this?

I try thinking back to when everything was normal, and fail. Has it only three months since she told me she was pregnant? I've been living a nightmare for so long now, and I want it to be over so things can get back to normal, but I know that before they can get normal they're going to get worse. A lot worse.

Who am I trying to kid? Things can never be normal again, and not just because of Nancy. Because of me. Because of what I've done. Because of what has been done to me.

This current headache is the worst so far, and I've had some humdingers lately. I can feel warm liquid leaking from my ear. My brain feels ready to split like a baked potato, but Nancy looks even worse than I feel. The whites of her eyes aren't white any more, but yellowish pink. Her cheekbones are protruding like ivory netsukes. Her hair is plastered flat against her head, and she's been perspiring so much the black hair dye has left a grey halo on the top pillow. She looks not just exhausted but half-drowned, like a witch after a session in the ducking stool.

And yet... and yet, I can't help noticing yet again there's something about her, something that wasn't there before, and only partly to do with the way she looks. It brings to mind such old-fashioned concepts as mettle, and grit, and backbone, though it's more than all of these. Whatever it is, it's forged in blood and fire, and she possesses it now, in spades. Despite the pink eyes and the ratty hair and the tatters of her streetwalker costume, it makes her look quite formidable, like a mythological creature from the pages of an ancient book. I feel quite proud, not just of her but of my part in her transformation.

When she sees me staring, she reaches over to grab my hand and squeezes it, hard. Then she pulls me towards her till my face is inches from hers.

'I'm sorry, Belinda.'

'What for?'

'Sorry I got you mixed up in this.'

'Hey, what are friends for.'

She chuckles and relaxes her grip, but almost immediately curls up in another spasm. Her eyelids start flickering as though she's being controlled by a dodgy electrical circuit. There's blood on the sheets, and not just streaks of it. Bright scarlet flowers. I can't tell if it's mine or hers. But I'm beginning to get the hang of this, and so I go out into the corridor and crouch, back against the wall, waiting for the crisis to pass. It's cool out there, and dark, but I have no intention of turning on the lights. I'm not going to broadcast our position to anyone outside who might be peering through telephoto lenses or rifle sights. They'll have this place surrounded, which is one of the reasons I haven't made a run for it. I wouldn't get far before Church or ComSec or one of Delgado's foot soldiers picked me up and started grilling me, or hacking away at my remaining ear.

But there's another reason I haven't taken off, and it's almost embarrassing to admit it. Nancy's my friend. She needs me, and she hasn't got anyone else. And I pride myself on being loyal, and reliable. You can always count on me.

I'm always here for you. Call me any time, any time at all.

I vaguely remember Lars saying something like that, half a century ago, when I still had both my ears. But I can't remember when, or why, or in what context. We were drunk, I guess. We were usually drunk, but I always managed to keep him and Nancy in separate compartments, the way I always try to keep people apart so they can't get together and compare notes. This was how you got caught out. This was where I'd gone wrong with Jules Delgado and Verity Wilson. I'd introduced them to each other, and look how *that* had ended.

But maybe it's time to knock down another of the dividing walls. I'm not sure how much longer I can hold out here on my own, and Lars has experience with sick women. The idea of sharing the burden is becoming more appealing with every nosebleed. I'm tired of having to deal with Nancy's contractions all by myself. Les Six isn't coming back, I know that now, and I desperately need a shoulder to lean on. Maybe it's time to summon the cavalry.

Nancy's bellowing has tapered off. Filled with fresh resolve, I rejoin her and tell her about my plan to call Lars. 'He always wanted to meet you,' I say, as though that will swing it.

She looks at me sceptically. 'I need a doctor, not

an accountant.'

I'm offended she thinks I've been hanging out with an accountant. On the other hand, I've never been entirely sure what Lars does for a living. Something in an office, something in the City, though I can't be any more precise because every time he'd mentioned Dow Jones or FTSE I'd switched off and stopped listening.

'Sure, call your boyfriend. Why not? What have we got to lose? He'll probably end up bleeding out like all the others, but what do we care?'

I start to snivel. Not like Nancy's elegant *Dame aux Camélias* weeping - more of a Punch and Judy convulsion in which slimy tears course down my cheeks to join up with the lava flow of snot and blood already streaming from my nostrils. Nancy gives me a long-suffering look, as though to remind me she's the one doing all the heavy lifting here. But I can't help it. I miss my ear. I'll probably be able to cover what's left of it with my hair, but what will Lars think when he sees it? What if he or one of his successors tries to draw that hair aside so he can whisper endearments? How will he react when he sees that nub of weeping gristle? How am I going to cope with the inevitable Van Gogh quips and snide gags about The War of Pringle's Ear? and *ear we go ear we go* and *'ello 'ello, what's going on ear then?*

'Belinda.' Nancy is stroking my hand, and whispering. 'Belinda. I've got a present for you.'

I sit up and sniff. 'What?'

She tries to sit all the way up too, but the effort is too much and she falls back against the pillows.

'My bag.' Nancy's bag is under the bed. I must have kicked it there at some point, possibly when I started bleeding from the eyes. I squat down and pull it open. It's full of the usual rubbish: make-up, tissues, volume four of *In Search of Lost Time*... I do a double-take; I knew Nancy had been reading a lot, but I hadn't realised she'd got as far as Proust. There are other things I'm not expecting: Fish Oil and Folic Acid, a fat roll of fifty pound notes, a silver crucifix on a chain, a small green velvet jeweller's case...

'That's for you,' says Nancy.

I pick up the jeweller's case and weigh it in my hands. It could be anything - an engagement ring, a pearl necklace - but I know it's not. The thought of what's inside makes me want to throw up. Presented to me like jewellery. Does she think I'm going to string it around my neck?

'Aren't you going to open it?'

'I know what's in there.'

'You can get someone to sew it back on.'

I laugh bitterly. 'Is there a doctor in the house?'

'Don't worry, Belinda,' she whispers, and her mouth is so cracked and dry that I dive back into her bag and start rummaging around for lip-salve. 'We'll look after you.'

'That's good,' I say. 'And we'll do our best to reciprocate.' We? Who the hell is we? What am I talking about? I can't find lip salve but there's some greasy hand cream. She puckers up as I rub it on her mouth. She touches my wrist, more lightly this time.

'Promise that if something happens to me, you'll look after Kitty.'

'Sure,' I say.

'Promise.'

'OK, I promise.'

'Because I'm starting to think I might not make it,

and I don't want ComSec taking her.'

'Of course you'll make it. No-one dies in childbirth.'

'Not if they have medical attention,' she groans. 'And guess what I don't have? It hurts, Belinda. I don't think it should be hurting like this.'

I don't know what to say. I wish someone else were here, to take control of the situation. I wish Lars were here. Nancy's eyes flick towards the object nestling in my hand like a large chrome kidney bean, and her expression changes. 'Verity Wilson had a recorder like that,' she says.

So here we are. I knew we'd get here sooner or later.

'Actually, she gave me it to,' I say. 'In a manner of speaking.'

'When?'

'I need to tell you something.'

She shakes her head. 'I already know it was you.'

I'm so exhausted I can't even summon surprise..

'Did you think I wouldn't guess? All that stuff she wrote about me? That could only have come from you, Belinda.'

'They were writing so much junk. I was just trying to set things straight.' This sounds feeble, even to me.

Nancy looks me straight in the eye. 'Who killed her? Delgado? Or Bull?'

'I thought you said Bull was on your side.'

'That's what he *said*. Doesn't mean he *was*. People lie all the time, Belinda. You should know that.'

This is it then. Time to come clean. I take a deep breath and tell her about what I did to Verity Wilson. And then, before she's had time to process that, I take another deep breath and tell her about Clive Mengers.

*****

'Belinda? Belinda?'

Hell's bells, where am I? Oh yes, with Nancy in the hospital.

'Are you OK? You drifted off.'

I'd been expecting her to make my head explode, like Delgado's, but she seems remarkably sanguine.

'You're not angry about me hitting Verity Wilson on the head with my crackle glaze celadon amphora?'

Nancy shakes her head incredulously. 'You really thought you sleepwalked across London with Verity Wilson's severed head in a bag?'

'Delgado said it wasn't me.'

'He was right. You're not capable of that.'

'But the clinic,' I say.

'What about it?'

'I started thinking that might have been my fault.' I laugh weakly, because it sounds ridiculous now. 'There were so many black holes in my memory.'

'You thought...?' She looks at me open-mouthed. 'Oh, my poor darling Belinda. No wonder you've been acting so strangely. *Of course* your memory has holes; it's been trying to blank out things no-one should ever have to see. Why didn't you say something earlier?' She bites her lip. 'What happened at the clinic was all me, I'm afraid. Me and Kitty. I wish it had been someone else. But not you, it was never you.'

She's looking at me as though I'm mad - not the cutting-off-head kind of mad, but the senile old grandma who wanders off down the lane and doesn't know who she is.

'You're sure Mengers was dead? You did say you were very drunk.'

'Not *that* drunk,' I say. 'Maybe. I don't know. I was there. Who else could it have been?'

'Let's run through the contenders, shall we. How about ComSec? Or The Agency? Or the bonkers Brotherhood of the Latterday Saints? There's a whole pack of professional killers out there, Belinda; any one of them could have done it. You're just not in their league.'

I stick out my chin. 'How would you know?'

'I know *you*. You're a good person, even though you don't want to admit it. A bit eccentric, and you do obsess over peculiar things sometimes, but that's understandable, with that godawful Croydon business. Why didn't you talk to me?'

'You weren't there!' I wail. 'You were lording it in your luxury mansion, or gadding about with your actor friends.'

She sighs. 'I should have been paying more attention. Someone's been playing a trick on you.'

'That's what Delgado said,' I say. 'But why?'

'To get at me,' she says. 'Did Delgado really say that? Look, I'm sorry about what happened. He didn't deserve...' She trails off.

'Even so,' I say. 'It doesn't make sense.'

'You're trying to make sense out of all this? No wonder you're... Sweetie, you need a good night's sleep. So do I. Can't remember when I...' She breaks off and curls up. Starts rocking back and forth again.

I can feel another nosebleed coming on. I dig Phoebe's phone out of my bag, where Delgado had dropped it, but when I switch it on, the screen asks me for a code, and locks when I keep getting it wrong. I rummage in Nancy's bag again, but it's like trying to find a needle in a haystack. So I tell her, 'Just popping out,' as though I'm nipping out for a packet of Ginger Nuts, and go out into the corridor and head towards the lifts, where I vaguely recall having seen a telephone at one of the nurses' stations. My memory is functioning properly, for once, because I find it straightaway. I have to hold the receiver to my right ear, which feels unnatural, but no dialling tone. I push a few buttons. Nothing.

Then my eye is caught by the small Perspex window where figures have been printed in blue Biro: hash sign, followed by 538. Internal exchange. Of course. I try pushing zero, and then, when there's no result, nine. Hallelujah! The mechanical burr of a dialling tone. The line hasn't yet been shut down. So I tap out Lars's number. Why is it, I wonder, that right-handers always hold telephone receivers to their left ears?

Brrrgghh. Like a foreign ringing tone. I'm used to this. What I'm not used to is Lars picking up almost immediately.

'Yup.'

Yup. Like a gunshot. Probably thinking it's Hong Kong on the line.

'Lars?' Feels all wrong, receiver on that side of my head.

'Lindy-Loo! Where are you?'

He sounds so pleased to hear me I let the Scooby-Doo greeting slide. 'St. Cuthbert's.'

A pause. It's a terrible line. Or maybe it's just my right ear, which isn't used to having a receiver held to it. Our conversation is punctuated with false starts and awkward pauses, like a primitive trunk call.

I say, 'St. Cuthbert's,' again, in case he didn't hear it the first time.

'Isn't that...?'

'I don't think I can take much more.'

'St. Cuthbert's?'

'Well...'

'Didn't they close it down?'

'You said to call any time.'

There was the briefest of pauses, then... 'I'll be right there.'

'She's bleeding.' I can hear my voice going up a pitch. '*I'm* bleeding. Can you bring a doctor? Can they sew ears back on?'

Silence, interrupted by sharp crackling. Then, 'How long?'

I try to think back to when I had my ear cut off. 'About one o'clock. Yesterday, I think.' I feel a wave of dizzy nostalgia for the bookshop, and Alain and Elspeth, and the vile coffee in Lou's Café. 'What day is it now? Should I put it in the fridge?'

'How long *between contractions?*'

Oh, I see. 'Not a lot.'

'You won't help her by panicking.'

'I'm not panicking,' I say, aggrieved he thinks I am. He has *no idea* what I've been through. 'I just don't know what's normal and what isn't.'

'Calm down,' he says, as though I'm losing it, which only annoys me more. I ask where he is.

'Near Euston.'

The receiver emits a crackle so earsplitting I have to hold it away from my head. But I can still hear his voice, tinny and distant.

'Don't worry, Lindy-Loo. The cavalry is on its

way.'

And he hangs up. I haven't told him what floor we're on, but when I try calling back, the line is engaged.

But the relief is immediate, and overwhelming. Lars will know what to do. Not my type, and it was never going to be serious between us, but he's exactly the sort of chap who'd know how to damp-proof a wall or put up shelves or deliver a baby. No wonder Eileen is so keen to hang on to him.

*****

As I go back to Nancy, there's a smile on my face for the first time since I lost my ear.

She sees the smile. 'What's so funny?' I tell her help is on its way, thinking this will cheer her up too, but she promptly curls up with another cramp and starts puffing and blowing, and my nose starts bleeding again, so I go down to the lobby and wait for Lars there.

I sit at the bottom of the stairs with the fire door propped open, facing towards the car park, where I can see the Skoda. Still no sign of Les Six. I wonder again what happened to him, and feel sorry that he's probably dead by now. He wasn't a bad sort, in the end. I check my watch; either it's run out of battery, or time is standing still. Ten minutes pass, or perhaps twenty. Just as I'm starting to nod off, the sound of an engine jerks me awake.

There's a car pulling up. Unlike Six, Lars is smart enough to stop right in front of the door so he won't get drenched crossing the car park. He gets out. He's wearing navy-blue tracksuit bottoms and a grey sweatshirt, which make his usual brogues appear a little incongruous, and carrying a holdall. I've never seen him in anything but a suit, but I should have realised he went to a gym. His hair looks silkier than usual, as though freshly shampooed.

I wave gaily as he comes through the doors and then stand up on tiptoe to kiss him. There's a strong smell of soap. He recoils, and I try not to be offended. He can hardly be blamed for not wanting my blood and sweat and grubbiness to rub off on him, not when he's all squeaky clean.

'You look like you've been in the wars,' he says.

We get into the lift, with him keeping as much distance between us as the small space will allow. I press the button for the seventh floor and the lift moves upward.

'Just got back from the gym?' I ask, as though everything were normal.

'The gym? Oh, the gym,' he says absent-mindedly, apparently unaware of the distaste playing across his features like a fine mist. 'How is she?'

I feel cheesed off that he isn't more concerned about *my* health. He doesn't show any curiosity about the sticking plasters holding the side of my head together. The lift doors slide open on the seventh floor, and he overtakes me before we've even crossed the reception area. I slow down, letting him get further ahead along the corridor. Only a few minutes ago I couldn't wait to see him. Now he's here, and I can't wait to get away. I've got what I came for, it's all in my journal, or on Wilson's cassette recorder, and if the world doesn't end I can go home and write it all up in the morning after I've had a good meal and a decent night's sleep. He's just in time to take delivery of the baby and watch Nancy die.

Then I remember him telling me about the miscarriage, and a small annoying voice pipes up at the back of my brain. *What if he wants to steal the baby and take it back to Eileen, so they can bring it up as their own?* I can't allow this to happen. Nancy's baby deserves better than being brought up by a boring businessman and his hypochondriac wife in dull suburbia. There's a heaviness around my heart. I'll have to stick around a little while longer. That baby will be my responsibility, and no-one else's. I did promise Nancy, after all.

Lars notices I've lagged behind, and slows down so I can catch up.

'Aren't you going to introduce us?'

He always did want to meet her, didn't he? Well, now he has his wish; at long last, Lars is going to meet my lovely friend. At least I can console myself with the knowledge that she isn't looking her best.

He looks me up and down again, more kindly this time. 'You don't have to stay,' he says. 'You look like you could do with a stiff drink, Belinda.'

'I'll have one later,' I say, leading him into the examination room where Nancy is bracing herself against the next wave of pain. She doesn't even have the energy to look up as we come in.

'Lars, Nancy,' I say. 'Nancy, Lars.'

At the sound of my voice she turns her head, just a fraction.

'How are you bearing up?' says Lars. 'Or should I say bearing down.' He chuckles at his joke, and she stares straight through him. Lars ignores the chilly reception. He's all touchy-feely concern. He drops his holdall and leans over to stroke her forehead, feel her pulse, place his palm against her swelling abdomen. A little presumptuous, I think, for someone who has only just met her. I wait for her to knock him back with a nosebleed, but she's totally passive. Cowlike, even. I feel a flush of shame on her behalf - letting strange men come up and put their hands all over her like that.

'I expect you'd like a shot of Pethidine,' he says. 'Well, I know just where to find some.'

And he's out of the door and gone again, just like that. Nancy stares at the empty doorway, then turns her attention to me. *Uh-oh.* Here it comes. *What Pethidine? You said you couldn't find any drugs, Belinda.*

She's pissed off, but not about the Pethidine.

'So that was Lars,' she says, as though hearing his name for the very first time. Heaven knows I've mentioned him enough, but since I'd been talking about my own boring life rather than her infinitely more exciting one, she probably hadn't been paying attention.

'Lars,' she repeats softly.

'I hear you.'

Oh God, where did he go? What if he's changed his mind and abandoned us?

'What kind of name is Lars, anyway?' asks Nancy.

'I told you, his parents were Norwegian.'

'Your boyfriend is *Norwegian*,' she says, summoning just enough stamina to be withering, though I don't see what's so awful about that. After all, she's been out with a Swede or two in her time.

'He's got an accent,' I say, as if this settles it.

'I didn't hear one.'

Now she mentions it, neither did I. But the accent was only ever slight to begin with.

'You let this man shag you and you were never curious about his name?'

'So what?' I bristle. 'Did you ever cross-examine Maurice about his? What kind of name is Pflum anyway? Get off my case.'

Nancy still has that withering look. If I were a flower, I'd be wilting. 'Did he ever tell you his surname?'

I have to think hard. What *was* Lars's last name? I've seen him sign for things. I vaguely remember making a feeble joke about it, a joke that made him sigh and roll his eyes, as though he'd already heard it before, many times. I'm sure it had something to do with fish.

'Turbot? No, *Tublut*. I guess that's Norwegian too.'

Nancy is staring past me now, into space. 'And you spell that... how?'

I humour her by spelling it out. 'T. U. B. L. U. T.'

'Lars Tublut,' she repeats softly, several times, and then more loudly, 'Lars fucking Tublut. I don't believe it.'

'Lars Tublut,' I repeat, thinking it has rather a lilt to it. If ever he got divorced from Eileen he could marry me and then I'd be Belinda Tublut.

Nancy is staring past me now. She seems calm enough, but I'm glad she's stopped looking directly at me; I can't take much more of that withering.

'Write it down, Belinda. Take another look.'

What's up with her now? OK, anything to keep her happy. The first writing surface I lay my hands on is the Bar-F matchbook from my Apocalypse Kit, which is a design classic so I'm loathe to deface it, but Nancy leans over and snatches it out of my hand, and then seizes my Edison Samurai, flips the matchbook open and starts printing in childish capitals on the inside flap, pressing so hard the nib all but punctures the card, which makes me wince. As she prints, I can feel pressure building up in my sinuses, and then all I can see is blood splashing like the first droplets of a tropical rainstorm on to my hands. Prepared for the droplets to turn into a gush, I grope for the roll of paper towel and tear off a sheet and blot myself dry, but Nancy has finished writing, and sinks back against the pillows, all emotion drained. The droplets promptly stop.

'And I thought you were the Scrabble fan,' she says.

I'm still too busy dabbing at my nostrils to reply. Nancy watches me silently, then says, in that same quiet voice that makes me wish she would start shouting again, 'You were seeing him all along.'

What she's saying doesn't make much sense. I hold my hand out, wanting to rescue the Edison. Nancy drops it into my hand as though it were a cheap ballpoint.

'It's a fucking anagram, Belinda.' She shakes her head, unable to believe my utter stupidity. '*Lars Tublut* is an anagram of *Stuart Bull.*

Only when I take the matchbook and examine the letters do her words sink in. *Lars Tublut is an anagram of Stuart Bull.* It's my turn to shake my head. Wow. Nancy and I each know a man whose name is an anagram of the other's. What are the chances?

'It's not even a good anagram,' she says. 'I mean, *Tublut?* Hello? I can't believe you never twigged.'

The truth sinks in, albeit more sluggishly than it ought to. But I've been bleeding a lot, and my oxygen-deprived brain hasn't been functioning at full speed for quite some time now. It's no coincidence, of course it isn't. How could it have been? What is left of my world gently crumbles into ruin. I'd always known Lars was a liar, but only now do I grasp how much of one. Lars Tublut and Stuart Bull don't just have the same letters in their names. *They're the same person.* Heavens to Betsy, how could I have missed that?

But I don't want Nancy to see how upset I am, so I say, 'It just proves you should never expect too much from a married man.'

Inside, I'm seething. Though, oddly, not as much as I could have been. It's as though my mind reached boiling point some time ago and cut off, for safety reasons, like a kettle. Lars owes me an explanation. Boy, does he have some grovelling to do.

But when he comes back with a stack of clean towels and a couple of unmarked cardboard boxes, he has eyes only for Nancy, even though all she does in return is snivel quietly, tears welling out of her pink-rimmed eyes and scoring pale trails through her smudged complexion. He sits down by the bed, and starts stroking her forehead again, whispering soft words and encouraging her to breathe as she curls up with another contraction. Who the hell does he think he is? Her boyfriend?

'I'm proud of you,' he says. 'You were great.'

'I messed up.'

'You gave them what they wanted.'

'You were there?'

'Wouldn't have missed it.'

'I thought you were dead.'

'Takes more than a pissy little electric shock to take me out.'

'And ComSec?'

'Ssh, don't talk.'

That's right, Nancy, I think. *Shut the hell up. You've*

done enough talking for today.

And I think back to all the times Lars and I have been together, and how I thought he was too good to be true. Well, news flash, it *wasn't* true, any of it. Raymond Radiguet, Wilkie Bunterberg, Van Merkens: the whole performance had been a ruse, to trick me into giving him the information he needed. About the clinic, first of all, and then about Nancy's friends, her habits, her history; he'd cajoled me into telling him everything, and convinced me it was for my own good. I recall how Eileen's ailments had got worse, a whole lot worse, once I'd told him what he needed to know. He led me on, used me, and dumped me.

How could I have been so gullible? It's not as though I hadn't already been around the block, several times, or had dealings with sociopathic narcissists who could twist me round their little fingers. I think back to what Delgado once told me, that I had a face that was just begging to be bamboozled.

And then my one functioning ear picks up Nancy saying, '...from Verity Wilson,' and I feel all the remaining blood drain out of my head, and the floor opens up and is about to swallow me whole when she takes a deep, shuddering gulp of air and starts to make new noises, ones I haven't heard before, gasping and grunting and cursing. I've heard her curse before, of course, but never this colourfully.

Lars straightens up and points at the towels. 'Hand me some of those, will you?'

What does he think I am? An orderly? Why do people keep thinking I'm some kind of domestic servant, with no purpose other than to tidy up their mess and provide towels and hot beverages? I push some of the towels over to him, trying to convey without words the disgust I feel at his betrayal, but he barely glances at me.

'Why me?' Maybe I don't say it clearly enough, or maybe it's drowned out by Nancy's grunting, but he gives no sign of having heard. Either way, our relationship has served its purpose and there's no longer any need for him to maintain the pretence. None of it was real, not for a second. This tender New Man act he's putting on now just makes me want to puke. He's acting as though...

A terrible thought occurs to me. Has he been shagging Nancy all along? *Has he?*

'How's your wife?' I ask loudly, hoping Nancy will hear through her cussing. *'How's Eileen?'*

He's bent so far over that I can't see his face, but I think I hear him say, 'She's dead.' Then again, it might be my imagination. Obviously I've been imagining a lot of things lately.

'Did she even exist? Or did you make her up as well?'

He says, 'Oh my God.' Hasn't been listening to a word I've been saying. Then, and only then, does he look up, though I don't think he's *seeing* me, even now. He's grinning like an idiot and all I want to do is smash his face in.

'Will you take a look at this?' He shifts to one side to give me an unobstructed view, and I wish he hadn't. Emerging headfirst from Nancy's womb is the most horrifying thing I've ever seen, worse than what I saw at the clinic, worse than the worst photographs in *Practical Homicide Investigation*. I'm so horrified, I gulp in more air than my lungs can cope with, and my senses begin to swim. I stick out an arm to stop myself swaying, but

there's nothing to grab hold of, and I'm falling, falling...
Falling through the floor.
Falling through the basement.
Falling all the way down.

Chapter 11
Fireworks

Hell is a sitting-room with brown vinyl wallpaper, porcelain figurines of ladies in crinolines, and a bowl-shaped lampshade made from dimpled amber glass. I'm sitting in front of a Cosi-Glo gas-fire, but my hands stay cold, no matter how much I tried to warm them, because although the flames are flickering in a realistic manner, no-one has switched on the heating element.

Someone is sitting next to me on the chintz-covered sofa. I turn and see Nancy. Not pregnant. Scatterbrained and thoughtless and fidgeting like a schoolgirl, just like her old self, and everything is all right between us. It's as though the last three months never happened, as though the last ten years never happened; it's just like old times, when we were the best of friends, before I gave everything up for Croydon and then had to recover from that and getting married and then it all went horribly wrong, all of it, and I somehow got left behind, with no career, no life, no friends except Nancy Loughlin.

'You wouldn't want to live here,' she says, looking around and wrinkling her nose.

'Not unless they let me redecorate,' I say. Just the thought of my fingertips zithering across the surface of that wallpaper is making me wince. Or maybe it's the chill in my bones. Funny, I'd always thought hell was supposed to be hot.

Nancy looks thoughtful. 'That could be arranged, you know.'

'It could?' I perk up. 'How?'

'It's up to you.' She's looking at me in a shifty way that seems very unlike Nancy, who has always been very straightforward. 'It was always up to you. You could say we're counting on you now.'

My icy breath is hanging in the air, a small cloud of white vapour. I prod it with a tentative finger, and it bursts into a million fragments. Aware any one single of them could pierce flesh and bone and pulmonary tissue, I try desperately not to inhale.

'Not sure I'm up to the task,' I say, still trying not to breathe.

'You haven't let me down yet,' she smiles. I glance down and see her feet are bare, and a most peculiar shape, not foot-shaped at all.

'I'm afraid I have,' I say, still staring at her feet. 'I've let you down terribly. I've been selfish and envious, because people always look at you, and never notice me.'

'Well, it doesn't matter now,' she says, and I examine her face more closely. She looks like Nancy, she talks like Nancy, but I'm not so sure it is Nancy, not any more. Her eyes are red - not the area around her eyes, as though she's been rubbing them, but the actual eye; the irises are a fierce burning crimson. And her teeth are different; some of them are sharper than they ought to be, as though she's been filing them into points.

'That's all in the past,' she's saying. 'Now we must address the future. You were right, you know, when you said it was a question of nurture, not nature.'

'I said that?' I decide to play along, even if I'm no longer sure who I'm talking to. 'What should I do now?'

'What's best for baby,' says the Nancy thing.
'Don't let them take him away. Don't let Lars take him.'

Lars. Oh Christ, for a moment there I'd forgotten about him. But why is she calling him Lars anyway? He's Bull. A load of Bull. The perfect name, and if *that* isn't his real one, then it jolly well ought to be.

'He's bigger than me,' I say. 'Plus he can do kung-fu.'

'No, you could never take him in a fair fight.' Her voice begins to fade. 'But *you* know how to play dirty, Pringle. And remember, you're not alone...'

*****

O HAVE YOU SEEN THE DEVLE WITH HIS MIKERSCOPE AND SCALPUL

Graffiti is the first thing I see. I'm cold. This isn't right. Nothing is right. Everything is off and I feel sick.

Shouldn't be here. Lying flat on my back. Flat on the floor. I squint up at the ceiling; the texture reminds me of cottage cheese, which makes me feel even sicker. Mustn't throw up, not lying down like this. Remember Jimi Hendrix. Aching all over. Head like an open wound. And a horrible, shrill, unrelenting noise, piercing my brain like a dentist's drill. Crying. No, not crying. *Keening.*

I roll over on to my side and try curling into a ball, but this position hurts even more because now my hip bone is digging into the floor, but from this angle I can see a pair of blood-stained scissors on the floor on the other side of the bed.

Cold, much too cold. Nothing for it. Need to sit up and find a blanket.

Where was I? Oh yes. *Oh no.*

'Welcome back,' Lars says through the wailing.

I could tell him I'm not back at all, but don't. The Belinda he knew has gone, but another Belinda has returned in her place. This is a Belinda he doesn't know. A Belinda he really wouldn't *want* to know, who has his number and no longer needs an evil alter ego to do what is necessary.

'All right down there?' he asks as I manoeuvre myself into a sitting position. Something's different. There's something missing from the room, but also a troubling new presence. I can feel it in my head.

'You fainted,' says Lars.

Does he think I'm stupid? Oh yes, I forgot, it's exactly what he *does* think. The recent past comes flooding back. I remember a shiny red homunculus with pursed-up lips, and eyes like currents. I'd never seen anything so revolting in my life. I struggle to my feet, flapping my hands, trying to keep the vision at bay.

'Oh God, what the hell *was* that? Did you kill it?'

Lars finds this funny. 'It's just a *baby*, Belinda. A perfectly normal baby. No horns. No tail or hooves. No wings or halo, either. What a nugget you are.' His face cracks into a wide smile, but not for me. His big hands are streaked with blood and he's cradling something wrapped in a towel.

'The girl done good,' says Lars.

'Nancy...?'

'Sssh, don't wake her.'

Clinging to the bedframe to stop myself keeling over again, I look at Nancy. Her eyes are closed, lips slightly parted. A feather of suspicion tickles the base of my spine. There's no movement in her chest, no gentle rise and fall. She is still, *too* still, even for someone asleep.

I gaze down at her face, and remember the scissors, and the truth strikes me like a hammer-blow. Her face doesn't look peaceful, though it's not as bad as some of the faces I've seen in the medical books. The way she looks, she might almost be alive. But the clincher: there's no more pressure in my head, and the insides of my nostrils are no longer moist, but caked and dry. For the first time since we got here, the nosebleed has stopped.

'You said you'd bring a doctor.'

'We didn't need one,' he says. 'No complications.'

Au contraire, I think. *There are more complications in this room than you'll ever know.* I can feel something building up inside me. Once again the kettle is coming to the boil, but this time I'm not sure the cut-out mechanism will kick in. And I'm not sure I want it to.

The words on an old demolition company sign pop into my head. *Let it come down.*

The thing has quietened down and is now mewling, like a kitten. Lars is chuckling and prodding it with his finger, as though testing to see if it's ripe. If I'm going to do something, I need to do it while he's off guard like this. But what?

'What will you do now?' I ask. 'Take it away for weapons testing?'

That gets a reaction. He looks scathingly at me. 'I won't dignify that with an answer.'

'But it's the truth, isn't it?'

'I'd stop talking if I were you, Belinda, before you...'

'Before I what?'

'Before you say something you regret.'

I suppress a guffaw of indignation. What could there possibly be left for me to regret? Unless it was being so stupid I let him lead me up the garden path, lock me in the shed and set fire to it.

A missing piece of the jigsaw puzzle suddenly snaps into place. I still can't see the whole picture, but now I've got the outline.

'The clinic was you!'

For a moment Lars looks perplexed, as though the hit list is so long he can't remember who did what to whom, but then his face clears, and he grins. 'Sorry to disappoint you, but no. We had a team in place, but she didn't need our help. She saw to that one all on her own. That's when I knew we had to bring her in.' He whistled. 'Quite impressive, actually. Wish I'd been there to see it.'

'Except she wasn't on her own.'

He tilts his head. 'You what?'

'And it wasn't Nancy who killed Verity Wilson and Clive Mengers.'

'The photographer?' His eyes flick sideways, as though he's running through his mental Rolodex again. 'No, I think that was Wheeler. Or Fisher. Whoever was assigned to you that day. But oh my God, we didn't expect you to go to *bed* with him. Do you go to bed with just anybody, Belinda? You're a bit of a slut, you know.'

I don't take this to heart; I'm wise to him now.

'What did Mengers ever do to you?'

He casts his mind back, and shrugs. 'We couldn't afford to have him sober up.'

'I deleted his files.'

'Not all of them. He was what you might call a loose end.'

'You made me think it was me!'

'I did nothing of the kind,' he chortles, still more preoccupied with the chirruping bundle in his arms than with what I'm saying. He begins to pace up and down, rocking it in his arms. 'I can't help it if you jump to conclusions. Though of course I might have planted a few seeds here and there.'

'*Why?* Why would you even *do* that?'

He shrugs. 'Why not?'

'Have you got a key to my flat? No don't tell me, you don't need one. You picked the lock, or you have some sort of master key which opens all the doors in town. You pop in and out as you please.'

'Only that once. Twice, if you count going back for the body. But I was doing you a favour there.'

'I *do* count it! And you hit me on the head!'

'You were making a mess of it.'

'I wasn't trying to *kill* her!'

He sighs. 'If it's any consolation, it was going to happen anyway. Just not in your flat.'

'But the head! In the fridge!' I wailed. 'So unnecessary!'

'We couldn't very well put the whole corpse in there, Belinda. We were working to a deadline.' He's talking to me as though I'm a child asking why the sky is blue.

'*Why the fridge?* No, don't tell me. You wanted Nancy to think Delgado had done it. But in that case you didn't do a very good job. *You forgot the Chihuahua!*'

He stops pacing. 'Chihuahua?'

I'm livid. Now I'll have to revise my journal, crossing things out and adding new stuff. It's going to play havoc with my lovely handwriting, and it's all Lars's fault. I glare at him, and ask, 'Am I a loose end too?' Then remember the cassette is still running in the kidney-shaped Miniguchi, and smile, because I'm getting all this on tape. Church will have to take me seriously now.

'What are you smirking about?' He peers at me suspiciously before returning his attention to the bundle. I stop smiling as it dawns on me I'll never get a chance to correct my journal, or deliver the cassette to Church. Lars can't let me walk out of here, not without some sort of major debriefing which will probably end up with me being pushed out of a high window.

'You didn't even have the decency to cover her face,' I say. All the sheets and towels are soaked in blood, so I go into my bag and bring out my Space Blanket. I tear open the packaging and unfold the contents, which is easier said than done; the golden foil is so fine it keeps clinging to my hands. But finally I get it under control. It rustles like tinsel as I spread it over Nancy's face. That's better. She's at peace now. I feel I should say something.

'I'm sorry things have turned out like this,' I tell her, 'but it wasn't my fault. It was your two-faced double-dealing serial-killing friend here.'

Lars glances up again. 'Get that stuff off her.' He tries to look menacing, but it's not so easy with the *thing* in his arms. I move towards him and catch sight of a tiny hand. It looks almost normal. Four tiny fingers and a thumb.

'Maybe I could help bring it up.' But as I raise my hand to touch it, Lars swings the bundle out of my reach.

'You, Belinda? Raise a child? I think not.'

Visions of the baby's future pop into my brain, fanned out like collectors' cards. Raised in sterile isolation in an impregnable cell. Fed on pellets of scientifically-approved diet. Prodded by a never-ending series of Dr. Smiths with clipboards. Stared at by bowler-hatted men from the ministry. Tutored in nuclear physics by stern-faced women with steel-grey hair pulled back into buns... Have I come up with these images all by myself, or has someone put them there?

'How will you feed it?' I ask.

Lars is looking as though he wants to knock me unconscious again, but he has his arms full.

'Bottle. Did it with my youngest.'

Yet another lie. 'You told me you don't have children. I don't suppose there's an Eileen either.'

'Oh Belinda, you should know by now the most effective lies are the ones that stick closest to the truth. There used to be children. There used to be a... Not Eileen. Her name was Elaine.'

'What happened to them?'

'Ended badly. Someone wanted payback.'

I must have looked shocked, because he added, 'Long time ago, before the world was wet. Now get that thing off Nancy's face, before she suffocates...'

'She made me promise to look after the baby if anything happened to her.'

Lars is becoming restless, as though my presence is preventing him from getting on with the important stuff.

'Look, I needed your help, Belinda, but that's over now. Get that gold crap off her face and get out of here.'

I stay where I am, thinking maybe if I look lugubrious he might feel a twinge of guilt about the way he's been treating me.

He raises his voice. 'What do you want? More money? Go home, Belinda. Go home and type up your story. Sell it to the highest bidder, whatever.'

But I know, without a shadow of a doubt, that even if I do go home, I won't be there for long. Lars won't want me around, knowing what I know, and he certainly won't want me writing a book about it. He'll kill me and burn my journal and destroy the cassettes. And then make it look like an accident. Or suicide. *Now you mention it, she* had *been behaving strangely. I guess her friend's death was the last straw.* That's what people will say.

'They'll never fall for that!' I say out loud.

'I know you've got problems, Belinda.' Lars is looking at me with distaste again. 'Not surprising, considering what you've been through. Have you considered seeking professional help?'

Why do people keep saying that? But I've already had counselling, truckloads of it, and none of it ever helped, though I sometimes pretended it did, just to make it stop.

'All right for you to say,' I glower at him. 'You've had your fun.'

Something bursts out of him. 'You think it was *fun?* Drinking disgusting wine, playing fucking scrabble, having bad sex, night after night? Having to talk about fucking French literature? Having to watch *Doing It Up*, for fuck's sake? Seeing you was part of the job, Belinda. I was bored out of my skull. The only enjoyment I ever got from that assignment was making you think you were some sort of schizophrenic mass murderer.'

Bored out of his skull? Now that was something he should never have said. But he's underestimating me again. He's been underestimating me from the start, the way everybody does. And I haven't told him everything. I've never told him, for example, about my Apocalypse

Kit. I dip down and extract another item from the case, and slide it up my sleeve. It's easy to do this without Lars noticing, because he's still paying more attention to the thing in his arms.

I straighten up and ask, 'Can I touch it?'

'*Her*. It's a girl.'

I give it one last try. 'You did fancy me at the beginning, didn't you?'

'Yeah,' he says. 'Of course.'

He could at least have made an effort.

'Just kick that over here before you go,' he says, pointing at his holdall.

'Why? Going to teach baby how to play squash?'

He sighs in exasperation. 'Phone. Inside pocket.'

I unzip the bag and find his mobile. 'This?' I hold it up.

He clicks his fingers impatiently. 'Let's have it.'

'Oops!' I let the mobile slip through my fingers. It bounces once, twice, and then I tread on it, but it's tougher than it looks. I have to stamp hard, several times, before I feel it crack beneath my heel. Lars rolls his eyes heavenward. Probably wants to slap me, but can't. Because he's still cradling the baby.

'Let me hold her,' I say. 'Just for a minute.'

His face sets into a mask. I've never seen him looking like this before. Correction: I *have* seen him looking like this, but only now do I realise what it means. It's the look of resolve. It's the look that means he's about to do whatever he thinks is necessary.

The baby lets out a small burble and Lars looks startled, as though I've annoyed him so much he's forgotten what he was holding, and it gives me an advantage. Just a small one, but I may never get another chance like this. He turns to set the bundle carefully on the chair, and I know if I let him turn all the way round to face me, I'm done for. So when he does turn, I'm right behind him, sliding the knife out of my sleeve and opening it up, and it's his own momentum which propels him on to the steel, which is sharp enough to slice off a boar's testicles. The blade doesn't slide in smoothly; it jams up against one of his ribs, so I pull back a fraction and thrust upwards, and this time I'm surprised at how easily it sinks in.

Lars grunts and looks down at the slowly spreading red stain. I wait for him to crumple, but it's like sticking a pin into an alligator. I let go of the knife and it falls out of him and clatters to the floor, and he lashes out with a foot, and the metal toecap of his brogue connects with my shin. It's a pain unlike any I've ever experienced, even worse than the pain of my sliced-off ear - a rocketing pain like the spreading heat from a space shuttle's thrusters - and I yelp and hop backwards, clutching my leg, which now feels like a long, thin sackful of shattered bone.

And now he's coming towards me, bloodstained fingers outspread as though he's preparing to apply them to my face. They look huge, like bananas. I know I can't let them come into contact with my head, or they'll wrap themselves around my skull and squeeze until my eyes burst out of their sockets like Delgado's did at the theatre. I'm beginning to wish I hadn't stabbed him, but too late now. I can't rewind. I'll just have to deal with the consequences.

I brace myself for the bananas, but they never arrive. He's wiping his fingers on his shirt, where the bloody smears became several among the many.

He says, 'Why couldn't you have just gone home?'
Then he bobs down and picks up the knife. In his hand
it looks puny, but he's inspecting it with interest. 'Hmm,'
he says. 'Étripouille. You really do have excellent taste,
Belinda.' He looks at me, and smiles coldly. 'But of
course, you have to know how to use these things.'

And now the knife isn't looking so puny any more.
It's no Kitchen Devil, but I know it's sharp, because the
first time I opened it up I accidentally sliced the fleshy
pad of my thumb. The thought of sliced thumb makes
my eyes water, so I avert them from the blade and look
at Lars's face instead. The features are so familiar, and
yet so alien. I don't know this man at all. I've never
known him.

A thin line of blood has started to trickle out of
one of his nostrils.

'You're bleeding,' I tell him.

'Well, that's generally what happens when you
stick knives into people,' he says. 'Let me give you
another demonstration.'

He doesn't raise the knife but lowers it, holding it
at hip level. He's preparing to gut me like a French boar.
I tell myself to wake up, the nightmare is over, but it's
not, I'm still there, he's still there and this is real. I never
imagined my last few moments on earth would be like
this.

I close my eyes. And then, as I wait for the sting
of the blade, I realise it's taking too long, and open them
again. It's as though time hasn't so much slowed down
but expanded as hundreds - no, *thousands* - of memories
are flickering through my head. Now I see what Nancy
meant by the slide-show, though I still don't understand
it. Falling off my bike, my mother playing tennis, Nancy

and me at the ice-rink, the devastating realisation that she's sleeping with my boyfriend, the Croydon house of horror, *We've Only Just Begun* by The Carpenters, finding the source of the smell under the floorboards, hours and hours of questioning, Charlie's trial, hours and hours of counselling, the awful films Roger made me watch, the devastating realisation that he's been sleeping with Marietta... Now the show is speeding up, riffling through the recent past: bookshop, entrails, Wilson, Mengers, Delgado, exploding eyeballs, Les Six, hospital... Lars is in there too. And so are the items in my Apocalypse Kit.

Something clicks into place in my head, like a Lego brick.

As it is written, so shall it be done.

I have no idea where *that* came from, but the words sound important, so I repeat them out loud.

'As it is written, so shall it be done.'

A look of uncertainty darts across Lars's face, but just for a microsecond, and then he takes another step towards me. The blade is so sharp I could slice an eyeball just by looking at it, so I close my eyes again, and feel a cool breeze on my face, and hear a soft rustling, like tinsel in the wind. I wait, and wait, tensed in anticipation of the piercing pain of the steel, but nothing happens. Just more of that soft rustling.

And the words of non-Nancy come back to me: I'm *not* alone.

I open my eyes.

It takes a moment to make sense of the Magritte painting being acted out in front of me. Lars has something wrapped around his head. He's struggling to get it off, but the more he wrestles, the more tightly it moulds itself to his features, until I can see the depressions of his mouth and eyes.

It's odd there should have been a breeze at all, because the window is closed. But the Space Blanket has blown off Nancy's head and has attached itself to Lars. I remember what it says on the packaging.

WINDPROOF. CHILLPROOF. WATERPROOF. ALSO REFLECTS RADAR. Someone out there is probably pinpointing Lars's position at this very moment. Well, it won't do him much good.

'Get this thing off me,' he says in a muffled voice. He's picking at the edge, trying to hack at it with the knife, but the foil is vacuum-suctioned to his face, and all he manages to do is cut his neck and chin, and his wrapped head is starting to turn into a streaky mess of red and gold. The empty packet is still lying on the floor. Since Lars is otherwise occupied, I pick it up and, out of curiosity, take another look at the words on it.

WARNING: THIS BLANKET IS NOT A TOY. KEEP IT IN A SAFE PLACE, AWAY FROM CHILDREN.

Oh yes. I read on.

INFLAMMABLE.

My gaze drifts to the floor, where it falls on the Bar-F matchbook with LARS TUBLUT printed on it in Nancy's hand. I look from the open matchbook to where he's flailing around, only a couple of feet away. He's stomping and shuffling, still trying to peel the space blanket from his features. I can hear him wheezing, and this time I don't think it's laughter. He's jabbing at the depression where his mouth is, trying to poke a hole in it, but the knife blade bounces off the foil as though it's made of rubber.

His wheezing is abruptly drowned out by an angry

crackle, like chips being plunged into a deep-fat frier, and the examination room flares green. I look towards the window just in time to see the sky burst into a gigantic glittering chrysanthemum. The petals fall lazily and fade, and then there's a lot of popping and another explosion of colour, this time purple. Fireworks! Lars spins round blindly, as though trying to dodge incoming artillery, the space blanket reflecting red and green and purple as the sky lights up and fades.

My gaze returns to the Bar-F matchbook. They're not safety matches, that much I know. I glance over to the chair, to the towel-wrapped bundle is gurgling in delight, and I know what will happen next. It has a classical inevitability to it, like all of Nancy's so-called accidents. Cause and effect. The baby doesn't want to go with Lars. It doesn't want to be raised in a sterile safe house and fed on pellets and tested in laboratories or whatever ComSec has planned for it. Ergo, the baby is going to make sure this doesn't happen. It's going to remove Lars from the equation.

More celestial chrysanthemums, lighting up the sky to the sound of distant ordnance. Lars and his toecaps are shuffling nearer and nearer to the matchbook, making a noise like scuffed gravel, doing the Space Blanket fandango.

Clever little thing.

Another rocket delivers its load, this time blooming purple, just as the metal edge of Lars's right brogue scrapes against the match-book. All it takes is a tiny spark. First one match ignites, then, after a dramatic pause, all the others follow its lead. There's a whoop and a fizz and another pop of light penetrates the murk outside, bathing the room in red, so the first lick of orange flame is almost invisible, and Lars manages to shake it out. The second, though, is easier to see as it snakes up his leg and attaches itself to a dangling corner of the space blanket, where it lingers, feeding on the foil.

'Happy New Year!' I shout.

Nothing else catches fire - it's a textbook case of spontaneous combustion, or might have been, had it not been precision-engineered. The flames feed on the foil like tiny dragons and start shooting up over his shoulders and the blanket starts to melt over his head, and he coughs and drops the knife and tries yet again to peel the foil from his face, but now it's no longer foil - just pure orange and purple and red and green flame. There's a sizzling noise and a thin plume of black smoke detaches itself and shoots straight up to scorch the cottage cheese ceiling, which gives off a sickening smell, like burning fat. Lars's arms are flapping. But not for long. The coughing is replaced by a hoarse retching as he inhales fumes and fire and melted foil. Then that too stops.

His legs support him for a short while longer, but once his top half has been reduced to crispy foil-baked chicken, like something cooked over a campfire, they give way and he topples sideways like a treetrunk. One of his hands is stretched out like a claw. His head seems to have melted into the floor. He doesn't look human any more. It looks as though a bored teenager has set fire to a pile of filthy bedclothes.

The sight reminds me of the scorch marks on Nancy's table, but that was a lifetime, literally several lifetimes ago, and this is now. I creep forward, and tentatively poke the bedclothes with my toe. The sound they make is pretty disgusting; a slooshy crinkling from what's left of the foil, and the gloop of something liquid. But I've seen and heard worse, not just in books but in real life. And at least we're not in my flat, so I won't have to worry about cleaning up. I draw back my foot and kick what remains of my boyfriend, again and again, even though the leg is hurting like hell from where he kicked me. *That's* for Nancy, you arsehole. And *that's* for Verity Wilson. And *that's* for Clive Mengers. And *that's* for making me think it was *me*.

I stop kicking and stand there, panting. All I can say is *wow*. If only Nancy had been alive to see it, she would have been proud of me. Of *us*. Because we're a team, me and the bundle on the chair.

I limp over to it and prod it gently with my finger. The tiny face is wizened, but its strange emerald eyes are shining out of its face, regarding me with unblinking curiosity and unnatural intelligence. Do all newborn babies look like this? Little black eyelashes? Tiny rosebud lips? A miniature hand reaches out and four miniature fingers and one miniature thumb attach themselves to my forefinger. Quite cute, I grudgingly admit, picking it up and rocking it the way I'd seen Lars do. But a bit slimy. Needs a wash. How do you wash a baby? I suppose I'll have to learn. It's all down to me now. Nancy had just been a temporary vessel. Let's face it, Nancy didn't have a clue. Nancy would have brought it up as a regular kid.

Whereas I... What was the betting it's had its eye on me all along? If only Lars Tublut and Verity Wilson had realised, they would have treated me with more respect. Respect. I'm going to get a lot of that now. Everyone will be falling over themselves to give me my own newspaper column and do book deals and make movies about us. Baby and I can go mountain-climbing, and deep-sea diving and blowfish-eating, and all the things Nancy never dared, and we'll write about it, a mother and daughter double-act. Though maybe not straightaway, because all I want - all *we* want - is to get out of this place and go and have something to eat and catch up on our sleep and lie low until we've recovered our fighting form, ready for our first press conference.

Delgado said the world was going to end, and it certainly looks as though we're in for another Flood. I wonder if the Thames Barrier is holding. But we're seven floors up, and and despite the unrelenting downpour there are still fireworks going off, glittering silver and gold now. Maybe the world isn't ending after all, at least not yet. Maybe it's not going out with a bang. Maybe it was always going to be a whimpering baby. Except this one isn't whimpering. I decide to call her Betty.

There's coughing behind me, and I go rigid. Then turn, slowly, prepared to see Lars rising from the dead with his face melting off his skull.

Nancy has propped herself up against the pillows and is rubbing her eyes.

'Jesus, Belinda. Something's burning.'

OK, so Nancy isn't dead after all. I'd leapt to conclusions again. But I can live with that. I do some rapid mental calculations. Plan A is out of the question now, so I'll just have to move on to Plan B. *There's always a Plan B,* Delgado once said. I don't actually know what it is, but I'm sure we can work something out. I'm happy, and relieved, that Nancy is still alive, even if it does complicate my partnership with Betty.

'It was Lars,' I say, limping over to the bed. 'Bull, I mean. He had a knife. He tried to kill us all. You, me, the baby.'

The lie comes easily. Nancy is shocked, I can see it in her eyes, but I can also see that, by a stroke of good fortune, I've opted for an untruth that strikes her as plausible. What is it he said? *The most effective lies are the ones that stick closest to the truth.* And I have no doubt he *would* have killed Nancy too, if she'd tried to stop him taking the baby.

'But you know what? Betty and I bonded, and we took him out! We're a team.'

She manages a feeble chuckle. 'Big mistake,' she says. 'He should have known better.'

I lower the gurgling bundle on to Nancy's chest, and she wraps her arms around it. I'm reluctant to part with it now, but it makes me happy when Nancy's face erupts into a broad smile. She's exhausted and her hair is plastered to her head, but she looks beautiful.

'Betty? For heaven's sake, Belinda. She's always been Kitty. Or The Shrimp. But Kitty now.'

'You don't need to decide on a name right this minute.'

I search in my head for the Lego brick, wondering if I can make something happen, nothing drastic, maybe give Nancy a small nosebleed. But it's too late, and I realise to my disappointment that the psychic link was only ever a temporary arrangement, and now it's broken. The baby has transferred its allegiance back to its biological mother. Baby-Mama-Bonding beats Godmother every time. Ah well, it was worth a try.

But there will be times when Nancy isn't awake. And then I'll be able to attend to Betty's spiritual needs, read her Bible stories and fairy tales, teach her beautiful handwriting and the principles of good design, make sure she doesn't turn to the Dark Side or anything, maybe reforge that link and test its limits...

My reverie is rudely interrupted by a yell of 'HAPPY NEW YEAR!'

I turn to see Les Six, propped up on a walking frame in the doorway. Jesus Fucking Christ, everyone's coming back from the dead! I glance down at the mushy heap on the floor to check that Lars isn't coming back as well, then back at Six. He looks drained, but very much alive. And he's not alone. Maurice and Phoebe are behind him, with a middle-aged woman in a white coat.

Oh heavens, have they come to take me away?

But White Coat Woman barges past without looking at me, and takes my place at Nancy's bedside.

'How are you feeling?' she asks. 'Who's this, then?'

'This is Kitty,' Nancy says proudly.

White Coat Woman opens a brown leather bag, and I spot an array of steel instruments sealed in plastic, and bottles of pills and coloured liquid. Now Maurice and Phoebe are at the bedside too, crowding me out and cooing over the baby.

White Coat Woman gently lifts the baby and hands it to Phoebe, and then she takes out scissors and starts cutting through the bloodied remains of Nancy's streetwalker costume.

'Hello Kitty!' says Phoebe.

'Who cut the cord?' asks White Coat Woman, and I realise she's addressing me.

I remember the bloodstained scissors on the floor and say, 'I did,' because lying seems simpler than having to explain about Lars.

'What the fuck happened here?' asks Six, prodding the charred mess with the edge of his walking frame.

'The Devil,' I say. 'But it's OK, we took him out.'

'How did you find us?' murmurs Nancy.

'Tracked my phone,' says Phoebe, glaring at me over the top of the bundle.

'Sorry about that,' I say. 'You know, back in your flat, when we...'

'It's OK,' she says, making a valiant effort to be nice. 'You weren't yourself.'

'They made me do it,' I say. 'They cut off my ear.'

Phoebe looks suitably shocked.

'Melinda!' says Maurice, patting me on the back so hard I nearly fall over. 'Well done! You delivered the baby! You're a star!'

There's a loud fizzing, and the sky lights up with another flurry of glittering silver and gold.

THE END

ABOUT THE AUTHOR

Anne Billson is a film critic, novelist and photographer whose work has been widely published. She is also well known as a style icon, wicked spinster, evil feminist, and international cat-sitter.

Her books include horror novels *Suckers*, *Stiff Lips* and *The Ex*; monographs on the films *The Thing* and *Let the Right One In*; *Breast Man: A Conversation with Russ Meyer*; and *Billson Film Database*, a collection of film reviews.

In 1993 she was named one of *Granta* magazine's 'Best Young British Novelists'. From 1993 to 2001 she was film critic of the *Sunday Telegraph*. In 2015 she was named by the British Film Institute as one of '25 Female Film Critics Worth Celebrating.'

She has lived in London, Tokyo, Cambridge, Paris and Croydon, and now lives in Brussels. She likes frites, beer and chocolate.

She has three blogs:

multiglom.com (the Billson blog)

catsonfilm.net (a blog about films that have cats in them)

lempiredeslumieres.com (a blog about Belgium)

She can be contacted on Twitter at @AnneBillson

SUCKERS

'Billson honours the rules of the genre, then proceeds to have fun with them... Dark, sharp, chic and very funny' (Christopher Fowler - *Time Out*)

'A superb satirist' (Salman Rushdie)

'Merits a post position on everybody's reading list, even those who don't usually like vampire stories. It isn't splatter fiction; it's an honest piece of literature' (Elliott Swanson - *Booklist*)

'A black and bloody celebration of wit, womanhood and slapstick, beautifully sustained to a thoroughly satisfying climax' (Chris Gilmore - *Interzone*)

'A very camp and hugely entertaining vampire novel' (Christie Hickman - *Midweek*)

'Wicked and vulgar and unsettling... rollicking knockabout gore... nasty and brutishly funny' (Patt Morrison - *Los Angeles Times*)

'Enchanting and ominous at the same time; a rare and impressive piece of literary juggling' (Jonathan Carroll)

'A distinctive, original and refreshing debut' (Kim Newman - *Starburst*)

STIFF LIPS

'A slick and remarkably controlled performance which more than equals her satisfying first novel Suckers. Ghost tales invariably leave me cold. I read this one in a single highly enjoyable sitting' (Paul Rutman - *Sunday Telegraph*)

'With Stiff Lips, Billson overturns the clichés of the horror genre, establishing, in their stead, her own original voice' (Lucy O'Brien - *The Independent*)

'Sexy, sardonic and distinctly spooky... a tale to make you shiver - if you don't die laughing first' (*Cosmopolitan*)

'Stiff Lips achieves an authentic and unsettling nastiness' (*Sunday Times*)

'A vastly entertaining story... As well as being a successful ghost story, Stiff Lips is an amusing satire... Funny and spooky - an excellent combination' (Sophia Watson - *The Spectator*)

'An absolutely terrific ghost story, taut and well-written with vivid characters and a spot-on blackly comic/satirical vein that does not detract from the very effective horror' (Lynda Rucker)

'Very creepy, thoroughly modern ghost story about frenemies, real-estate envy, going-for-the-gold bitchery and what makes the perfect boyfriend' (Maitland McDonagh)

THE EX

'Great wit, great dialogue, great scares, genuinely disturbing yet never less than thoroughly entertaining, this book is a terrific read' (Stephen Volk)

'Witty, blackly comic, pacy and original. Seedy anti-hero John Croydon is the supernatural version of Len Deighton's Harry Palmer. Or as if Harold Lloyd had strayed into *The Omen*. Slapstick as well as chills. It moves expertly from set-piece to set-piece in locations both grubby and glamorous. Totally recommended' (Lawrence Jackson)

'a fast paced, supernatural detective novel with a welcome vein of black humour running through it' (Oliver Clarke)

'Another page-turning spine-chiller from the author of *Suckers*... contains Billson's usual mix of dark humour, social satire and imaginative creepiness (Simon Litton)

'Another clever, creepy, wickedly funny book from Anne Billson, a great follow-up to *Suckers* and *Stiff Lips*... A thoroughly entertaining read, jolly good fun' (Esther Sherman)

Made in the USA
Middletown, DE
12 September 2017